MYSTERY AMONG
THE STARS

Tariq's radiotelescope stretched for 200 kilometers across the dark, icy surface of Charon, its flat phased-array dishes laid neatly in a complex pattern across the moon like a thousand dishes awaiting a picnic of giants. The delicate, steady radio hiss of interstellar electrons was picked up by the dishes and sent to the center of the array, where the signals converged on a little plastex igloo. Inside stood Tariq, crowded by amplifiers, signal processors, computers, test equipment, and wiring. The signals passed through his gear until, amplified, processed, and artificially colored, they formed the glowing image of the complex swirl of plasma and magnetic fields on the screen.

Tariq stared intently at the picture. For months he had been doing a routine sky survey. Reds and oranges dominated the screen, marking the hot galactic plasma. The computer added black magnetic field lines threading complex paths through the plasma.

Ordinarily, the pattern changed little from day to day, apart from occasional ripples in the plasma, perhaps the ghosts of long-dead supernova explosions. But on this day a hot, red blotch suddenly appeared in a place where there should have been nothing but blue.

Ask your bookseller for the Bantam Spectra
science fiction titles you have missed:

The Next Wave
BOOK 3

THE MISSING MATTER

THOMAS R. McDONOUGH

BANTAM BOOKS
New York • Toronto
London • Sydney • Auckland

THE MISSING MATTER
A Bantam Spectra Book/January 1992

*SPECTRA and the portrayal of a boxed "s" are trademarks of
Bantam Books,
a division of Bantam Doubleday Dell Publishing Group, Inc.*

ISBN 0-553-29364-8

Published simultaneously in the United States and Canada

*Bantam Books are published by Bantam Books, a division of Bantam
Doubleday Dell Publishing Group, Inc. Its trademark, consisting of the
words "Bantam Books" and the portrayal of a rooster, is Registered in
U.S. Patent and Trademark Office and in other countries. Marca
Registrada. Bantam Books, 666 Fifth Avenue, New York, New York
10103.*

PRINTED IN THE UNITED STATES OF AMERICA

RAD 0 9 8 7 6 5 4 3 2 1

THE
MISSING
MATTER

Dark Matter
by ISAAC ASIMOV

Cosmology—the science of the Universe as a whole—began in 1916 with Albert Einstein's Theory of General Relativity. For the first time, a set of relationships was set up that seemed to govern the behavior of the Universe as a whole.

One of the things that was consistent with the equations was first pointed out by the Dutch astronomer Willem de Sitter (1872–1934). He suggested that the Universe had to be expanding. And, indeed, in the 1920s, the American astronomer Edwin Powell Hubble (1889–1953) demonstrated that it was. (It was this Hubble for whom the ill-fated Hubble Space Telescope was named.)

The reason for the expansion, it would seem, is that the Universe began as a random fluctuation in an endless sea of "false vacuum," and did so under conditions in which the initial matter that made it up had to undergo a vast and explosive inflation ("the big bang"), the effects of which still exist today. The clusters of galaxies still recede from each other by force of that initial explosion.

This explosion is taking place against the inward pull of the gravitational forces of the Universe as a whole, so a question arises: Will the Universe continue to expand forever, albeit at a slower and slower rate; or will the Universal expansion slow to the point where, eventually, it comes to a halt, and turns into a contraction so that it ends in a "big crunch" that will return it to the false vacuum from which it arose.

If the former condition is true and the Universe is fated to eternal expansion, we have an "open Universe." If the latter condition is true and the big crunch awaits us at the end, then we have a "closed Universe." Open or closed, that is the question.

The situation is similar to that of throwing an object into the air. Gravitational pull slows the rate of its rise, brings it to a halt, converts the rise to a fall, and down it comes. The harder we throw it, the higher it will rise before falling, but it may seem to us that no matter how hard we throw it, it must eventually come down again.

However, Earth's gravity weakens slowly with distance, and if we throw an object hard enough, then it reaches distances in which the steadily weakening gravitational pull can never quite bring it to a halt. It turns out that if an object is hurled upward at a speed of seven miles a second, it will outrace the gravitational field, so to speak, and never return. Thus, seven miles a second is the "escape velocity" from Earth's surface.

What we are asking with respect to the Universe, then, is whether the rate of its expansion is beyond the escape velocity. If so, it is open; if not, it is closed.

How do you determine the escape velocity of the Universe? If you knew its mass and volume, the escape velocity could be calculated. Of course, we don't know its total mass and its total volume and we may never know what those values are. Fortunately, it isn't the total mass and volume that counts—merely the amount of mass crammed into each unit volume of the Universe. In short, we must have the *density* of the Universe.

To get the density, we consider how far apart the galaxies are; how many stars there are in each galaxy and how far apart those stars are; how much mass each star has. The results we get are pretty approximate, but astronomers end up with the feeling that there are, on the average, 10^{-29} grams of matter in every cubic centimeter of the Universe. That amounts to one hydrogen atom in every hundred cubic centimeters of the Universe. (That doesn't sound like much, especially considering the vastly higher densities of matter within stars and planets

—but it does show how essentially empty most of the Universe is.)

Now, then, we have the density of the Universe, and we can also measure the rate at which galaxies are expanding. Both figures are highly uncertain, but using the best we have, it turns out that the galaxies are racing apart at speeds that are at least ten times the escape velocity. To put it another way, the density of the Universe is only about 1/10 of what it would have to be to bring the expansion of the Universe to a halt some day.

Verdict: the Universe is open and will expand forever.

But then, in the 1930s, the Swiss astronomer Fritz Zwicky (1898–1974) brought up a puzzling fact. He was one of the first to study distant galaxies, and he noticed that galaxies that existed in clusters moved about within those clusters. The velocities with which they moved were greater than the escape velocities calculated for those clusters and so the clusters ought to pull apart and "evaporate." But they don't. There is reason to think that they are stable and continue to exist for enormous lengths of time.

The conclusion can only be that the clusters have a higher escape velocity than they seem to have. That, in turn, means the total mass of the cluster must be greater than it seems. Since the total mass is calculated from the number and size of stars, that brings us to the conclusion that there is mass in the clusters that are *not* stars, and that therefore cannot be seen. This is called "dark matter."

In 1970s, a similar problem arose in connection with individual galaxies.

When small bodies revolve about large bodies, the rate of revolution decreases with distance. Thus, Earth travels in its orbit more slowly than Venus does since Venus is nearer the Sun than we are. Mars, which is farther from the Sun than we are, moves more slowly in its orbit than we do, and the outer planets move more slowly still. In fact, the rate at which orbital speed decreases with distance can be calculated from the laws of planetary motion, enunciated by the German astronomer Johannes Kepler (1571–1630) as long ago as 1609.

The situation in galaxies is somewhat similar to that of planets in the Solar system. It would seem that about 90 percent of all the mass of a galaxy is to be found in a relatively small region at its core. The core therefore takes the place of a "sun." The individual stars in the outer regions of the galaxy revolve about the core. Thus, our Sun revolves about the core of the Milky Way Galaxy, making one revolution in about 200 million years. Stars closer to the core than the Sun is should move more rapidly than the Sun in their orbits; while stars farther from the core than the Sun is should move more slowly.

It is possible now to tell just how fast different parts of different galaxies are rotating by measuring the shifts in the dark lines in their spectra. It is not a simple technique but it can be done.

When such measurements are made it turns out that the rate of orbital motion does *not* decrease with distance from the core, but remains more or less steady as one moves outward from the core of a galaxy toward its outskirts. This implies that the mass of the galaxy is *not* heavily concentrated at the core, but is spread throughout the galaxy much more evenly than we thought. Nevertheless, the matter we *see* in a galaxy *is* concentrated. The conclusion can only be that there is a great deal of mass, especially in the outer regions of the galaxy, that we *don't* see. It's the dark matter again.

The amount of dark matter in the Universe, judged from what would be required to produce the gravitational pull needed to hold the clusters of galaxies together and to keep galaxies rotating the way they do, would seem to be considerably greater than the amount of visible matter. In fact, there seems to be enough dark matter in the Universe to raise its overall escape velocity to the point where the Universe is closed.

This is rather a relief to astronomers, for recent theories of the formation of the Universe seem to require that the Universe have just enough mass to close it.

The question arises, though: What is the nature of the dark matter that we don't see?

There *is* dark matter in the Universe, we know. There are pieces of matter too small to shine right here within our own Solar system: planets, satellites, asteroids, comets, and so on. There are pieces of matter too massive and dense to shine: black holes. There are clouds of dust and gas between the stars that don't shine.

We can imagine, then, that the Universe is filled with these dark objects of one kind or another, and that they have, altogether, a far greater mass than the stars that we see and therefore automatically think of as constituting all the Universe there is.

The problem is that astronomers can't bring themselves to think that there are enough planets and other small bodies, and even enough in the way of black holes and dark clouds, to outmass the stars by so much. After all, in our own Solar system, the one star, our Sun, outmasses all the dark matter put together by something like one thousand to one. There's no reason why this preponderance of visible matter over dark matter should not exist in the Universe generally.

Besides which, all ordinary material objects, including stars, planets, asteroids, comets, dust clouds, and black holes, are made up essentially of protons and neutrons, in about a ten to one ratio. There are also electrons equal in numbers to the protons, but the total mass of the electrons is not much more than $1/2000$ the total mass of protons plus neutrons. Therefore, in judging the mass of the Universe, we are really judging the mass of its protons and neutrons.

There are ways of judging how much mass of the Universe is tied up in protons and neutrons from a consideration of conditions at the start of the big bang. The result seems to be that the amount of protons and neutrons is more or less what we would expect if we counted in only the stars we can see. That, in turn, means that there is very little in the way of protons and neutrons that can exist outside of the stars, and whatever the dark matter is, it is not anything that consists of protons and neutrons.

What, then, can it be?

The only known particles—aside from protons, neutrons, and electrons—that exist in the Universe in quantity are gravitons, photons, and neutrinos.

These exist in far greater numbers than do protons, neutrons, and electrons. However, gravitons, photons, and neutrinos are all massless objects and therefore cannot ordinarily contribute to the gravitational effects of the Universe.

This is not *entirely* true. As massless objects, gravitons, photons, and neutrinos all travel at the speed of light and this gives them a certain amount of energy, which is equivalent to a certain amount of mass. However, it takes a great deal of energy to be equivalent to a small amount of mass, and all the energy of motion of these three types of particles are not sufficient to add appreciable mass and gravitation to the Universe.

Of course, if one of these particles *did* have mass, that would multiply their gravitational effect enormously. As far as gravitons and photons are concerned, we are quite convinced there is no mass, but neutrinos have not entirely been eliminated.

There are three types of neutrinos known: electron-neutrinos, muon-neutrinos, and tauon-neutrinos. These are apparently distinct particles, which interact with matter (when they do interact, which is very seldom) in three different ways. This means there must be some difference in properties among them, but so far, scientists have not been able to detect those property differences.

The best bet seems to be that the neutrinos do have tiny masses, and that each of the three types of neutrinos has a different tiny mass. Because neutrinos so rarely interact with ordinary matter it is difficult to detect such tiny masses, however, and the point remains in dispute.

Nevertheless, that *might* be the answer. It is estimated that there are a billion times as many neutrinos in the Universe as there are protons, neutrons, and electrons. Even if an individual neutrino had a mass that was no more than 1/5000 that of an electron, or 1/10,000,000 that of a proton, there are so many neutrinos that the total mass of the neutrinos would be enough to produce the additional gravitation required to keep galaxies rotating as they do, to keep clusters of galaxies firmly together, and to make the entire Universe a closed one.

Two points keep astronomers from jumping at the neutrino solution. One is the fact that no experiments have yet shown, beyond doubt, that the neutrinos have mass. The other is that if the Universe's mass did consist almost entirely of neutrinos, it would not explain the formation of the galaxies, something that is much exercising the imaginations of astronomers at the moment.

Well, then, what is the dark matter? Perhaps it consists

of particles that we have never detected and that are very difficult to detect.

At the moment, there are two kinds of particles that seem to be in the lead as candidates for dark matter.

One type of particle are WIMPs, which is an abbreviation for "weakly interacting massive particles." They are supposed to be massive so that they would effectively close the Universe if they existed in the quantities that might be in existence. Then, they are weakly interacting, like the neutrinos, meaning that they tend to ignore the existence of ordinary matter, so that they can't easily be picked up by the many detecting devices we have for various subatomic particles.

Why should we think that WIMPs exist? Scientists are trying to work out the rules that would place all four known fields of interaction (gravitation, electromagnetism, weak, and strong) under a single set of equations. In order to make such a "grand unified theory" work, they must suppose whole new families of subatomic particles, some of which are included among the WIMPS.

The second possibility among the unknown particles is one that has been given the name of "axion." Axions, like WIMPs, are weakly interacting so that they are hard to detect. In addition, they are not massive. Their masses are as small as those that might possibly characterize neutrinos. Again, the Universe may exist in such a sea of axions that even if each individual axion had only a tiny mass, the sum total would be enough to explain the dark matter and to close the Universe.

And what makes people think that axions might exist? Well, all massive particles of ordinary type, including protons and neutrons, are made up of combinations of still more fundamental particles called "quarks." Scientists have devised the theory of "quantum chromodynamics" to explain how quarks work, and the theory has held up very nicely. There were some difficulties to it, however, that could not be surmounted till 1977, when the existence of axions with certain properties was postulated.

There are physicists laboring to find some way of demonstrating the existence of WIMPs, or axions, or both, but, so far, all attempts have failed. The question of dark matter remains open, therefore, and is an exciting venture for scientists.

And, in fact, in July of 1990, something turned up that calls into question the very existence of dark matter.

The Dutch astronomer Edwin A. Valentijn has reported that spiral galaxies may be much dustier than had been thought. Vast clouds of dust may be obscuring much of their structure.

This, in turn, could mean that in estimating the visible matter of a galaxy, we are routinely indulging in a gross underestimate because so much of the matter is hidden by dust. In other words, there *is* dark matter in the galaxies, but it is not intrinsically dark. It is merely unseen because it is hidden. If the dust could be miraculously removed, then all the dark matter would not be dark at all but would become visible.

Somehow, I don't find this convincing. It seems to me that stars, seen or unseen, should be concentrated greatly at the cores of galaxies. If the mass of the galaxy is spread more or less evenly through its structure, the mass outside the core must (it seems to me) consist of something other than stars.

So the puzzle continues—for which we may all be grateful. A Universe without puzzles would be unfit to live in.

CHAPTER 1

Tariq Salib's radiotelescope stretched for two hundred kilometers along the dark, icy surface of Charon. Its flat phased-array dishes were arranged neatly across the anti-Pluto side of the moon like plates awaiting a picnic of giants. The delicate, steady hiss of interstellar electrons the dishes picked up was sent to the center of the array, to Tariq's lab in a little plastex igloo.

Inside, the Egyptian scientist stared intently at the complex swirl of plasma and magnetic fields his equipment translated the signals into on the screen of his computer.

Tariq liked to think of Charon as a beach on the galactic shore, where the subatomic debris of exploded stars and microscopic dust grains washed up—the flotsam and jetsam of deep space. He and his fellow astrophysicists were studying the area for clues to the genealogy of the galaxy.

For months, he had been doing a routine sky survey. Ordinarily, the pattern changed little from day to day. Reds and oranges dominated the screen, marking the hot galactic plasma, with patches of blue indicating relatively cool spots. The computer added black magnetic field lines, making the picture look like a street map of a mad megalopolis.

Suddenly, as Tariq watched in disbelief, a hot red blotch appeared in a place where there should have been nothing but blue.

"Tondemonai! What *'afrit* is that?" he muttered in a mixture of his native Arabic and the Japanese in which he had been schooled.

He increased the magnification until the splotch filled the screen. It grew slowly as he watched. Concentrated magnetic field lines grew out of the object like strands of spaghetti and merged with the interstellar field. Tariq quickly accessed previous records of that part of the sky from his sky patrol database. There was absolutely nothing like it.

The blob started to drift off the screen. *Either that thing is moving ridiculously fast or it is incredibly close*! he thought, startled.

He ran a parallax calculation to fix the distance, then hit the commline and said in English, "Get me Hades! I want Father Fitzpatrick!"

The computer analyzed his voice and connected him via communication satellite to Pluto. The planet lay directly beneath his feet on the other side of Charon. The satcom was needed to carry the signal to Hades, Pluto's major mining station and administrative center.

"Please stand by," said the comm-puter.

Tariq tapped out the rhythm for an Arabic sword dance he often hummed when he was impatient.

At last, the screen lit up with the face of Father Al-Hajji Brian Fitzpatrick, SJA—member of the Society of Jesuits for Allah, and chief Eurafrican scientist on Pluto. Tariq and the priest had often videoed each other, but had never met face-to-face.

"Father Fitzpatrick, you have got to see this!" Tariq hit the command button and said to the computer, "Dump last ten minutes of data into commlink!"

Tariq watched the expression on the priest's face change from irritation to puzzlement to amazement in the space of a minute. "What in the name of Mary and Khadijah is going on?" He spoke with the strong brogue of the west coast of Ireland, from which he hailed. It contrasted dramatically with Tariq's heavily Arabic-flavored English.

"I do not have the faintest notion," said Tariq, "but somehow, particles and fields are being created out of nothing!"

"How far away is it?" asked Fitzpatrick.

"Less than two A.U. away." Two astronomical units—twice the Earth–Sun distance—was nearby as astronomical distances went, far closer to Pluto than any other planet.

"That is well within the range of the *Ulug Beg*," added Tariq, referring to the experimental near-interstellar spacecraft stationed at Pluto. It was the first hesitant step in the direction of piloted missions to nearby stars, but so far it was limited to exploration of transplutonian planets and comets. "That's why I called. I want to use the ship to take a closer look."

"Well, she just got back from a trip, and she needs to be serviced, which usually takes a month. Also, the crew has earned planet leave. And then, she's scheduled for another transplutonian trip."

"Listen to me, Father. This could be a once-in-a-life-time opportunity! No one has ever seen anything like this! Admit it!"

"It sounds as though you've caught a really wild interstellar fish in your net. And if there were any way to get the *Ulug Beg* out there, I'd be the first to recommend the mission."

"So, what is stopping you?"

"There are channels you have to go through."

"The laws of physics do not wait for man!"

"I'm afraid the laws of red tape are as immutable as those of physics."

"I do not care about red tape. Something wonderful is happening there, and I want to see it. It might disappear as quickly as it came."

"I'll tell you what I can do. I'll authorize you to visit Hades, and perhaps we can talk the chief into expediting things. If anyone can move those crats on Malta, she can." The island of Malta was the capital of the Eurafrican Federation for which the priest, the Egyptian, and their chief all worked.

Fitzpatrick gave him a travel authorization number

and signed off. Tariq called for a skimmer, put the radio-telescope into auto mode, and grabbed some gear from a locker. While he threw his things into a duffel bag, he kept glancing at the display, watching as the strange radio emissions intensified.

CHAPTER 2

The one-man shuttle traveled along a permanent metal-whisker cable linking Charon to Pluto, like a cosmic ski-lift twenty thousand kilometers long. Unique in the Solar System, the moon and planet kept the same sides facing each other, gravitationally locked. Like a dumbbell, they spun around their center of mass every six days.

At last the shuttle decelerated. A bright spot on the dark surface of Pluto grew rapidly into a patch of randomly scattered buildings, extravagantly lit by lights, which were outlawed by astronomers on Charon. Hades was an oasis of light in a dark universe, reminding Tariq of Kyoto Vegas.

"Welcome to Hell!" announced the shuttle computer over his suit radio. "Abandon hope, all ye who enter! Prepare to meet all your ex-bosses, ex-spouses, tax auditors, mothers-in-law, and everyone else you thought you'd left on Earth!"

"Your messages," muttered Tariq, "would crash a man's brain if he had to go to Hades regularly." In fact, he thought, that could explain a few of the people he had seen on Charon.

He slammed into the ground with a jolt. A Charon cargo barrel automatically ejected from the shuttle, bounced a dozen meters, and rolled until it slammed inaudibly into a cluster of similar containers.

Tariq shook his head and unstrapped himself. "Ah, the joys of first-class travel," he muttered. He looked forward to a nice pressurized hut, where he could take his helmet off a breathe "fresh" air once again.

Tariq jumped up through the open cockpit, but only rose a meter before descending to the ground. So accustomed had he become to the 1 percent gravity of Charon during his three months there that Pluto's 4 percent made his arms and legs leaden. It reminded him of the first, painful time he had returned to Earth for a vacation after a year on the Moon.

It was a lot easier to get used to Pluto's feeble gravity, especially since he had spent a part of each day running around the vertical hooptrack on Charon. He wondered if they had hooptracks on Pluto, and whether one could run upside down on the inside of the ring here. Probably, he decided, then returned to his urgent business.

He switched the suit radio over to Hades' main channel and identified himself to the base operator.

"This is urgent," said Tariq. "Connect me to Father Fitzpatrick."

"Roger. Switch to channel red–green–blue."

Tariq hit the color combination on his wrist.

In a moment, the priest's brogue filled his pressure helmet: "I'm really glad you could get here so quickly. Come right over to the Eurafrica complex."

"Where is that?" asked Tariq.

"It's about three hundred meters northwest of Styx Station. Right next to a geodesic hydrodome."

Tariq automatically looked to the stars for orientation, but the bright lights of the Sun-starved metropolis made it difficult to see them, so he glanced at the navigational pack on his wrist, hit the PLUTO button to reset the inertial guidance, and located north.

Something brushed against his leg, and he looked down, startled. It was a cat—a cat in a tiny white pressure suit.

"*Oya ma*!" Years of study at Toyota University had given him a rich vocabulary of throaty Japanese curses, the language having a satisfying Samurai bite lacking in Arabic.

The cat rubbed against his leg and looked up at him. A furry gray face was visible inside the small bubble helmet. Its mouth opened wide, and an AI voice interpreted its meow over the radio as "I need affection." It had become popular on Earth to use artificial intelligence to translate pet sounds.

He shook his head in amazement and awkwardly petted it, rubbing his glove across the velvety little pressure suit. "Sorry, *neko*," he said, "but I have to go."

He put the sample cases on a rack labeled HADES INMAIL. The cat bounced away, jumping a couple of meters off the ground each time, putting its ancient orientational talents to good use as it landed neatly on its feet with every hop.

Tariq, duffel in hand, kangarooed rapidly toward the northwest.

After three months in the tiny settlement on Charon, Hades looked like a thriving metropolis. It had at least a hundred glowing buildings. The slipshod construction and flimsy structures reminded him of research stations on the Moon, except that these lacked the thick layers of solar-radiation-absorbing dirt needed in the inner solar system. Out here, even the worst solar flare was diluted by distance to a tenth of a percent of its terrestrial intensity.

He hopped past a transparent geodesic dome with a green jungle inside, visible through glowing frost, its warmth beckoning. The crescent flag of Eurafrica glowed electroluminescently on the Quonset hut next to it, and as he approached, a short, pressure-suited figure bounced toward him.

"I've just finished evening prayers," said Father Fitzpatrick.

Tariq glanced at his navpac. "I forgot it was that time of day."

"I'm sure Allah will forgive you. Once I fouled up and we prayed to Mars instead of Mecca."

Tariq chuckled. It was startling to see how short the priest was in person. Through the visor he looked singularly inappropriate, like a leprechaun playing astronaut.

"I'm really glad you're here," said Fitzpatrick. His ruddy face glowed with excitement. "I want you to meet the station chief."

They hopped over to the Quonset hut and into the airlock. The priest hit the pressurization button. "She's the one we've got to convince to let us launch the *Ulug Beg*. I've told her to expect us."

Air hissed in. And soon a green light lit up and they removed their helmets. Hot, humid air greeted them, with a distinct animal smell to it.

No sooner had the inner door opened than a white fur ball with wings flew by screaming, chased by a fat orange cat. The feline screamed, "Hunger alert!"

"What the hell was that?" exclaimed Tariq.

The priest shrugged. "It's a long story, but in a byte, that's the station chief's pet. She loves cats. But she's also imported some critters engineered back on Earth that are a cross between sheep and chickens. Some of them got loose this morning and the cats have been having a field day chasing them through the corridors."

"I saw a cat in a pressure suit out by the shuttle terminal."

"Yes, she had those suits custom-made. Cost the taxpayers a fortune, but then she says nothing's too good for her little friends."

Tariq noticed strains of Hawaiian music in the air. The nearest computer monitor showed a screen of waving palm trees and crashing surf on a tropical beach. The priest said, "She hates the cold. She's got the whole station rigged up so it looks like Hawaii."

"Is that where she is from?"

"No, she's English," he said with a faint trace of dismay on his ruddy Irish brow. "I guess every Englishman has this lust for the tropics under his skin, and living on this ice ball has brought out the worst in her."

They bounced down the corridor, an activity more than walking but less than hopping, thanks to a ceiling that kept them from kangarooing freely. They paused outside a door painted with a palm tree while its annunciator murmured in English and Arabic, "Eurafrica Station Chief Sybil Ollerenshaw."

"It's very important that you impress Dr. Ollerenshaw," said the priest. "She runs the whole shebang and she can make you or break you."

"I do not know much about her, other than that she

approves my requisition forms after you. What is her doctorate in?"

"Personnel management, but it's said that she majored in Machiavelli."

The priest pushed a button and said, "Dr. Ollerenshaw, I've got Tariq here."

"Just a minute!" replied the annunciator.

"Is she hard to get along with?" asked Tariq.

"Not if you can convince her that what you want is going to help her plans in the long run."

"What are they?"

"Mainly, to get back to Earth."

The door opened and a woman's voice called out, "Come in, gentlemen." They bounced into a large, well-furnished office that was swelteringly hot.

As the door opened, a black cat ran out.

Dr. Sybil Ollerenshaw, a black woman in her thirties, sat behind her desk. Her skin testified to African ancestry, but its light shading intimated that it was not recent. She was a good ten kilos overweight, and her curly, dyed red hair was slightly rumpled. She wore a sarong, fitting in with the Pacific island decor. Everywhere was artificial bamboo, and the furniture was pseudorattan. A large hammock was stretched out at one end of the office, where slept a hulking man, naked from the waist up.

Tariq noticed that all four walls, the floor, and the ceiling of the office had been covered with video display paint. The walls depicted palm trees swaying gently in the wind, while fluffy white clouds floated by overhead. Waves lapped behind the woman. The effect was almost three-dimensional.

Large circular golden earrings dangled from Ollerenshaw's pierced lobes, and a golden chain necklace hung around her neck. She studied Tariq slowly, surveying his tall, lean frame, his swarthy face, and the black knit watch cap that concealed his bald forehead. She smiled.

"So," said the woman, "you're the Dr. Tariq Salib that Father Fitzpatrick has been telling me all about. An excellent scientist, he assures me."

He spread his hands wide noncommittally, never quite sure how to respond to praise. Waves splashed across the floor and merged into golden sand, which Tariq found disconcerting as the swirls splashed intangibly beneath his feet. He noticed the tang of salt air and the musty smell of jungle, emanating from a hidden olfactorator, and he mused at the man in the hammock, who resembled Tarzan. With his headband, he looked vaguely familiar, but Tariq couldn't quite place him.

She continued. "I've been getting reports about you ever since you arrived on Charon, and they've all been first-class." Her voice was halfway between cockney and BBC—the speech of a lower middle class Londoner attempting to swim against the currents of upper class British society. "Well, then. What can you do for me?"

"I was hoping you could do something for me," Tariq said.

"Such as?"

"Such as," said the priest, "letting him take the *Ulug Beg* out for a jaunt. I think he's really found something. If he's right, this could mean big stories about us in the media back home."

Her interest intensified noticeably.

"So, as I understand it," she said, "there's some kind of bother going on in space that's got you all excited, with visions of a Nobel in your head, no doubt."

Tariq's eyes flared at the belittling of his discovery.

"Tariq, here," said the priest quickly, "has done some very important work in understanding the universe's dark matter, including the interstellar metamatter particles that fuel the *Ulug Beg*. And he thinks this phenomenon might be as important as metamatter." Metamatter promised to revolutionize space travel, allowing the energy of metastable, ultradense interstellar matter to be harnessed for experimental spacecraft, though it was too expensive for routine commerce.

Searching for clues to the chief's psychology, Tariq studied the holoplaque on her desk, framed by artificial seashells. Its message floated in space: THERE IS NO LIMIT TO WHAT CAN BE ACCOMPLISHED IF YOU KNOW WHERE THE BODIES ARE BURIED.

"We've been getting good PR from the *Ulug Beg*," she said. "After all, everyone's curious about the transplutonian planets, and it's done a rather good job of exploring them so far. But it's only been back for a couple of weeks. Normally, we like to take a month or so to refurbish it after an expedition, and it's already scheduled for three more flights. Why don't I just put an application in to Malta administration. We should get the appropriation next year, with a little luck."

"We cannot possibly wait that long!" exclaimed Tariq.

"It would be a *haraam*!" said Fitzpatrick, showing off his meager Arabic, quoting a Koranic "sinful act."

"I don't think you quite understand the subtleties and complexities of life here," said Ollerenshaw. "You scientists never think about politics." Tariq grimaced. "On Pluto, Eurafricans are just one of several blocs. We're always jockeying with the Latins or the Norams or the Asians or the Antarkies. The Israelis even have a little base on the other side of the planet."

Tariq's lips wrinkled with distaste. They were the one group he could not tolerate.

"It's a very delicate situation, isn't it?" she said.

With Earth divided into half a dozen geopolitical power groups at war with each other commercially but in an uneasy peace politically, there were constant economic battles for control over the diminishing resources of the grotesquely overpopulated home world. Only the development of the rest of the solar system offered hope. Mines, processing plants, and research stations had been established on almost every solid planet, moon, and major asteroid.

There was only one resource on Pluto valuable enough to justify the expense of mining and shipping to Earth: metastable matter, the power source of the most advanced rocket engines and power generators. The discovery of pockets of the matter on Pluto, laid down by billions of years of interstellar meteorites, had led to the patchwork of mining settlements around the planet. Pure scientific research such as Tariq's was reluctantly funded by the power blocs in the hope that it might lead to further practical discoveries of use back home.

"Reminds me of World War II Switzerland," said the chief. "Back then, the whole European continent was in flames. All these countries were battling each other. But in the center of it all was Switzerland, the eye of the hurricane. The Swiss just stood there, *absolutely* neutral, oiling their guns and eating chocolate, while all the warring nations sent them their diplomats and spies.

"History's a bit of a hobby with me—especially diplomatic history and political intrigues—and I'm always amazed at places like that where the competitors from the different warring nations could chat at lunch and spy on each other at tea. And here on Pluto, we have to do a real juggling act to keep ourselves from ripping one another's throats out. So our beloved leaders in Malta, resplendent in their wisdom," she said sourly, "always take forever to do anything out of the norm. 'Protect your gluteus maximus' is their motto."

Ollerenshaw steepled her fingers and said, "If you can figure out some way your discovery could give us an edge in competing with the Asians or the others, I might be able to find a way to get approval for your proposal."

"Look," said Tariq, "I cannot promise anything, but this could be a whole new physical principle at work. It could be as revolutionary as anything on Earth. History is a bit of a hobby with me, too, except that it is the history of science that fascinates me. It was parlor tricks of electric sparks that led to the entire electrical revolution. It was the fogging of photographic film that led to the discovery of nuclear energy. This could be as big as either of them!"

She nodded. "Father, do you really think this could be as big as he says it is?"

"I think so," he said, nodding his head. "I've never seen anything like it. It's matter created out of nothing, like the white holes that theoreticians have speculated about—the opposite of black holes. If that's what it is, the possibilities are dazzling!"

"Worth headline coverage on the video?" asked Ollerenshaw.

"That and a good bit more!" said the priest enthusiastically.

Tariq reached over to the desk and turned her keyboard around, saying into its microphone, "Access Charon database blue-red-yellow." Immediately, a window appeared on the Hawaiian scene behind him, showing a seething turmoil of colors. *"Miwakuteki-na!"* he exclaimed. "It's growing phenomenally!"

"Could it be dangerous?" asked Ollerenshaw.

"Certainly," said Tariq. "The synchrotron radiation hazard could be great if we got too close to the heart of the emission—like Earth's Van Allen belts. But we can avoid the worst regions. Whatever it is is well worth the danger!"

She nodded dubiously. "I'll see what I can do. I'll put together a memo and photon it off to Malta as quickly as possible. Theoretically, I should have at least a preliminary answer tomorrow, but we usually get bogged down in red tape. However, I have some friends who owe me favors down on Malta. Perhaps I can get my authority extended to cover this."

"In the meantime," said the priest, "let's get the *Ulug Beg* running on three shifts for minimal turnaround, just in case we get launch approval."

"Done!" said Ollerenshaw.

"I would really like to take a look at her," said Tariq.

"That can be arranged," said Fitzpatrick, "but first, I'd like to show you something we've just recently discovered. We've been keeping it under wraps until just the right moment, to max the PR value."

"What is it?" said Tariq.

The Jesuit smiled. "I'd rather show it to you."

The chief shooed them out as she began dictating a memo.

"I think you're going to find this as interesting in its way as your discovery in space," said Fitzpatrick.

CHAPTER 3

"Have you ever been on a submarine?" the priest asked as the helmeted men climbed down a shaft from the main Eurafrica station.

"No, all my life I have been looking up, not down," said Tariq.

"This shaft is about a hundred meters deep," said Fitzpatrick. "That's nothing on Charon, but here you could break a leg if you're not careful."

The shaft was two meters in diameter and went straight down toward the center of Pluto. It was as black as the rings of Uranus; Tariq strained in vain to see the bottom.

Fitzpatrick pointed at a three-centimeter-wide strip of tape fastened to the ceiling that went straight down the center of the shaft. "That's our fireman's pole," he said. "Use it to keep yourself from bumping into the walls, and to slow yourself down when you're twenty or thirty meters from the bottom. Just watch me."

He stepped nonchalantly into the shaft, which lit up around him immediately. He sank slowly, loosely encircling the tape with one hand to keep from bobbing to the opposite side of the shaft. In a few seconds, he was well below the surface. Tariq joined him with the confidence of a man used to low gravity. As they sank they accelerated gradually. The lights kept up with their passage.

Fitzpatrick craned his neck up toward Tariq. "This is equivalent to about a four-meter fall on Earth," he said.

"How long does it take to get to the bottom?"

"Oh, about half a minute."

No sooner did he say that than they passed a red zone in the shaft and Fitzpatrick said, "Now, grab the tape firmly!"

They squeezed it with their gloved hands and quickly decelerated until they were within a couple of meters of the bottom, at which point the Jesuit let go and dropped out of the shaft, bouncing gently off the rubber surface on the bottom. Tariq followed and said, "How do you get back up?"

"Well, if I need exercise, I just climb up. Otherwise, I push a button and the tape rises. It's actually an endless loop, with the return hidden in the wall."

It was chilly in the great chamber they were in. They were surrounded by a mixture of the methane- and water ices that comprise much of Pluto. Notches like steps were carved into the ice floor. Tariq mimicked Fitzpatrick as he pushed off the steps and bounced off the ceiling periodically, cushioning the impact with his outstretched hands. They left a trail of small white clouds above their footprints, where their warm boots had vaporized methane.

After bouncing and skidding along for a couple of minutes, they came to a chamber in which sat the strangest-looking vessel Tariq had ever seen.

"This is my baby," said Fitzpatrick.

It was a large oval shape, reminiscent of the flying saucers of twentieth-century movies. The top front consisted of a transparent window through which Tariq could see controls vaguely like those of a spacecraft. The hull was of red metal and plastex; several hatches were now open.

"I've worked on the *Talg* for almost four years now. We built the first model on Earth, tested it in the Arctic. We made a lot of improvements, then shipped this one in pieces from the Moon."

At one of the hatches, an elderly but spry woman was working.

"How are you, Yildiz?" said Fitzpatrick.

"Great," she replied.

"What are you doing?"

"Checking out the engine." She spoke with a Turkish accent, in nearly a monotone.

Fitzpatrick introduced Tariq and said, "Yildiz is our engineer. I had the crew get the boat ready so I could give you a tour."

A middle-aged man stuck his head out of the hatch and called out a greeting.

"That's Einar, our captain," said the priest.

"Hop in," said the captain in a musical Norwegian accent.

Tariq paused for a moment to study the strange vessel —its hydrodynamic shape, the tiny steerable fins on the side and rear. The pond in which it sat was evidently the result of massive melting of the surrounding ice. The name *Moby Talg*—the latter meaning "ice" in Arabic— appeared on the stern in Roman and Arabic characters. Massive icicles grew fore and aft of the craft.

They effortlessly climbed into the vessel. Only three meters in diameter, it was cramped, with tubes, wires, and fibers running every which way. It reminded Tariq of a research lab, and he felt at home.

They pulled themselves through a small opening into the transparent canopy at the bow of the vessel. Icicles were clearly visible in the cavern wall in front of them.

"Ever been on a cryoscaph?" asked the captain in his singsong accent.

"I have never even heard of one," replied Tariq. "You have really kept this thing secret."

"Then I think you will find it most interesting." The captain turned his focus to a computer screen, and began reading off commands to the engineer. The hatches were closed.

The two visitors lay on their bellies on thin shelves like bunks, overlooking the control panel, while the captain lay on the bottom left of the vessel, his hands firmly holding one set of controls. Yildiz crawled into the space to the right of the captain and grabbed another set of controls.

"Prepare for melt," said the captain.

"Roger," said the engineer. She hit several switches,

and floodlights turned on the front, rear, and top of the vessel, making the cavern glisten. A ventilation fan began to whir in the background.

After the captain and engineer had gone through a lengthy checklist, the captain said, "Meltdown," and hit a blue switch.

The icicles in front of the vessel began to soften, and the ice in front of them, a bluish-white wall flecked with particles of rock and dirt, began to liquefy and run down slowly.

In a minute, the cavity ahead of them enlarged and the water formed a pool deep enough that the vessel floated.

"Electromagnetic induction?" asked Tariq.

"Check," said the engineer as she studied the colored indicators on her video display.

Fitzpatrick smiled and said, "Yes. The vessel produces an intense AC electromagnetic field that melts the ice ahead of us."

The captain turned up the intensity and the cryoscaph moved forward. The water began to melt more rapidly. Occasionally, a small rock broke off the ice ceiling and thunked onto the canopy. Soon they were moving forward at barely more than a turtle's pace, but enough so that they had covered a greater distance than the diameter of the vessel in just two minutes.

"What keeps us moving forward?" asked Tariq.

"Hydraulic pumps," said the captain. "We slurp the water in and shoot it out the back. I'm afraid we won't set any speed records, but we'll get wherever we want to go."

Tariq looked at the rearview monitor on the panel between the captain and the engineer. The cavern behind was now a wall of ice. "I hope we do not experience a quake while we are inside the ice," he said. As Pluto moved away from the Sun, it cooled. Tremendous pressures built up as the planet contracted, sometimes exploding into great plutoquakes that splintered vast stretches of ice and shook the entire world.

"This is one tough boat," said Yildiz. "We can withstand almost anything without being crushed."

"Just the same," said Fitzpatrick, "I hope we don't have occasion to test your calculations."

They traveled on for two hours in this fashion, angling downward, slowly going deeper. The captain studied a screen depicting contours of different colors.

"Radar?" asked Tariq.

"Yes, and sonar. Some radio frequencies penetrate fairly well, but sonar is the best for subtle short-range discrimination. We mix both types of data to produce this display."

He tapped at a large red blob. "Rock. There are boulders mixed in with the ice. Some of them are meteoric, like in Antarctica, only here they're more likely to be cometary or interstellar."

"What are the blue concentrations?" said Tariq, studying the screen.

"Areas of higher-density ice. They're tougher to go through, so we usually avoid them, but they help us navigate."

They passed through veins of black flakes that Tariq suspected were signs of Pluto's ancient passage through an interstellar cloud. He thought of the solar system history the flakes could help unravel. At his insistence, they took samples.

"This is fantastic!" said Tariq. "We could get bits of every interstellar substance that the solar system has passed through in billions of years of history!"

"That's why this vessel was built in the first place," said Fitzpatrick.

"But, why keep it secret?"

"The minerals we find might be commercially valuable," replied the priest.

"*My* great desire in life," said the engineer, "is to take this sucker to Europa, dive through the ice, and see what's there." Europa, one of Jupiter's four large moons, contained an unexplored liquid ocean.

By now they had gone to a depth of two kilometers, as measured by the inertial navigation unit, and suddenly, the character of the ice changed. In the lights of the vessel it became translucent, almost to the point of transparency. It had a greenish, glassy look.

"Is this the only such vessel on Charon?" Tariq asked.

"As far as we know," said Einar.

"Yes. If we have a breakdown out here," said Fitzpatrick, "we might be frozen here for centuries."

Tariq suppressed a shudder.

"Sounds like a good time to ask for a raise for us engineers," said Yildiz, smiling. "How about it, Father?"

"I'll think about it when we get back," he replied with a wink.

"We're here," said the captain. He turned off the melters, and they stopped in a cavern. The vessel gently rocked in a small pool of water.

Tariq suddenly felt claustrophobic. Memories came back to him of his boyhood, when he lived inside an Egyptian pyramid at the time of the Arab–Israeli Antimatter War. He had felt as sealed off from the universe as the pharaoh inside his tomb.

The pyramid had been a great comfort during the war, when much of the Middle East had been vaporized. He had often fantasized about what it would have been like to be the pharaoh's priest, sealed inside the tomb with the gutted mummy and his possessions for eternity.

His clammy reverie was interrupted quickly by the engineer, who pointed to a side porthole where a dark object lay entombed within the ice.

"Know what that is?" asked Fitzpatrick.

Tariq stared at the blurry image for a long time. Then recognition suddenly hit. "A fish!" he exclaimed. "A frozen fish! On Pluto? That's absurd!"

The Jesuit chuckled. "Yes, that's the amazing thing—fish on Pluto!"

Tariq stared at the dark object in front of him. It was about thirty centimeters long, with curious projections hanging below it—something like an angler fish, but unlike anything he had ever seen in the Tokyo Aquarium. Even its fins were different—they jutted out at strange angles from the sides of the body, instead of vertically or horizontally. The fish was a dark blue, and covered with netlike scales.

"This is utterly impossible!" said Tariq.

"Of course," said the priest. "There's no way that Pluto could have evolved life. It's always been far too cold out here. But somehow, it did!" He shook his head. "Sometime, millions of years ago, Pluto had a warm ocean, and creatures different from anything we have on Earth arose here."

"What about their DNA?"

"They don't have DNA, as we know it—they're not even carbon-based. Germanium plays the role of carbon, along with some chemical structures I would have sworn were impossible. There is some kind of complicated chemical structure that has a vague similarity to the DNA molecule, but instead of a double helix, it has a pair of chemical backbones running parallel to each other, rather like mating snakes. It's nothing like Martian algae or the Titanian slime molds."

"Then it must have evolved completely independently from Earth life!"

Fitzpatrick nodded. "That's why I wanted you to see this with your own eyes. It probably has nothing whatsoever to do with that weirdness of yours out in space, but who knows?"

Tariq wrenched his eyes from the strange fish and looked around the cavern. There were other fish suspended in the ice. Larger shapes loomed in the distance, some the size of whales, indistinct, dark, hovering, like caged monsters waiting to be released. Despite the warmth of his suit, he shivered.

CHAPTER 4

The next day, Tariq and Fitzpatrick were called back to the chief's office. The Tarzanoid man was swinging lazily in the hammock when they entered, while ukulele music played in the background.

Ollerenshaw smiled. "Good news! You can go!"

Fitzpatrick smiled and Tariq beamed.

"You got permission?" asked Tariq.

"No, I didn't actually get it," said the woman. *"I'm* authorizing this expedition."

"But you don't have the authority," said Fitzpatrick hesitantly.

"True, but when it's all done, and we're headline news on the video, they're not going to notice that I've shuffled the funds for the next transplutonian flight."

She leaned back in her flimsy pseudorattan chair. "You see, the more I thought about it last night, the more I realized that this could be my ticket out of here."

"Why didn't you submit our request?" said Fitzpatrick.

"Oh, they're always worried about someone getting killed out there. Bad PR. And they're worried chipless that our expensive transplutonian spaceship might get totally malfunctioned. I just know that if I asked them, they'd say the *Ulug Beg*'s going to get gobbled up by that black hole, or whatever the hell it is. They'd have told me just to send robotic probes."

"That would be a waste as long as the *Ulug Beg* is at hand," said Tariq. "We do not even know what we should be measuring out there, let alone know how to program the probes for it."

"All I know," said the woman, with a crafty smile, "is that no robot ever won a commendation. It's people who win medals, and get on the video, and get promotions when they do something spectacular, even if it's not by the rule book. That's why *I'm* going along, too."

The two scientists looked at her dubiously.

"But you don't know anything about spacecraft or scientific instrumentation," said Fitzpatrick. "You can't even stand being on a vessel without a tankful of drugs."

Tariq looked at Fitzpatrick and said, "Then how did she get out here?"

"Same as you. She was frozen on the Moon, put into a can, and shot by rail gun."

The chief's mouth wrinkled as if she had bitten a lemon. "Not one of the more memorable trips of my life, let me assure you," she said. "Getting to the Moon was bad enough. When I squeezed into that miserable, cold, confining, tiny little tin they call the lunar shuttle, I could barely keep myself from jumping out the airlock, even when I was drugged to my follicles. And *that* was an orgasm compared to walking into the freeze room on the Moon wearing nothing but that paper gown they give you, knowing I was about to become an ice cube and be shot out of a cannon across the solar system." She shuddered.

"Then," said Fitzpatrick, "why the hell don't you stay here in this nice, comfortable little station?"

"Because I don't want to be a footnote to history. I want to be a chapter title! It's the only way to climb to the top of the bureaucratic tree."

"Well, as the chief Eurafrican scientist on this station," said the Jesuit, "I absolutely forbid you to join this mission."

"Father, either I go, or nobody goes," said the woman, with the confidence of one who has stacked the deck. "And remember, *I* control your funding."

"We cannot just stand around here all day arguing,"

said Tariq. "We do not know how long this phenomenon will continue. If she wants to come, so be it. Just let us *go*!"

The Irishman knew a losing hand when he saw one. He shrugged and said, "I guess there's no alternative—"

"You're damn right," said Ollerenshaw.

"—though I'm sure we shall all regret it." Fitzpatrick sighed. "Then, you will authorize the refurbishing of the vessel?"

"I already have," she said sweetly. "They're working on it now. I pulled them off every other project. They'll be working all night long—two crews, in two shifts."

Tariq and Fitzpatrick stowed their gear and boarded the Hades shuttle craft. This vessel was a long metal crate on skis, set at the base of what looked like a toboggan run at least a kilometer long, carved out of the ice, running up the base of an extinct nitrogen volcano. After some routine checks, the pilot gave them the thumbs-up, and the ion drive fired. The shuttle craft raced up the run, accelerating.

There was a stomach-churning moment as they passed the top of the "ski jump" and continued to fly higher. After a few minutes, they could see the hull of the *Ulug Beg* in the distance, gently glowing in the light of the sun in the distance, above Charon's beautiful huge crescent.

The *Ulug Beg*, named after the great Tartar astronomer, grandson of Tamerlane, stretched three hundred meters from stem to stern. It was a conical silver vessel with a large collar around the base—a disc extending a kilometer away from the ship, made of a fine wire mesh. This was the dustcatcher—a device containing electromagnetic fields to sweep up interstellar particles for fuel. Technicians worked on the outside, looking like ants.

They flew past the edge of the halo and mated near the base of the cone, joining an airlock. They transferred their equipment, duffel bags, and supplies into the lock, floating in the zero gravity.

Pluto's ghostly surface drifted by, twenty kilometers below, occasionally lit up by the sparkle of landing lights and commlasers from mining camps and laboratories.

Fitzpatrick sealed himself, Tariq, and their baggage inside the hatch. The Egyptian glanced through a porthole into the ship. An entrancing woman floated inside, her arm casually wrapped around a stanchion, talking with and gesticulating at someone hidden from view. Her shoulder-length black hair floated in the air, drifting to one side like seaweed in the gentle debris-sweeping breeze maintained on the spacecraft. When she shook her head, her hair scattered capriciously.

Tariq had a vision of her as a mermaid in the Tokyo Aquarium, where he had spent many a leisure hour during his education. He smiled.

She was in her midtwenties, of medium height, with a slender figure delineated by her red jumpsuit. Tariq, who had not seen a truly beautiful woman in three months, remained transfixed by the porthole, not needing the handgrip, thanks to the crowded gear. He was grateful that he had put his black watch cap on, concealing his balding forehead.

Fitzpatrick activated the air supply, and after a minute, the gas hissed in and equalized the pressure. The inner hatch slid open automatically. The woman looked up at them and Tariq heard her mutter, "Fresh meat!" in Arabic. His eyes narrowed in disapproval.

The men removed their helmets and telcroed them to their belts. "Ahoy, Fairouz," said Fitzpatrick.

"How are you doing, Father?" replied the woman in English, floating toward them.

"Pretty fair," he replied. Grabbing a duffel bag, he kicked away from the hatch and floated down the corridor toward her. He expertly grabbed a handhold just before reaching her and floated to a stop.

Tariq followed him almost as gracefully, thanks to his three months on Charon.

The priest introduced them and said to Tariq, "Maybe you two know each other. Fairouz has lived a lot on the Moon and you did quite a bit of research there."

"Why is it," said Fairouz, "that people think everyone knows everyone else on the Moon?"

Tariq chuckled. "They do not realize how many millions of people live there," he said.

"It's tough to get experienced pilots out here," said Fitzpatrick. "Fairouz is an independent contractor we hired on the Moon."

"Yeah," she said. "I'm nearly through my three-year hitch. Never could resist a challenge." She pointed at Tariq's bag. "Stow your equipment. Then I'll give you the grand tour."

"Let me give you a hand," said a voice with an Italian accent.

Only then did Tariq notice the young man floating behind her.

"My name is Arnaldo," he said, shaking their hands.

"Arnaldo's our commperson," said Fairouz.

"So, you're the captain?" asked Tariq.

"Yeah," said Fairouz.

"You look pretty young, for such a major responsibility."

"Listen, I've been shipping terries like you since I was knee-high to a micrometeorite crater. I was born on the Moon. I used to fly out to the Druze asteroids all the time."

"Are you a Druze?" asked Tariq.

"You bet your booster I am," she said.

Tariq looked at her with new respect. Druzes were legendary for their abilities with spacecraft.

"So, what's the latest word on your white hole?" she said.

"We do not really know that it is a white hole," said Tariq. "But whatever it is, the vortex is now several thousands of kilometers in diameter, and still growing. Furthermore, the data show a periodic increase and decrease in the intensity of radio emissions every thirteen hours."

"What does it mean?" she asked.

"Damned if I know," he replied.

"Then, let's get going!" said the diminutive Irishman. "We've got space to cover and mysteries to solve!"

CHAPTER 5

After they stored their gear, Fairouz showed them the vessel, starting with the massive engine rooms in the aft. In this spacecraft, designed for prolonged acceleration, aft was "down" and forward was "up." Above the engines was the hangar deck, containing storage rooms and a small shuttle craft. Next came the hydroponics and cabin decks, with quarters enough for two dozen crew members—male on one deck and female on the other, in Islamic space-vessel tradition. They saw at least twice that number hard at work in various parts of the ship, readying it for emergency takeoff. Many of these were ground crew who would not be going on the mission, and many more were at work down in Hades getting supplies ready.

In the center of the crew decks was the main ship's computer. Above this lay the recreation deck, also serving as the mess hall and prayer room. Then came the flight deck, with command, navigation, communication, and monitoring stations running around the periphery, and the captain's cabin and a VIP room in the center. Higher yet was the cramped data deck, with scientific instrumentation for observing planets, and finally, there was the tiny radar/lidar room in the very tip.

Two shafts ran down the central axis of the spacecraft, side by side, like a double-barreled shotgun. One was empty but for handholds—just wide enough for two people to conveniently go up or down in zero gravity; the other was a small elevator shaft used when the vessel was under acceleration.

After the tour, Tariq and the priest began installing their gear on the data deck.

They worked around the clock, fueling up, loading consumables, doing routine maintenance, and the thousand and one chores needed to get ready. By postponing minor maintenance and low-priority work, they were ready for launch in two days.

After the ground crew had left the ship, and the last of the flight crew members had boarded, Tariq found himself strapped in on the flight deck in the privileged seat just behind the pilot. To her right were the Byelorussian copilot/navigator, the commmperson Arnaldo, and Chief Science Officer Fitzpatrick. To Tariq's right, the chief was strapped in, and next to her was her Tarzanoid companion. Everyone was wearing green government-issue jumpsuits. The remaining crew members were in the lower decks.

While the pilot ran down the checklist, Tariq whispered to Ollerenshaw, "I don't believe I've formally met your assistant."

"Oh, him?" She spoke drowsily. Tariq could see in her half-open eyes that she was speaking through a drug-induced smog that insulated her brain against the claustrophobic challenge of the spacecraft. "That's Sly."

"Yo!" he called out, saluting.

"I keep thinking I have seen him somewhere," said Tariq.

Ollerenshaw chuckled. "You probably have."

"Has he ever been on the Moon?"

"Only when he was shipped here," she said.

Tariq stared at the man. He was big, square-jawed, and muscular, in his thirties, wearing a headband.

Tariq shook his head. "I just cannot place him."

"That's Sylvester Stallone," said Ollerenshaw, smiling.

"Who?"

Her smile turned to a frown. "You don't know who Sylvester Stallone is?"

Tariq shrugged.

"He's only the greatest actor of the twentieth century!" she said. "Didn't you take *any* humanities courses in university?"

Tariq experienced the humiliation he so often felt when conversing with truly cultured people. "He's a *robot*?" he said weakly.

"Yes, but a *fully functional* robot," she said, winking. "Nothing's too good for our taxpayers."

Fairouz announced over the intercom: "Final warning! Prepare for launch." Then, to Arnaldo, she said, "Comm clear?"

Arnaldo nodded and said, "On-board commlines clear; commlink to Hades Control on channel one."

Fairouz spoke with the Byelorussian copilot, who was completely bald. Nobody could pronounce his name, so he was simply known as Grodno, after his hometown. "Systems nominal?" she said.

"Good enough for government work!" he replied with a Slavic accent.

"Hades Control," said Fairouz over the radio. "Are we clear for ejection orbit?"

"Roger," replied Hades. "You are clear for escape. Good luck!"

Fairouz hit the thumb switch on the joystick, and the metamatter in the main fuel tank began to flow in microscopic bits into the combustion chamber. There, laser beams heated it until it destabilized and shot out the rear, magnetohydrodynamically channeled out in a great burst of optical and thermal radiation.

Fairouz smiled. Not only was she in her element, but by interplanetary law, she was now in command. Until they returned, the chief was merely second in command; Father Fitzpatrick, as science officer, was number three. The chief could order the destination changed or even abort the mission, but Fairouz was obliged to obey only if, in her judgment, it did not endanger the spacecraft and crew. It brought back happy memories of roaming the asteroids alone, where not one soul could challenge her decisions.

Slowly, with an acceleration barely perceptible to the crew, the great ship began to leave its orbit. Gradually, the acceleration became noticeable.

Minute by minute, it grew until it equaled one Earth gravity. After living in low gravity for so long, it felt like an elephant on their chests.

Pluto drifted away gradually as they spiraled out.

Soon they were free of the planet's gravity and were moving away from the Sun, out toward interstellar space. At this point, Fairouz turned on the dustcatcher. Powerful currents of electricity flowed through it. The huge network began to attract dust particles ionized by extreme ultraviolet starlight. Interstellar and solar protons, electrons, hydrogen, and helium atoms also were swept up and separated from the dust. Electrostatic fields pulled the particles in and squirted them like a fluid through the web and into the engines.

They continued to accelerate until they reached two gees, the maximum the structure could handle, and twice the normal cruising acceleration of the vessel.

Despite the fact that he worked out religiously on Charon, even Tariq was tired out by the constant weight pulling on his muscles. He glanced around the deck. The chief was barely conscious. Fitzpatrick was reciting suras from the Koran with his rosary. Arnaldo was watching a TV show from the ship's entertainment database. The co-pilot was asleep. Only Fairouz and the robot seemed to enjoy the acceleration.

CHAPTER 6

After they had accelerated at two gees for two hours, Fairouz announced, "Pit stop." She pulled the joystick back and reduced the acceleration to a steady one gee.

"Oh, my aching bod!" said the chief, blinking her bleary eyes. There was a rousing chorus of groans as bodies used to low gravity protested the acceleration they had endured. After two hours of double-gee acceleration, one gee felt almost pleasant.

"I see we've all been doing our low-grav exercises, haven't we?" said Fairouz sarcastically. She was answered by more groans. "That's what I get for hiring myself out to a bunch of civil servants," she muttered.

Tariq snickered inwardly at the thought of all his colleagues who had stopped doing the prescribed workouts. He could see that most of the members of the crew were in a similar dilapidated condition. He noted with approval that Fairouz seemed indifferent to the acceleration.

"Fifteen minutes only!" she said.

"Do we have to go this fast?" asked Ollerenshaw plaintively.

"All I know," said Fairouz, "is Father Fitzpatrick said we should get there as quick as possible, so I've plotted the fastest course this ship can take without falling apart."

"What good does that do if *we* fall apart?" muttered Ollerenshaw.

"Speed is imperative," said Tariq. "We have no idea how long this phenomenon is going to last. It could disappear in a second."

"Heaven forbid!" said the priest. "That's all I need to make my day complete—arrive just as the damn thing is disappearing."

"It would not be the first time the path of science has been impeded by unexpected changes," said Tariq.

"Yes," said Fitzpatrick. "Murphy's Law is universal!"

"My job is to get this ship where it's needed for scientific observation," said Fairouz. "That's what it says in my contract, and I'm not going to screw it up just because some of us have been exercising our perks more than our bodies."

After a moment the flight deck was empty of all but Tariq, Fairouz, and Grodno, who was still asleep. The others had hobbled away to pursue personal housekeeping chores.

Tariq looked up from his keyboard. "What brought you to the Moon?" he asked in Arabic.

"At the time, it seemed like a good place to be born," she replied in the same tongue. "My parents moved there just after the war, with my five brothers—"

"Five brothers?" said Tariq.

"Yes. No sisters."

"Must have been quite a tough upbringing," he said.

"Not so bad. I was the youngest of the litter, so they treated me like a princess. It had its advantages. I never had to worry about anyone beating me up, because my brothers were always around protecting me. It did wonders for my self-confidence."

Tariq smiled.

"Where were you born?" she asked.

"A little village between Cairo and Tura. Or, it used to be—before it was vaporized."

"But now and then I catch you using Japanese."

Tariq smiled. "I was lucky enough to win a scholarship to Japan, where I did my undergraduate and graduate studies."

"That must make you a little suspicious to some Eurafricans."

"Some of the narrow-minded ones think I've been corrupted into the godless ways of the Japanese. They call me a Zen Arab."

"Are you?"

"Well, I can see more points of view than many of my countrymen. I sometimes feel like an outsider."

"I know how you feel," she said. "I've always been one."

"Because you're lunar?"

"No, because I'm a Druze."

He nodded.

"To traditional Christians," she said, "we're just Muslims. To Muslims, we're heretics, even though we believe that Muhammad was a prophet of the Lord. They're bothered by our rejection of the five pillars of Islam—even though we have moral principles just as good—and by our belief in reincarnation."

"Reincarnation?" said Tariq, startled.

"Yes. Of course, a scientist like you will just laugh."

"No, I won't laugh." His mind drifted back to Egypt. He had never admitted it to an adult, but there had been times when he lived in the pyramid, during the war, when he'd had the eerie feeling that he'd once been a pharaoh, or at the very least a scribe, thousands of years ago. His adult mind knew it was only a silly childhood fantasy, a natural consequence of living in that ancient tomb. Yet even now, on rare occasions, it was his secret pleasure to imagine himself in command of the forces of ancient Egypt, with thousands of slaves to do his bidding. They reminded him of the engineers, secretaries, bureaucrats, and technicians who had built the greatest monuments of all time—the observatories scattered throughout the solar system, where he and the select few of the scientific priesthood peered into the face of God Himself.

Fairouz was speaking, bringing him suddenly back to reality. "It doesn't help that we keep our rituals secret." She waved her hands helplessly. "The wise Druzes a thousand years ago decreed that most knowledge of our religion should be hidden from the ignorant. Even I am not permitted to know the innermost rituals. I am only a *juhhal*, an ordinary Druze—not an *'uggal*, with the complete sacred knowledge. Anyway, I'm not really religious. Even some of the Druzes are suspicious of me."

"It also didn't help that some of you fought on the side of the *Israelis.*" He spat the word out, a host of less pleasant wartime memories surging forth.

Just then, a small voice said in sauerkraut-flavored English, "Vhere can a guy get a little affection around here?"

They both looked around, and an orange tabby cat ran past.

"Oh, no!" said Tariq. "She didn't bring her cats with her, did she?"

The cat sniffed around the base of the main control, then walked over to Fairouz.

"I'm afraid so," said Fairouz. "She blackmailed me. Wouldn't get some stuff I wanted if I didn't let her. But I put my foot down. I wouldn't let her bring more than one."

The cat paused, sniffed her boots, and jumped into her lap. She embraced him affectionately.

"He's certainly adapted all right to one gee," said Tariq, "after all that time on Pluto."

"And what's your name?" she asked the animal.

"My name iss Schwarzenegger," replied the cat. Its artificial-intelligence collar translated the question and answered automatically from its limited vocabulary. "But you can call me Schwartzie," it added.

The cat purred loudly, and the AI unit said, "I am experiencing contentment."

"And that's not all she brought aboard," said Fairouz leering.

"You mean Sly," said Tariq.

"Yes. She thinks of everything. Nothing's too good for our administrator."

The elevator opened up and Arnaldo ran out in a near panic. Immediately Fairouz tensed up, and the cat in her lap did likewise, staring at the man. Her hands leapt over to the control panel, to the red emergency section. "What's wrong?" she said in English.

"I almost missed it!" he said in his thick Italian accent. *"Police Witch!"* he exclaimed, hitting the keyboard and talking to the comm-puter.

She laughed, and Tariq looked at her inquisitively.

"That's one of his favorite shows," she said.

"I forgot to record the damn thing," said Arnaldo.

Tariq's nose wrinkled with disdain. "Here we are," he said, "on what could be the greatest exploration of this century, and all you can think of is television?"

Arnaldo shrugged. "It's a helluva lot better than life."

"Don't be too hard on him," said Fairouz. "We're lucky. Like most of the crew, he's civil service, but he's good anyway."

"I was assigned Pluto," said Arnaldo, his eyes glued to the TV monitor, earphone in place, "and I didn't have any friends in the right coordinates to get me sent somewhere nice. I requested Paris, but they gave me Pluto!" He made an obscene Italian gesture.

"He's a whiz at communications," said Fairouz. "When we're in space, he uses our high-gain antenna to pick up satellite TV transmissions from Earth."

"It's pretty tricky, lemme tell you," said Arnaldo. "What with the antennas orbiting around the Earth, the high directionality of the beams, and our changing position, it's one *macro*-headache to lock onto a signal long enough to get a whole program."

She nodded. "Yes, he's got it all figured out. He's calculated where the satellites will be around Earth at any given time and he's got the whole programming schedule for all the satellites he's interested in stored on his database. He knows the antenna patterns on the satellite transmitters, and he can figure out when one of them will be pointing close enough in our direction so he can pick up the programs he wants."

On the comm video monitor there appeared an image of a female police officer, chasing after a criminal in some great metropolis.

"Thank God," said Arnaldo. "I just missed the beginning. I should be able to get the rest of the program."

The police officer waved a wand and the man she was chasing froze in a storm of sparkles.

Tariq cringed and shook his head.

"You know, what we really need right now," said Fairouz, "is a little music to entertain us." She hit a key on the console and said into the microphone, "Let's hear a little of the Interstellar Zits."

Immediately, the wailing sound of one of Earth's

greatest hits filled the flight deck. The Zits were one of the biggest tooie groups, singing only two-tone songs.

Tariq cringed again and gave Fairouz a look indicating that his opinion of her had fallen by several quantum levels. She ignored him.

Arnaldo began snapping his fingers to the tune of the music, while the earphone kept him connected to the TV show.

"You like that stuff?" said Tariq to the Italian, pointing to a speaker blaring the music.

Arnaldo nodded absently, and said, "Coherent stuff! Don't you like it?"

"I prefer more serious music," he said. "Like cyber-Beethoven."

"No accounting for taste," replied Arnaldo with a shrug.

Fairouz looked at Tariq as if he had suddenly become a hundred years old.

"I will never understand popular music," said Tariq. "How can anyone listen to it when there are hundreds of symphonies and chamber works of great synthesized composers—all the wonderful compositions that they might have written had they lived, produced with the aid of some of the most brilliant programmers in the history of AI!"

"Is there anything else on that's good?" Fairouz asked.

Arnaldo verified that his show was being recorded and skimmed through a series of other channels on the same satellite. He stopped at one and switched on the speaker.

A man was saying, "—so I say unto you, brothers and sisters, listen to the word of the Lord!" He spoke with a deep South Noram accent, and was dressed in a white suit and a cowboy hat.

"What is that?" said Tariq.

"Obey the Good Book," said the speaker, "and don't let the devil catch you with his hellish brew!" He stood on a floodlit stage with a glowing halo floating over his head.

Arnaldo shrugged. "Just one of those videvangelists they love in Noram."

"Remember what the Good Book says," the evangelist continued. " 'And when Jesus Son of Mary said: O Children of Israel! Lo! I am the messenger of God unto you, confirmin' that which was revealed before me in the Torah, and bringin' good tidin's of a messenger who cometh after me, whose name is the Praised One. Yet when he hath come unto them with clear proofs, they said: This is mere magic.' "

"These guys are really popular in Noram," Arnaldo said. "People travel from kilometers around just to see them live."

"Yay, verily! And elsewhere in the Koran it sayeth: 'He hath ordained fer you that religion which He commended unto Noah, and that which We inspire in Thee Muhammad, and that which We commended unto Abraham and Moses and Jesus, saying: Establish the religion, and be not divided therein. Allah chooseth fer himself whom He will, and guideth unto Himself him who turneth toward Him.'"

"Sermons bore me," said Tariq.

"So key those dollars to your lovin' brother, Billy Bob Arafat, so we can keep the message of Allah alive, and clobber the forces of the devil!"

"Me, too," said Arnaldo, switching to another channel.

A trio of electric lute players appeared. Each pluck of the string was synchronized by an audivid processor so it produced images from modern Chinese sitcoms, while the music itself consisted of the old neorock classic, "I'm Just a Lonely Pubernaut."

"Hey!" said Fairouz. "It's the Raging Fungus! Great group when you're feeling nostalgic."

Arnaldo shrugged. "Too dense for me, person."

The cat began to howl, and its AI box said, "Zis is my kind of music!"

Tariq groaned, closed his eyes, and lay back in his chair.

After three days, Fairouz reversed the ship's direction and began to decelerate in order to match velocity with the target vortex, which by now had grown to over sixty thousand kilometers in diameter.

When traveling backwards, they monitored their progress on television monitors, radar, and lidar mounted on the aft of the spacecraft, similar to the equipment in

the nose that detected and automatically evaded interstellar debris.

At last they approached the mysterious vortex. They
matched velocity with it and rotated by 180 degrees
again until they were drifting slowly toward it and to one
side, aiming to miss it. By now it extended almost one
hundred thousand kilometers. Against the blackness of
interstellar space, it glowed red and blue, and occasional
discharges of intense electric currents raged in the mysterious plasma.

On the flight deck, the forward screens that filled the
ceiling of their cabin showed seething plasma.

The crew remained belted in, to keep from floating
around in zero gravity now that acceleration had
stopped.

Tariq hunched over a portable terminal attached to his
seat, talking softly into its microphone, hitting keys, and
studying the colored graphs of the display.

"It's still growing," he said to Fairouz. "God only
knows what it is, but it's still growing."

CHAPTER 7

While the others stared in awe at the eerie sight of the vortex on the main screen that filled the ceiling, Tariq quietly continued to murmur commands to his computer. Glowing swirls of plasma rotated slowly in front of them.

"What the hell *is* that?" asked the chief.

"Glory be to the Father, the Son, the Holy Ghost, and the Prophet Muhammad!" said the priest.

"In all my days," said Fairouz, "I've never seen anything like that. Except maybe it's a little like the time I was doing a fast flyby through Jupiter's shadow and caught a glimpse of the Io torus."

"Ah-ha!" said Tariq.

"What have you found?" said Fitzpatrick.

"It all fits in with my observations back on Charon. We found a thirteen-hour periodicity in the signal. I've just done some Doppler measurements, bouncing radar off plasma blobs. The plasma you see up there on the screen is rotating as if it were a solid body," said Tariq.

"How can it do that?" said Fairouz.

"A magnetic field strong enough could do the trick," said Fitzpatrick. "It happens all the time in magnetospheres on the Earth, Jupiter, and several other places in the solar system."

"But the sixty-four eurafrodollar question is," said Tariq, "where is the magnetic field coming from?"

The Jesuit nodded. "There's no body out there that we can see. Is there anything on the radar besides plasma?"

"Nothing I can see," said Tariq. "The higher frequencies penetrate all the way through the plasma, and there doesn't seem to be anything solid there."

"It's got to be a tiny black hole," said Fitzpatrick. "Imagine, a black hole, just waiting for us to visit it."

"A black hole!" exclaimed Ollerenshaw. "No one's ever found one of those things, have they?"

"Not within light-years of our solar system," said Fitzpatrick.

"That would be a fantastic discovery, wouldn't it?" said Ollerenshaw.

"It would be fabulous, indeed," said the priest.

"Easily worthy of major press coverage?" she added.

"Certainly. Many a physicist would give his right brain for a chance at a close look!"

"But it still doesn't make any sense," said Tariq. "If that is a black hole, then the whole magnetosphere should have been visible all at once, instead of gradually appearing out of nothing."

"Like the Cheshire cat in reverse," said Ollerenshaw.

The bald copilot began to look agitated. "Something weird is going on here!"

"You're telling me!" said Fairouz. "I've been checking our position with the Pluto beacon, and we're drifting toward that thing, whatever it is."

"How much is the drift?" asked the copilot.

"Around five meters per second."

"That is not much," said Tariq.

"It's too much," said Fairouz. "I put this sucker in here at zero meters per second, and believe me, I'm used to slow approaches to asteroids. It's too soon for us to have drifted that much unless it's heavier than it looks."

"And we're accelerating!" said the copilot, pointing at the digital display.

Fairouz switched her screen to the same data link and, sure enough, they watched as the relative velocity reading slowly increased in the third decimal place:

5.413 MPS
5.414 MPS
5.415 MPS

"That's an awfully small acceleration to get excited about," said Fitzpatrick.

"Yes, but it shouldn't even be measurable at all yet," said Fairouz. "Our drifts with respect to any gravitating body around here are so small and our errors in these measurements are so tiny that any acceleration is significant."

"Will someone explain to me what is going on in plain English?" said Ollerenshaw.

"Whatever that thing is, it's pulling us toward it slowly," said Fairouz.

"Are we going to crash?" Ollerenshaw asked.

"Not if I have anything to say about it!" said Fairouz. "Grab on," she said into the intercom. "Prepare for minor course correction." She hit a thruster and they felt a gentle acceleration.

In a moment, she had neutralized the acceleration. "There!" she said. Into the intercom, she said, "Maneuver complete. I've established a large circular orbit around the thing." To the flight deck crew, she added, "That takes care of that."

"But how can a blob of plasma have enough gravitation to attract us?" said Tariq. "Unless it is a black hole."

"Maybe it's got an unusual amount of ultradense metastable dark matter," said Fitzpatrick.

"But that still wouldn't explain its sudden appearance out of nothing," said Tariq.

The copilot tapped the velocity display again impatiently. It showed an acceleration of 0.03 meters per second.

Fairouz said, "Oh, no! We're drifting again! There must be an eccentricity in my orbit." She touched the thruster again for a moment and the reading fell to zero.

"Give me an estimate on the mass," said Fairouz, "assuming it's some kind of point mass attracting us."

The copilot talked rapidly to his computer and hit a series of keys. On his screen and on Fairouz's, there appeared the line:

ESTIMATED MASS: 7 E9 KG

"Seven times ten to the ninth kilos. It's like a small asteroid," said Fairouz.

"Yes," said Fitzpatrick. "It could be one with an anomalously intense magnetic field. That would explain a lot."

"I wonder," said Tariq. "Have that thing display some more decimal places."

Fairouz nodded to the copilot. He spoke into his computer and immediately the display read:

7.87 E9 KG

"So what?" said Fairouz.

"Wait a minute," said Tariq, watching the screen, and as he spoke, it changed to:

7.88 E9 KG

"Aha!" said Tariq.

"Just measurement error," said Fitzpatrick.

"We'll see," said Tariq. As they watched, another decimal point was added to the figure, and then another and another:

7.89 E9 KG
7.90 E9 KG
7.91 E9 KG

The changes began to increase so rapidly that it became hard to read the last digit.

"The mass really is increasing," said Tariq, nodding his head slightly.

"What does it mean?" said Fitzpatrick. "How can that be? It must be an artifact of the measurement."

The numbers continued to increase.

8.33 E9 KG

Periodically, Fairouz adjusted the position of the ship to remain at a safe distance.

8.79 E9 KG

Tariq studied his instruments and said, "We are being bombarded by energetic particles."

9.26 E9 KG

"Is it dangerous?" Ollerenshaw asked.

9.58 E9 KG

"It depends on how long we are going to be here," he said, "and how well shielded the vessel is."

1.04 E10 KG

Fairouz ordered all personnel to strap in, and began firing the ship's thrusters frequently, trying to keep the orbit in step with the increasing mass.

2.37 E10 KG

Tariq and Fairouz heatedly discussed the radiation shielding on the spacecraft and the intensity of the energetic particles bombarding them.

7.51 E10 KG

By now, even the first digit was changing so rapidly that only the exponent was readable.

3.27 E11 KG
1.99 E12 KG
5.08 E13 KG

"This is crazy!" said Fairouz.
"I do not think we have any problem from the radiation," Tariq said. "The main source of danger is proton bombardment, with megavolt protons being emitted from the magnetic field of the vortex. Our shielding can absorb these fluxes."

7.44 E15 KG

"That thing's gaining mass like crazy!" said the priest.
"Maybe it really is a white hole," said Tariq.

2.13 E16 KG

"I thought they'd been discredited a long time ago,"
Fitzpatrick said.
"Can you think of anything better?"

8.05 E19 KG

"Look!" said Fairouz, pointing excitedly at the screen.
A small black circular "opening" appeared in the center
of the vortex. The mass measurement kept rising.
"A black hole!" said Ollerenshaw.

7.79 E22 KG

"No," said Tariq after a moment's calculation. "Magnetic field intensity is only a few gauss at the surface—
much weaker than if it were an honest-to-God black hole.
Besides, it would be sucking matter in, not spewing it
out. Fairouz, can you magnify that image?"
"Roger," she said, hitting a key.
A square fiducial mark appeared on the screen. She
manipulated it until it enclosed the black circular region.
Then she expanded it until the black region filled the
main screen over their heads and became gray.

2.63 E25 KG

"Let's have some contrast enhancement," said Tariq.
Fairouz nodded and hit some more keys. Suddenly
the subtle variations in the gray were exaggerated until
they became clear markings. They could see a mountain range, a sinuous river valley, and a desert swept
by dunes.

2.63 E25 KG

"It's a planet!" exclaimed the Jesuit. Even Tariq was awed by the sight of it. Around the edges the planet expanded, revealing more territory: vast craters, patchy clouds, and rolling hills. Lakes appeared, and then a volcano spewed smoke across a large stretch of the world. There was a haze around the edges of the planet—an atmosphere.

2.63 E25 KG

"The mass has leveled off," said Tariq. "I guess it's here to stay."

They sat in silence, watching the planet slowly rotate beneath them.

CHAPTER 8

The planet floated outside—tantalizing, mysterious, enticing.

After a while, Tariq said, "It must have tunneled from some other part of the universe."

"That makes as much sense as anything I can think of," said Fitzpatrick. "Or as little. Do you mean quantum tunneling or some kind of general-relativistic wormhole?"

"It could be either, or both," said Tariq. "Obviously, conventional quantum tunneling would not be enough."

"It would take an absurd length of time for such a massive object to get anywhere."

"But there may well be some kind of quantum tunneling that just is not dreamed of in our current theories—something that only occurs in higher dimensions. A quantum wormhole, perhaps."

"Perhaps," said Fitzpatrick, "but wormholes are unstable and wouldn't last long enough to be of any use."

"Only if current theory is complete, and it never is. The only thing that is certain is that we do not know all the laws of physics yet. Maybe we never will."

"Well, at least now we're in a stable orbit," said Fairouz. "I hope."

"How far are we from the planet?" Tariq asked.

"About a hundred thousand kilometers," she said.

"Ah, we are still in the magnetosphere, but that should not hurt," said Tariq.

"How big is it?" Fitzpatrick asked.

She looked at the radar data and did a quick calculation. "It's almost twice the diameter of Earth."

"Imagine!" said Arnaldo. "An entire planet bigger than Earth has just materialized in front of our eyes. Truly it is a miracle of God!"

Fairouz said, "It's a miracle of the laws of physics."

"Same thing," said Fitzpatrick, who then touched a button on his belt.

A voice from a small device there said, "Him unto whom belongeth the sovereignty of the heavens and the Earth and Allah is of all things the witness." It paused, then said, "Sura eighty-five, 'The mansions of the stars.' "

"What's that?" Arnaldo asked.

"My hafiz," said Fitzpatrick.

"Your what?"

"A hafiz is a man who has memorized the Koran," said Fitzpatrick. "I'm afraid I'm not quite up to that task," he said, "so I carry around a little electronic one containing some AI that listens to my conversations and pops out with an appropriate chapter from the Koran when I ask it to. You should attend my sermons."

"But I'm a Mormon," said Arnaldo.

"A Sicilian Mormon?" The priest looked at him as if suspicious of a prank.

"Oh, yes," said Arnaldo quite seriously. "Thanks to a century of Mormon missionaries, there's hardly a gentile —a non-Mormon—left in Sicily now!"

The Jesuit chuckled. "We'll turn you into a believer yet!"

"Or I'll do it to you!"

"Allah forbid!" Fitzpatrick laughed. "It was tough enough converting an old Catholic like me into a good Muslim. I don't think I could handle the transformation into a Mormon, too!"

"And now we face the most serious question of all," said Ollerenshaw.

"Yes," said Tariq. "Do we land?"

"No," said Ollerenshaw. "Don't you know anything

about history or politics? The important question is: What do we call it?"

"May God save us from politicians," said Tariq vehemently.

"I've got it," said Arnaldo. "Deseret."

"What the hell is a deseret?" Fairouz asked.

"Deseret," explained the Italian, "was the state we Mormons tried to establish in the nineteenth century in the Noram province of Utah."

"There's no way in Hades," said Ollerenshaw, "that an expedition funded by Eurafrica is going to let us give this planet a Mormon name."

"I think we ought to call it the Big Pain," said the copilot, "in honor of our sore muscles."

"And in honor of the crats who've made our lives so full of joy," added Fairouz.

A gleam came into the chief's eye, and she said, "I know a perfect name: Ollerenshaw."

"You have an even bigger ego than I thought you did," said Fairouz indignantly. "It takes a lot of nerve to name a planet after yourself."

Ollerenshaw shrugged, and said, "It takes a lot of ego to get anywhere in this world, but my ego is insignificant compared to the advantage this would give me in my career. Can you imagine having a planet named after you? No one would ever forget your name. I could do anything I wanted, and the bureaucrats of Malta would kiss my feet."

"I think we're overlooking a point of etiquette," said Fitzpatrick. "Traditionally, the discoverer gets to name the object." He bowed toward Tariq.

"I personally could not care less," said Tariq.

"There you are." said Ollerenshaw. "Planet Ollerenshaw it is!" She savored each delicious syllable with her tongue. "The world of Ollerenshaw!" She put on the voice of a mock BBC newscaster: " 'The news from Ollerenshaw today is . . .' 'This just in from Ollerenshaw!' 'The colonists of Ollerenshaw met with diplomats from planet Earth.' 'The Ollerenshaw–Pluto trade balance.' 'There were fireworks over Ollerenshaw City, capital of planet Ollerenshaw, as they celebrated their greatest festival, Ollerenshaw Day, held on the anniversary of the discovery of the planet by Lady Sybil Ollerenshaw.' " She drifted off into a silent daydream, a smile upon her face.

"Sorry to rain on your fireworks," said Tariq, "but I am afraid it would not stick. When William Herschel discovered the planet Uranus, he was as politically astute as you, and he named it after his king. George, he called it, or *Georgium Sidus* in Latin: George's Star."

Ollerenshaw's dreamy smile deflated.

"A planet named George?" said Fairouz, chuckling.

"No one else wanted to honor King George with a permanent billboard in the sky," continued Tariq. "Certainly not the French, the other nation great in astronomy then. Nor the Americans, who had just fought for their independence from him."

"Nor the Irish," added Fitzpatrick. "And besides, every name has to be registered with the Interplanetary Astronomical Union. So we're back to you, Tariq. Name your planet."

"By George, I've got it," said Ollerenshaw, lighting up again. "This is brilliant. Let's name it after the President of the Federated States of Eurafrica! I don't care what the astronomers call it, but *we* can call it anything we want to right now, and they can always change the name later on."

"True," said Tariq. "Calling it George's Star did not hurt Herschel at the royal court, and in fact, it got him a royal pension, too."

"A royal pension?" said Ollerenshaw. "Sounds good to me!"

"As the chief scientist of this expedition," said the Jesuit, "I must insist that the honor of naming the planet belongs to Tariq. That's your job," he said, looking at the Egyptian, "and no one can do it for you."

The chief's eyes narrowed and she sat back, craftily resolving to withdraw from the discussion and to put her suggestion in the official report, regardless of the outcome of the debate.

Grudgingly, Tariq thought for several moments and then brightened, "I have it." Everyone looked at him expectantly. "Ronin!"

He was greeted by blank faces.

"In Japan, the Ronin were samurai warriors without a feudal lord. They were, one might say, free-lance. And to this day, students who fail the entrance exams to get into universities but continue to try again and again are known as Ronin. This planet, like the samurai of old, wanders from place to place, never finding a home."

"Excellent!" said Fitzpatrick. "It kind of breaks with the Greco–Roman tradition for naming planets, but it's sure going to please our Asian friends."

A calculating look came over Ollerenshaw's face. "Maybe that's not such a bad idea," she said. "We've been trying to improve our relations, but Allah knows we've come to the brink of war with them more than once. Maybe this will do the trick. If I present it right to Malta, they might give me a couple of brownie points for being a fantastic diplomat. In any event, I can let *them* make the decision. I'll give them a choice between Ronin and the President. Passing the buck is always the safest way to promotion, anyway."

"Which brings us to the second most important question," said Tariq sarcastically. "All in favor of landing on Ronin, say aye."

The whole flight deck crew, with the exception of Ollerenshaw, enthusiastically cried out, "Aye!"

"And," Tariq continued, "all opposed, signify by jumping out the airlock without a pressure suit."

Ollerenshaw glared at him.

Fairouz turned to her main screen and increased the magnification of the planet's image.

"Ronin, here we come." said Fitzpatrick. Everyone but Ollerenshaw cheered.

"Maybe," said Fairouz quietly, "instead of naming the planet now, we should wait and see if the inhabitants have already got a name for it."

The flight deck fell silent.

"What inhabitants?" Tariq asked.

"Those," Fairouz said, pointing at the main screen. "The ones who live in those cities." The dark side of the planet was approaching, and several regions there glowed vividly, like the megalopolises on the night side of Earth.

CHAPTER 9

All over the ship, the eyes of the twenty-four crew members were on screens showing the dark side of the planet. On the flight deck, even Grodno, who seemed to have only two states—sleep and yawning—was riveted to the screen.

Long stretches of blue and red streaked across the blackness, like vast superhighways. Other, huge areas of the night surface were covered with great blue splotches like vast cities. Visions of an advanced civilization, populated by strange inhuman creatures, flashed through their minds.

And then Tariq laughed.

A moment later, Fitzpatrick joined him.

The crew looked as if the men were crazy, until the priest explained, "Those are auroras—northern lights!"

Fairouz turned red.

Tariq said, "Who wants to go down there?"

"We've only got room for five people in the shuttle," said Fairouz. "That's me and four volunteers."

"Obviously, I have to go," said Tariq immediately.

Fairouz nodded approvingly at his willingness.

"And I, too," said Fitzpatrick.

Fairouz arched an eyebrow toward Ollerenshaw.

"It is my duty to go," she said.

"May Allah save us!" said Fairouz.

"And I'm going to bring along a friend," said the chief.

"You have a *friend*?"

"Sly."

"*Sly*? Your fully functional solid-state Don Juan?"

"That's not as bad an idea as it sounds," said Fitzpatrick. "Sly's a general-purpose robot built for rugged planetary work."

"I just added some optional extras to the requisition," said the chief with a wink.

"He could come in very handy down there," added the priest.

"I'll buy that," said Fairouz. "So now we have our shuttle crew. But we're going to take some sensible precautions first—we're going to send down some robot probes."

"That is a wise move," said Tariq softly as he bent over a data display. "Especially since there is something living there."

All eyes turned toward him.

"I have just gotten the spectral analysis of the atmosphere. It is loaded with oxygen."

"And only life can produce oxygen in large quantities," said Fitzpatrick excitedly.

There was silence.

"As far as we know," added Tariq.

It took them an hour to prep and launch the three grapefruit-sized planetary lander probes. They watched anxiously as they descended through the atmosphere on the sunlit side of the planet, a metal mesh spread out behind each one like a badminton bird, to maximize atmospheric drag and slow it down with a minimum of fuel. One went to a northern midlatitude, one to the equator, and one to a southern midlatitude.

There was surprisingly little variation across the planet. There were no polar caps and no equatorial deserts, other than patches similar to those at other latitudes.

The images from the television system aboard the robotic probes were displayed side by side on the main monitor screen in the flight-deck ceiling. They watched the surface of the planet slowly approach, as mountain ranges became distinct hills, and valleys resolved into streams cutting through orange plains.

The first to land was the southern probe. It showed a bleak desert landscape of rippled sand dunes. Nothing moved.

The second landed near a lake, where gentle waves lapped against a sandy beach. Orange weeds fringed the far shore.

The third flew north. The probe decelerated and automatically ejected the metal badminton mesh, replacing it with three small paragliders. In the thick atmosphere, it slowed to a reasonable rate and drifted down.

The image descended, revealing treetops rushing by. Fairouz manipulated the paragliders with her joystick, and aimed the lander for a clearing.

Suddenly the image stopped, tilted at a crazy angle. "We're on the ground!" said Fairouz with satisfaction.

Cheers resounded on the flight deck.

Automatically, the lander sprouted six insectlike legs and stood up, righting the camera. The image leveled off. The robot stood like a metal spider and began to scan the surface. There was a profusion of colors, as if from fields of flowers. Reds, oranges, and fuchsia predominated.

All of them watched the monitor screen, except Arnaldo, who kept one eye on a snowy image of the TV signal he was picking up from Earth—the ever-popular series, *Psychic Dentist.*

Tariq studied the telemetry readout from the lander. "Incredible!" he exclaimed. "The temperature really is about thirty-two degrees centigrade!"

"So it confirms the IR measurement," said Fitzpatrick, nodding with a puzzled expression.

"I thought," said Tariq, "that it might have been some freak atmospheric phenomenon that heated the upper layers so much, but it is real."

"Wonderful," said Fairouz. "Imagine, it's just a little bit warmer down there than it is in this room right now. Maybe we can even go swimming! Nothing like those icy transplutonian planets, thank God. How can it possibly get that warm?"

"It must be internal heat," said Tariq.

"Yes," said Fitzpatrick, "like on Earth."

"Even I," said Ollerenshaw, "sense something weird here. Why isn't this thing an ice ball like the others?"

"Why is Earth hot inside?" asked Tariq. "Radioactivity. Practically everything in the universe is radioactive, and there is enough in the rocks to melt the insides of the Earth."

"That's what gives us volcanoes and geysers and drifting continents," added the priest.

"So something like that could be happening on this planet," said Tariq. "And since it is much larger than Earth, the surface-to-volume ratio is going to lead to a hotter planet."

"The bigger you make a planet," explained the Jesuit, "the more slowly its heat radiates away. The volume goes up rapidly, as the cube of the radius, but the area goes up slowly, as the square."

"I suppose," mused Tariq, "we shouldn't have been too surprised because Jupiter, Saturn, and Neptune all were much warmer than they should have been so far from the Sun. In fact, they radiate more heat than they receive."

"But they're gas giants," said Fitzpatrick. "They're still contracting from their formation eons ago. It's not surprising they're hot. Ronin is a terrestrial planet, so it can only be getting its heat from radioisotopic decay."

They returned to the screen, where the robot's slowly panning camera absorbed the attention of the rest of the crew. In the distance they could see strange orange-colored trees, shaped rather like the onion domes of Russian churches. Flaming red grass grew everywhere, except in patches of blue that seemed to be dry areas. There were low rolling hills, and in the distance, behind some trees, was a white stalk culminating in a mushroom cloud that pulsated visibly.

"So there really is life here," said Fitzpatrick softly.

In the sky, tiny dark splotches flew by, indistinct, resembling birds, yet without the hint of wings one would expect.

Suddenly Tariq felt queasy. A tingle ran down his spine, making him shake his head and shudder. He chalked it up to the excitement of seeing an alien world for the first time.

"Let us get those samples back up here," said Tariq,

impatiently. "The sooner we do, the sooner we can go down there ourselves."

Fairouz nodded and spoke into the microphone. "Probe-con, take a few samples and bring 'em back up."

Down in the satellite control room, an engineer manipulated a joystick and the robot began to walk around the planet. On the flight deck, the scene bobbed up and down.

Tariq and Fitzpatrick selected spots from which to take samples and the engineer pushed the joystick thumb switch. A metal proboscis descended from the robot body and collected microscopic pieces of soil and plant life. Another probe sucked in an air sample.

"That's enough," said Fitzpatrick after the third sample.

Fairouz said, "Okay, probe-con, bring 'em back up."

After a moment the screen vibrated as a tiny subassembly within the sphere unlatched itself, fired a miniature metamatter-fueled rocket, and shot up into the air. The robot's camera followed it, but in a moment it was too small to see.

The surface roiled with dust from the microrocket, as the camera resumed recording the scene around the robot.

Within an hour, they had rendezvoused with the five-centimeter-long, one-centimeter-wide rockets, and the scientists were anxiously putting the samples they had collected through spectroscopic, magnetic resonance, and chromatographic tests.

After a few minutes, Tariq and Fitzpatrick returned to the flight deck to make their report to Ollerenshaw. They were both smiling.

"It's safe," said Fitzpatrick. "The air is definitely breathable, although the life-forms, the bacteria, are quite different from anything I've ever seen. They don't seem to like our cells and our cells don't seem to like them, and as best we can tell, there doesn't seem to be a risk of them infecting us or vice versa."

"Of course," said Tariq, "we can never be sure at this stage. There could always be some strange microbe that likes us—perhaps a virus—but I for one am willing to take the chance."

Ollerenshaw clearly did not like the last remark. "You mean, we could come down with a plague?"

"Not if we all wear pressure suits," said Fitzpatrick.

The chief looked unconvinced.

"Che figura!" said Arnaldo, staring at his snow-filled video screen and throwing his hands up in frustration.

With a pained expression Fairouz said, "What's the matter?"

"I can't get *My Three Clones*. Over and over I've calculated it, and it *still* isn't coming in."

"That's one of my favorites, too," said Ollerenshaw, with an expression of genuine disappointment.

"We're awfully far from Earth," said Fitzpatrick. "It's amazing you're able to get *anything* at this distance. Can you get *The Sister Sisters*?"

Arnaldo consulted his master schedule in the main data bank.

"What's that one about?" said Fairouz.

The Jesuit replied with some embarrassment, "Three nuns who are biological sisters. They work undercover for the Pope, going on secret missions for the Vatican, reporting to a mysterious bishop known only as Carlo. Used to be called *Carlo's Angels*. Actually, I don't watch it much."

"Not on for a couple of hours," said Arnaldo.

"You'd better not fail to record *my* favorite show," said the chief.

"What's that?" asked Arnaldo.

"Gidget Goes to Mars."

"That's one of *my* favorites, too!" he said.

"It's on tonight," she added.

"It's a *crime* they don't make shows like that anymore," he said.

"I see you are a man of taste," said Ollerenshaw approvingly.

Tariq oriented himself toward Earth with the aid of the navigation screen, and said a little prayer toward Mecca, an expression of martyrdom on his face.

CHAPTER 10

The next day, they packed the shuttle with gear and supplies. During the night, Fairouz had slowly built up the
air pressure in the *Ulug Beg* to match the somewhat
higher pressure on Ronin, to avoid problems with the
bends when going to and from the planet.

Down in the shuttle bay, just above the engines, three
crew members pushed the now-weightless shuttle craft to
the edge of the closed bay door. When the *Ulug Beg* was
underway, the shuttle was stowed in the center of the
deck, like a seed in a great pod, where its mass would not
create stability problems during acceleration.

The shuttle was a small, sleek vessel, looking rather
like a streamlined flatiron, designed for minimal weight
and maximum efficiency. Its borosilicate hull dissipated
energy with minimum use of fuel, and its sturdy wings
and tail gave it control on planets with atmospheres.

After breakfast and morning prayers, the five crew
members crammed aboard. Fairouz, Tariq, Fitzpatrick,
and Ollerenshaw wore pressure suits, with sidearms
belted to them; Sly did not need a suit. Their faces were
grimmer than they had been in the comfort of the flight
deck. They realized too well they were soon to step onto a
world filled with unknown dangers.

As they strapped themselves in, Tariq again felt a moment of queasiness and a tingle down his spine, which he attributed to the adrenaline now pumping in his veins.

Fairouz twisted around to face the crew and pointed to a black box on the floor below her seat. "Now, this is the most important device on this vessel."

"Is that where you keep the barf bags?" said the chief with genuine interest, though she was half asleep from anticlaustrophobia drugs.

"No," said Fairouz with a snort. "That's the emergency autopilot. If anything happens to me, push the red button on that sucker. It will talk you through the lift-off procedures, so you can return to the *Ulug Beg*. It can't handle every contingency, but it should be able to get you out of ninety percent of the messes you might find yourself in without me."

Ollerenshaw looked doubtful.

Fairouz went down the checklist on the video screen and chatted with the *Ulug Beg*'s copilot. Then she looked over her shoulder at the rest of the shuttle crew and said, "Is everybody all set?"

They mumbled their assent, none too enthusiastically in the sardine-can environment.

"Good enough for government work," said Ollerenshaw dreamily.

"Prepare for lift-off," said Fairouz. "By the way, night has fallen down at the probe site, so check your lights."

While the crew followed her order, she hit a key on the console and an alarm began to pound in the small hangar. A synthetic voice boomed outside, "All personnel leave hangar immediately. Air will be evacuated in sixty seconds." The announcement repeated and a countdown began.

At the end of the minute, a pump began to operate noisily, sucking the air out of the hangar. For the next few minutes, the crew sat and fidgeted.

Finally, the door opened a crack and the small amount of remaining air whistled out until the silence of vacuum shut it off.

In the darkness of space outside, illuminated by the hangar lights, a faint cloud enshrouded them where the moisture in the air had frozen out.

Fairouz hit another key and two actuators inside the

hangar reached out their long, cushioned arms and gently pushed the vessel sideways out the hangar doors.

They drifted for a few seconds to clear the ship safely for rocket firing. Then Fairouz fired the verniers and moved them farther away.

Though the hull above the crew compartment was made of the same opaque borosilicate as the rest of the fuselage, it was riddled with microscopic fiber optics that made it seem transparent, like a picture window on the universe. The huge planet loomed up in the sky, its details becoming clearer as their eyes adapted to the dim sunlight.

The dark planet rotated slowly beneath them. Up near the North Pole, now in darkness, they could see the blue glow of the auroras, still looking ever so much like the great megalopolises of the nighttime Earth.

Fairouz fired the reaction-control thrusters and oriented the shuttle so the planet was directly overhead, and they were traveling backwards, the aft pointing in the direction of their orbital motion.

"Stand by for descent burn," she said.

"Three, two, one," she said calmly, as if it were a Sunday jaunt around the Moon. "Fire." She hit the thumb switch on her joystick and the aft engines, miniature versions of the metamatter engines of the *Ulug Beg,* fired.

The deceleration pushed the crew into their seats. Fairouz glanced back at Ollerenshaw, who looked green behind her faceplate.

Over a period of minutes they descended toward the planet as the engines slowly decreased their orbital energy.

From his seat behind her, Tariq studied Fairouz's control panel. He recognized a data display on a small screen showing telemetry from the robot lander they were homing in on. "We're still getting data back," said Tariq, "even though it's on the other side of the planet. Did you put up a relay satcon?"

"No," said Fairouz. "It wasn't necessary. That's a smart little lander down there. It just aims its signal at the ionosphere, calculating where it has to point so that the signal will be bent back toward us. We automatically keep it informed of our current position, and changes in the signal strength from the probe let us adjust for changes in ionospheric conditions."

"Impressive," said Tariq.

They crossed the terminator between the dim sunlight side of the planet and the night half. Fairouz switched the cockpit lights to red so their eyes would be dark-adapted by the time they landed.

As the planet's night side slipped by below, they saw patches glow momentarily and turn back to black. "Strange," said Fitzpatrick. "I wouldn't have thought you would get auroral phenomena so far from the magnetic poles."

"Sometimes you get that even on Earth," said Tariq, "when there is really strong solar activity. It distorts the magnetic field and lets energetic particles slip in where they would ordinarily be forbidden. There are even cases on record of auroras seen near the equator, but they are extremely rare."

"Maybe it's some kind of luminescence," said Fitzpatrick.

"Could be," said Tariq. "Like deep-sea fish, perhaps."

As their eyes grew skilled at discerning the spots, more phosphorescent glows became evident in many places, often varying erratically.

"Look at that!" said Ollerenshaw, pointing to the receding edge of the terminator, near the north. On the dark side, a flash of whiteness surrounded by pitch black appeared.

"It is almost like a volcano," said Tariq.

"It reminds me of Io," said Fairouz. "When the volcanoes approach the day side, and they're erupting, the plumes spurt out into space, where they hit the sunlight, and then they glow like magic. It's a gorgeous sight—you ought to see it!"

"It fits," said Tariq. "There are lots of sulfur compounds in the atmosphere—not enough to be dangerous, but enough to suggest extensive active volcanism."

"Prepare to lose your breakfast," Fairouz said. "We're going to reorient for final descent."

Fairouz gave their stomachs a real trial as she reoriented the shuttle craft so it was nose first and right side up as its belly felt the first touches of the outer atmosphere. Ollerenshaw, who had fallen asleep, awoke with a start when the ship started to flip, took one look at the dizzying sight of the planet rushing across the sky, and fainted. Tariq tore his eyes from the land for a moment, glanced at Fairouz, and noted with satisfaction her calm, confident control of the vessel.

The shuttle craft heated up until the bottom was white-hot, dissipating the energy of entry, and they descended on a flight path directly toward the robot probe. The shuttle creaked and a hiss of thin air rushed by, growing in intensity until the noise filled the cabin.

Fairouz hit the air brakes, and small projections across the surface of the shuttle stuck out into the airflow. The craft fell like a rock, while the conscious members of the crew felt their stomachs lift as if in a falling elevator.

The ground came up to them at breakneck pace, illuminated by the glow of an aurora, and Ollerenshaw awoke to see the planet rushing by. Her eyes opened wide in hazy panic. Fairouz selected a smooth patch of ground and hit the forward and bottom thrusters. With a roar, the vessel settled down onto the surface of the planet.

There was a bang as they hit the ground, shaking up the crew. "We're down!" said Fairouz, as she began to shut down the thruster fuel lines one by one.

The chief looked green, and everyone else looked relieved. With the thrusters silent, they sat quietly for a moment, listening to the creaking of the super-heated parts of the spacecraft as they cooled off, and watching the dust raised by the thrusters settle around them.

"Thar she blows!" said Fairouz, pointing off to left field.

By straining, they could barely make out a tiny flashing light atop the tiny sphere of their robot probe thirty meters away.

"Good, the welcome wagon's here," said Fitzpatrick.

"All ashore who's going ashore," said Fairouz. She turned back to Ollerenshaw. "Okay, Chief? Ready for that one small step for a woman, one giant leap for womankind?"

Ollerenshaw stared at the dark, dimly lit landscape, straining to make out fuzzy objects in the distance that slowly wandered across the plains. The bright colors that had seemed riotous in the image-enhanced views from space were now dark shadows and barely discernible reddish hues. It was a cold, forbidding, alien terrain, and even with her doped-up courage, Ollerenshaw had no desire to escape from the comfortable womb of the shuttle. She took a deep breath and said, "I think it's my responsibility to stay here and supervise the activities, while you chaps get outside and set up the ground station."

"Wise move," said Fairouz sarcastically.

"In that case, I have no objection to leaving right now," said Tariq.

"Not so fast!" said Fairouz. "As the captain of this vessel, I will be the first person on the planet."

"No," said the Jesuit. "As the chief scientist, as well as your chaplain, I think I should be the one who first tests the surface of this world."

"Okay, okay," said Fairouz. "Out in the 'roids, we use a random cycle program to settle things like this." She turned to the console and spoke into the on-board computer's microphone.

"Random cycle program loaded," replied the computer. "Request labels."

"Fairouz, Tariq, and Fitzpatrick." She turned back to the men and said, "When I say the word *go*"—she whispered it to keep from triggering a false start in the computer—"it will cycle through the three names so fast that you won't be able to see them. When you call out *stop*, the voice recognition circuitry will freeze whatever name is on the screen at that moment. Can't get fairer than that, can you?"

"Sounds reasonable," said Tariq. The priest nodded.

Fairouz turned back to the microphone and said "Go!" The main video monitor in front of her lit up with the three names in rapid-fire succession, but so fast that all three seemed to be on the screen simultaneously.

"Stop!" said the priest. Immediately, the screen froze and FAIROUZ appeared on it.

Fitzpatrick shrugged. "You win," he said.

"Fan-tastic!" she said as she got up out of her seat and squeezed back to the airlock at midship.

She looked back at the crew. "Continue to use the airlock until we're sure the planet's clean." She opened the hatch, squeezed into the small space, and closed herself in. Fitzpatrick struggled out of his seat in the heavy gravity and moved back to watch her through a small porthole. She sealed up the inner hatch and opened the outer one with a pop, as a tiny pressure imbalance equilibrated.

Tariq got up suspiciously and sat in her seat. He reactivated the random-cycle program and said, "Go." The names flashed on the screen and he said, "Stop." The name FAIROUZ froze on the screen. He said "Go" and "Stop" again and FAIROUZ came up once more.

"Damn!" he muttered, and then said over the radio, "Fairouz, that program is rigged, right?" By now, she was halfway out the outer hatch.

She laughed. "It's a sucker's game."

"Do you also have a program that *never* brings up your name when you do *not* want to get called?"

"Of course," she said, happily stepping down onto the surface. "I programmed both of them a long time ago." She stood where the thrusters had burned away the vegetation. The landscape was eerily lit by the glow of a great blue auroral curtain slowly rippling in the sky. "Fan-tastic!" she exclaimed.

A moment later, she added, *"Yarabb!"* and pointed. "Look at that!"

Out in the dim distance, a glowing blob approached.

CHAPTER 11

Tariq rushed through the airlock as fast as the mechanism allowed, slamming the outer hatch against the hull so hard it shook the whole vessel. He recklessly jumped to the ground, landing with a great thump, almost breaking a leg in the process in the heavy gravity. He cursed and painfully stood up. Fairouz was walking toward the glowing, pulsating blob near the flashing light of the robot probe.

"For God's sake," he said in Arabic over the suit radio, "don't go any closer!"

Fairouz pulled her sidearm from her holster. Tariq did likewise.

He ran toward her ungracefully, in the painful stomping style necessitated by the gravity. There was enough light from the aurora overhead that their dark-adapted eyes did not need the flashlights at their sides.

The great blob resolved into a group of small, luminescent creatures.

The animals reached the robot probe, with its pulsating light on top, and paused. Tariq could now hear their little birdlike whistling sounds.

"Oh, look," said Fairouz in English. "They're curious about the robot." She paused about ten meters from it, and Tariq caught up with her. He grabbed her shoulder with his free hand, holding her back, and aimed the gun toward the creatures.

Each animal was the size of a mouse, and there were hundreds of them swarming in a long line that went off into the distance. Each one pulsated erratically, its blue glow turning on and off in an unpredictable rhythm; sometimes, groups of them pulsated in synchrony, as if part of a distinct family.

"I think they are communicating with each other through their flashes," said Tariq.

Fairouz shook his arm off and stepped several meters closer. Dozens of the little creatures swarmed over the robot excitedly. The rest milled around the spacecraft, sniffing at it.

Tariq reluctantly joined her, looking suspiciously at the animals.

Now they could see that each was furry, with one huge red eye in front of its head.

"I guess light sensitivity is more important than stereoscopic vision on this planet," said Tariq.

"Why do you say that?" Fairouz asked.

"They have just that one big eye to gather in as many photons as possible, so they cannot have three-dimensional vision."

"Makes sense."

Fitzpatrick joined them. "Well, I'll be damned!" he said, excited as only a scientist can be by the sight of something new to study. He leaned closer. The little bodies had four legs each and two long furry tails. The glow seemed to emanate from their fur. They had small round noses underneath the eye and thin, black-lipped mouths with a goatlike beard running down the chin. All the fur —from the whiskers to the tips of the tail—glowed together, whenever it was turned on.

"They're cute," said Fairouz. She stepped closer, as if to pet one.

"They could be poisonous!" said Tariq. "Don't touch them," he added in Arabic.

"They can't hurt me in my suit," replied Fairouz in English, reaching down.

"Maybe they can bite through a glove," said Fitzpatrick.

Fairouz hesitated. The creatures seemed to be fascinated by the robot.

"Maybe they're trying to mate with it," said Fairouz. "They probably think that blinking light on it is really sexy." She again started to lean over to pet one.

"Wait a minute," said Tariq. "Let us do a little experiment. Tell the robot to move back a meter."

Back on the *Ulug Beg*, an engineer monitoring the radio transmissions of the explorers spoke the appropriate command to the robot's master-control computer and it started to move. Suddenly, it was as if someone had shouted "free beer" in a university lecture hall. The creatures went crazy, jumping at it, covering it with their bodies.

In a moment, the robot fell to the ground. "Look!" exclaimed the priest. "They've chewed its legs off!" They had reduced the legs to broken segments, which individuals gnawed on energetically.

"Telemetry indicates malfunction in manipulator legs," radioed the engineer.

"Roger, we copy," said Fairouz.

"I guess the flashing light is not very sexy after all," said Tariq. "It probably resembles something they like to eat for breakfast."

Their blue pulsations grew in frequency until the creatures were an almost constant blur of light, and their cries increased in pitch and intensity. They jumped on top of one another until they enveloped the robot. In a couple of minutes, the pile of creatures was flat, as they spread out and lay down with plump little bellies, their glows dying. Occasionally, the sound of tiny burps was audible.

"Total malfunction," radioed the engineer.

"The little pigs!" said Fairouz with a smile.

"Somehow," said Tariq, "these creatures have evolved a taste for metal, and teeth—or acids—powerful enough to do the job."

"But where on Ronin would they find metal to live on?" asked the Jesuit.

"Nickel–iron asteroids," said Fairouz. "Bombarding the planet as meteorites. There are lots of them on the Moon and Mars and out in the 'roids."

"But they're rare out beyond Pluto," said Fitzpatrick.

"We do not know where this planet has been," said Tariq. "It could have passed through a cloud of asteroids around some other star."

There was nothing left of the robot except a few pieces of plastex. Most of the creatures were motionless; they uttered low trills periodically.

"They snore!" said Fairouz affectionately.

Some of the less sated animals began edging toward the three astronauts, their noses sniffing the air. Suddenly, Tariq became conscious of the flashing light on the top of his helmet, and the metal fittings on his pressure suit.

"I suggest we move back to the ship, friends," said Tariq, grabbing Fairouz's arm, "unless you want your suit to become their next meal." This time she did not resist, and the three of them beat a hasty, clumsy retreat toward the ship, while those of the creatures without full bellies moved hesitantly toward them.

As they stumbled in the heavy gravity, Tariq said, "Shut off your helmet light." Following his own advice, he muttered, "Attention suit. Helmet light off." The suit computer complied.

The glowing creatures, seeing the tall spacers retreating, were emboldened. They began to move quicker, glow brighter, and pulsate more rapidly.

When the humans reached the airlock, Tariq said, "You first," to Fairouz.

"No way," she said, aiming her gun at the approaching horde. "A Druze is never the first one to run away."

With a look of disgust on his face, Tariq turned to the priest and spat, "Get in!" Fitzpatrick scrambled up into the airlock.

As he slammed the hatch closed on the priest, Tariq said, "Why the hell didn't you put a bigger airlock on this thing?"

"We had trouble getting money for this project," said Fairouz. "We had to cut corners *somewhere*."

He turned around and saw the blue, furry blobs pulsating toward them, several meters away. They both looked at the flashing light on the top of the shuttle and grimaced. Tariq said, "For Allah's sake, kill the goddamn shuttle light." Immediately the light went out.

"That must look like the biggest banquet," said Tariq, aiming his gun at the advancing creatures.

"Oh, I hate the thought of killing them," said Fairouz. "They're so cute." But she took a bead on the lead animal.

"I do not think they would look so cute if they were eating your toes," said Tariq.

Suddenly, one of the creatures jumped at Tariq's boot and began to chew on the metal fastener that held it sealed.

As the crowd of creatures surged toward them, Tariq unhooked the flashlight from his belt and turned it on with its beam narrowed to a bright pencil of light. He shined it in the big eye of the leader of the pack. The animal whistled shrilly and pushed back for a moment.

"Aha!" said Tariq. "They may like light, but this beam's brighter than anything they've seen in their lives."

The entire horde moved back a bit.

"Shuttlecomp," shouted Fairouz. "Turn on the floodlights."

Immediately, the ship lit up like a Christmas tree in a dazzling brightness unknown to this part of the solar system.

The creatures squealed and turned away. And then, mysteriously, they began digging furiously into the ground.

While Fairouz, Tariq, and the shuttle crew watched in astonishment, the animals buried themselves underground. Soon there was nothing left but mounds of earth to show where the creatures had been.

Fitzpatrick gestured from behind the cockpit window and said over the suit radio, "Now's the perfect time to get a sample."

"Of what?" Tariq asked suspiciously.

"Of the creatures," said Fitzpatrick.

Fairouz laughed.

"You mean, you want us to get one of her darlings?" Tariq asked.

"Of course. Two would be better," said Fitzpatrick.

"If you seriously think I am going to bring a metal-eating creature aboard this spacecraft, you have got vacuum inside your skull," said Tariq.

"Well," said Fitzpatrick, "I suppose if they escaped, it would be a bit of a bother."

"Damn right it would be," said Tariq.

"I'm not letting one of those little monsters inside my ship," came the voice of the chief.

"Well," said Fitzpatrick, "it doesn't have to be alive, though it would be a lot better for biology if it were."

"Aaw, you're not going to kill the little dears?" Fairouz asked.

"It's in the name of science," said the Jesuit.

"Okay," said Tariq. "If you are so anxious to have one of these walking sharks, then you go get it!"

Even with the shining lights and the several layers of glasstex between them, Tariq could see Fitzpatrick turn pale.

"I'm not a biologist," said Fitzpatrick. "I'm not competent to do this."

"I'm not a biologist, either," said Tariq.

"I'm very inexperienced at handling weapons. I've never had any lessons in firing a gun," Fitzpatrick said.

"Oh, hell," said Tariq. "Give me some kind of sample bag and I will go get one of the damn things."

"You're not going to kill Mickey Mouse?" Fairouz asked accusingly.

"So, now it is Mickey Mouse? They almost eat you alive, and suddenly they are something out of a Disney video?"

"I was quite prepared to shoot them when my life was in danger," said Fairouz indignantly. "But I'll be damned if I'll stand around while someone kills defenseless little animals."

"They are as defenseless as my former mother-in-law," said Tariq with a grimace. "Listen. This is a scientific expedition, in case you have forgotten. No one has *ever* found living creatures this complex anywhere in the solar system. It is our *duty* to bring back samples. Sure, you have got the strange crystalline life-forms of Mars, and the sludge dwellers of Titan, and the floaters on the Jovian planets. But here we have a radically new ecology— something unlike anything we have ever seen. We *have* to bring back samples of it. Dammit, you women are so softhearted!"

Ollerenshaw pressed her face to the cockpit and said,

"Hurry up and shoot one of the little bastards so we can get out of here."

Fitzpatrick passed a collection bag and a digging implement through the small tool airlock next to the main one. Tariq grabbed it and stomped heavily out to the nearest mound.

Fairouz looked away. In a minute he returned, an expression of distaste on his face and a dead critter inside the sample bag. Grimly, he passed it in through the tool airlock and said, "You had better keep this thing sealed and refrigerated, in case it carries any diseases or parasites."

"Of course, of course," said the priest.

Fairouz glared at Tariq. "Now, if I may suggest," she said, "we ought to move this sucker somewhere where we'll be safer."

"Amen," said the Jesuit.

For a moment, Tariq felt queasy; an electric tingle went down his spine. The ground trembled slightly.

"Oh, no," he said. "An earthquake!"

"Is that what that was?" Fairouz asked. "I thought it was something I ate."

"Oh, no," said Ollerenshaw, who was disastrously close to clearheadedness, as her drugs had almost worn off. "Please, not an earthquake, too." Panic could be seen in her eyes through the shuttle window.

"I suppose it is a Ronin quake," Tariq observed dryly. "Anyway, it was insignificant. No one in Japan would pay any attention to one this size."

She and Tariq reentered separately without a word. When they were back inside the cramped quarters, Fairouz went down the launch checklist.

Arnaldo's face lit up on the monitor. "Something weird's going on with my equipment. I can't pick up the normal frequencies from Pluto or Earth or any other planet in the solar system."

"He is just mad," muttered Tariq, "because he cannot pick up *Sam O'Dracula, Transylvanian Private Eye.*"

Ollerenshaw looked at him approvingly and said, "Oh, you're a fan, too, eh?"

Tariq rolled his eyes toward Mecca and muttered a silent prayer.

CHAPTER 12

They argued over where to go next. The chief wanted to leave for home, but the scientists insisted on at least one more landing. They pored over the computer maps of the planet, and finally settled on a spot on the daylight side.

Half an hour later they landed in the caldera of a crater, where the bed was mostly rock and sand. There were few places for creatures to hide. The crater was in some ways the most prominent spot on the planet, with a curious dark region at the very center. A kilometer away, there was a series of lakes of great potential scientific interest. By now, everyone was feeling claustrophobic and tired from the constant high gravity.

Tariq and Fairouz got off first and carefully scouted the region around the shuttle. The land was barren. Cracked rock predominated, much of it covered by a greenish mosslike substance that Tariq took samples of, but apart from that, there were no signs of living things on the ground. Occasionally, creatures more resembling Frisbees than birds flew overhead, but none landed near them.

After the two were confident that all was safe, the rest of the crew disembarked and unpacked the gear stored in the equipment lockers in the aft of the shuttle. In the heavy gravity, they awkwardly assembled the inflatable hut and attached the air recirculator that filtered out carbon dioxide, carbon monoxide, and other poisons.

They pumped up the hut, which filled a large duffel bag but quickly grew into a huge geodesic dome. It was made of an extremely thin organometallic synthetic that grew into a hemisphere the size of a football field, complete with a dozen separate partitions inside. There was a self-sealing layer underneath the outer surface, which automatically repaired minor punctures. A cellular structure ensured that even the loss of a large portion would not cause immediate collapse of the whole hut.

By now everyone was happy to get out of their pressure suits and to take advantage of the showers cell, where water was carefully collected and recirculated after purification.

While the others retired to the soft, inviting hammocks within the inflatable dome, Tariq volunteered to stand watch with Sly.

He and Sly, who carried a heavy-duty laser rifle, exited through the dome's airlock.

"Sly," said Tariq, "I want you to walk with me, look for anything suspicious."

"Check," said Sly. He stomped awkwardly ahead of Tariq, constantly on the brink of falling over. He had not been well designed for heavy gravity.

Tariq noted the robot's artfully torn T-shirt, the sweatband around his forehead, and the too-tight jeans he wore. He shook his head. *I will never understand women's taste in men,* he thought.

"Do you speak Arabic?" Tariq asked.

"No, I don't talk no A-rab."

Tariq shrugged. Then something caught the corner of his eye. The "something" scurried along the rock and disappeared almost immediately.

"Damn! I hope it's just a lizard."

He double-checked the charge in his sidearm and his cartridge of microdarts.

He thought back to his year in the Egyptian army, sandwiched between his schooling in Japan. At the time, he had regretted it as a waste of his life, but now he was grateful for the knowledge of weapons it afforded him. He began to walk around the perimeter of the camp in the opposite direction to Sly. He moved slowly, tiredly, muscles aching.

His faceplate started to fog up a little, and he made a mental note to check the dehumidifier.

A moment of electrifying queasiness struck him again, and the ground vibrated. Irritated, Tariq looked around and saw the spaceship and the encampment apparently undisturbed. He shrugged.

He sat down on a rock, first glancing around to be sure it was unoccupied. Sly paused and began circling around Tariq, constantly on the lookout for danger.

Tariq faced away from the encampment and toward a black peak that rose up gradually in the distance—the center of the volcanic crater.

He stared at the cracks in the ground. *Something funny is going on here,* he thought. *This should be a lava field, but it looks a lot like dried mud.*

The ground began to vibrate again. Tariq just sat there wearily, as he had often done during earthquakes in Japan, after they had ceased being sources of worry and become a mild diversion.

This time the vibration continued, and rumbling sounds grew, until a shrill whistling sound came from the distance. The source was a black hill in the center of the crater. A great gush spurted out of the hole up into the air, ever higher, until it was at least a kilometer overhead, spreading out as it went, into a mushroom cloud.

"My God," exclaimed Tariq. "There must be incredible pressure for it to shoot that high!"

"My thoughts exactly," said the robot.

The water continued to shoot into the air. Tariq estimated that it must be a good twenty meters wide, like a giant's fire hose aimed straight up.

Something knocked on his helmet. He laughed. "It's raining!"

It came faster and harder. He bent his head back and looked up. The mushroom cloud towered above, and fat droplets of rain fell in the heavy gravity.

"Of course," Tariq said. "This is not a volcanic caldera, it is a crater produced by the water—a giant geyser!"

"Of course," said Sly.

"That is very perceptive of you, my dear colleague. It

must erupt frequently. That explains the ground. It is not volcanic—it is dried-up mud."

Suddenly Tariq felt a movement under his right foot. He jumped aside clumsily. A tiny purple bud appeared where his foot had been—something like a tulip bulb, with petals folded on top of one another, barely a centimeter in diameter. It pushed its way out of the earth. Tariq drew his gun. "Maybe it's a snake," he said.

"I hate snakes," said Sly. "I like to bite their heads off."

"You would."

But the "snake" opened its petals and revealed pulpy orange filaments. "It is a flower," said Tariq.

Sly was unimpressed.

All around them, strange flowers burst through the cracks in the mud, growing ever larger, struggling visibly to grow taller. The petals unfolded until they became as large as an opened cabbage. They oriented themselves toward the distant sun, trying pitifully to pick up photons.

All around them, the delicate flowers unfolded in the cracks of the now-softening mud. The crater became a riot of color: oranges, reds, and fuchsia predominated. The rain splattered down on Tariq's pressure suit. Each drop hit with the impact of a grape, and warmed the suit noticeably. A pump whirred inside his backpack as the thermoelectric air conditioner turned on.

"The water must be pretty hot in that geyser," said Tariq. "Even after it got cooled falling from up there, I can feel it through my gloves."

Sly grunted. They stood there watching the rain for several minutes, when suddenly something banged off Tariq's helmet, knocking his head to one side like a blow from a fist.

An object fell to the ground and lay fluttering there. It looked almost like a green pigeon, with a triangular head terminating in a long, pointed beak. It shook its head, as if the encounter with Tariq's helmet had done it more damage than vice versa. It then stuck its beak into the softening mud and pushed itself up in the air until it was standing nose-deep in the mud. It wiggled mightily and burrowed deeper, until in a moment it was completely buried.

Around them, more of the green creatures fell from

overhead and plowed into the ground. Their short wings let them spiral down at a terrific rate of speed, like live drills. When they hit the wet ground, most of them were buried almost instantly.

Suddenly over the radio, came a yell, "What the hell?"

"We've got a leak!" came another voice.

Tariq looked back at the dome. It was sagging in spots. Numerous tiny holes showed where the creatures had penetrated. He cursed and ran heavily toward it, followed by Sly.

Sly quickly overtook Tariq and reached the dome first. They entered the airlock. Inside, all was a shambles. The crew hid underneath packing crates and canisters of equipment. There were holes in the floor of the dome, as well, testifying to the passage of the pointed creatures. Some were still fluttering around inside, frustratedly looking for mud.

"Anyone hurt?" Tariq asked as one of the creatures hit him in the shoulder and bounced onto the floor.

He found Fairouz inside a crate. She looked very pleasing in her red jumpsuit.

"I don't think anyone is hurt," she said, extricating herself, "because when this infernal rain started, it woke us all up. Then, when those damn things began falling through the roof, we all dived for cover. What the hell are they, anyway?"

"I suppose we ought to call them kamikaze birds," said Tariq. He glanced around. "The bird rain seems to be letting up."

"Well, there goes our atmospheric seal," said Fitzpatrick, emerging from a large canister.

"We had better hope that there really are no dangerous bacteria here," said Tariq. "You are breathing Ronin air now, for better or worse."

After checking on each of the crew members, Tariq went back outside. It was still raining water, only now an even stranger sight appeared in the sky. Thousands of pink objects began to float down. They landed softly, and Tariq chuckled.

"What are you laughing at?" Fairouz radioed.

"These creatures have evolved parachutes," he replied.

Fairouz emerged from the airlock with a sidearm and radio strapped to her belt. She looked around. Countless creatures now fluttered down from above, their tiny parachutes slowing them in the thick atmosphere. When they landed, they crawled rapidly away in different directions, some of them to eat flowers, others to slip into holes left by the pointed falling creatures. Still others rapidly ran to unknown destinations.

Tariq knelt and picked up one of the parachute creatures in his gloved hand as it munched happily on a flower. It squirmed, and its four legs struggled mightily to escape. He held it firmly but gently. It had two green eyes, a large gaping mouth, and a body like a sparrow but with scales like a fish. The pink parachute was a floppy membrane delicately attached to its tail.

Fairouz joined him. Water glued her long hair to her face. She pushed some strands from her eyes.

"Aren't you going to put on your pressure suit?" Tariq asked in Arabic.

"What's the point? I've breathed the air, and nothing's happened."

"At least it would keep you dry."

"I got soaked in the dome, and it's not any worse out here."

He showed the creature to her, and she put out her hands to take it.

Tariq hesitated and said, "Better not touch it. Could be poisonous." He got a porous sample bag and placed it inside. It fluttered around, trying to escape.

Fitzpatrick emerged in his jumpsuit and joined the pair. "There's a helluva weird ecology here," he said.

"Yes," said Tariq, returning to English. "The creatures must live in the hot water underground. They seem to have evolved to take advantage of the fact that they get squirted up into the air now and then."

"Yes," said Fitzpatrick, "a good dispersal mechanism. And then they find their way back underground."

"Some of them bore their way through the ground," said Tariq. "Others seem to crawl over to the nearby lakes, which are probably connected to underground water channels."

"Then those volcanoes we saw from orbit," said Fairouz, "could be geysers."

"Right," said Tariq. "At least, some of them. But this place has so much internal heat that it probably has real volcanoes, too. The earthquake we just had must have triggered this outburst."

"Could be," said the Jesuit.

"I wonder what other surprises Ronin has for us?" said Fairouz.

CHAPTER 13

The chief burst through the airlock, soggy and bedraggled, followed by Sly.

"That does it," she said. "I've had enough of this goddamn planet. We're getting the hell out of here."

"I was gettin' tired of this burg, anyway," said Sly.

Wearily, Tariq walked over to her and said, "We have barely begun to explore this world."

"We've landed here," said Ollerenshaw, "we've spent more time than Neil Armstrong did on the Moon, and we're going home *now*!"

"But we have just begun to gather samples," Tariq said.

"All right. You've got as much time to gather samples as it takes to get the goddamn shuttle loaded."

"I could spend years gathering samples."

"Well, you're just going have to take minutes." She paused. "What the hell difference does it make? You've already got all the glory of being the discoverer *and* the first scientist on this planet. You're going to be the most famous person in the whole bloody solar system when we get back."

"I do not give a damn about fame," said Tariq. "Here

we have the most fabulous experience in the history of man—a whole new planet to explore. I could spend the rest of my life here."

"Maybe you could, but I certainly could not," she said.

"Why not leave me here after we have repaired the dome, with enough supplies to last me a year? That should be enough time for you to get a new expedition financed. You will not have any trouble now. That way you get what you want, and I get what I want."

She stood deep in thought for a moment. "Not a bad idea," she said. "If you went back with us, you'd be the one they'd be interviewing the most, and this way you could just stay here, while I do the interviewing. Sounds like a good idea. Okay, it's a deal." They shook on it.

"Anyone want to join me?" he said. "Father?"

"I think I've had as much of this planet as I can handle, for now," said Fitzpatrick.

"Fairouz?"

"I really should fly the *Ulug Beg* back. Just between you and me, I'm a helluva lot better rocketjock than our copilot. He's spent most of his time on lunar runs." She smiled a little. "But I'm tempted."

"It would be nice to have someone to talk to," said Tariq.

"Yeah," she said, smiling. "Among other things."

"How about leaving Sly?" Fitzpatrick asked.

"No way!" said Ollerenshaw. "He's government property."

"So is practically everything else here," said Tariq. "We'll just be using him for a year."

"Sly was designed according to my personal specifications," said Ollerenshaw.

"That's obvious," said Tariq dryly.

"A lot of taxpayers' dollars went into making sure that he would satisfy the chief Eurafrican administrator of Pluto in every possible way," she said.

"Damn right!" said Sly.

"And you have no idea how much finagling it took to have him sent out here instead of the plain-vanilla industrial robot that was supposed to be shipped," added Ollerenshaw.

"Dammit!" said Tariq. "I could use someone or something to stand guard while I am sleeping. Even that stupid robot is better than nothing, though not much."

"Thank you," said Sly.

The robot put his arm tenderly around Ollerenshaw. "You aren't going to leave me here, are you, chief?" he asked plaintively.

"Of course not, my dear."

"Look at it this way," said the Jesuit. "When you get back, you're going to be so famous that you won't have to remain on Pluto any longer. You'll be able to go back to Earth."

This brought a smile to her face.

"And there you'll be, surrounded by all the robots and even all the real Slys that you could possibly ask for," said Fitzpatrick.

Ollerenshaw's lips pursed. He had hit the mark. "You've got a good point there, Father," she said, nodding slowly.

"You can't leave me here," said the robot. "It would violate the three laws of robotics!"

"Which three are those?" said Ollerenshaw.

An unaccustomed solemnity came into his voice. He quoted the regulations: "The first law: 'A robot may not injure government property, or, through inaction, allow government property to come to harm.'

"The second law: 'A robot must obey the orders given it by authorized government representatives, except where such orders would conflict with the first law.'

"The third law: 'A robot must protect its own existence as long as such protection does not conflict with the first and second laws.'"

A decisive look came to her face, and the chief said, "I requisitioned you for outer planet use, and you can't get much outer than this planet. Sly you're staying."

The robot slumped, looking as dejected as possible, given its limited facial expressions.

"After all we've been to each other," he said.

"I knew I shouldn't have had so much affection intensity programmed into him," replied Ollerenshaw. "A factory rep warned me about that."

"Ain't love wonderful?" said Fairouz.

Tariq said, "All right. Start unloading all the supplies I can use, and get someone to work patching up the dome.

Then we will move it to the rim of the crater, out of kamikaze range."

"And we can make another couple of shuttle trips with more supplies," said Fairouz.

Tariq nodded. "I am going to gather as many samples now as I can, for you to take back home."

"I'll help," said Fitzpatrick.

"Thanks," said Tariq. "You go west, I will go east. Let us meet back at the dome."

While the rest returned to the dome, Tariq and Fitzpatrick gathered up sample bags and tongs from the shuttle cargo holds.

Tariq walked slowly away from the dome, sloshing through the mud. He paused every now and then to pick up a bloom or a particularly interesting rock sample.

He caught a four-legged, segmented insectoid creature as it scurried from one flower to another and put it into a bag. Then he pinched the tag, checked the inertial guidance unit on his wrist, and said, "Live specimen, caught at Ronin, 47.90322 north, 136.49827 east." The tag contained a nanoelectronics crystal with enough memory to store a minute's worth of verbal data and automatically record the date and time.

He flipped the bag into his backpack and walked on wearily, wishing for a chance to rest. The geyser had died away, leaving a damp botanical fairyland in its wake. Everywhere the mud flats bloomed with colorful flowers; tiny creatures skittered from blossom to blossom. Occasionally, he checked his sidearm and searched for dangerous creatures, but as nothing intimidating appeared, his inspections became less frequent.

At one point, he paused and saw a small green object in the distance, just to one side of a blossom, that was different from anything else he had seen. He walked over and examined it. It was a damp, crumpled kelparette package, its tantalum-mylar wrapping reflecting the distant Sun.

"Slob!" he muttered, and ground it into the mud with his boot. *First thing people do,* he thought, *whenever they go into a pristine, beautiful place, is throw their garbage away!*

He walked to a low rise and climbed to the top. It was nearly dry—the porous ground had absorbed most of the water. Looking beyond, he saw a little blue lake on the other side. He resolved to visit it at his leisure. *I'll be the first human ever to scuba there,* he thought.

He turned around and looked back. He was just barely able to see the dome in the distance.

So, this is going to be my home for a year. He sat down heavily on the top of the hill, among a field of flowers that reminded him of the exquisitely tended gardens of Japan. He closed his eyes for a moment and thought about the future. *I guess I really will be another Robinson Crusoe. And Sly will be my Man Friday.* He gagged at the thought.

In the background, he half heard the radioed conversations of the people back at the dome, but paid no attention.

He was ready to doze off. He shook his head, pushed a helmet button that sprayed his face lightly with mist, and forced himself to stand again. The Sun was starting to set. It was low on the horizon. *Better go back now,* he thought. *Don't want to be out here in the dark.*

He walked back slowly toward the dome, following his footprints in the mud, his backpack loaded with samples. The light from the Sun, though feeble, was much better than nothing, and the hazards of the night remained to be discovered.

He noticed the spot where his boot had made a particularly messy imprint, and he recalled the kelparette pack. He walked on, thinking of how wonderful the hammock in the dome was going to feel.

Then he stopped, turned around, and looked back at the spot where the kelparette pack lay buried. How could it have gotten there? He was the only one who had been out here this far—unless someone had sneaked out. But they all had been wearing their pressure suits until the geyser had erupted. These were government-issue suits—they didn't have the smoker's mouth hatch of the top-of-the-line private suits. The crew *couldn't* have been smoking!

He backtracked to the boot mark, fished around in the thickening mud with his glove until he felt the pack, and picked it up.

He rinsed it off in a puddle and unfolded the foil. It was crinkled silver with a green logo—a stylized pair of triangles with curved sides—but the printing was unfamiliar.

He stared at the square characters. They resembled nothing he had ever seen before, either in the Middle East or the Far East. Could it be one of the more obscure Indian languages? They had dozens, many with their own alphabets.

He looked in vain for "Registered Trademark," or "Patented by" or "Made in," or the international symbol for NO SMOKING AT HYDROGEN STATIONS normally found on such products.

A thought surfaced that had been gnawing at the back of his mind—one too absurd to be given credence till now: *Could it be that we are not the first beings to visit Ronin?*

He stared at the pack for a long time, then put it in his pocket and returned to his homeward journey, slowly, trying to think of a reasonable explanation.

By the time he got back, the Sun had set. Signal lights on top of the dome and the shuttle flashed, serving as beacons to the crew members who were still outside. Floodlights had been set outside, illuminating parts of the dome where work was being done.

Tariq looked back one last time before entering the dome, and saw the whole mud flat aglow with phosphorescence. Each flower shined pink or yellow or blue, and tiny radiant flying creatures flitted in and among the flowers, like the offspring of fireflies and butterflies.

Tariq walked behind the dome, where it was shaded from the floodlights, and looked up at the sky. Distant as the Sun was, it was already dark enough to see the Milky Way. He bathed in its glow. It filled him with a feeling of awe at the mystery and vastness of the galaxy.

It was easy to see the bright stars and he automatically searched for familiar constellations. There was the great "W" of Cassiopeia, and next to her was Perseus.

And then his heart froze. Something was terribly wrong about the stars! That wasn't the orange Schedar—it was too close to cream-colored Caph. And the yellow supergiant Mirfak was too far away from Cassiopeia to be in Perseus. He whirled around, peering at every point in the sky not blotted out by the camp lights or the dome. None of the constellations was quite correct. They were all lopsided or stretched, as if viewed through a distorting lens. He ran to the other side of the dome and found even more warped constellations.

He stood in the dark shadow of the dome for long minutes, silent, his mind racing, until at last he reached the inescapable conclusion that somehow, they had been transported very, very far away in space—or in time.

CHAPTER 14

Tariq stared at the stars for a long time, contradictory emotions racing through him: excitement at being the first to discover something incomprehensibly beyond the experience of any other human being in history; and a sick feeling that he would never see his home world again.

"There you are," said Fairouz in Arabic, shining a flashlight at him.

"Put that out," he said, closing his eyes and turning away.

"Put what out?" said a voice over his suit radio.

"Sorry," he said. "I will switch the radio off."

He touched a button on his suit and killed the radio, leaving only his suit microphones activated.

Fairouz was dressed in a fresh jumpsuit. "I was getting worried about you," she said, continuing in Arabic.

Tariq stared up at the unfamiliar stars. "We have a problem."

"What kind?" she asked.

"We're not where we think we are," said Tariq. "Take a look at the stars."

She glanced up and scanned for familiar constellations. Slowly, an expression of puzzlement crossed her face.

Somewhere the chattering of an air pump started, and repaired sections of the dome began to reinflate.

"This is impossible," she said. "It must be some kind of optical illusion."

"There's no optical illusion that can rearrange the stars," said Tariq.

"Well, we got here somehow, so we ought to be able to get back."

Tariq shrugged.

"Maybe we can get some advice from Earth." She unhooked a transceiver from her belt, pushed a key, and said in English, "Arnaldo, are you there?" Her transceiver signals were relayed via the shuttle to the orbiting spacecraft.

There was silence.

"Arnaldo!" she said again. "Turn off the goddamn *Bowling Beauties* or whatever the hell it is you're watching and get on the shuttle frequency pronto, or I'll have every last one of your videos erased from the data bank!"

"Hey, Skipper," replied the Italian, "what's glitching you?"

Tariq switched to the same frequency.

"Did you ever have any success in talking with Pluto?" Fairouz asked.

"No, my captain," he replied. "I tried again and again, and just couldn't get through."

"Did you ever get anything from Earth?" asked Tariq.

"Not one bloody signal."

"Nothing at all?" asked Tariq.

"Well, I got occasional weird signals that didn't sync, but nothing that would tune in properly. Maybe it's Jupiter acting up. It sometimes interferes."

Tariq began tapping his leg rhythmically, and after a moment said, "Tune in those weird signals anyway, and play around with them. See if you can pull in anything."

"Do you think it will do any good?" Fairouz asked.

"I do not know," he replied, "but we seem to have gotten scrambled in some way. Maybe this world is warping space-time. Perhaps the signals are trying to get through here but are transformed in some way that we have to figure out."

"If that's so, maybe we can go back just by leaving this accursed planet."

"Perhaps."

"I think we should tell the rest of the crew," said Fairouz. She spoke into her transceiver. "Arnaldo, put this on shipwide squawk."

"Roger, Skipper!"

Fairouz and Tariq walked over to the brightly lit entrance of the dome. The Egyptian sat down on a crate. Small flittering creatures darted through the air, like moths heading toward the bright lights, but now the humans paid no attention to them.

"Listen to me, guys," she bellowed to the ground crew in her loudest, most commanding voice. "I've got something important to say."

She waited until Fitzpatrick, Ollerenshaw, and Sly had gathered around. Tariq felt an urge to lie down and sleep for a year. His weary, worn body screamed for a hammock and some quiet.

Fairouz set the transceiver down with the switch on, transmitting the talk up to the orbiting spacecraft. "Tariq has made a really disturbing discovery," she said.

"I don't think I'm going to like this," said Ollerenshaw. "This planet is really beginning to disagree with me."

"Why don't you explain it?" Fairouz said to Tariq. "I certainly can't."

Tariq shrugged wearily and stood up.

He looked at the assembled crew and then up at the sky, and was partly blinded by the floodlights. "Can we kill the lights?" he asked.

Sly aimed his rifle at them.

"No, you idiot," said Fairouz. "Don't take everything so literally." Sly put his weapon down with a puzzled expression. "Just march around the goddamn dome and warn us if you see anything dangerous."

"Danger! Love it!" said the robot. He cradled his weapon and stomped off happily into the darkness.

Someone reached over and shut off the floodlights, plunging the front of the dome into darkness. There was a flutter of beating wings as confused birdlike creatures crashed into one another.

"Look up at the sky," said Tariq. "Something's wrong."

"Where the hell are Jupiter and Saturn?" asked the priest. "And what's happened to the constellations?"

"Jesus Christ and Muhammad the Prophet!" exclaimed Ollerenshaw. "Does this mean we're lost?"

"Something about Ronin has changed our relationship to space or time," Tariq said.

"What do you mean?" Ollerenshaw asked.

"I do not know how," he said, "but we may have gone forward or backward in time. Or we could have been transported to another part of space."

"But then the Sun wouldn't be here," said Fitzpatrick.

"How do we know it is the same Sun?" said Tariq. "Ours is just a miserable little G2 star, about as ordinary as you can get."

"I don't think we're in Kansas anymore, Toto," Ollerenshaw whispered in a small, plaintive voice.

Tariq ignored the unfamiliar reference.

They all stared at the sky, except for Ollerenshaw, who stared at the ground. "There's another explanation," she whispered. "I'm simply going neuro."

"We can't *all* be crazy," said Fairouz.

"How could this have happened?" Fitzpatrick asked.

Tariq shook his head. "Perhaps this planet stumbled into our universe from somewhere else or some other time. It could be from some place in our galaxy, or from a parallel universe."

"But why didn't it just go out again?" said Fitzpatrick.

"It may have," said Tariq, "and dragged us along."

"It should just have disappeared in front of our eyes, the same way it appeared," said Fitzpatrick.

"I guess," said Tariq, "that when we matched velocities with it and orbited around it—when we had less than escape velocity—we became trapped in its gravitational field, and it just dragged us along with it wherever it went."

"I suppose that makes a kind of sense," said the priest. "General relativity says a planet distorts the fabric of space and time. So when we entered the gravitational sphere of influence of Ronin, we merged with the distortion."

Tariq nodded. "And that means that as soon as we leave the planet, we will leave its influence forever."

"Yes," said Fitzpatrick.

"You mean there's hope?" said Ollerenshaw.

"Of course," said the priest.

"Perhaps," said Tariq. "But the problem is that if we do leave this planet, and return to normal space, God only knows where we will end up."

"What do you mean?" Ollerenshaw asked.

"We could find ourselves stranded a hundred light-years from home or a million years in the past or future. We have no idea."

"Great," she said softly, staring at the ground. "That's just what I wanted to hear."

"When we get back to the ship," Tariq said, "we can run a spectral analysis on the Sun and some of the other stars and see where we are. We should even be able to figure out 'when' we are—at least if we are in the same universe."

In a very small voice, Ollerenshaw said, "I really don't think I want to hear this, but what do you mean 'if we're in the same universe?'"

"There could be other universes existing alongside ours."

"It's as if we lived in a pack of cards," elaborated Fitzpatrick, "and we were on one of the cards. On the next card is another universe, and on the next card yet another. There could be dozens, or hundreds, or an infinite number of parallel universes."

There was silence as the idea of endless alternate universes filtered into their minds.

"We'd better get our boosters back up to the ship," Fairouz said. "All right, guys. Pack it up, and don't damage anything. We don't know when we'll be able to repair it. And don't leave even a chip behind."

"Wait a minute," Tariq said, pulling out the kelparette pack. "I found this today. I think it must bear on our problem. Have you ever seen any language like that?"

Fairouz showed the pack to the vidcamera that broadcast to the monitors on the ship. Not one member of the multilingual crew had ever encountered such writing.

"Someone dropped it on a visit," said Tariq. "And since we see no evidence that this planet is inhabited, it must have been a visitor from another world—or another universe."

"Wonderful," said the chief sourly. "Not only have you taken away my universe, you've given me a monster to watch out for in the night."

"It looks like you're not alone in your Robinson Crusoe effort after all," said Fairouz to Tariq. "Now we're all in the same boat."

Tariq held the kelparette pack in his hand, and said, "And who is our Man Friday?"

CHAPTER 15

A glum shuttle crew returned to the *Ulug Beg*, Tariq included. They floated up to the flight deck, where Arnaldo was hunched over his communications panel next to the copilot, who was asleep, strapped down in his seat.

"Any luck?" Fairouz asked.

"No," Arnaldo replied. "I'm getting what looks like it ought to be a TV signal, except it doesn't sync up." He pointed at an oscilloscope display showing a periodic signal with bursts of what looked liked noise on it.

"Could it be sabotage?" said the chief.

The Italian threw his hands in the air. "That would explain it. Someone could have screwed up the comm gear." He turned back to his control panel and began to push keys feverishly.

"What about sound?" said Tariq. He had meditated on the flight back up, and his energy was partly restored.

"I've just been concentrating on video," said Arnaldo. "I've never been that interested in radio."

"Well, do me a favor," said Tariq. "Scan the lower frequencies on Earth and see what kind of signals you get."

Arnaldo hit a couple of keys on the computer, spoke commands into his microphone, and played with the joystick, controlling the spectrum analyzer that scanned frequencies throughout the microwave range. It showed numerous spikes, as if there were many radio transmitters operating.

"Tune in to one," said Tariq.

Arnaldo moved the joystick and centered the cursor on one of the stronger signals. Immediately, sounds like a man's voice came from the loudspeaker. He seemed to be speaking a foreign language.

"Thank God," said Ollerenshaw. "At least there's someone out there. I was beginning to think we'd gone off to another galaxy!"

They listened to it for a while, then Fairouz said, "Does anyone recognize this language?" They all shook their heads.

"Try another one," said Fairouz.

The Italian moved the cursor to another strong frequency, and a different voice came in—this time, a female.

Again, no one recognized the language. They tried every signal on the screen. Mostly they heard human voices; occasionally, there were chirps of data transmission. But not once did they get a recognizable language.

"I'm afraid," said Tariq, "that we may not even be in contact with human beings."

"You sure do know how to brighten my day," said Ollerenshaw. "You mean these guys may be little green men who want to come over here and barbecue us?"

"This is wonderful," said Tariq. "We will be the first people to make contact with another civilization!"

"I've had enough honors to last me ten lifetimes," said Ollerenshaw.

"If they are alien," said Fitzpatrick, "this will be a fascinating opportunity to solve some of the riddles of theology. What if they have never heard of Muhammad or Jesus Christ?"

"What if they worship thirty-nine gods?" said Fairouz. "What's that going to do to our religion?"

"Simple," said Arnaldo, half seriously. "We'll make them all Mormons."

Ollerenshaw slouched down in her chair after fiddling with the telcro straps that kept her from floating away, and closed her eyes. "What did I do to deserve this?" she asked plaintively.

"Cheer up," said Tariq, the adrenaline of scientific excitement overwhelming the fatigue he ought to have been feeling. "Think of it as an exciting new challenge."

"I swear, if I ever get back," said Ollerenshaw, "I'll accept any assignment, even Antarctica, as long as it's on planet Earth. I will *never,* ever again do anything that deviates by one micron from the book."

"Let us see if we can do something with those television signals, or whatever they are," Tariq said.

"What can we possibly do?" Arnaldo asked. "I've already done everything I can think of and nothing comes in. And you're talking to a guy who has managed to pull in reruns of *My Mother, the Cyborg* from a tiny transmitter on Easter Island—on Mars."

"Well, I've got some ideas," said Tariq. "If I'm right, we might be able to pull in some real television pictures from this system. The problem is that you are used to thinking about human transmission systems, and there is no reason to suppose that this universe has the same Interplanetary Communications Commission. Is your monitor using the shipboard main computer data processing system?"

"Sure. The regular ship's receiver doesn't pack the processing power you need to pick up these signals, and I couldn't get the brass to pay for a really expensive video receiver when this is supposed to be a scientific expedition. So I simply reprogrammed the data-analysis subsystem so it would feed onto the computer monitor screen right here."

Tariq nodded. "Then all we have to do, if I am right, is modify your programming so we can experiment. They may be broadcasting with a different number of scan lines, a different aspect ratio, and a different color-encoding scheme. Chances are, they also use different data compression algorithms."

"Hey, you might be right!" The gleam of the closet hacker came into the Italian's eyes. "This is almost like breaking into the main admin computer on Malta— which I, of course, would never do," he said with a quick glance over his shoulder at the chief, "only it should be easier. As far as we know, no one is trying to prevent us from accessing."

Tariq spent the next few minutes talking shop with him, discussing different strategies and suggesting software packages to test. Then Tariq turned to Grodno, the copilot/navigator, whose eyes were closed. He shook him.

The bald Byelorussian jerked up and rubbed his eyes. "I wasn't asleep," he said, stifling a yawn. "I was just resting my eyeballs."

"Okay," said Tariq. "Any idea where we are?"

"No," he said. "I'm used to navigating around the solar system. I don't even know what galaxy we're in now."

"How do you normally locate your position?" Tariq asked.

"Okay. You've got your Pluto beacons, your Earth beacons, your Mars beacons, and a few others. Usually I use Pluto because it has the strongest signal out here. You monitor the Pluto beacon continuously and you integrate out your position by Doppler tracking. Then, occasionally, you double-check with some of the more distant beacons, and once in a while, you do a star check just to be safe. Also, you've got your inertial navigation, which isn't quite as accurate, but it serves as a useful check, and it's handy for navigating when you're eclipsed by a planet and can't see a beacon."

"What does your inertial navigation system say about where we are now?" Tariq asked.

He studied the readouts. "It says that we're right where we thought we were—several hundred million kilometers from Pluto, orbiting around Ronin."

"What about your beacon records?"

The copilot dumped the data onto the screen and graphed their position as recorded by the beacon since the start of the trip. Everything was normal for a while—then there was a sudden halt in the signal.

"When did the cutoff occur?" Tariq asked.

Grodno hit a few keys and muttered instructions to the computer. "A few hours after we arrived here."

"That's about when I had that strange feeling," Tariq said quietly. "What about the stars? They may be able to tell us if we've gone forward in time—at least if it's a large amount."

"How?"

"They will have moved into different positions—at least, the nearby ones."

"I see," said the copilot. "How do you know we haven't gone backward in time?"

"The radio transmitters are a sign of an advanced culture," Tariq said. "Let's measure the positions of some of the planets, too, and see whether we can fit them to any reasonable date. Rack the ephemeris forward as far as necessary to get a good fit."

The copilot nodded. "Gotta call upstairs."

"Why?" said Tariq.

"That's data deck, where Ng'ethe does optical tracking."

"Oh, yes, the Kenyan."

"Right." He called up, and Ng'ethe's ebony face appeared in his monitor. "Have you figured out where the planets are?"

"Yes," replied the Kenyan. "They're all there, thank God. Just in different places."

"Dump the positions down here, okay?"

"Roger."

The parameters of the planets appeared on the copilot's nav monitor. "What now?" he said. "They aren't where they should be."

Tariq nodded. "Command the computer to calculate the future positions of the planets as a function of time."

"Standard subroutine," said the copilot, whispering into the computer microphone.

"Now compare the measured positions of, let's say, the Earth, Jupiter, and Saturn with the predicted values."

"I'll calculate the angular separations between Ng'ethe's positions and the computer's predictions."

"Good. And you can compute the sum of the squares of the deviations as a simple measure of how large the discrepancy is."

"Done. They're all over the place."

"Right. Now, start moving the computer positions forward continuously on the calendar."

"How far?"

"A century."

The computer displayed the deviation of the actual positions of the planets from the positions they would have tomorrow. Then, it began to jump forward a day at a time.

"Lousy fit," said the copilot.

"Tell it to stop when the discrepancy is small. Then accelerate."

The copilot hit the keyboard and talked to the computer. The days began flashing by too quickly to see, then the years. The discrepancy fluctuated, growing larger and smaller, but never became tiny.

They watched the calendar race forward into the next century with only a very poor fit. "Keep on going."

The display showed two hundred years in the future, then three hundred years, and on and on. Occasionally, the copilot paused when there seemed to be a good fit, but in each case it was just a local minimum.

The calendar reached a thousand years into the future, and then two thousand. Finally, more than seven thousand years into the future, they got a fairly good fit. The copilot announced this to the flight deck.

"Oh, my God!" said Ollerenshaw. "You mean the year is nine thousand something?"

"Yeah, A.D."

"Apparently," said Tariq. "It's the only combination of positions that gives us a reasonably good fit."

The Jesuit made the sign of the cross, and said, *"Inshallah!"*

"There is one way to be sure that we really are seven thousand years into the future," said Tariq. "Star positions."

"Ah-ha," said Fairouz. "We know that some of the stars have moved. If they've moved by seven thousand years, then the whole picture will be consistent."

"Right," said Tariq. "The nearby ones would be the most sensitive."

"We need a bright star—a nearby one," said Tariq. "Is Sirius visible?"

The copilot spoke into the computer microphone: "Scan sky near Sirius."

The image on the screen shifted rapidly.

"The planet's in the way," said the copilot.

"Try Procyon," said Tariq.

The copilot spoke again, and the edge of the planet moved off to one side, replaced by a star field.

"There," said the copilot.

"Good," said Tariq. "Now, measure its angular separation from several neighboring stars, then calculate its position with respect to the other stars in the data base."

The copilot issued a few commands into the computer, and the screen listed a series of angular separations.

"It's moved!" said Fitzpatrick, looking over Tariq's shoulder.

"Right!" said Tariq. "Now, the only question is, is it consistent with seven thousand years?"

"What's Procyon's proper motion?" Fitzpatrick asked.

Tariq looked inquisitively at the copilot, who called up the data on the computer.

"One point two five seconds of arc per year," said the copilot.

"That means that the star moves around the sky a rather large amount, due to its motion in the galaxy," whispered Fitzpatrick to Ollerenshaw.

Tariq did a mental calculation and then frowned. "Something is wrong. Procyon should be a lot farther away than it is."

"Let's try another star," said Fitzpatrick.

"How about Epsilon Eridani?" said Tariq.

They went through the whole routine again, and once more, the star had not drifted nearly as far as it would have in seven thousand years.

"We're not in the future," said Fitzpatrick.

"But we must be—the stars have drifted from their proper places," said Tariq.

He did some more calculations on his own computer and then said, "Now I am more confused than ever. The drifts are inconsistent. Not only that, but they're not even in the right directions."

They did measurements of several more bright, nearby stars.

Tariq shook his head, and Fitzpatrick said, "This is absolutely insane. These stars are moving around like bees in a swarm."

"There is only one explanation I can see," said Tariq. "We are in our old solar system, and the planets are all here, so we *must* be in a parallel universe."

"Maybe something has damaged the database," said Fairouz.

"That is worth checking," said Tariq. He returned to

his own terminal and hit keys furiously for several minutes, then floated over to the copilot's terminal.

"It does not hold water," said Tariq. "The database I brought with me in my own computer agrees with your shipboard one. They could not both malfunction in the same way."

"Scratch one great theory," said Fairouz.

"I've got it!" exclaimed Arnaldo. "Look at this."

They all rushed over to his console, bumping each other in midair in the process. They hung on to assorted handles and brackets as they clustered around him. On his screen was a quiz show with a gaudily dressed man in a green suit next to a scantily clad female in a purple wisp of a garment. There were small desks to his left and right—one occupied by a man in a suit, the other by a neatly dressed woman. Arnaldo turned up the volume and they heard a strange, almost musical language. It sounded rather like Chinese, but none of the people looked Asian. Occasionally someone would hit one of the desks and a light would appear above him, accompanied by music.

"Praise Allah," said the chief. "TV. Arnaldo, you're a genius!"

"True," said Arnaldo.

Ollerenshaw unstrapped, flew over to the Italian, and hugged him.

Fairouz smiled at Tariq. "You know, you've really got something under that hat of yours."

Tariq self-consciously pulled his watch cap down a bit and beamed back at her.

"It was a real bitch," said Arnaldo. "Everything was different—scan lines, the whole works."

"Just your type of show," said Tariq.

"Yeah. I wish I could understand it," he replied seriously.

"How did you do it?" Fairouz asked.

"I just experimented," said Arnaldo, "until I had the right combination of raster, interlacing, and data-compression algorithm. I had forgotten how many different ways there are to put a video signal out."

On the TV, the woman behind the desk shouted something enthusiastically and the light above the host began to flash blue. Then the hostess jumped up and down excitedly as the men in the group watched appreciatively. Lettering appeared in white at the bottom of the screen. The letters were mostly mixtures of triangles, squares, and dots.

"Has anyone seen anything like that?" Ollerenshaw asked.

"It doesn't resemble any language I've ever seen," said Fitzpatrick.

Several others shook their heads.

"Not even the kelparette packet," said Tariq.

"And look at the clothing of the man behind the desk," said Fairouz. "Have you ever seen a jacket like that?"

It was mauve, and each lapel was a semicircular arc with two notches. There was no collar; instead, the man wore a red belt around his neck, with a blue buckle in the middle of it where his Adam's apple was.

"And look at the hairstyles," Ollerenshaw said. "Never seen anything like that."

On the men, the hair was very short on the left side, and covered the ear on the right side. With the women, it was the opposite.

"Maybe this is some kind of freak show," Fairouz said. "Let's find another channel."

"I hope I don't have to go through this rigmarole all over again," Arnaldo said.

He brought up the spectrum of terrestrial signals and chose another strong television channel. On the screen, a band of horsemen were chasing something through a prairie.

"Oh, good, a Western!" Arnaldo said.

"You like them, too?" said the chief. "No question about it, you're my kind of guy." She squeezed his shoulders.

The scene cut to a man on horseback riding as fast as he could, being chased by the others.

"Let's try another channel," Fitzpatrick said.

"Wait a minute," Tariq said. "Look at that carefully."

The details were eerily at variance with their expectations. The Indians wore metallic togas, almost like those of Roman legionnaires. Instead of feathers in their headbands, their own hair had numerous braids flying in the wind. Their weapons were crossbows, and every now and then a warrior stopped to rewind.

Even the cowboy was strangely different. Instead of a ten-gallon hat he wore a visor, and his leather jacket had semicircular lapels like the man on the quiz show. And instead of a handgun, he carried a seemingly endless supply of hand grenades, which he periodically tossed back toward the Indians.

"Another channel," Tariq said.

Reluctantly, the Italian tuned in a different one.

This time, there was a smiling gentlemen in a suit with the now-familiar lapels. He spoke in a guttural language quite different from the previous one—more like Arabic—yet without a single familiar word. He screwed a blue cylinder the size of a milk packet into a rectangular box on the ceiling above his head and pushed a button. There was a flash, a door on the bottom of the device opened, and some clothing fell out onto the table below. He picked up a shirt and held it up admiringly.

"A commercial," Fairouz said.

"They put their laundry machines in the ceiling?" said Ollerenshaw.

"Sounds like a good way to save room," Tariq said, thinking of the cramped quarters of Japan.

The commercial dissolved and was replaced by a man with graying hair in a suit standing in the middle of an empty stage. He slowly and somberly spoke in the same guttural sounds as the preceding man, then the scene was replaced by the image of hundreds of people yelling a slogan while waving triangular placards in the air. They swarmed up a ramp toward a large building with curved walls, rising toward the sky to a point. The announcer's image returned and he continued to speak in the same somber style.

"Well," Ollerenshaw said, "at least now we've got a news broadcast."

"Damn," Arnaldo said. "I'll switch to something more interesting."

"You do that," Tariq said as he studied the scene intently, "and I will break your arm."

Arnaldo looked at him with new respect.

"This may be the most important thing we could watch," said Tariq. "We could learn a tremendous amount about their culture, perhaps some clues to their language. Are you recording this?"

"Of course."

A scene of aircraft replaced the announcer on the screen. They were flying in formation, but they were unlike any aircraft in the history of videos. They all had three fuselages side by side, and two tails, jutting out at odd angles. In front, there were canard wings above and below each of the cockpits. A wing jutted out of each side of the exterior fuselages. It looked like a delta wing, except that it was tremendously curved, almost as if it were made of paper and were bending with the breeze. The announcer returned and made some lengthy remarks.

This went on for a while, interrupted by more commercials and more news items on farms and schools.

They were startled to see an image they recognized. It was the seething, glowing vortex of plasma that had drawn them there in the first place. The image cut to a scene of a large angular spacecraft, clearly incapable of landing on a planet, orbiting around Mars. The announcer came back on, and Tariq said, "I would give my left brain to know what he is saying."

A second face came on, with the visage of a stern lecturer. A computer graphic appeared, showing the orbits of the planets. A red line shot out from Mars, past the orbit of Pluto, and terminated in a pulsating blue dot.

"They've mounted an expedition," Fairouz said. "Quick," she said to the copilot. "Check for any signs of alien vessels."

Grodno hunched over his console.

"It will take them a while to get here," Fairouz said. "They were starting from Mars."

"Maybe they have faster vessels than we do," said Tariq.

Fairouz checked her own console, and chattered back and forth with the copilot. After a lengthy examination of all the optical, radar, and other sensors available to them, she reported, "There's no one detectable within a hundred million kilometers."

"How do we know that was a recent news photo?" Tariq asked. "They might have made it weeks ago, and this might just have been a news update on the expedition."

"But we've only just arrived here," Ollerenshaw said. "They didn't have weeks."

"Sure, they did," said Fitzpatrick, "if they started out as soon as they detected the phenomenon, like Tariq, instead of waiting to act."

"They could be planning to knock on our front door any moment now," said Tariq.

All eyes stared out into space, peering beyond the mysterious planet, looking for a moving speck among the myriad stars.

CHAPTER 16

"I wonder how fast their spacecraft can travel," said Fairouz, staring out the screen into the depths of the inner solar system.

"No way to tell," Tariq said.

"I've never seen any design like that," she added.

"Just think of the knowledge we can get from them," said Tariq. "This is even better than meeting with aliens, because they are human. We have everything in common with them except language. And we could work that out eventually."

"How do we know they're not hostile?" the chief said.

"At least they don't know we're here yet," Fitzpatrick said.

"I wouldn't bet on that," Arnaldo said.

All eyes focused on him.

"I've been trying to contact Pluto ever since we lost contact with it. I've been sending out all kinds of signals. I also tried to beam a signal to Earth. It's been going on automatically for days."

Ollerenshaw groaned.

They stared out at the faint red dot that was Mars, trying to imagine where the other spacecraft was.

"Search the spectrum again," Tariq said. "See if there are any signals being beamed at us."

"Roger," said Arnaldo, adjusting his panel instruments.

"What will we do if—" Fairouz said.

Just then the too-familiar queasiness struck, accompanied by the tingle in the spine.

Tariq looked around. "Did everyone just feel that?"

"My stomach feels like I just ate at the Two Guys from Venus taco stand," said Ollerenshaw. "The three barf bag special."

"It felt like someone just gave me a spinal tap with a Tesla coil," the priest said.

"It felt like the first time I landed on Earth," said Fairouz. "I'd never been on a high-gravity planet before. It was awful."

Tariq peered over Arnaldo's shoulder at the spectrum on the screen and said, "Look!"

"The frequencies are different," Arnaldo said.

"Then we have crossed into yet another universe," Tariq said.

Ollerenshaw groaned again.

The Jesuit made the sign of the cross and muttered a prayer to Allah.

"We must have gone through half a dozen of these universe changes since we arrived," Tariq said.

"Oh, my God!" Ollerenshaw said. "Does this mean we've got a new set of people and politics and dangers to face?"

"I am afraid it does," Tariq said.

"Can anyone tell me what the hell is going on here?" Ollerenshaw asked. "Isn't there any explanation for it? Is it all magic? Is there some god on Mount Olympus who's doing this to us? Or am I simply crazy and you're all a bunch of hallucinations?"

"Somehow, Ronin travels through parallel universes," said Tariq. "That is just a fact of life, like the constancy of the speed of light. We simply must accept it." He tapped out an Arabic rhythm on the panel. "In fact, we might even be back where we started from."

The crew brightened visibly. Tariq looked at Arnaldo. "How do those frequencies compare with the allocations of the Interplanetary Communications Commission?"

Arnaldo scanned the frequency spectrum in front of him and shook his head. "It's all screwed up."

"Delete that hypothesis," Tariq said. "For all we know, there could be an infinite number of parallel universes."

"You mean, we may never get back home?" said Ollerenshaw sorrowfully.

"That is right," Tariq said.

"And I thought Pluto was the end of the universe," she added. "Now I'd give anything to see Hades once more, even if it meant never being able to leave that ice ball again for as long as I live. Oh, please, Allah, let this be a mindhack. Let me wake up on dear, sweet Pluto, and I swear I'll give alms to the poor for the rest of my days!" She floated back to her seat and belted herself in, looking more dejected than any human Tariq had seen since the end of the Antimatter War.

"It looks like we may have wandered into the quantum-theoretic parallel universe," Tariq said.

Fitzpatrick nodded and said, "Personally, I've never accepted the many-worlds interpretation of quantum mechanics, but I must admit I'm beginning to take it seriously."

"Every second," said Tariq, "there could be trillions of universes splitting off, side by side, where every conceivable event happens. At least, every event that does not violate the laws of physics."

"But what does Ronin have to do with it?" Fairouz asked.

"Somehow," Tariq said, "Ronin acquired a velocity perpendicular to all these universes, perhaps when it was created. I see no hope of our ever returning home, unless Ronin cycles among alternate universes and returns to its place of origin."

"Fascinating idea," Fitzpatrick said. "It could be like an electron going up and down in an atom, without ever leaving it. So we might find ourselves returning back to our old state. There's hope after all."

"You're just saying that to cheer me up," the chief said. "We're never going to see our home again, are we?"

"No, no, you mustn't think that way," the priest said. "There's always hope. In fact, I know just what we need right now—we need to put our faith in God. Yes, let's all go down to the rec deck and say a little prayer—unless anyone has objections?"

"Not as long as critical personnel stay at their sta

ions," Fairouz said. "Now hear this," she said over the
ship intercom. "All personnel not rated A-one critical,
report to rec deck immediately."

One by one, the crew floated down to the rec room,
which also served as the prayer room five times a day.
Only Fairouz and Arnaldo remained on the flight deck,
while a half dozen other critical crew members manned
the data, life-support, and engine decks.

On the recreation deck, they removed the booties they
wore while on board and performed the required ablu-
tions, washing their faces, feet, hands, and forearms up to
the elbows. Then they knelt in the direction of Earth,
holding onto hand- and footholds in the floor to keep
from floating away.

Fitzpatrick knelt at the front of the group. Behind him
on the wall was a little crescent-shaped red light that
flickered erratically with the passing of gamma rays from
a tiny, sealed radioactive relic of the antimatter-bomb
annihilation of Jerusalem. Which one of the many fanatic terrorist groups had set off the bomb would never
be known, but the Muslims blamed the Jews, just as the
Children of Moses blamed the followers of the Koran.

"You realize," Tariq whispered to him, "that Mecca
probably does not exist anymore, so there is really not
much point in bowing toward it."

"I'm sure God will understand," he whispered back.
"And if Mecca doesn't exist there, I'm sure there's some
other city just as holy. Just as I am sure that Jesus Christ
and Muhammad have walked that planet, even if they
were called by different names. Or, if they haven't been
there, then perhaps it is our job to bring the word of the
Lord to these heathen worlds."

He bowed his head, and said in a loud voice, "In the
name of the Father, the Son, the Holy Ghost, and
Muhammad.

"In the time of adversity, we find comfort in the Koran, and especially in the sura *Ya Sin*." He tapped the
hafiz on his belt and turned its volume up.

"Excerpts from sura thirty-six, *Ya Sin*, revealed at
Mecca," said the hafiz.

"A token unto them is night. We strip it of the day,
and Lo! they are in darkness.

"And the Sun runneth onto a resting place for him. That is the measuring of the Mighty, the Wise.

"And for the Moon, We have appointed mansions till she return like an old shriveled palm leaf.

"It is not for the Sun to overtake the Moon, nor doth the night outstrip the day. They float each in an orbit.

"And a token unto them is that we bear their offspring in the laden ship.

"And have created for them of the life thereof, whereon they lie.

"And if We will, We drown them and there is no help for them, neither can they be saved;

"Unless by mercy from Us and as comfort for a while.'

To Tariq, each red flash of the relic behind the Jesuit counted the transmutation of an atomic nucleus from one state into another, much like the transition to a different universe.

"When it is said unto them: Beware of that which is before you and that which is behind you, that happily ye may find mercy (they are heedless).

"Is not He Who created the heavens and the Earth able to create the like of them? Aye, that He is! For He is the All-Wise Creator.

"But His command, when He intended a thing, is only that he sayeth unto it: Be! and it is.

"Therefore, glory be to Him in Whose hand is the dominion over all things! Unto Him he will be brought back."

"Amen," said the Jesuit.

CHAPTER 17

Back on the flight deck, Arnaldo was trying to watch TV again. He sat at the keyboard, playing with a strong signal. The rest of the flight-deck crew floated anxiously around the communications monitor, while he fiddled with the number of scan lines, frequencies, and other parameters. Zigzags, diagonals, rolling bars, and lots of snow appeared across the screen.

Gradually, an image began to form. "It's pretty crude," he said. "They seem to be using only two hundred scan lines."

"Even worse than twentieth-century television," Tariq said.

A woman's face began to form on the screen. At first the colors were strange, with the face purple, but Arnaldo adjusted the screen until the picture was black and white. "There's no color information in the signal," he said. "It's really crude."

The woman spoke, using a language rich in nasal sounds, much like French.

They watched scenes of city life, in which horse-drawn vehicles were the main mode of transportation, although the coaches contained radio antennae.

"It's like Victorian England," said the chief. "Almost."

"Strange," said Fitzpatrick. "They have television technology, but not internal combustion engines."

"It could have happened to us," Tariq said. "It is all a matter of who invented which device first, and whether the inventor received support or opposition from his society."

"Well, one thing we don't have to worry about," Fairouz said, "is whether or not they're going to be visiting us."

"Doesn't look they will be able to do that for another couple of centuries," said the priest.

"Maybe this is where we should get off," said Ollerenshaw, brightening.

"Get off?" Fairouz asked.

"Sure," Ollerenshaw said. "We've got to do it sooner or later. We're just getting farther away from home."

"She may be right," Tariq said. "It may get stranger and stranger as we move along."

"With my luck," added Ollerenshaw, "this is as good as it gets."

"But who would want to live on such a primitive planet?" Fitzpatrick asked.

"Oh, I don't know," Ollerenshaw said, "it wouldn't be so bad. They undoubtedly don't know half the tricks that we do about manipulating public opinion, mindhacking, and tailoring socioeconomic algorithms to modify people's behavior."

"Yes, they are definitely primitive," Fairouz said sarcastically.

"Just think," said the chief, deep in thought. "A whole planet out there, completely unaware of the advanced techniques of mass mind manipulation, which have allowed us to bring religious, political, social, and economic order to the world—or, at least, our part of it. And instead of having battles between our algorithms and those of the Japanese or the Antarkies, we could unite the whole planet under one."

"Those algorithms do not work a hundred percent perfectly even in our time," said Tariq. "Some are resistant."

"But it doesn't have to be a hundred percent perfect, especially when you have a virgin world where they are only acting under the ancient, crude algorithms of the rabble-rousers, preachers, and politicians. With modern sociometric techniques, we could take over the whole planet."

"I wouldn't be able to stand it," Arnaldo said.

"Why not?" Ollerenshaw asked.

"Because the TV is so lousy."

"You've got a point there," Fairouz said with a smile. "Well, anyone who wants to get off here is welcome to do so. But I'm not going to take the *Ulug Beg* away from Ronin and get myself stranded on this primitive, barbaric planet. I think we should hold out for a better universe."

Everyone but the chief nodded in agreement.

"Very well," said Ollerenshaw. "I can't do it myself. Maybe there will be some better world up ahead, but mark my word, you're going to regret we didn't get off here. I'll wager it's all downhill after this. A great twentieth-century philosopher once said, 'You've got to go for the gusto,' and I think we've lost our chance."

"Well, if that is settled," Tariq said, "let us do some serious thinking. There has got to be a pattern here—some kind of underlying order, simplicity. I think the first thing we have to look at is the possibility that this shift between universes is something that occurs regularly. I wish I could remember exactly when I had those queasy feelings."

"Maybe there's some kind of record," Fairouz said. "We keep a continuous monitor of the ship's instruments —you know, temperature, pressure, status of different optical and wired data lines, things like that."

"Excellent!" Tariq said. "Let's look for glitches."

The three of them pored over the data in the ship's computer. They found six instances of data glitches. In each case, the data ran smoothly, except for a little blip that occurred simultaneously in several systems on board the ship.

"It reminds me of the electromagnetic pulse of an antimatter explosion," Tariq said, "only a lot less powerful."

"Yes," Fitzpatrick said. "If an EMP had hit us, it would have zapped half the computers on board."

"Five of these glitches, I remember feeling," said Tariq. "The sixth occurred while I was asleep."

The computer listed the intervals between glitches:

DELTA T
(HOURS)
13.70328
12.56124
11.55625
10.66724
9.877020
9.171472

"That is ominous," Tariq said.

"The time interval is decreasing steadily," Fairouz said.

"The important thing is that it comes every few hours," said Tariq. "Let's plot it."

Fitzpatrick spoke into the computer microphone: "Plot *delta t* versus *t.*"

A curve formed on the screen, showing vertically the interval between glitches as a function of the horizontal time axis. It was a gentle curve, nearly a straight line, running from the top left to the bottom right.

"I wonder what will happen if the interval goes to zero?" Tariq asked.

They stared at the screen.

"At least," he added, "now we will be able to predict when the next one will strike."

"If it continues to remain as smoothly varying as this," said Fairouz.

"When's the next one?" Fitzpatrick asked.

"A simple polynomial fit should do," Tariq said.

The priest spoke to the computer: "Do a fourth-order poly fit to the data. Extrapolate to next data point."

The screen displayed:

DELTA T
(PREDICT)
(HOURS)
8.538917

TIME FROM PRESENT:
(PREDICT)
(HOURS:MIN:SEC)
7:26:41

"Seven and a half hours to go," Ollerenshaw said, looking over their shoulders. "Gives me something to look forward to. Thanks."

"Program the computer to announce the future glitches," said Fairouz, "and sound an alarm."

Fitzpatrick attacked the keyboard enthusiastically and muttered into the microphone.

"But what could cause the interval to vary?" Fairouz asked. "Why isn't it a constant?"

"It is as if Ronin is traveling through a series of universes of decreasing thicknesses," Tariq said.

"How do you mean thickness—centimeters?" Fairouz asked.

"Yes," Tariq said. "Or kilometers or light-years, or God knows what units. It is like in the twentieth century, when many physicists thought the universe had only ten dimensions. They thought that three dimensions of space plus time had infinite extent, or at least near-infinite extent, depending on whether the universe was open or closed. They believed that the other six had collapsed in the big bang that formed the universe, and that the thickness of the universe there was almost infinitesimal. Now it appears that there is this dimension that Ronin is traveling through which is perpendicular to all other universes."

"Does that mean we'll never get back home?" Fairouz asked.

"Not necessarily," Tariq said. "Perhaps we will stop moving through these universes and fall back through the ones we have just been through, like a star in the galaxy."

"You mean, like a star orbiting the center of the Milky Way?" Fairouz asked.

"No," Tariq said. "I am really thinking of stars that bounce up and down in the Milky Way perpendicular to the plane of our galaxy. There are many stars and star clusters that are moving up and down, above and below the plane of the galaxy, and the gravitational field of the galaxy pulls them back, so they are doomed to bob up and down forever. If something like that happens with Ronin, we might bob back to our home universe."

"So we had better be careful to identify each universe," said the Jesuit, "in case we come back." Otherwise, we might never know. How do you fingerprint a universe?"

"We will have to take careful measurements of the positions and velocities of the planets and nearby stars," Tariq said. "And especially, we will have to record the frequency spectra of all the transmissions from Earth. Each universe seems to have its own frequency allocations—thanks to the differing legislative bodies, presumably. Whenever we get a match of a previous set of frequencies, we will know we are in a universe we have been in before.

"In fact," he added, "it is our obligation as scientists to record as much as we can on each of these universes, so that if we ever get back we will be able to share this knowledge with other people."

"Who cares what happens to the dusty data?" Ollerenshaw asked. "All I care about is getting back."

"Even if we ourselves do not survive, our data might," said Tariq.

"What a lovely thought," Ollerenshaw said.

"But what puzzles me the most," Tariq said, "is the law behind this. Is there some fundamental physical process that we could understand if we could only put together all the data? Some trivial mathematical relationship?"

"All we need is an Einstein," said Fitzpatrick, "plus a research grant and a few decades of work—none of which we have."

"There is one thing we can do," Tariq said.

"What's that?" Ollerenshaw asked. "As if I wanted to know."

"We can make more measurements. Beyond Father Fitzpatrick's fingerprinting of the universe."

"Good idea," Ollerenshaw said sarcastically. "That'll sure solve our problems."

"What kind of measurements?" Fairouz asked.

"I want to check the spectrum of the Sun to see if there is something strange happening to it, too," Tariq said.

"That's not a bad idea," said Fitzpatrick.

He and Tariq floated up through the shaft to the instrumentation deck just above the flight deck. There were relay racks of electronics connected to sensors all over the spacecraft—data analysis computers, spectroscopes, and other instrumentation designed primarily for the exploration of transplutonian planets.

Ng'ethe, the engineer, was strapped into the main seat, running a routine reliability check on the magnetometer. He turned around and faced his guests.

"Good to see you," he said in his soft accent, a blend of African and British dialects. "It gets lonely up here."

"I am glad that we can keep you company," Tariq said.

"But our visit," added Fitzpatrick, "as you might have suspected, is not entirely social, I'm afraid."

Tariq explained what they wanted, and the Kenyan set about interfacing the necessary astronomical instruments to the main data computer.

"I'll have to put some filters in the spectroscope," said Ng'ethe, "because we normally have it set so that it shuts itself off whenever it points near the Sun. It's a very sensitive instrument, designed for studying the atmospheres of faint planets."

Tariq nodded. "I once ruined a photometer on the Moon. I was setting it up for nighttime observations during the day. I accidentally aimed it at the Sun and burned out the sensor."

Ng'ethe smiled knowingly and entered some commands on the computer. He unstrapped himself, floated over to one of the relay racks, unscrewed one unit, and pulled it out. Where the unit had been, they could see a small window—a fiberoptic porthole opening to the outside world. It was a transparent hemispherical dome—a small bubble on the outer surface of the spacecraft. He retrieved some neutral density filters from a locker and placed them over the lens of the spectroscope. He then reassembled the apparatus so the lens stuck out into the bubble.

He spoke into the intercom. "Captain, can you rotate us about forty degrees clockwise?"

"Roger," came back Fairouz's voice. "Now hear this. Prepare for minor maneuvers."

Slowly the ship rotated, and the Sun shined into the bubble.

After a few more computer commands, the solar spectrum appeared on the computer screen in false color, with the infrared red, the ultraviolet blue, and the visible spectrum compressed to intermediate colors. Bright and dark absorption and emission lines of numerous elements and ions in the solar atmosphere sliced the spectrum like salami. The chemical symbols of the major spectral lines appeared along the top of the screen.

"Can you put a normal solar spectrum up there for comparison?" Tariq asked.

"No problem," Ng'ethe said. He spoke into the computer mike. "Solar comparison spectrum, two centimeters below current spectrum."

Another spectrum appeared immediately below the first, looking exactly like the first—the same colors, the same bright and dark lines, the same positions and intensities.

"Well, that's a relief," Fitzpatrick said. "They're identical."

"I suppose so," Tariq said. "But let us take a closer look. Can you difference them?"

"Sure," said the Kenyan. He spoke into the microphone; "Subtract current spectrum minus standard solar spectrum, and put the result two centimeters below second spectrum."

Nothing appeared except for a fine rectangular line outlining where the third spectrum should be.

"See?" Fitzpatrick said. "They're identical. Pure black."

"Stretch the contrast," Tariq said.

The engineer moved the cursor with the joystick into the third spectrum and adjusted a dial.

"Contrast enhancement ten times," said Ng'ethe.

Still nothing appeared on the third line.

"Try a hundred times," Tariq said.

Ng'ethe adjusted the dial and several faint lines, scattered across the difference spectrum, began to appear.

Fitzpatrick grunted, "Maybe it's just noise."

"Another factor of ten," Tariq said.

Ng'ethe made the adjustment and hundreds of lines appeared on the screen.

"Well, I'll be damned," said the Jesuit. "Look at that! Heavy on the iron, calcium, magnesium, sodium."

"Somehow, the Sun has acquired more heavy elements," said Tariq.

"What could do that?" the engineer asked.

"I guess the solar composition is different in this universe," said the priest.

Tariq nodded and thought intensely. He began tapping out a rhythm on the console. After a while, he said, "You know, this is just what you would expect if the Sun got older."

"I see what you mean," Fitzpatrick said. "It's as if it has evolved a little bit further along, and the hydrogen has been burnt up a little bit more, producing heavier elements."

"Yes," said Tariq. "It is aging more rapidly in this universe, but maybe in the next one it will be older yet."

"How long before it starts to die?" the engineer asked.

"I do not know," Tariq said. "I will have to do some calculations."

Fitzpatrick stared glumly at the spectrum and muttered, "Maybe this *is* as good as it gets."

CHAPTER 18

Tariq sat in his cabin, lightly strapped to the bed, staring out a porthole. The light was off and he could see the Milky Way outside, tantalizing, filled with mystery.

His thoughts turned to Fairouz. Her face floated in his mind, her long black hair drifting gently, her black eyes flashing. For a moment, he smiled softly. If he had to be stranded in another universe, better to be with her than any other woman he had ever met.

He had never felt so hopeless, not even inside the damp pyramid in Egypt during the Antimatter War, when the breath of the crowded refugees left moisture constantly on the walls. His cramped cabin reminded him of that time, when he had had to bend over uncomfortably to get through the long corridors within the pyramid. To the younger children this had not mattered, but he was a tall teenager.

He stared at the stars. Here in a tiny vessel they orbited a bizarre planet, so far from home that they did not even have words to express the distance. His left hand brushed the hull and passed over the videograph he had attached when he boarded. Although he could not see it in the darkness, he knew every square millimeter of the picture. There was a couple standing in front of the Sphinx, with two young boys and a girl at their knees.

The photograph had been taken shortly before the war that vaporized so much of the Middle East.

The slender, beautiful woman and her tall, mustached husband were his parents in happier days. The boys were his rascally brother and himself, and the girl his dear sister, now married and herself the mother of two. He thought about how his parents had survived those years living in the pyramid, only to die in the famine when they finally resettled. His brother had immigrated to Mars where he had found a wife, and continued to this day to work a hydrofarm with their seven children— back in a universe that got farther and farther away by the moment.

His hand brushed across the book he had telcroed next to the porthole. It was probably the only real book on the entire spacecraft—the only one with printed words and a leather cover instead of bits of data preserved inside crystals. It was a two-hundred-year-old copy of the works of Sadi, the great Persian poet, translated into Arabic. These were the golden maxims he would dip into when in search of wisdom, only now it was doubtful that the words of a man who had died over seven centuries ago could get him out of this hopeless situation.

One of Sadi's lines flitted through his mind in archaic Arabic: "Wise Lukman for his treasure patience chose. Who have not patience, wisdom ne'er attain."

As he stared at the Milky Way, its view soothingly familiar, he remembered the rock garden where he had so often meditated in Japan. His wise *sensei* at Toyota University, Professor Shidehara, had encouraged him to go there whenever his mind was overloaded with the complexities of his studies.

He had spent many an hour sitting on the low bench, staring at the sinuous grooves in the sand symbolizing water. The simplicity of the garden, its elegance, had symbolized to him the essence of the universe. It made him understand why the Japanese had produced so many world-class physicists. The search for simplicity and elegance, and above all, harmony, that dominated the aesthetic of the Japanese was what motivated the greatest physicists everywhere.

As he thought of his happy hours in the rock garden, away from the stress of student life, he let his present problems evaporate, as his *sensei* had taught him. He spent a timeless hour bathed in the gentle white light of the Milky Way, while the vessel completed nearly an orbit around the planet Ronin.

He breathed in carefully, slowly, deeply. The Milky Way came and went outside.

"Life hangs on a single breath," Sadi had said, "and the world of existence is between two nonexistences."

His thoughts began to crystallize. He felt the excitement of new insight, while still beclouded by puzzles.

He hit the switch and the door slid open, blinding him momentarily with light from the corridor. He unstrapped himself and raced up to the flight deck, where the crew was huddled around the television monitor.

"We are safe," he said. "We cannot be in grave danger."

"You mean you've figured out a way back home?" the chief asked eagerly.

"No," Tariq said. "I just mean that the fact that all the life-forms on Ronin have existed for billions of years means that the transformations we go through cannot be too severe."

"That's encouraging," Ollerenshaw said doubtfully.

"Right," Tariq said. "In fact, it strongly suggests that everything is cyclical."

"You mean," Fairouz said, "that Ronin really does go bobbing back and forth between universes, coming back to where it started?"

"Exactly! These changes cannot go on forever, or the creatures would have died out long ago."

The priest looked at him doubtfully. "That doesn't mean that things are safe for us. You just said it yourself: these creatures must have evolved to survive whatever changes there are."

Tariq looked momentarily crestfallen, but then he brightened, and said, "Well, if these dumb creatures could survive whatever changes the universes fling at them, then surely, with our brains, we ought to be able to do the same."

"Of course," Fairouz said. "Human beings have adapted to everything from the bottom of the oceans to the outer solar system. There's nothing we can't do."

"There are a lot of things we can't do," Ollerenshaw

said. "You can't make twenty billion people agree about anything, or make a cat eat food it doesn't like, and they tell me you can't go faster than the speed of light."

"I doubt very much," Tariq said, "that we are going to have to deal with any of those particular problems. The laws of physics got us into this difficulty, and if we are smart enough, they will get us out."

He began to tap the console rhythmically. "I need to think some more," he muttered, and went back to his cabin.

CHAPTER 19

Tariq was falling down a black hole, his legs stretching out like licorice toward the fierce gravitational field. He awoke. An alarm was shrieking. He tried to jump out of his bunk, and realized he was still belted in.

"Universe change alert," said the dispassionate voice of the main computer.

"Damn," he said, "a computer alarm." He looked at the clock and saw that it was 4:07 A.M.

He tore off the telcro restraining strips, reached over to open the exit hatch, then realized he was wearing nothing but his shorts. He threw on a crew jumpsuit and exited his cabin. The corridor lights were at half intensity; several crewmen stuck their heads sleepily out of their cabins as he passed. On board the ship, they kept Universal Time, dimming the lights arbitrarily to simulate nighttime.

He raced up the shaft to the flight deck and saw Fairouz poring over the computer console. Soon they were joined by other members of the ship's crew.

"The radio spectrum looks even weirder than usual," said Fairouz. "What do you think of it?" she asked Arnaldo.

Arnaldo scanned every interplanetary-communication wavelength, from shortwaves to microwaves, pausing occasionally to expand certain regions.

"There doesn't seem to be any television transmission," he said. "But there are what look like voice radio signals." He tuned in one of the strongest and put it on the speaker. It sounded almost like the howling of dogs. Tariq felt the flesh creep on his neck.

"Maybe it's a planet of werewolves," Arnaldo said.

"Oh, my God!" the chief said, emerging from the shaft. "A planet of werewolves? Now you've really done it, Tariq!" Her face was pale, and sweat beaded on her brow.

The Italian laughed. "Just a guess," he said, reaching over to her hand, rubbing it.

Tariq eased away from the group and traveled up the shaft to the data deck. He found the Kenyan engineer huddled over his instruments.

"Glad to see you're here," Tariq said. "I thought you might still be sleeping."

"That alarm all but scared the moondust out of me," replied the engineer. "I figured I'd better come up here and monitor whatever data I could. Never can tell what might be useful."

"What I'd really like to see right now is the Sun," said Tariq. He glanced out a porthole and saw that they were orbiting over the sunlit side of Ronin.

"Good," he said. "It's up. Let's do a spectrum."

The engineer began calling up the data. Tariq moved over to a porthole so he could see the distant Sun with his own eyes. "Always use your eyes and ears and fingers whenever you can. That is what my teacher in Japan taught me." Ng'ethe grunted and continued the data analysis, oblivious to Tariq's philosophizing.

" 'The finest instruments in the world can never give you a complete feeling for the universe.' That is what he would say right now. 'You need to have as many data channels flowing into your mind as possible. You need to awaken your dormant senses so that your brain can function as a true whole. The analytical part of it is a finely trained computer. The intuitive part is an idiot savant, with the power to make foolish associations and brilliant leaps of the imagination. Either one alone is a Frankenstein's monster at best. But put the two together, and sometimes you get genius.' "

Despite the distance, Tariq had to squint at the Sun, much as one squints at a candle in the dark. Something disturbed him about the sight, but he could not put his finger on it.

"Here's the spectrum," the engineer said.

It was arrayed as before, with the normal spectrum, the observed spectrum, and the difference side by side. Only now, the difference between the two was so dramatic that it stood out even without contrast enhancement.

"Wow!" Tariq said. "Look at those heavy metals."

"Yeah," the engineer said. "Even without any training in spectroscopy, I can see a humungous difference between them."

"This Sun is much older than ours."

"Do you think we're traveling into the future?" the engineer asked.

Tariq contemplated that for minutes. At last he replied, "Maybe. Maybe not. Perhaps time flows the same in all these universes, but the Sun is getting older more rapidly in this one."

"But why?"

"I don't know." He looked back out the porthole. "Can you measure the absolute brightness of this Sun? It seems a lot brighter than it ought to be."

"I can measure the absolute incident intensity, assuming that we're the same distance from it as when we arrived here."

"Do it," Tariq said.

The engineer hit several keys and muttered some commands to the computer. "Here's the absolute bolometric magnitude," he said. "Four point four seven."

"My God!" Tariq said. "It has heated up tremendously. Its bolometric magnitude is four point seven five back in our universe." They were both well aware that the smaller magnitude number corresponded to a brighter, hotter Sun.

"That's not much of a magnitude change," said the engineer.

"Oh, but it is, when you realize how delicately life is suspended on Earth. Even a small change in the Sun's intensity could cause the oceans to boil."

"How big a picture can you give me of Earth?" Tariq asked.

"Our largest optical imager is a microfiberoptic phased-array sensor with an equivalent aperture of seven meters."

"Is it up?"

"Sure. We've been using it to study the surface of Ronin."

"Then aim it at Earth."

"I'll have to call the skipper. We'll have to rotate the ship."

The engineer called down to the flight deck, and in a moment, Fairouz had rotated the vessel so that the instrumentation was facing Earthward. The photodetector was built flush into the hull so that it was not even obvious to astronauts floating next to the spaceship. Electronic tuning of the fiberoptics allowed the antenna to be aimed.

"Where is Earth today, anyway?" the engineer asked, looking at a starry screen.

"Oh, yes. We will have to scan for it. It should not be difficult, if the Earth is still in the same orbit. It has got to be close to the Sun."

Fairouz and Fitzpatrick entered the data deck.

"We were kind of wondering what you were up to," said Fitzpatrick.

"There it is," Tariq said, pointing to a starlike object on the screen. "That's Earth."

"Give us a real good close-up," Tariq said.

Ng'ethe increased magnification, and the tiny dot that was Earth swam into view. He centered it on the screen, hit a switch, and moved the joystick around until the Earth was bracketed by two parallel horizontal white lines and two vertical ones, the fiducial markings of the telescope electronics.

"Blow it up," Tariq said.

"I hope you don't mean that literally," Fairouz said.

The engineer touched a key and the rectangle outlined by the fiducial markings expanded to fill the whole screen. The tiny white dot became a fuzzy little dot.

"Again," said Tariq.

The engineer repeated the procedure and the fuzzy dot started to look like a Ping-Pong ball in the distance.

"Again," said Tariq.

This time, the Ping-Pong ball filled the screen. It was still white and almost featureless. There were streaks here and there, but it was completely cloud-covered and looked much like the planet Venus. The four of them stared at the screen a long time, each thinking about their home planet turned unrecognizable.

After a while Tariq said softly, "Down there, it is hot. The Sun has undoubtedly melted the ice caps. There is not as much land area as we knew. The greenhouse effect is operating—even worse than the one at home. It would be a wonder if any life at all exists down there, much less a civilization advanced enough to give us radio signals."

Each of them reacted differently. Tariq looked around, analyzing what was going on in their minds. Fairouz showed uneasiness, tempered by the fact that Earth had never been her home. The Jesuit looked like he was feeling a great emptiness in his soul, as he contemplated being stranded forever from his beloved home world. The engineer looked as if he was wondering why he had ever volunteered to come out on this crazy expedition. And Tariq himself was experiencing a modest fear of the unknown, but simultaneously an exhilaration, much like what he had felt when he had left Egypt to travel to the distant, alien land of Japan.

The engineer threw a switch and tapped the radio line that Arnaldo monitored. Horrible howling sounds filled the room. Tariq's flesh crawled.

"Maybe it is the devil himself," said Fitzpatrick.

CHAPTER 20

They scanned the solar system at all wavelengths for signs of space travel and found none. This civilization was confined to Earth.

"Anyone want to get off here?" Fairouz asked quietly. No one answered.

Gradually, the flight-deck team drifted down to the rec deck, except for Fairouz and Arnaldo. Most of the remainder of the crew was there, stuck like flies to every wall, eating glumly. The rec deck also served as mess hall, in which machines surrounding the central shafts dispensed rehydrated Arabic, English, and Italian foods.

"I guess no one could get back to sleep," Fitzpatrick said to Tariq. "We'll have morning prayer early today. I sure wish I knew which way Mecca was."

"I am just going to grab something and go somewhere to think," said Tariq. Fitzpatrick nodded. Tariq selected a chocolate food bar from the dispenser and a container of pomegranate juice.

"We've certainly got a lot to think about," Fitzpatrick said. "Does it just get worse? Does Ronin ever go backwards? Is there any way out of this?"

"My *sensei* always used to say that there had to be a solution to every problem. Sometimes the solution is crude, and sometimes it is elegant. The crude solutions give you another paper to publish, but the elegant ones make it all worthwhile. Those are the ones every scientist strives for. They are the catnip of the scientific life."

"I'll settle for an inelegant solution," Fitzpatrick said.

"But he was wrong," Tariq said. "Sometimes there are no solutions. Gödel proved that."

The Jesuit helped himself to an almond breakfast bar and a plastibubble of tea. He put the nozzle of the tea to his lips, squeezed the hot fluid, and frowned. "Nothing tastes right anymore. I guess I'm just getting old. Like the Sun."

"How much food do we have on board?"

"Almost another month. Fairouz always makes certain we carry a lot more than we expect to need. Old asteroid habit. You break down out there, you can't stop off at the nearest ultramarket to resupply."

Tariq waved good-bye glumly and went down to his cabin. He hooked his feet around a toehold and stretched out. His body barely fit into the confined space. He took a bite of the food bar and grimaced. *He's right,* he thought. *Nothing tastes good anymore.* He held the juice bulb away from him, pointing at his mouth, and squeezed it expertly. A stream of liquid shot onto his tongue. It tasted slightly bitter.

He stared out at the planet slowly rotating beneath them. A supergeyser was erupting just below, and its cloud drifted slowly by. *Time sure flies when you're having fun,* he thought.

He removed the book of Sadi from its confinement and thumbed through it.

"There's always an underlying logic," *sensei* used to say. "All you have to do is find it."

He rubbed his eyes as he gazed at the book, then blinked. The letters were still slightly fuzzy. *Damn! I guess I should get my eyes checked,* he thought, *as if it matters.*

"Perhaps the biggest mystery of all," the *sensei* had said, "is the simplicity of the universe. All of its most fundamental laws can be written on the back of an envelope."

Whenever he was immersed in a difficult problem, Tariq liked to write down the fundamental equations of the universe and try to see them with a fresh eye.

He pulled a sketch pad out of a pocket and applied the

stylus to the input surface. Keep it simple. Just the basic equations.

First, he wrote down Maxwell's four equations connecting the electric and magnetic fields to electric currents and charge. Even Maxwell himself in the nineteenth century didn't know that his Victorian equations contained the basic concept of relativity that Einstein was to decipher. If he'd been just a bit smarter, he might have discovered $E = mc^2$.

He added Einstein's equation to the list. It was the process that was producing all the extra metals in the new Sun.

Next, he wrote down Newton's law of gravity: the force between two bodies is inversely proportional to the square of their distance and proportional to the product of their masses.

And then there was the quantum theory. He wrote down the equation for *psi*—the probability that a particle would be found at any given point in space inside a force field.

He added a separate line: spin equals one-half, measured in units of Planck's constant. It was valid for the most important particles: the electron, the proton, and the neutron. If electrons had no spin, solid bodies would not exist.

He stared at the white letters on the black screen of his scratch pad. Those eight little equations covered gravity, chemistry, and biology.

He blinked his eyes as the lettering on his display blurred and looked outside. The Sun was now visible through the porthole. Its brightness was somehow chilling. He visualized the many nuclear reactions taking place inside the star, the endless number of small nuclei gluing themselves together.

He glanced down at Einstein's equation and his eye fell on the letter *c*. And it was at that moment that he had the greatest insight of his life. "I've got it—*c*!" he exclaimed aloud.

CHAPTER 21

Tariq burst onto the flight deck. Fairouz, Arnaldo, Fitzpatrick, and the chief were huddled together. "I've got it!" Tariq shouted excitedly.

"A way out of here?" the chief asked.

"No, better than that," Tariq said.

The chief groaned. "What could possibly be better than that—another brainstorm, like your last one?"

"The reason behind everything." He waved his scratch pad in the air.

The chief took a slug from a beersphere. She no longer bothered to hide the illicit brew she had smuggled aboard. The Jesuit looked at her disapprovingly, though he knew the drinking of alcohol was probably the worst-observed proscription in the Koran, and was not entirely unacquainted with its pleasures himself.

Tariq waved his scratchpad toward him. "It's all in the fundamental constants," he said.

He was answered by uncomprehending stares.

"Don't you see, Father?" said Tariq. "The fundamental constants have changed."

Fitzpatrick looked at him as if he had not had a bath in a decade.

"I know it sounds crazy, but it fits! It explains why the Sun is getting older and why the planets are in different positions. It even explains why things taste funny. Haven't you noticed that? Doesn't everything taste funny now?"

"Yes!" said the chief.

"Haven't tasted such bilge since I was on Callisto," said Fairouz. "This is even worse than broccoli ice cream on the last trip, and I didn't think *anything* could be that bad."

"Tastes great to me," Arnaldo said seriously.

Everyone groaned.

"He's the one," Fairouz said, "who thought it was wonderful when we had the Martian pizza party on Pluto and we all got food poisoning except him."

"But constants are constant," said Fitzpatrick, "as sure as God reigns in the universe—in all universes."

"Would someone please explain to me," the chief said, "what all this bother about constants is?"

"We live in a world controlled by constants," said Tariq. "There are just a handful of them—the fundamental constants of physics. Most people never think about them—even physicists."

"He means things like the universal gravitational constant, and the speed of light," said the priest.

"Yes, and the charge of the electron, and the mass of the electron, and Planck's constant, and Boltzmann's constant."

"These," elaborated the Jesuit, "are the things that determine the size of the atom, the rates of chemical reaction, the evolution of stars, the length of the year—in fact, everything in the universe depends upon a handful of constants."

"You physicists are always trying to snow us laymen with your goddamn equations," said the chief. "Why can't you keep things simple?"

"That's what physicists try to do," said Fitzpatrick.

Tariq ignored her and gestured agitatedly at Fitzpatrick. "The Sun should have given us our first clue. It is more sensitive to these constants than probably anything else in our life. That is because it is driven by nuclear fusion, which needs hundreds of millions of degrees to operate efficiently. The temperature inside the center of the Sun is only around ten million degrees. But whenever you have a whole bunch of particles that are ten million degrees, there will always be a few of them, the statistical rarities, that just happen to have, for a moment, some much higher energy. These are the ones that trigger the fusion, right? So the temperature of the Sun is incredibly sensitive to changes in anything— Boltzmann's constant, or the gravitational constant, or the others."

"Okay," said Fitzpatrick. "If you did change any of the constants, the Sun could get hotter or colder and it would burn much faster or slower. Yes, it would be fantastically sensitive."

"You see, this mess we have gotten in may be depressing to us, but there is a bright side," said Tariq.

"A sunny side?" Fairouz said, making a halfhearted attempt at a joke.

"Yes," Tariq said, oblivious to the worldly concerns of his companions. "Humans have always wondered if they were the center of the universe. It always looked that way. After all, the Sun and the Moon seemed to revolve around us."

"What in hell does this have to do with our predicament?" the chief asked. She was fairly well lubricated.

"What we are discovering is that there are apparently a great number of parallel universes, and in each of them the constants are different. In some of them, the conditions for life are right. In others, they are not."

"So this means we might be coming to one where they're not right for us," said Fairouz.

"That is certainly a possibility," said Tariq. "It does not necessarily·mean it will kill us. It might just mean that life did not have a chance to get started there. But since we already got started ourselves, it may not be so bad."

"My God," said the chief. "That *was* as good as it gets!"

"Back in the twentieth century," said Tariq, "some scientists actually held that God must have created the universe just for us alone—that there was no one else."

"We've found all kinds of new elementary particles out here in interstellar space," said the priest, "and we've found interstellar planets and bizarre objects that they never dreamt of back then. But a large portion of matter is still missing, detectable only by its gravity, completely invisible to our instruments."

"Yes, just like Ronin. Its gravitational and electromagnetic fields stretch out into adjacent universes and influence matter there. There must be a lot of Ronins to explain the missing matter. Maybe even more Ronins than there are stars."

Fairouz interrupted. "What does this do to your idea that the life on Ronin means we've got to return back home eventually?"

Tariq tapped his fingers on the control panel for a moment and said, "I still suspect that is right. The fact that there is life on Ronin means that it must be capable of evolving over billions of years, despite all the strange changes that it undergoes in traveling between universes. So that means that the changes cannot be too harsh." He slapped his head. "Of course! That explains why those creatures buried themselves in the ground so quickly."

The others stared inquisitively.

"When they saw our bright floodlights, they thought they were a bright Sun. That means they have adapted to universes where the Sun gets much brighter than ours. There are probably all kinds of changes going on down on Ronin right now. Maybe we should go take a look."

"Like hell we will," the chief said. "We got off that planet alive by a miracle, and we're not going back as long as I have one molecule of oxygen in my lungs."

"Ronin must return," said Tariq. "I just do not see how it could have evolved without being periodic. There must be some mechanism that causes it to move back and forth for all eternity, or else surely, sooner or later, the changes would be too extreme for life to endure."

"So, when do you think Ronin will start going back?" Fairouz asked.

"Who knows? It could be centuries. It could be millions of years."

"Millions of years?" the chief said sourly. "At least I should have a lot of accumulated back pay." She expertly squirted some liquid into her mouth from the beersphere, swallowed with no evident pleasure, and said, "Moondust! At least your theory explains why this beer has lost its taste. If our atoms are different, so is our chemistry, and taste is just a bunch of chemical reactions. See, I'm not as dumb as you thought."

"You are a genius, Chief," said Tariq, smiling.

"True," she replied, "but what's it got me?"

"If only all our problems were so inconsequential," said Tariq.

"The ruin of good beer is hardly inconsequential," said the chief. "I'd feel a helluva lot better if someone could come up with a way to make it taste better."

Tariq looked at his hands with a new curiosity. "Imagine—everything in our bodies is a result of all these fundamental constants. Change just one of them—say, the charge of the electron, or Planck's constant—and the size of the atoms changes, their energy changes, the speed at which the electrons revolve around the nuclei changes. Everything!" He paused, "And the reaction rates—oh, my God! The reaction rates are all different."

He turned pale. "Our whole body is run by thousands of chemical reactions, maybe millions, delicately balanced."

"It's a wonder we're still alive," said Fitzpatrick.

"Yes. Have you had any difficulty focusing your eyes?" Tariq asked Fitzpatrick.

"Yes, now that you mention it." The others nodded.

"I thought it was strain—not enough sleep," Fairouz said.

Tariq nodded. "The amount by which light is bent and the chemical reactions inside the little muscles that focus the eyes are different."

"Yet we're still alive," said the Jesuit. "It must mean that the changes are still very small."

"Yes," said Tariq.

"I don't like this a bit," said the chief. "How long can it go on?"

Tariq shrugged.

"If this keeps up," Fitzpatrick said, "we won't even be able to digest our food."

"Yes," said Tariq. "Would it not be ironic to be surrounded by food, and unable to eat it?"

"*Santo cielo!*" shouted Arnaldo, gesturing angrily.

"What's wrong now?" Fairouz asked resignedly.

"The main CPU is out," he replied.

"No!" shouted Fairouz as she flew over to her own console. She began hitting keys furiously and barking into the computer's microphone.

They crowded around her as she frantically rerouted some of the smaller computers. Then she stopped and turned to them. "This is bad. Practically everything on the ship depends on that main computer. It's completely dead. I was able to call up some peripheral computers and link them in as substitutes. They should be able to handle the environmental systems, so we can keep on breathing. But they don't have all the software of the main CPU—they're not programmed to handle all the contingencies. Only the main one is." Looking at Tariq, she said, "Is this another one of your goddamn fundamental constants?"

"Probably," he said. "I do not know how sensitive the solid-state electronics is to changes in the constants. We do not even know which constants are changing or by how much. There could come a point where nothing works anymore."

"Tariq," the chief said, "how is it you always know just the right thing to brighten my day?"

CHAPTER 22

There was pandemonium as crew members called in to complain about their equipment. Fairouz and two computer technicians frantically ran through diagnostic programs, searching for the malfunction. The cat flew howling through the flight deck, with its AI voice crying out, "I schmell a rat!"

While the technicians began to open panels on the console and in the hull, inspecting fiberoptic cables, Tariq retreated to the relative quiet of the instrumentation deck, where Ng'ethe and a technician were frantically checking instruments controlled by the main ship computer. Tariq brought with him the gray metal attaché case containing his personal computer and its own scientific database.

Strapped into a seat, Tariq drummed on his computer's metal lid, oblivious to the excitement around him, pushing out the mundane with the discipline taught him by his *sensei*. He needed to figure out a way to measure the fundamental constants with the equipment available. He opened the case and spoke into its microphone. "List the main fundamental constants," he commanded, and the screen displayed:

SPEED OF LIGHT	C	3.00	E8	M/SEC
ELECTRON CHARGE	E	1.60	E-19	COULOMB
ELECTRON MASS	M_e	9.11	E-31	KG
PROTON MASS	M_e	1.67	E-27	KG
AVOGADRO CONSTANT	N_A	6.02	E23	/MOLE
FINE STRUCTURE CONSTANT	α	7.30	E-3	
BOLTZMANN CONSTANT	K	1.38	E-23	JOULE/K
GRAVITATIONAL CONSTANT	G	6.67	E-11	N M²/KG²

He tried to see the speed of light from different angles, the way his *sensei* had taught him—3.00 E8 m/sec.; 3×10^8 meters per second; 300,000 kilometers per second. One light-year per year. Eight minutes per A.U. Universal constant. Any laboratory would get the same value for it, regardless of how fast it was moving, as long as it moved with constant velocity.

He stared idly out the porthole at the planet revolving beneath him. They were over the night side now, and glowing, ghostly auroral blobs slowly drifted past.

He stared again at his list of constants, and his eye fell on gravity.

"That is easy!" he exclaimed. "It is not coupled to the others." The technicians looked at him strangely and then returned to their work. "Listen," he said to them. "We have to measure our orbit carefully."

"All you need to do is tap into the navigational database," said the Kenyan. He spoke into the computer microphone. "Oh, damn. It's down, too. It's tied into the main CPU."

"I would not want it anyway," said Tariq. "I do not know how many assumptions went into its software—like, what did it do when it lost Pluto's beacon, and when it went through all these transitions between universes?"

"Well, we do have a backup—a cruder system, for emergencies like this. It's not as accurate as the main system, but it's good enough for short-term operations. Good enough for government work." He spoke into the microphone again and the display lit up. "There you are. That's our orbit."

Tariq ran his eye down the list of the semimajor axis, the eccentricity, the velocity components, and other parameters. He looked at the numbers skeptically and said, "My *sensei* always said that numbers do not mean a thing, no matter how many decimal places they have, if you do not know how they were made."

"Well, these measurements are based on Doppler radar."

"So," said Tariq, "what you have basically, then, is a transmitter here sending a microwave signal to Ronin and bouncing it off."

"Right. The change in frequency tells us how fast we're moving with respect to it. We do solutions for the orbit based on our measurements since we arrived here, given the planet's distribution of mass."

"Precisely how do you calculate that?"

"We use the spherical harmonics based on our orbit around the planet. Every time we go around the planet we get a better measurement of the distribution of matter. You know, whether it's highly concentrated in the center, or whether there are masscons, et cetera."

"How often do you update this model?"

"The mainframe updates constantly, but the backup uses the model obtained on the first orbit when we arrived."

"Well, we cannot use that. Things may have changed since then. Can you replace it with the measurements from the last orbit?"

"Sure. We can use the last measurements from just before the computer went down. The data was stored in a buffer. I can dump it easily."

"Excellent," Tariq said. "This will give us an uncontaminated measurement of what our orbit is in terms of our standards here on board."

At that moment, Fairouz was in the CPU bay, deep in the bowels of the vessel, near the entrance. So important was the computer to the life of the ship that it had been placed where it would be safest from collisions and other accidents.

She unlocked the access hatch to the CPU, which was normally kept secured to prevent tampering.

Soft white lights came on, illuminating the cylindrical room. She floated in, followed by two computer technicians. The room was a sphere six meters in diameter, almost filled with a slightly smaller sphere made up of hundreds of small, truncated octahedrons with tiny apple symbols embossed on them, fitting into each other like atoms in a crystal. Each octahedron was a powerful computer in its own right, but collectively, they were interconnected in a multidimensional way by fiberoptics, so each unit could think independently, yet still share its data with the other units. Fiberoptic cables, which were the nervous system of the computer, ran every which way. The room was warm. A wind blew noisily by—the cooling system in operation.

The computer was held by strong supports connecting it to the outer sphere. A float space a meter deep between the outer sphere and the computer allowed the crew access between the cables. The technicians whipped out their test instruments and plugged them in, while Fairouz floated farther in, surrounded by the complex wiring.

She drifted around to the far side, tumbling slowly, surveying it all, trying to absorb it. It could take weeks to trace down all the possible problems that could have arisen.

And then she spotted it. One of the cables floated free, several centimeters above where it had been attached. Slowly she drifted closer, like a spaceship preparing to dock. She could see several other cables that had been similarly cut. She reached them and held them in her hand. Each ending was sliced off cleanly, as if by a knife. Several centimeters of gap lay between the endings, and several centimeters of fiber were missing completely. She could see where thousands of fibers came to an end at the cut.

"I think we've found the problem, guys," she said.

The technicians floated over to her and stared as she waved a loose fiber end around. They bounced off the wall and excitedly examined the breaks.

"Take it easy," she said. "We don't want to make things even worse."

One of the technicians looked at her and said, "Sabotage!"

"Yes," Fairouz said. "On my vessel. What kind of slime mold would do such a thing?"

"Only a lunatic," said the other technician.

"Or someone who doesn't want to see us succeed," said the first technician.

"Who wouldn't want us to succeed?" Fairouz asked.

"A lot of people," said the second technician.

"Antarkies," said the first. "Israelis, Japs, Norams."

"But it would have to be someone who's on board *right now*. It would be suicidal," she said.

"Hara-kiri," said the first one thoughtfully.

"It's got to be a psychoid," said the second technician. "We were already as good as dead before this happened. Only a nut would do this to us now."

"That's great," Fairouz said. "Not only do we have to worry about the goddamn fundamental constants killing us, but there's some guy with neurobugs and a suicidal subroutine!"

CHAPTER 23

While the technicians repaired the computer, Fairouz returned to the flight deck.

"I think we found the problem," she said to Arnaldo.

"Sabotage," Arnaldo said.

"How did you know?"

"I was just talking to a comptech over the voice line to the CPU room."

"Great," Fairouz said sourly. "It's probably all over the ship by now."

"You can't keep any secrets on this ship. You ought to know that."

"You're right."

Tariq came flying into the room and Fairouz brightened.

"What is this universe coming to when constants are not constant?" he exclaimed. "It is driving me crazy! I can measure changes in the product of the gravitational constant and the planet's mass, and there is a change, but the problem is that we use radar to make the measurement. What if the speed of light is different here? And what if the charge of the electron is different? I cannot even trust the time standard, because the time standard you are using on board the ship is based on atoms of krypton eighty-six, and if the charge of the electron is different, or its mass, or Planck's constant, then even the time standard will be wrong. That means that I do not know how to interpret the radar data, since that depends on the speed of light, and the frequency of the transmitter. But those are probably different from what they used to be."

Fairouz sighed. "Is it my fault that the constants are variable?"

"How am I suppose to measure anything if my measuring rods are all different?" Tariq complained. "It is like trying to measure a pyramid with a writhing snake."

"I've got a ship to run," Fairouz said. "Don't bother me with this trivia."

"This trivia is the closest thing to a compass we have to navigate these universes."

"So, go measure the hell out of everything and don't talk to me until you've figured out a way back home."

The chief, relieved at last to see a problem she could grasp—interpersonal relations—unbelted herself from her chair and floated over between the two.

"There, there, now," she said. "Fairouz, you do what you're good at, and Tariq will do what he's good at."

Tariq floated off in a huff, back to the shaft.

"It sounds to me like things are pretty much under control, for the moment," Ollerenshaw said.

"Sure," Fairouz said. "We can repair the computer, but how did it happen?"

"Yes, indeed, how did it happen? Well, I guess I'd better get some rest and think about it. I'll go to my cabin."

"Give my regards to Sly," Fairouz said drily.

"Oh, I will," Ollerenshaw said, winking.

The cat bounced through the flight deck shouting, "Mouse alert!"

"Goddamn it," Fairouz shouted. "That's the last straw! You lock that flea-bitten cat up before he bumps into some switch and vaporizes us all."

"Heeeere, Schwartzy," Ollerenshaw called, floating off in the direction of the cat.

The alarm went off and the computer announced, "Universe change alert."

Fairouz exclaimed, "Megacrap!"

In the distance, the cat howled, its AI collar shouting, "Intolerable annoyance!"

"You said it, cat," Fairouz muttered.

The new universe was not much worse than the last one. There were no signals at all coming from Earth, although it still had an oxygen atmosphere, indicating life.

"We have done it," Tariq said, smiling.

"Yes," Fitzpatrick said. "I didn't think we could with the instruments on board, but we did."

Fairouz, also in a better mood, said, "So, you measured the constants?"

"Yes," Tariq said, "and I think they are now self-consistent."

"We started out by measuring the ship itself," said the Jesuit. "Since we had a laser interferometer, it was convenient to make a few measurements of the size of the hull, and compare that with the ship's blueprints in the database. At first it looked like the hull had grown larger, but when we measured the other constants, we realized that in fact it had shrunk, but the wavelength used in the interferometer had changed to make it look like a bigger measurement."

"You mean we've shrunk?" Fairouz asked.

"We sure have," said Tariq. "By about two percent."

"Everything looks the same," Fairouz said, glancing around.

"Of course," said Tariq. "That's because everything has shrunk."

"Well, if it looks the same, how do we tell the difference?" Fairouz asked.

"That is what we have just been spending all these hours doing," said Tariq. "We had to measure the charge-to-mass ratio of the electron in a magnetic field, and the magnetic field, then the current generating it, and a lot of spectra of different kinds, to disentangle the dependence on the electron charge, the mass, Planck's constant, and the speed of light."

"And don't forget the Josephson's junction," said Fitzpatrick. "That gave us the ratio between the electron charge and Planck's constant, by using a superconductor."

"And then, of course, we had to measure the ratio of the electron and the proton masses," Tariq said.

"And only then could we begin to interpret our orbit around Ronin," said Fitzpatrick.

"What's to interpret?" Fairouz asked. "You just look at the radar display and the computer tells you the orbital elements and the mass of the planet."

"Nothing is that easy," said Tariq. "The numbers you read on your computer were calculated using the fundamental constants back in our home universe. The computer doesn't understand that those numbers have changed."

"Of course, we can enter in the new numbers," said Fitzpatrick, "but we'll have to change them every time we go to a new universe."

"But our orbit is determined by Ronin's mass," said Fairouz.

"I wish it were," said Tariq. "Actually, it's determined by the product of the gravitational constant and the mass of Ronin. It turns out that both of those have changed."

"We had to do all these other measurements first, to figure out what the mass of Ronin really was now. The fact that the proton mass had changed was the most important factor that we had to measure."

"What does the proton mass have to do with anything?" Fairouz asked, growing impatient. "Mass is mass!"

"But Ronin," said the Jesuit, "is made up of zillions of atoms. Most of the matter in atoms is in the protons and neutrons, which weigh about the same and have changed about the same. We had to measure that, too. We assumed that the only thing that hasn't changed is the *number* of atoms in Ronin. So once we had recalibrated the radar, using the new fundamental constants—especially the faster speed of light in this universe—and the new time standard, since the krypton eighty-six atom is whirling around at a different speed now, our orbital period gave us the product of the gravitational constant and the mass of Ronin. The change in the proton mass then told us what Ronin's new mass was, and from that, we could deduce what the new universal gravitational constant is."

"So how much did gravity change by?" Fairouz asked.

"A few tenths of a percent," Tariq said.

"A few tenths of a percent," Fairouz said. "Who cares? What's the big deal?"

"That's enough to scramble the positions of the planets over billions of years," said Tariq.

Fairouz nodded, a look of understanding beginning to appear on her face. "I see. Just change the strength of gravity a *teensy-weensy* bit, and Earth will go around the Sun a tiny bit faster or slower. And during billions of years, its position along its orbit could be tremendously different from our universe."

"The biggest effect we've detected so far is in Planck's constant," Fitzpatrick said. "It's decreased by almost one percent." He paused dramatically, as if he had just delivered the most mind-boggling news in history.

Fairouz stared at him blankly.

"The changes in the other constants are rather small compared with this one," the priest elaborated.

"Oh, look, Father," said Fairouz, "I understand about gravity because that's how I earn my living. If there's a mistake in the measurement of some gravitational field, then I could miss my target by millions of kilometers. And I've been around enough electronics to have a feel for electrons and protons and such dust. And, of course, the speed of light has been a fact of life for me ever since I can remember. Practically all of my long-distance conversations have delays created by the size of the solar system. But I never had the foggiest idea what the hell Planck's constant was all about."

"Planck revolutionized our understanding of energy—," the Jesuit said. "What he said was that you couldn't have just *any* amount of energy—it comes in lumps. It's like money. You have eurafrodollars and cents, but you don't have coins for half a cent or a seventeenth of a cent."

Fitzpatrick continued. "There had long been a debate about whether light consisted of waves or particles. Gradually, it was becoming clear that it was both. What Planck realized was that in order to explain the properties of matter, you had to assume that light came in little lumps that he called quanta. He came up with an equation, just as simple as Einstein's later $E = mc^2$, and just as profound: $E = h f$, where h is Planck's constant and f is the frequency.

"Where Einstein was to find that matter had an enormous amount of energy always associated with it, and that energy always behaved like matter, Planck found that each frequency of light had a certain amount of energy associated with it. He introduced this constant h—six point six times ten to the minus thirty-four joule-seconds. So low-frequency light, like red light, doesn't have as much energy as high-frequency light, like blue light.

"Anyway, this started a revolution, and shook up a lot of people, until several of them put all these different ideas together, including some of Einstein's, and came up with the quantum theory. It was the first thing to successfully explain the atom. Without quantum effects, the atom would have collapsed in a tiny fraction of a second. The electron would have radiated away all its energy, and would have spiraled right down into the nucleus. The only reason atoms exist, or we do, is that the energy of the atom is quantized, just like light, and the atom can't collapse.

"All of the behavior of atoms, apart from details of the nucleus, are determined by the quantum theory. Whether two atoms will stick together and form a molecule is determined by it. And the fact that carbon atoms stick together so readily and form long chain molecules, allowing life to form.

"In ancient days, people used to perform chemistry by pouring chemicals together and seeing what happened. Now, most chemistry is done on a computer, using quantum theory to predict the results. That's why we've seen an outpouring of synthetics in this century unlike anything in history. All kinds of new medicines, materials, cloth, building materials, have been made possible, all because of this theory developed so long ago. You see?"

Fairouz shrugged.

"And that's why we've shrunk," said Tariq, rejoining the conversation. "Planck's constant has gotten slightly smaller, and the size of atoms is determined by this constant. In fact, since the size of the atom is proportional to the square of Planck's constant, a one percent reduction in Planck's constant means that we are now two percent smaller than we used to be."

"Can this go on forever?" Fairouz asked. "Will we become little things the size of microbes?"

"Maybe," Tariq said, "but long before that happens, our chemistry will break down, because it is nonlinear."

"All of our reaction rates are being screwed up in different ways by this change," Fitzpatrick said. "That's why I've been having indigestion."

"Haven't we all?" Fairouz asked.

"There could come a time," Tariq said, "when it would interfere with our heart or our brain, and we might not be able to recover."

"Isn't there anything we can do?" Fairouz asked.

"Perhaps," Tariq said. "Something the Father said gave me an idea."

They looked at him eagerly.

"There is a chemical database in the lab," he said. "We can easily simulate the changes in our biochemistry by simply changing the value of Planck's constant in the software. That will tell us what is going to happen—at least with some of the reactions in our bodies. We probably do not have enough data to simulate every single reaction, but at least we can do the more important ones. And then, we can figure out if there is a way we can create new chemicals to moderate these changes, and see whether we can synthesize chemicals that will help us, using what is on board."

"You mean, you can come up with an anticonstant pill?" Fairouz asked with admiration.

Tariq shrugged and said, "Maybe we can at least slow down the processes that are endangering our bodies, but there is going to be a limit to how much we can do, with the time available, and with our ignorance of all the details—the thousands of different chemical reactions taking place inside us at any moment."

"It's a hell of a lot better than doing nothing," Fairouz said.

In the distance the cat howled and said, "Get me some Alpha Seltzer."

CHAPTER 24

Tariq and Fitzpatrick were on the laboratory deck amidships, surrounded by test instruments and three computer technicians, plus the ship's physician, Dr. Isingoma. The smell of chemicals and medicines permeated the air.

They pored over the flow chart of the human body displayed on the main computer screen that filled the ceiling. A casual observer would not have realized that the intricate series of boxes, arrows, and multicolored wiring diagrams on the screen were not those of a large computer, but were symbols representing a schematic diagram of the chemical reactions of the human body and their interrelationships. It resembled a chart of the ecology of Earth, where the interrelationships of foxes and rabbits were replaced by connections between glands and enzymes.

Tariq stared at the screen glumly, and remarked, "It looks pretty hopeless to me. Chemistry was never one of my strong suits."

"Oh," said Dr. Isingoma, a white smile gleaming on his pitch-black Ugandan face, "it's not all that bad. Ninety-nine percent of it is repetitive trivia. It's just the 1 percent that can kill you."

"I'm certainly glad I took a lot of biology at university," the priest said.

"These days," Dr. Isingoma said, "medicine is mostly a matter of computer models of the human body, expert systems, and measurements to find out which parameters have changed when someone gets sick."

"They've reduced us to a bunch of differential equations and reaction rates," Fitzpatrick said. "They've never managed to make a mathematical model of the soul, but fortunately, that isn't what we need to repair right now."

"Speaking as a mere astronomer," Tariq said, "the problem is the reaction rates. If Planck's constant is smaller, the atoms are also smaller; therefore, cross sections are smaller, and most chemical rates should be slower."

"Well," said Dr. Isingoma, "what controls the reaction rates is enzymes, for the most part."

"So, basically, we're dealing with biochemical catalysts," said the Jesuit.

"If we can just find a way of tweaking up the critical enzyme rates a bit," said Dr. Isingoma, "we should be able to help our bodies ride out this difficult period."

"What I worry about," Fitzpatrick said, "are our antibodies and white blood cells. Suppose they aren't as efficient as they used to be. That could cause our bodies' normal contingents of nasty viruses and bacteria to get out of hand."

"That would be very serious," said Dr. Isingoma. "We could come down with all kinds of diseases."

"I will let one of you tell that to the chief," Tariq said. "She has already gotten enough bad news from me."

An alarm sounded.

"Damn," said the Jesuit. "Another universe shift."

"But it is not time," said Tariq.

Fairouz's voice came over the ship's intercom. "Now hear this. This is an emergency. All personnel put on oh two gear. There are poisonous gases in the life support system."

The alarm rang again, and Fairouz repeated the instructions, while everyone converged on the red locker marked O2. Tariq reached it first and hit the key. The door slid open. He reached in and pulled out half a dozen

O2 respirators, threw them at the other crew members, then put one on himself.

The face masks resembled those of fighter pilots of a bygone era, but the tiny tank beneath the chin contained liquid oxygen and a recycler that guaranteed up to several hours of precious oxygen.

When the commotion settled down, Tariq called up to Fairouz. "What's going on?"

"There's a leak in the coolant lines."

"Where?"

"In the engine room."

"What are you using for coolant?"

"It's a very volatile organic chemical that is also, unfortunately, very poisonous."

"Any idea what caused it?"

"I don't know, but I'm beginning to think about the psychoid who sabotaged our computer."

CHAPTER 25

Tariq left the Jesuit and the doctor deep in a conversation full of polysyllabic biochemical jargon and floated down to the engine room. In the shaft, he saw the cat approach, bouncing skillfully from one side to the other. He was pleased someone had thought to put the animal's pressure suit on him, so he was safe from the fumes. As he bounced by, the cat meowed in his Austrian accent, "I schmell a rat! I'll get him if it takes the rest of my nine lives!" Tariq marveled at how easily Schwartzy adapted to zero gravity.

In the engine room, there were technicians and mechanics everywhere.

Access hatches were open, exposing a bewildering array of pipes and coils, fiber cables and electrical wiring. There were massive coolant pumps, magnetohydrodynamic suspension coils for ultradense metamatter, and other indefinable pieces of hardware.

"Found the trouble yet?" Tariq asked a mechanic squeezed inside an access hatch filled with blue and red glass pipes.

"Sure have," she said with a German accent muffled by her face mask. "Sabotage."

She pointed at a gap in one of the blue pipes. "Someone cut right through the coolant lines. They must really be afraid we are going to get back."

"Evidently," mused Tariq, studying the break. She removed a short section of pipe from one side of the break and gave it to him. It was an industrial-strength glass pipe of the sort used for highly corrosive liquids. He sniffed at it.

"It's clean now. The coolant has evaporated."

The break was smooth, not jagged, and there were faint parallel grooves across the edge of the glass. "May I keep this?" he asked.

She looked at him suspiciously. "I'd better check with the captain." She muttered into the intercom, then turned back to Tariq. "Okay, but only after we video it."

After they had recorded it from every angle, he took it back to the flight deck. The whole gang was there except for the priest. Sly was massaging the chief's back.

Tariq floated lazily around the deck, holding the pipe casually in one hand while studying the crew's eyes. No one gave the pipe more than a momentary glance except Fairouz, who stared at it long and hard.

She reached out and examined it carefully. "How could such a thing happen?" she murmured.

"How, indeed?"

She turned away silently and he belted himself in at the keyboard, deep in thought.

The Jesuit came bouncing out of the shaft. "I think we've come up with something," he said. "The doc's downstairs, mixing up a batch of bacteria he's engineered to serve as an enzyme thermostat. We'll ingest the little buggers, and they'll accelerate some of the enzymes when we need it."

Ollerenshaw belched. Tariq noticed the air was not too fragrant. He was not sure whether it was due to his changed sense of smell, or to the frequent breaking of wind that had become a recent manifestation of their upset digestive tracts.

The automatic alarm went off and the synthetic voice said, "Universe change alert." They experienced the standard symptoms.

"Ho hum," said Ollerenshaw. "Another new universe. I feel like I'm on one of those quickie tourist excursions. You know—seven continents in seven days."

"They're coming faster and faster," Fairouz said.

"*Fenomenale!*" shouted Arnaldo. "TV!"

Everyone brightened up. "Does this mean that things are getting better?" Ollerenshaw asked. "It must."

Tariq went over to an intercom and called up to Ng'ethe. "Got the measurements yet?" he asked.

"Working on them, Tariq. It's not perfectly automated, you know."

"I know there is a lot of work involved. I am just impatient. Please give me a call as soon as you have the new values. We have got to do this every time we shift universes."

"Roger." They signed off.

"Maybe we ought to get off here," the chief said. "At least there are people. It's more than I can say for the last couple of universes."

"How do you know they are *people*?" Tariq asked quietly.

Nobody answered.

To Fitzpatrick, he said, "Will your bugs still work in the new universe?"

"We think we've come up with a few tricks to make them self-adjusting, so that each time Planck's constant changes, they'll change in an appropriate way."

"This TV spectrum is really weird," Arnaldo said.

On the screen, he had a blowup of a two-megahertz strip of the spectrum. It showed various spikes, flattened portions, and rapidly varying patterns within the overall steady one.

"I'm no expert on television," Tariq said. "It looks pretty much like what I've seen in the textcrystals."

"But these spikes are varying all over the place," said the Italian. "I've never seen anything like it."

"Well, you are the expert," Tariq said. "In fact, you are the *universe's* greatest expert, having seen more kinds of TV signals than any other human being in history."

"I have faith in you," Fitzpatrick said to Arnaldo. "Just play around with it like you did the other signals, and I'm sure you'll figure it out."

"Let's take a look at the planet," Tariq said. They floated over to a data keyboard and entered some commands, accessing the main telescope via the data deck's computer. Earth floated into view.

It was now a greenish globe, covered with yellow clouds, with darker shadings hinting at strange continents. What drew all eyes was not the planet, but the series of silvery rings encircling it, which gave it the appearance of Saturn. These extended much farther than Saturn's in proportion to the size of the planet—nearly twenty times Earth's radius.

"Are you sure this is Earth?" Ollerenshaw asked hesitantly.

"It has to be," Tariq said. "It is in the right orbit." He zoomed back and they saw the Moon, which looked familiar, yet somehow different.

He quickly made some measurements, and then announced, "The Moon is bigger than ours, and farther out. I guess I should have thought of it earlier, but even details like the sizes of moons and planets will be affected by changes in the fundamental constants during the evolution of the solar system.

"Just a minute," he added. He entered a few more instructions into the computer and then said, "Earth's spin has really slowed down. One day down there is now one hundred thirteen regular Earth hours."

"Almost a week," exclaimed Fitzpatrick.

"How did you find out so fast?" Fairouz asked.

"I did a Doppler measurement on the spectral lines of the planet's atmosphere. But that is what you would expect, with the Moon farther away. Tidal drag must have been greater."

"Even today," said Fitzpatrick, "the Moon—I mean, our own Moon back home—is moving away from Earth a few centimeters every year due to tidal drag. It also slows down the planet's rotation by sixteen seconds every million years."

Occasionally, strange squeals and chirps came out of the loudspeaker as Arnaldo fiddled with the controls.

"My God," said the Jesuit. "Can you imagine what effect that would have on evolution?"

"Unpredictable," said Tariq. "The tides would have been enormously greater, and life would have been stirred up far more viciously than on Earth. And yet, ours was a pretty violent environment at that."

"I wonder," said Fitzpatrick, "what effect it would have had on our civilization to have had days almost a week long? They would get much hotter, and the nights much colder. Weather and climate patterns would be radically different."

Tariq zoomed in on the rings. "That's strange—the rings go right down to the planet."

"That's weird," Fairouz said. "I've never seen them do that—not on Saturn, Jupiter, Uranus, or Neptune."

"Right," said Tariq. "Once you get inside the Roche limit, bodies tend to break up."

"If a moon gets too close to a planet," Fitzpatrick amplified for the chief, "the tidal forces can break it apart. If the Moon got within a couple of radii of the Earth, it would break up and form a ring. The particles tend to get swept away by the magnetosphere or the outer fringes of the atmosphere."

Tariq magnified the image further, until the tilted rings dissolved into an intricate tracery of fine bright lines.

"It's beautiful," Fairouz said.

"It's like the finest Islamic art," Fitzpatrick exclaimed.

They stared at it for several minutes, and then Tariq remarked after a calculation, "The rings end at the geosynchronous point."

More strange growling came from Arnaldo's speaker.

"You mean, at the equator, where you would put a satellite, like in the Geosync War?" Ollerenshaw asked.

"Right," Tariq said. "You really know your history." He magnified the outer portion of the ring that ended sharply at the geosynchronous point. There were thousands of regularly spaced tiny bright dots along its rim. In between each of the dots ran a gently curved line connecting every dot to every other one in an intricate geometric tracery. And from each dot hung a bright thin line that went straight down to Earth.

"This is an artificial structure," Tariq said. "Maybe it got its start with a natural ring around the Earth, from a small Moon that got too close and broke up. And then the civilization used the raw materials to build these connections between stations out at the geosynchronous points."

"But why connect every single point?" Fitzpatrick asked. "It's not very economical."

"Man does not live by economics alone," Ollerenshaw

said. "Maybe there are esthetic reasons, or religious ones—"

"Like the pyramids," Tariq said. "Immortality for the pharaoh."

"Yeah," continued the chief. "Or maybe there is such an advanced civilization there that this is economical in a way that's not obvious to us puny representatives of a more primitive Earth."

"Or us representatives of our particular Planck's constant," added the Jesuit. "Structural engineering may be different here due to the changed constants."

"After all," said Ollerenshaw, "economically, it would make sense to have just one road going from Rome to Paris, but in fact there's a dizzying variety of all sizes, with all kinds of purposes."

"Okay," Fairouz said. "If there are a lot of people living out there on the ring, there might well be a lot of traffic, perhaps in tunnels. That could be what we're seeing."

"Or, it could be like the infamous advertising projects of the early part of the century," said Ollerenshaw. "Flying mausoleums, so you could see your dear departed from Earth. And the huge mylar 'Drink Guaca Cola!' reflector that orbited every couple of hours."

"Astronomers got that kind of thing banned," Tariq said with satisfaction. "Except for political slogans," he added with disapproval.

"And religious ones," said Fitzpatrick.

"*Ma no!*" said Arnaldo. They looked at the TV screen. At first, it was difficult to comprehend the image, because the raster of the screen was stranger than anything they had seen before. Instead of a series of horizontal lines, as on most of the previous television systems, or vertical lines, in one case, the screen traced out an intricate hexagonal spiral, like a spiderweb. And on the web was a moving image of a head with four bulging eyes. Its mouth opened and closed, making a horrendous screeching sound like hail falling through a fan. Four flexible proboscises emerged from the mouth, and a curled tongue darted out.

The camera cut to a room whose walls were filled with hexagonal chambers. In front of the wall, little carts slowly wheeled by, containing large white, squirming, mummylike objects.

After a moment, Fitzpatrick said quietly, "Those are the larvae."

"I think I'm going to be sick," said Ollerenshaw, reaching for the barf bag under the seat.

The screen cut back to the first creature, who emitted the hideous sounds.

"It looks like he knows we're here," Fairouz said. "I have the feeling he's speaking to us."

"Nuke 'em!" said Sly.

"It's probably just a newscast," said Arnaldo. "Newscasters always look straight into the camera. At least, in most universes I've been in."

The camera cut to an exterior shot, showing a thriving metropolis covered by lush, junglelike vegetation. Huge hemispherical mounds rose in the distance, interconnected by metallic highways with fast-moving vehicles on them. Weblike lines connected two of the mounds. Tiny aircraft crisscrossed the sky regularly. The voice continued to screech throughout the scene, reminding Tariq of fingernails scraping across a sheet of silicate.

The scene cut to another interior, showing an enormous, pulsating hairy body, with dozens of small, dark creatures scurrying around it. Now they could see the structure of the creatures more clearly. They had ten legs, and a body divided into four parts, terminating in the four eyes.

Their bodies were bright green, except for the eyes, which were deep red. The eyes were multifaceted, like a fly's. And some of the creatures had wings on their backs.

"I'm only guessing at the color balance, you know," said Arnaldo.

Tariq spoke over the intercom to the data deck, and the Kenyan made measurements of the atmosphere. He called back to Tariq, who whistled. "Now *that* is a thick atmosphere," Tariq said. "It is more than a hundred times denser than our Earth's."

"Ah," said Fitzpatrick. "That would allow big, heavy creatures to fly around. It would be impossible, otherwise."

"I suppose we should not be surprised," Tariq said. "It's not much worse than Venus's atmosphere, and it is what our own Earth's air may have been shortly after it formed."

"I guess that big guy is the Numero Uno," Ollerenshaw said weakly, after trading her barf bag for a beersphere, which she quickly emptied.

"I think Numero Uno is a lady," Fitzpatrick said. "The queen."

"It looks like this is some kind of social type of insectoid species," Tariq said.

"Or arachnoid," the Jesuit said. "They have a lot of spiderlike qualities."

"Yes, the webbing and the multiple eyes. There are spiders on Earth with eight eyes, you know," Fitzpatrick said.

"I did not," said Tariq.

"You say insectoid, and I say arachnoid," Ollerenshaw sang feebly to a Gershwin tune.

"Yes," said Fitzpatrick. "I always wondered, if we hadn't come along, whether perhaps the hives of social insects would have taken over."

"Insectoid, arachnoid; arachnoid, insectoid," she sang.

"Individually," continued Fitzpatrick, "a bee, or an ant, or a termite, is pretty stupid. But you put a bunch of them together in a hive and they act almost human. They have a collective intelligence—something like what we're achieving for our whole civilization through modern communications and computers. Given a little more time, and less competition from us, one of those hives might have evolved into intelligent creatures."

"Let's call the whole thing off." The chief closed her eyes and became silent.

Suddenly Fairouz turned away from the screen and hit her keyboard. "Moondust!" she said. "We've got company!"

On her screen was displayed an infrared scan of the sky. Three bright dots showed in the middle, artificially colored by the computer as blue, meaning they were approaching.

"Better shine your shoes, guys," said Fairouz, "and brush up on your insectoid, because company's coming for dinner."

"I hope we're not the main course," Ollerenshaw said softly.

"Nuke the bastards!" Sly said.

"With what?" murmured Tariq.

CHAPTER 26

Tariq's heart skipped a beat. The crew stared wide-eyed at the screen.

"How far away are they?" Tariq asked.

Fairouz threw up her arms. "Too far for radar, thank God! No contact yet."

"What's the limit?"

"If they're about the same size as us," Fairouz said, "we could detect them up to a couple million kilometers."

"Good," Tariq said. "That means that they're at least ten light-seconds away."

"That's not very far," Fairouz said. She muttered into the computer microphone, "Calculate distance of target using infrared, assuming it is three hundred kelvins."

"Ah," said Tariq. "I see. You are using their infrared brightness to estimate their distance, assuming they are as hot as we are."

She manipulated a cursor to one of the targets.

The number 5.3 E6 KM appeared on the screen next to one of the dots.

"Five million kilometers," Fairouz said. "When's the next universe change due?" she asked the computer.

"Three hours, forty-one minutes," replied the computer.

"Tariq," called Ng'ethe over the intercom. "I've got the results."

"Good," said Tariq. "Put them on data line two."

He floated over to a console near Arnaldo and called up the data. A list flashed onto the screen.

"Great," Tariq said. "Planck's constant is going up."

"Is that good?" the chief asked.

"Yes," Tariq said. "It means we're going back toward normal."

"You mean we're going back home?" she asked.

"No," Tariq said. "Because we would have seen a familiar universe by now. We're still going in the same direction. It's just that this universe happens to be more like the one we are used to, at least as far as Planck's constant."

"Good," Fairouz said. "We've now got parallax measurements on those vessels. I'm treating them as if they were unknown asteroids." She studied the screen. "Damn! They're closer than we estimated—less than four million kilometers and closing fast."

The updated velocity measurements appeared next to the three dots on the screen.

"What's the estimated time until arrival?" she asked the computer.

Next to the dots on the screen, adjacent to the velocities, appeared these numbers: 2:13, 4:17, 6:29.

"Two hours till the first one arrives," she said. "They're really moving. They must have come from a Pluto-type base to get here this quickly."

"So the whole solar system is infested with these creatures," Fitzpatrick said.

"Damn," Fairouz said. "When the first one gets here, we'll still be in this stinking universe."

"Of course," Ollerenshaw said dejectedly. "Heaven forbid that we should slip away to a quiet universe without having a chance to shake feelers with our charming visitors."

"Let me at 'em!" Sly said, waving a well-muscled arm. "I'd like to rip their guts out."

"Will somebody shut that goddamn robot up?" Fairouz asked.

Ollerenshaw looked at Sly and put a finger over her mouth.

The robot winked.

"At least they probably haven't detected us yet," said Fairouz.

"But if we can detect them," Tariq said, "they can detect us."

"Not necessarily. It's a lot easier for us—we're detecting them against the cold of space. They'd have to pick us up against the background of Ronin's heat, and it's almost the same temperature as us."

"Ah so," said Tariq.

Fairouz starred intently at the screen, running her fingers through her long hair, as if to tear it out at the roots. "This reminds me," she said, "of evading the customs cops in the asteroids."

"Why would you do a thing like that?" Fitzpatrick asked naively.

She looked at him in disbelief. "Because sometimes, I just happened to have cargoes that your Earthcrats wanted to impose really big duties on or confiscate for their own use. I mean, not that I did this for a living, you understand," she said quickly. "But it was sometimes necessary, due to the complicated economics out in the roids, what with Eurafricans, Israelis, Druzes, Australians, and Japanese all claiming the same 'roids—always the most valuable ones."

The priest looked embarrassed.

"How do you know their radar is not more powerful than ours?" Tariq asked.

"Because an alarm would have gone off automatically. That's another trick I learned out in the 'roids. Always buy the most sensitive radar detector you can find. That way, you pick them up before they pick you up."

"If only we could go down to the surface of Ronin and hide," said Tariq. "Until we get into another universe."

"Yes," said Fairouz, absentmindedly.

"Why can't we?" the chief asked.

Fairouz went through an intricate series of system checks and the Jesuit replied, "The *Ulug Beg* isn't designed to land on the planet. The shuttle can only hold half a dozen of us."

"Well," Ollerenshaw said, "there's only half a dozen of us who really matter."

Fairouz turned around and looked at her as if she had

just turned into one of the insectoid creatures. "As long as I am captain of this vessel, we're going to save every man, woman, and robot, or die trying."

"I'll drink to that," whispered Sly, waving a fist.

In her most soothing voice, Ollerenshaw replied, "I didn't mean abandoning everyone. I was just thinking that if we're going to be captured anyway, it's better that a few of us escape than everyone die."

"How do we know that these creatures are going to kill us, anyway?" Fairouz asked.

"Perhaps they just want to invite us down to their planet so they can lay eggs in our bodies," Ollerenshaw said, giggling nervously.

"Ain't nobody going to lay eggs in my body," Sly whispered. At a gesture from the chief, he resumed massaging her back.

Fairouz stared at the screen with the approaching three dots, nodded, and said, "I think there's a way to hide."

"You have our complete attention," Fitzpatrick said.

"I once wanted to do this on a 'roid flight, when the customs cops were hot on our tail, but the 'roids are too small, and spin too fast. Ronin is different."

"What's the bottom line?" Ollerenshaw asked.

"We go into Ronin's shadow. They're going to be looking mainly at the planet. That's going to have their attention for the next few hours. They may do a routine scan for moons, but we're a really tiny moon, and if we're hiding in the shadow, they won't be able to detect us easily—at least, not with visible light."

"But we'll only be in the shadow a few minutes," Tariq said.

"Not if we go into a highly eccentric orbit."

He thought about it a moment and said, "Brilliant!" Fairouz smiled slightly, basking in his first praise.

Seeing the uncomprehending expression on the chief's face, Fitzpatrick said, "She'll put us into a higher orbit—an extremely elliptical one that will stay in Ronin's shadow for a couple of hours, until we're safely in another universe."

"Why don't you do it now?" Ollerenshaw asked.

"Right!" said the Italian emphatically. "We have a saying—you have to move when the devil is at your heels!"

"Perfecto!" said Ollerenshaw, mixing her meager Spanish with her feebler Italian.

"But if they're using infrared detectors," said Fairouz, "as soon as I fire our rockets, they'll pick us up, like a fireworks display at midnight. We've got to wait till our orbit takes us to where Ronin is between us and them. Then I can safely fire, and we can hide in the shadow."

"One thing that worries me," Tariq said, "is the lead ship. If it gets here before the universe changes, then it will orbit around Ronin and be locked together with us."

"Yes," said Fairouz, nodding. "It worries me, too."

Tariq stared at the rapidly decreasing distance figures on the lead spacecraft. "Maybe there is another way," he said. "I mean, in addition to hiding."

"What else can we possibly do?" Fairouz asked. "We're not equipped with heavy weapons. This is just a scientific exploration vessel."

"Yes," said Tariq. "So let us use our scientific payload and send out a decoy."

"By God, that might work," Fairouz said. "We can put out one of our probes, and head it straight toward those vessels with its radio blaring."

"It'll be just like your fireworks at night," said Fitzpatrick.

"Fabulous!" Ollerenshaw said sincerely—the first time in days that she had looked genuinely cheered. "As long as they're chasing after the wild goose, they won't get here until we shift into a different universe, right?"

"Right you are," Fairouz said, furiously punching commands on the keyboard.

"Let's hope we have the monopoly on dirty tricks," said the chief more contemplatively.

CHAPTER 27

While Fairouz frantically went down her checklists, Tariq floated over to Arnaldo. "I hope we aren't giving ourselves away to them," he said. "Are we transmitting any signals now?"

"No," replied Arnaldo. "The skipper shut down the radar and told me to shut off the transmitters till further notice."

"Evidently a skill she learned while dodging customs out among the asteroids," said Tariq dryly.

"Oh, yes. She's got a million stories about them. Those Druzes are the best 'roid dodgers in the business."

Fairouz paused in the midst of a checklist and gave the Italian a dirty look. He shut up.

Tariq watched Fairouz as she bent over the control panel. His mind was a jumble of conflicting thoughts. Increasingly, he found it hard to take his eyes off her, and more than once, he'd caught her gaze lingering on him. Too often of late, when he should have been thinking about the terrible problems facing them, he found his normally clear, cool mind filled with images of her.

The minutes dragged out as they watched the edge of Ronin slowly cross the screen toward the three alien dots, while the *Ulug Beg* swung in its circular orbit toward the night side of the planet. The crescent on the sunward side

f the planet shrank noticeably, its edge approaching the
rst of the three ships on the screen.

"Now hear this," Fairouz said on the ship's intercom.
Fasten your seat belts." Her words echoed down through
he shaft.

Ronin's edge eclipsed the first of the blips, and Fairouz
aid, "Stand by for high-gee acceleration."

The next blip was eclipsed, and then the third.

Her thumb squeezed the red button on the top of her
main thruster joystick and she shouted, "Fire." Nothing
happened. "Moondust," she spat, and hit a rapid succes-
ion of keys, muttering commands into the computer.

"That Earth-lickin' main engine won't start. Some-
hing's screwed up the command line." She toggled on
he intercom and shouted, "Engine room. Find out what
acuumhead has nixed the commline to the MEs! I'm
oming down." She unbuckled and kicked off from the
ontrol panel, pulling herself into the shaft.

Discreetly, Tariq floated over to the entrance to
airouz's cabin. While everyone's attention was on the
eadouts or absorbed in excited chatter with their neigh-
ors, he pushed the button to her cabin, and the door slid
uietly open. He slipped inside, and the door shut behind
im.

The cabin was shaped like a piece of pie, sandwiched
etween the two shafts in the center of the vessel. Al-
hough somewhat cramped, it was still several times the
olume of his own little cabin, and in zero gravity, it felt
uite comfortable. Much of the outer circumference was
aken up by a bed on the floor, a luxury in zero gravity,
ut a necessity during high acceleration. Normally it was
towed in the wall, but Fairouz had left it out unmade,
vrinkled sheets floating like a ghost in the ventilator's
reeze. There was a slight, vinegary odor in the cabin.
ariq guessed that it was perfume, distorted by his al-
ered sense of smell.

On one wall was a full-length mirror. Next to it was a
lank sheet of metal which, when he touched it, sprang
pen into a sink and toilet. On his deck, a private head
vas unheard of.

On the other side of the entrance was a little transpar-
nt case filled with small figurines. They were whimsical
rolls, of the sort found in the tourist traps of the Moon,

made from pieces of asteroid. These were of nickel-iron held in place by a magnet. One end of the cabin bore a full-length mirror; the other had a series of drawers built into the wall.

Hung on the ceiling were moving videographs of asteroids spinning slowly, and scenes on the Moon with traffic flying and crawling across craters. One showed a group of pressure-suited astronauts on an asteroid—two adults and seven children of ages that, judging from their sizes, ranged from about two to teens. Each wore a suit of a different color.

One image was oddly out of place among the lonely videographs. It was an old-fashioned still picture of a couple on Earth in front of a little house with palm trees in the background—a typical prewar Middle Eastern scene.

He felt a twinge of guilt at invading her privacy, but he forced himself to continue.

He floated over to the drawers and stuck his feet into the toeholds. Systematically, he went through them, starting at the top. Each one had a net to keep the contents from flying out in zero gravity. The first three held clothing, cosmetics, and other feminine articles. In the fourth was an assortment of jewelry—necklaces, bracelets, anklets, and all kinds of trinkets that are made out in the asteroid belt and on the Moon, found abundantly in tourist shops. Many of them were carved from asteroid —either the black obsidianlike beads of carbonaceous chondrites, or pieces with the shiny metal sheen of the nickel-iron. He was about to close the drawer when a small blue jewelry box caught his eye.

He removed it from under the net and opened it. Inside was a ring of black nickel-iron asteroid material with a stone fastened in the center. The "jewel" was an irregular bubble of colorless, dirty glass with tiny black specks. It was strange and ugly. Puzzled, he put it back in its case and closed the drawer.

The next drawer contained hundreds of viewcrystals with books encoded in them. He held up several of the coin-sized crystals and read the tiny titles. *I, the Jury,* by Mickey Spillane. *The Maltese Falcon,* by Dashiell Hammett.

Even with his poor cultural education, he recognized private detective stories.

The last drawer contained numerous little tools. He picked up the largest—a cylinder that fit his hand nicely, like a flashlight. It was a laser torch. Just the sort of thing for cutting pipes.

He put it back and closed the drawer, then went back to the fourth drawer and pulled out the ring again. He studied it carefully. Inside it, he could just make out some characters—three Hebrew letters, worn almost to invisibility. He stared at the unfamiliar language. It brought back boyhood memories of the war. He remembered stories of the Druzes who had fought on the side of the Jews.

He toyed with the ring distastefully, then put it back.

He searched the cabin further, but was unable to find anything else of interest.

He floated to the door and touched the transparency panel. It lit up, showing the scene outside on a one-way screen.

Two technicians were floating by. As soon as they were out of sight, he opened the door and floated out, feeling slightly guilty, and went back to the main control area, taking the long way around the circular flight deck.

Everyone was still there, except Fairouz. The copilot, as usual, was asleep in his chair.

"Any news?" Tariq asked.

"They found another cut in the fiber cable, from the CPU to the engine," Arnaldo replied.

"Sabotage?" Tariq asked.

"Yes, just like before."

Fitzpatrick pursed his lips. "I wonder why the damage has been so mild."

"Mild?" Tariq asked.

"Yes. Nothing has really endangered our lives."

"Yet," said the chief.

"If I were a saboteur," the priest said, "I should very much want to do more severe damage than has so far been the case."

"Maybe he was frightened away before he could complete the job," the chief said.

"Or maybe," said Tariq, "he is trying to divert us from his *real* target. While we are focusing on repairable damage, he could be doing God knows what somewhere else in the ship." He stared at the screen thoughtfully for a minute, although the approaching ships were still invisible, behind the crescent of Ronin. "How long before the repairs are finished?"

"Just a couple minutes more," Fitzpatrick said.

"What about the decoy?" Tariq asked.

"It's all set," said the chief.

"They shot it into a retrograde orbit at very high speed a couple minutes ago," Fitzpatrick said. "So our buggy friends should be picking up the signal soon."

"Excellent," Tariq said. "So all we have to do now is relax, wait for the engines to be repaired and the new universe to arrive, and everything will be all right."

"I swear to Allah," Ollerenshaw said, "to anyone else who's listening, and to whatever God calls himself in this godforsaken universe, that if I ever get back to Earth, I'm going to stay so close to that planet for the rest of my life that I will not even wear high heels."

Fairouz came bursting through the shaft and flew over to her console. She rapidly hit a series of keys, and barked commands into the computer. "Now hear this," she said over the ship's intercom, "the repair is just about finished, so tuck yourselves in. We're going to go on a high-gee ride."

Two minutes later, a message came over the intercom: "Engine is go for firing."

Fairouz triggered the short countdown voice, and the computer counted: "Three, two, one, fire!"

The engines vibrated and the acceleration pressed them back into their seats until they were going over two gees.

For five minutes this continued. Then the pressure mercifully died as Fairouz killed the engines. The crew returned happily to zero gravity.

"We're now in a highly elliptical orbit," she announced over the intercom. "One that will keep us in shadow for another half hour, by which time we'll be safely in the next universe.

"All we can do now," she added to the flight deck, "is wait."

They relaxed a bit, feeling that at last they were in command of the situation. Though still tense, they made quiet conversation. The minutes passed by, with the dark

ide of Ronin showing through the window, occasionally
it up by auroral flares.

"This reminds me of those old movies," Ollerenshaw
aid. "You know the ones, where the guys are in a subma-
ine and they're hiding from the Nazis or the English or
vhoever."

"Yes," Arnaldo said. "They're always afraid to make a
noise because they don't want the other guys upstairs to
near them."

"Funny," Fitzpatrick said. "We're all talking softly, as
f they could hear us."

"No danger of that!" shouted Fairouz playfully.
There's a lot of vacuum between us and them. Unless
ve start sending out radio signals—that would be like
houting."

"Aye, aye, Captain," said Ollerenshaw. "And the first
nonster off the starboard bow gets a torpedo right down
ts gullet."

"Let 'em come," whispered Sly. "I'll tear their lousy
neads off and shove 'em up their boosters."

"I can see it now," said Arnaldo. "The monster captain
s scanning the skies looking for us, and finds the bright
lecoy instead. In a few minutes he'll get to it, and I'd love
o see the expression on his face. 'Zose bastards! Zey did it
o us again!'" He spoke in a stage-Nazi voice that could
not completely override his Italian accent.

"Let's hope they don't have depth charges, like they
ilways did in the movies," said Ollerenshaw.

"By then," said Fairouz, "we'll be in another uni-
erse."

They watched the countdown to the next universe,
vhile monitoring for any strange signals that might be a
ign of the creature's spacecraft. At last, the alarm rang
ind the computer called out, "Universe change alert."

When they felt the change, many sighs of relief
ounded aboard the ship. The crews' cheers echoed
hroughout the vessel.

"I wish we had some champagne," Fairouz said.

She glanced guiltily at the Jesuit, and he said, "I think
Allah would forgive us."

After the cheering had died down, Tariq said quietly,
How do we know this universe is any better than the
ast one?"

"It can't be any worse," said Ollerenshaw.

"Earth's just become visible again," Arnaldo said. "I'm getting some signals. It's definitely an inhabited universe. No TV. I guess they're not as smart as our bug friends." He tuned in a radio channel, and the sound of erratic clicking filled the air.

"I guess," said Ollerenshaw, "this must be the planet of the spastic crickets."

The crescent of Ronin's sunlit side began to approach rapidly, until the ship was bathed in the delicate glow of the distant Sun. Suddenly, an alarm went off.

"Son of a chip!" exclaimed Fairouz.

"What is it?" Tariq asked.

"Radar," Arnaldo said. "Someone else's. It's triggered the alarm."

"Do you have coordinates?" Fairouz asked.

"Roger," Arnaldo said, punching some keys and transferring the data to Fairouz's console. She brought the main telescope up on the screen, and focused in on the spot from which the signal had come. At maximum magnification, an alien ship floated on the screen—the same one that had led the three in the previous universe.

There was stunned silence.

Tariq cursed in Japanese and said, "They must have sent one of the other ships after the decoy, and the lead ship continued. Now it is gravitationally bound to Ronin too!" Looking at Fairouz, he said, "Do you think they know we are here?"

"Well, at this range," she said, "it only takes a few seconds for signals to get from here to there. Of course we don't know how sensitive their receivers and antennas are. We may be too far away."

"And even if they do detect us," Tariq said, "at this distance, they can't resolve us, unless they have a good telescope like we do. So they may think that we are just another tiny moon of Ronin, not worth investigating. We would not have wasted our time on a small moon like this when Ronin appeared."

"As long as we keep cool," Fairouz said, "and don't draw any attention to ourselves, they'll probably just ignore us and go explore Ronin."

"Unless our saboteur tries something funny, like

roadcasting 'Come and get it' to the bugs," said Fitzpat-
ck.

"It had to happen," whimpered Ollerenshaw. "Now
e're hopelessly trapped in a new universe with those
umbugs." Sly comforted her.

"Take it easy," said Fairouz. "If we keep our heads,
e'll get out of this. As long as we remain quiet, we're
afe."

"On those infrequent occasions when the customs po-
ce were after you," Tariq said sourly, "did they ever
atch you?"

"Once or twice," she replied, "but for a few kilos of
steroidal platinum or some zorn crystals, they were only
o happy to let me go."

"How do you bribe a creature that looks like a cross
etween a tarantula and a wasp?" Ollerenshaw asked for-
rnly.

"Good question," Fairouz said. "Look, we're both orbit-
g in the same direction as Ronin's spin—clockwise, as
iewed from above.

"Is that good?" Ollerenshaw asked.

"Well, it's the natural way any explorer would ap-
roach, and it means that they'll be going behind the
lanet, from our point of view."

The dot on the screen flared.

"They're doing orbital maneuvers," said Fairouz. "I
ish I could read their minds."

"What has me bothered—" Tariq said.

"I'm always happy to hear what bothers you," said
llerenshaw sarcastically.

"—is what they have deduced from our decoy."

Fairouz sat in her seat pensively. "They know it's arti-
cial. They don't know much about it but they've lost
ontact with their buddies. They're probably mad as hor-
ets that someone has stolen their universe."

"They're probably thinking the probe's from Ronin,"
aid Fitzpatrick, "and wondering whether there's a civili-
ation down there."

The image of the alien spacecraft dimmed, and
airouz said, "They finished their maneuver. Let's see
hat orbit they're in now."

As the alien spacecraft approached the far side of Ro-
in on the screen, she made some more measurements.

After several minutes, she said, "We can't be very precis
without radar contact of our own, but based on the paral
lax measurements, they put themselves into a low Ronin
orbit, and they'll probably circularize as soon as they ge
there—inside an hour."

The spacecraft approached the edge of the planet and
disappeared behind it.

"Now we're blind again," Fairouz said. "I sure wish we
could land this sucker."

"What do we do now?" Ollerenshaw asked.

"We've got two choices," Fairouz said. "We can con
tinue in our present orbit, which will take us out and
back and down to Ronin again. And if we're lucky, they
won't pay any attention to a little moon like us. The
other possibility would be for us to take off right now a
max-acceleration—just get the hell out of here and disap
pear before they notice us."

"Of course," Tariq said. "Then we would be stranded
in this new solar system, which we do not know any
thing about."

"Yes," Fairouz said. "We'd never be able to leave it."

"Couldn't we just hide behind Ronin all the time?"
Ollerenshaw asked.

"If we knew their orbit precisely, we could," Fairouz
said. "The problem is, with just optical tracking data, we
wouldn't be able to match it exactly, so there'd be some
drift, and sooner or later they'd see us. There's no way
we'd be able to monitor any changes in their orbit, so
they'd overtake us eventually. Plus, we don't know ex
actly what altitude they're going to be running at.

"It reminds me of the time when the customs cop
were chasing us out around Ceres. We picked up their
radar, so we could tell they were going in for a circular
orbit to search out smugglers and illegal mining opera
tions."

"Another one of your infrequent encounters with the
customs authorities?" muttered the chief.

"So I put the ship into a grazing orbit just like they
would use, only a hundred eighty degrees out of phase
with them. So while they skimmed the surface of Ceres
we were skimming the surface on the exact opposite side
of the 'roid. If only we could do that here . . ."

"What you need, then," said Tariq, "is their precis

altitude, so you can know what circular orbit they are in."

Fairouz nodded.

"Then why not use one of the probes on Ronin?" Tariq asked.

Fairouz blinked uncomprehendingly, and then brightened. "That's right—two of them are still okay. It just might work."

"I do not know if they are in the right places for us to observe them yet," Tariq said.

"We'll find out soon enough," Fairouz said. She uttered rapid-fire commands to the computer.

The Jesuit, who had looked puzzled throughout this exchange, suddenly brightened. "I see," he said.

"Well, I sure as hell don't," Ollerenshaw said.

"Nice," Fairouz said happily. "One of them's in a good position."

While Fairouz talked with the probe control room, Fitzpatrick explained. "If we can still command the probes, we can tell them to look for that ship in the sky and send us pictures. Then we'll be able to tell how fast it's going, which will tell us what its altitude is. If it's in a low orbit, it will go across the sky fast; in a high orbit, it will be slow."

"Now hear this," said Fairouz on the intercom. "One of the alien vessels from the last universe is still with us, but I think we've got a way out. Prepare for rapid acceleration. We're going back to Ronin, in an orbit that will keep us hidden."

Everyone strapped in.

"Send those signals in a really tight beam," she said on the intercom to the probe control room. "As tight as you can! We do *not* want any signals leaking out to the bugs."

"By beaming the signals down to the ionosphere," Fitzpatrick explained to Ollerenshaw, "and focusing them so they channel down toward the probe, we can keep the leakage to a minimum, and it's not likely that they'll pick us up. I hope."

The ship computer's voice spoke: "Three, two, one, fire!"

Terrific acceleration hit them again, and they sped off into a new orbit that raced toward Ronin.

"Why do we have to send any signals?" Ollerenshaw

asked. "Couldn't we just pick up the signals it was already sending us? It hasn't been turned off, has it?"

"The problem is," said the priest, "that the probes have been sending the signals to where they thought we were. We haven't been able to inform the probes of our new orbit, since we've maintained radio silence. We've got to send out some new commands so they can aim their tiny transmitters in the right direction, and the ionosphere will bend the signals up to us."

A few minutes later, some cheers echoed up through the shaft from the probe control room on the lab deck.

"We've got it," said the probe control manager over the intercom.

"I copy," said Fairouz excitedly. "Send down the new commands."

"Roger."

"Now we have to tell it to stop looking around on Ronin," explained Fitzpatrick, "and look up at the sky."

"I've calculated that the probe ought to be able to see the spacecraft pretty soon," Tariq said, "but the problem is that it is daytime down there right now, and it will be a few more minutes before it is dark enough for the probe to see the spacecraft. So, what kind of an orbit are you giving us?"

"I'm taking us on a grazing orbit around Ronin," said Fairouz. "It's my best guess as to what the aliens are doing. We'll circularize just outside the fringes of the atmosphere, where these guys are going to go, and then we'll update our orbit based on what the probe sees."

Minutes later, Fairouz fired the engines again, and put them into a circular orbit roughly the same as the aliens', but on the opposite side of the planet.

On the main monitor, they watched the sunset as seen by the probe. As it darkened, image enhancement brought out the tiny speck of the alien spacecraft in the sky. They monitored it until it had disappeared below the horizon, while Fairouz updated its orbit, occasionally firing their own thrusters until they were in precisely the same orbit as the aliens.

"What about the other probe?" Tariq asked.

"It's in heavy terrain," Fairouz said. "It can't see the sky. But we're all set now, as long as they don't change their orbit."

"How long until the next time the probe sees the liens?" said Ollerenshaw.

"A couple of hours," said Fairouz.

"A couple of hours," repeated Ollerenshaw. "While ιey're doing God knows what on the other side of the lanet?"

"That's the hand that Allah has dealt us," said the Je-ιit.

A tiny flare appeared on the screen, off in black space, ιr from the planet.

"Moondust!" Fairouz whispered.

They all focused on the screen.

"Those little buggers have gone off into a highly ellipti-ɑl orbit—just like the one we had. And they must have ιst made another course change."

"What do we do now?" Ollerenshaw asked.

"A better question is," said Fairouz, "why did they ιake that course change just now? I have an awful feel-ιg that it's because they just spotted us."

The flare continued, and Fairouz frantically began to ιake parallax measurements. After a couple of agoniz-ιg minutes, the estimated distance between the *Ulug Beg* ιd the alien spacecraft appeared on the screen. The ιmbers were decreasing.

"How could they do this?" Fairouz asked. "Why?"

"Perhaps they are smarter than we have given them ʾedit for," Tariq said. "Perhaps they noticed that that ny moon they'd seen on the way out was missing. Per-ɑps they wondered whether it was connected to the ecoy probe they saw. Perhaps they have even been able detect our ion trail in the magnetosphere of Ronin. If ιey can, it is an arrow pointing straight at us, even ιhen we were on the other side of the planet."

Fairouz nodded. "Their orbit will kill much of their ιgular velocity, so they can just sit up there while we ιom right into their mouths. Perhaps our eerie friends ʾe not dummies."

"Perbacco!" exclaimed Arnaldo. They stared at the pat-ʾrn on the spectral screen—a series of regular pulses ith high-frequency components. "It looks just like our ʾcoy's signal," he said plaintively. "But stronger."

"So, what do we do now?" asked the white-ced chief.

"What the hell can we do?" said Fairouz. "We can hightail it out of here at full blast, but then we leave the gravitational field of Ronin and get trapped in this lousy universe forever. Or we can just wait for the bugs to come and give us their neighborly greetings."

"Which do you recommend?" the chief asked, aware that she would not like either answer.

"I recommend that we stay and aim our main engine at our visitors. If they try anything funny we fry them and hope that we can fire our engines before they fire whatever they have."

"It is worth a try," said Tariq.

"I think they're trying to talk to us," Arnaldo said. He waved an agitated finger at the screen above his console.

The strange, spiral hexagonal raster showed a four eyed creature staring at them and muttering the skin crawling, incomprehensible sounds they had come to know and loathe. He turned down the volume.

"Want me to say anything back?"

Fairouz said fatalistically, "They know we're here, and they're coming our way. We might as well try to ex change pleasantries."

"What should I say?"

"Doesn't matter," Fairouz said. "They can't understand us anyway. Just make yourself look kindly and peace loving."

Arnaldo threw up his hands and hit a key. "Attention alien vessel. This is the *Ulug Beg* of planet Earth, wher ever that is. I know you can't understand this, but we come in peace. So I hope you'll appreciate that we haven't come to rape your females, however lovely they may be, or to steal your larvae."

"Are you sending out the same kind of TV signal you're receiving?" Tariq asked.

"Of course not. Our transmitter isn't designed to send out anything except standard stuff. I'm just broadcasting a regular, human-type TV signal."

The creature on the screen jerked strangely, looking offscreen with all four of its eyes to something that emit ted another of the horrendous voices.

"It looks like they're picking it up," Arnaldo said. "It will take them hours to figure out our kind of scanning

Fairouz glumly noted that the distance between the pacecraft was rapidly diminishing.

The screen went blank, and was replaced by some agged noise lines. Suddenly, the image of the Italian ap-peared on the screen. "Attention, alien vessel."

"*Mamma mia!*" said the real Arnaldo.

His image repeated his entire message.

Tariq laughed. "They're just retransmitting our signal. Nothing to get excited about."

"We ought to do the same," said Fairouz.

Arnaldo hunched over his console and began to dump the recording from the computer memory. "I just stored the video data," he said, "and now I have to recon-truct the RF signal."

The image of Arnaldo disappeared and was replaced by snow and jagged lines.

"Damn!" said Arnaldo. "They're sending another sig-nal now, and it's not modulated the same as the last one."

"Do a spectral analysis," Tariq said.

"Gotcha," said Arnaldo as he leaned over his console. "Son of a clone—it looks just like one of our signals."

"Switch over to normal mode," said Tariq, "as if you were tuning in a signal from Earth."

The screen cleared, and there was the image of the alien, only this time, instead of the hexagonal raster pat-tern, it was the old familiar terrestrial style of horizontal scan lines. It spoke, however, in the familiar incompre-hensible, chilling sounds.

"Incredible," said Tariq. "They deciphered our signal and figured out how to convert theirs into our pattern, all in just a couple of minutes."

"The only thing I like less than horrible monsters," moaned Ollerenshaw, "is horrible, *smart* monsters."

"Prepare for emergency maneuvers." Fairouz com-manded over the intercom. "Everyone remain strapped in until told otherwise. We may have to make sudden changes."

She fired the altitude control thrusters, and the ship began slowly to rotate. She kept the main screen locked onto the alien vessel, so they continued to see it. Ronin moved until it seemed to be in front of the spacecraft. They were still orbiting around the planet, but now their

main engines faced the approaching spacecraft abov
them.

On the main screen, the alien vessel suddenl'
whipped around until its main engines were pointed te
ward them.

"Touché!" said Fairouz. "Boy, they sure whipped tha
thing around fast. Their hull must be strong as hell, an
their stomachs even stronger."

"A Mexican standoff in space," said Ollerenshaw
"Kinda like *The Magnificent Seven*."

"I don't feel very magnificent now," said Fairouz. Sh
concentrated on the navigation plot. "If we continue thi
way, we're going to collide. They can't fire their engine
to slow down without vaporizing us or starting the firs
interuniversal war."

"It's a game of chicken," said Ollerenshaw.

"We're only a few hundred kilometers apart now,
said Fairouz.

The alien vessel reoriented itself slightly, revealing
dark egg shape, and the screen flared. White-hot ion
blazed across the space in front of the vessel.

"Either that was a warning shot across our bow, o
they were decelerating to match velocities, or both."

"I'm going to do likewise," said Fairouz.

The alien vessel quickly reoriented itself so its mai
engines faced the humans again, only now they were les
than a kilometer apart.

The ship loomed in the screen, dark, ominous, an
growing visibly larger each moment. With no familia
features to guide the eye, at times it seemed tiny, an
other times, enormous. The alien thrusters gaped at then
—six clusters of them, each one hexagonal, with six en
gines within each hexagon.

Suddenly, the space was filled with thousands o
white lines and the hull reverberated with loud thump:

"What the hell?" Fairouz said.

Even before her words were finished the ship jerkec
twisting the crew in their seats.

A curtain of white lines surrounded them and th
alien vessel approached them more rapidly.

"We've been harpooned," Fairouz said. "They'v
twisted us so we can't fire our engines at them. They'r
reeling us in."

"It's like a spiderweb," Ollerenshaw said unhappily.

"Perhaps it is like that ring around the Earth," said Tariq. "They must have developed fabulously strong materials to build it."

"Maybe we can get them to give us some lessons in basket weaving," Fairouz said helplessly.

"Now I know how Moby Dick felt," the chief said, reaching for another beersphere.

CHAPTER 28

The *Ulug Beg* swayed horribly as it was towed in by the alien vessel. Inexorably the vessel approached, turning slowly, so that they now began to see the extent of the dark, egg-shaped hull.

Fairouz called into the intercom to the mechanic Abdullah MacTavish.

"Aye, Cap'n," came the burred voice.

"Take your biggest torch out in the vac, and see if you can cut away these lines that are holding us."

"Aye, Cap'n, I'll see what I can do."

"Attention all hands," Fairouz said over the intercom. "I'm breaking out the weapons locker, and I want every man, woman, and robot who knows anything about fire arms to go to shaft A, where they'll be distributed. We only have about a dozen, so don't take one if you have no experience with them."

"*All right!*" Sly exclaimed, flexing his robotic muscles. "At last, I'm gonna get me some monsters!"

"Only a dozen?" the chief said. "If I get out of here, I swear I'm going to have the head of whoever short changed this expedition!"

"We were exploring uninhabited planets," Fairouz said. "Besides, you're the one who cut back our last allo cation."

"Well," Ollerenshaw said, "there were certain things we needed on Pluto."

"Like an anatomically correct robot?" Fairouz said. She motioned to the copilot and floated with him to the far side of the flight deck, where she unlocked the weapons locker. She took a sidearm and told him to distribute the other weapons. "I sure wish this was a battleship instead of a research vessel." Back at her seat, she gave detailed orders over the intercom, deploying the armed personnel at the likely entry points.

On the screen, without magnification, they could see what seemed to be hatches in the other vessel, and began to get an impression of substantial size, but the markings were still too unfamiliar to be sure. The alien ship stopped turning when it was parallel to the *Ulug Beg*.

"We might as well use our radar," said Fairouz, "they sure as hell know we're here." She flipped a switch, and said, "My God—they're half a kilometer away. Look at the size of that thing. It's over a kilometer long!"

Now that they knew how far away it was, its immensity became obvious. What had seemed like personnel hatches before were now revealed to be the size of cargo hatches or hangar openings.

"What about the shuttle?" Tariq asked. "Is there any chance we could get away in that—at least, some of us?"

"You sound like the chief," Fairouz said.

"God forbid!" muttered Tariq. "But it is better that some people should have a chance than none at all."

"I suppose it's possible that they might let a little ship slip away," said Fairouz.

"It's worth a try," Ollerenshaw said excitedly. "Let's go down there right now."

"Computer," Fairouz said into her microphone, "do a randomization of the ship's crew, selecting five names."

The five names appeared on the lower screen. None of them were of people on the flight deck.

"Your name isn't there," Tariq said to Fairouz.

"I used the randomization program that omits mine."

Tariq nodded with new respect. He ran his eye over the list and recognized Ng'ethe's name and two members of the engine room crew.

"There are six spaces," Tariq said. "Why are there only five names?"

"Because she realizes that the chief administrator of this project has to be on board," Ollerenshaw said.

"What about me?" Sly asked.

"You're needed here to defend these people from those awful creatures," Ollerenshaw said. "You'll be able to slaughter them like crazy."

"I'm in heaven," said Sly, beaming.

"The reason there are only five," Fairouz said, "is that there is only one person besides me qualified to fly that shuttle, so he's got to go. That's our copilot."

The shock on Ollerenshaw's face was familiar by now, and almost poignant.

"Now hear this," said Fairouz. "This is an emergency. The following people will report immediately to the shuttle. This is not a drill." Then she read off the names of the five, plus the copilot.

She spoke into the intercom again, and said, "Shuttle prep crew on the double. Prepare for emergency launch."

While Fairouz busied herself with numerous chores, Tariq observed the chief and her robot quietly slip away down the shaft. He shook his head in disgust.

"Now hear this," Fairouz said on the intercom. "All hands will don pressure suits, in case of loss of atmosphere."

Fitzpatrick floated over to the locker and removed the pressure suits.

Fairouz worked frantically at the console while everyone else suited up.

The alien ship drew ever closer.

"Skipper," came a voice over the intercom. Tariq recognized the Slavic voice of copilot Grodno.

"Roger," Fairouz said.

"The chief is down here, trying to bump someone off the shuttle. Did you authorize it?"

"Negative," Fairouz said. "You tell that dust licker to get back up here in the next microsec, or I'll kick her out the airlock without a helmet."

"But her robot has other ideas."

"Oh, hell," said Fairouz. She thought a moment, and spoke into the intercom, "Now hear this. Sly, report to the flight deck immediately—and shut off your voice recognition circuit *now*!"

A moment later, they heard the chief's cursing from the shaft.

The robot came bursting back onto the flight deck, carrying a heavy duty laser rifle, and floated over to Fairouz, grabbing a handhold in the ceiling.

"Yo! Robot Sly reporting for duty as ordered, Captain."

She glanced at him, and said, "Go down to the hangar, immediately!"

The robot remained attached to the ceiling.

"Oh, of course," she said. "He can't hear me." She turned to the computer microphone and said, "Computer, put the following words on the main screen: 'Sly, resume voice analysis circuitry function.'"

The words appeared on the screen overhead, and she pointed at them vigorously while facing the robot.

"Understood," said Sly. "Voice recognition resumed."

"Sly," said Fairouz, "get your shiny booster down to the hangar and prepare to repel boarders."

"Way to go," said Sly, turning.

"But take the elevator down," Fairouz added quickly. "No one else would be using the elevator in zero gravity, and Ollerenshaw would not be likely to see him.

"Roger, Captain." The robot propelled itself toward the elevator on the far side of the deck. "Scumbugs of the galaxy, here I come!"

"Captain," Grodno said on the intercom.

"Roger," Fairouz replied.

"We're ready to launch."

Ollerenshaw burst onto the deck, sputtering, "Where the hell did you put my Sly?"

Fairouz ignored the chief, and Fitzpatrick grabbed her before she could reach the captain. Muttering soothing words, the priest gently pushed her into a chair and strapped her in.

"Abdullah," said Fairouz, "how are you doing?"

"Terrrible!" came the burred Scots voice over the radio. "I canna cut through this line to save my life!"

"Stand clear of the hangar; the shuttle's going to launch."

"Rrrroger."

"Shuttle," said Fairouz on the intercom, "is the hangar clear for launch?"

"Roger, Captain. All clear and systems ready."

"Emergency launch the shuttle," commanded Fairouz

Without waiting for the pumps to evaporate the chamber, the hangar door slid open and the shuttle popped out.

It drifted away from the *Ulug Beg* for several seconds while the pilot oriented it. Then the engines fired and it shot off, accelerating rapidly.

While the flight deck watched on screen, a line shot out of the alien vessel and snagged the shuttle.

The craft wriggled like a fish being reeled in, until the pilot killed the engine.

"Looks like we're caught," Grodno radioed.

"Damn," said Fairouz. "Abdullah, how do those things work, anyway?"

"They've got somethin' like a big sucker on the end o' 'em. I've never seen the likes of it," said MacTavish. "The material is almost organic, wi' a mixture of a metallic sheen and a fiber structure. It ends in a giant sucker that seems to grow into the surface, like a barnacle. It's not magnetic; it might be molecular. I wouldna' believed it if I hadna' seen it!"

"I copy," said Fairouz, defeated.

"Captain," MacTavish said excitedly. "Somethin's happenin'—somethin's makin' the tether vibrate."

They all looked up at the alien vessel, toward which the white lines converged.

"Somethin's comin'!" said the Scot. "I can see black dots movin' toward us."

Fairouz quickly turned up the magnification, and they saw on the screen hundreds of black, tentacled space suits scurrying along the lines, heading directly toward them.

"Prepare the welcome wagon," Fairouz said fatalistically into the intercom. "Company's coming."

CHAPTER 29

"Abdullah," Fairouz said over the radio, "get inside."

"Aye, aye, Cap'n," said MacTavish, "You dinna have to ask me twice."

On the screen, the tentacled creatures rapidly approached the ship. They got so close that Fairouz switched to exterior cameras. The first creature landed on the nose line a few meters above their heads with a muffled thump.

The creature was a grotesque sight. It looked like a black tarantula half as tall as a man, wearing a spacesuit that covered each of its ten legs. The close-fitting helmet was transparent, revealing four eyes—two above and two below on the head. It had four sets of wings, encapsulated in the same black material as the suit, and they seemed to vibrate as if to fly off. But in the vacuum of space, the motion accomplished nothing.

There were more thumps, and additional creatures joined the first. They approached the flight deck, their feet sticking to the surface as if by chemical adhesion. They moved jerkily, like marionettes on a string. The four front legs were shorter than the rest, and appeared to serve the purpose of arms, terminating in pincers. When the first one reached the screen directly outside the flight deck, Fairouz turned it transparent and they watched the creature touch the hull, almost as if it could see them.

While the chief made good use of a barf bag, Tariq commented, "Looks like they have gas jets on their backpacks. I think that is how they slide down the lines."

"Can they see us?" Fitzpatrick asked.

"No," Fairouz said. "The window is made of active fiber-optics cable in a metal matrix. From the outside, it just looks like dark paneling."

The alarm sounded and the master computer voice said, "Universe change alert." The usual queasiness and tingling struck.

"Just great," muttered Ollerenshaw.

The first creature twitched as if shocked. It paused uncertainly, then opened a pack on its underside and pulled out an instrument and placed it on the window above them. The device looked like an old-fashioned stethoscope, but what would have been the earpieces fitted over the face of the creature's helmet.

"He sees us!" shouted Ollerenshaw. "He's looking right at us with some kind of a microscope."

"Could it be?" Fairouz asked.

"It is possible," Tariq said. "If you put an instrument right onto a fiberoptic—say, another fiber optic with a matching end piece—in theory, you might be able to look right through the lens back at us."

The creature pulled another instrument out of his pack—a copper-colored cylinder about fifteen centimeters long and three centimeters in diameter. He placed it on the window, pressed a button, and a high-pitched sound came through. In a moment, a tiny wire appeared, drilled right through the hull.

"Oh, my God!" said Ollerenshaw.

Everyone pushed away from the hull.

The copper-colored wire snaked down through the hole and moved around, as if looking at each of them.

The creature looked through the stethoscope connected with the cylinder, and the wire snaked slowly, pointing in every direction around the flight deck. It paused at each of the human figures, and then focused on the control panel. It weaved closer to the panel, almost touching the controls, and paused at each screen, as if to read the displays.

In the meantime, other creatures swarmed over the hull. Occasionally, they heard scraping sounds.

After poking around in all the nooks and crannies of the flight deck, snaking every which way, the wire probe withdrew and the creature "walked" aft.

Fairouz shoved over to the place where the probe had come through and anxiously examined it. "There's no leak. Maybe a little damage, but they must have used some kind of filler to maintain hull integrity. Amazing!"

She turned on the damage-control cameras amidships, and they popped out of patches in the hull.

Hundreds of the creatures skittered about, tapping, probing, touching, and attaching strange-looking instruments.

Reports came in over the intercom of other coppery probes entering the ship, but none stayed.

She turned on the engine-inspection camera. It telescoped out among the aft nozzles and showed dozens of the creatures climbing into the nozzles and around them.

"Turn on the damn engines and fry a few of them," said the chief.

"No need to make them any angrier than they already are," Tariq said. "If they can do what they have done to us already, imagine what they could do if they were mad."

There was a loud thump, and Fairouz turned the hull camera around until she saw a creature larger than the others—one with the same charming shape, but at least twice as much mass as its mates.

"The boss," Ollerenshaw said.

The new visitor scampered to a point amidships, where it was surrounded by dozens of underlings.

"I wish I could read their minds," Fairouz said.

"It would probably just give you a headache," said Fitzpatrick. "Who knows what kind of thought processes they have?"

"Maybe we can," Arnaldo said. "I've been getting all kinds of radio stuff since they approached us." He turned on the speaker and an ungodly chorus of screeches sounded.

"Not much good unless someone here speaks bug," Fairouz said. She gestured to Arnaldo and he cut the disturbing noises.

The alien workers unstrapped a large, black, egg-shaped container from the back of the boss, and carefully placed it on the hull. The boss touched a spot on it and a thin leg sprouted, attaching itself to the hull.

"It's a bomb," Ollerenshaw said. "They're going to blow us to bits."

The boss made some more adjustments to the egg, and the top began glowing blue and flickering.

"Nobody seems to be in any hurry," Tariq said. "And why did they choose that point? There is no hatch, is there?"

"There's nothing there," said Fairouz.

"What's under the hull at that point?" Tariq asked.

"A data nexus, where a bunch of fiberoptic lines come together in a local node."

"Could they be trying to tap into our system?" Tariq asked.

"That's crazy," she said without conviction. "There are thousands of lines in each of those cables, and they don't even know the data format, much less our computer languages or English. I don't care how smart those spiders are, they're not going to be able to read our data."

"Suppose they just cut the line?" Fitzpatrick asked.

"Like our saboteur," added Ollerenshaw.

"They could do that," said Fairouz, "but it wouldn't be a big hassle for us. All our main data lines run down the central spine of the ship, where they're protected from meteoroid impacts and other potential disasters. What I'd like to know is why they haven't tried to break into the ship, other than poking little holes." She floated over to the main data display and said, "Well, at least we can see if they broke into the line." To the computer she said, "Sysop display."

The computer displayed:

SYSOP SYSTEM STATUS
NODES OPERATIONAL: 48
SUBSYSTEMS: ALL OPERATIONAL
ACTIVE USERS: 7

"Life support systems," she said. The computer gave a readout of the temperature, pressure, air composition, drinking water supplies, and food supplies.

"All's well with the environment," she reported.

"Could you tell if someone was tapping into your computer?" Tariq asked.

"It depends," said Fairouz. "If he was just listening to the data, then we couldn't detect it unless he interrupted the data flow as he tapped in. But if he's interacting with the CPU, then we should be able to." To the computer she said, "Sysop."

The previous display returned, and Fairouz focused on the number of active users: seven.

"List users," she said to the machine.

Six names appeared on the screen.

"Oh-ho!" she said. "Someone is using the machine who isn't logged on."

"An interplanetary hacker," said the Jesuit.

"Can you tell what files are being accessed?" Tariq asked.

"Map file usage," said Fairouz.

A multicolored display appeared, showing dozens of files in groups labeled NAVIGATION, LOG, MAINTENANCE HISTORY, SCIENCE INSTRUMENTATION, LIFE SUPPORT, INVENTORY, ENGINES, and ENCYCLOPEDIA.

"Who's using what?" Tariq asked.

"Delete usage by logged-in users," said Fairouz.

All of the entries disappeared except for the word *encyclopedia*.

"How thorough is your encyclopedia?" Tariq asked thoughtfully.

"It contains several large scientific data bases, plus a general-purpose encyclopedia, a Koranic data base, and a selection of the best videos of the last hundred of years or so," Fairouz said.

"Thank God," murmured Arnaldo.

"Can you map the encyclopedia usage in detail?" Tariq asked.

"Roger." She spoke the commands into the computer.

The screen filled with a hundred major areas of the encyclopedia data base, with the major categories represented by different colors. Active areas flashed. The display flickered erratically, as different sectors lit up for a moment, and then disappeared.

"It looks like the bug is hungry for information," said Tariq. "He is jumping around from one subject to another, cross-referencing, integrating, analyzing, synthesizing, correlating."

"Is it possible," said Fairouz, "for this to be of any use to him? I'm quite sure he doesn't speak English or Arabic."

"But with an encyclopedia," said Tariq, "especially one filled with illustrations, you do not need a language in common. Sooner or later, he will figure out how pictures are stored, and then he will recognize diagrams of atoms and molecules, and he will see the entries on arithmetic, and he will begin to understand our mathematical notation. There are probably millions of pictures in there, identified by their names and highlighted, making it easy for him to tell that, say, a picture of a spider is what we call 'spider.' And there are undoubtedly articles on grammar," said Tariq. "So, eventually, he is going to figure out what this information says."

"But that will take him years," the priest said.

The main screen flickered on the ceiling, and the televised image of the activity on the hull was replaced by a large, hairy, alien face in a space suit. The loudspeaker crackled and said, "Acknowledge contact, beings of an alternate universe!"

CHAPTER 30

There was complete silence on the flight deck, except for the faint whooshing of the ventilation system.

"Do you understand?" the creature asked. It spoke in a strange singsong. Each word came out in a completely different voice, sometimes male, sometimes female.

"We hear you," Fairouz said softly into the computer microphone.

Tariq noted that the mandibles of the creature moved when he spoke, but not in precise synchrony with the screen. There was a slight delay, as if it were a badly dubbed old foreign film. As he studied the features, it became obvious that this was the one they had been calling the "boss."

"You do not have any knowledge of how to return to your universe," the creature said. "Now we are both separated from our universes."

"What do you want from us?" Fairouz asked.

"The first datum we wished for was to learn whether or not you are hostile."

"We don't mean you any harm," the chief said.

"From your records," said the creature, "that is difficult to believe. However, it is clear that you could not offer a threat to us."

"What other data do you require?" Tariq asked.

"Information on your planet, and your universe, and on this body you call Ronin. But this we have acquired from your data bank."

"Please tell me," said Tariq, "did you find anything wrong with our science?"

"Many things. Although we did learn some new things about astronomy, so it was not a complete loss."

Tariq's eyes glowed, but before he could ask his next question, Fairouz said, "I think I understand how you learned to understand English, but how did you learn to *speak* it?"

"After we understood written English and Arabic," said the creature, "we read articles about phonetics and analyzed the video programs in the entertainment section of your data base. We are now using excerpts of words from many videos."

"I thought I recognized Clint Eastwood," whispered Ollerenshaw.

"What do you know about the alternate universes?" Tariq asked.

"Only what we have learned since we left our world, and most of that is from studying your records."

"Do you know a way back?" Fairouz asked.

"No. This is completely beyond our understanding."

"I still don't understand how you could have digested so much information so fast," said Tariq. "Are you considered a genius by your species?"

"No. When I am not speaking for the queen, I am an ordinary member of my species, in the middle level. However, it would be difficult for you to understand our structure, since your society is so different. Apparently, humans think of themselves as individuals. Is this correct?"

"Yes," said Tariq.

"We are social creatures. We evolved from creatures similar to your arthropods, much as you arose from the apes. Individually, we are not especially intelligent—not much smarter than you humans. But collectively, our intelligence exceeds yours by a large margin."

The humans glanced at each other, inferiority written on their faces.

The creature continued. "The cosmic accident that destroyed the dinosaurs and other species on your planet did not happen on our world. The creatures that were similar to your ancestors remain small and unintelligent. On our world, our ancestors developed the ability to communicate chemically, as many of your insects do. We also developed intricate body languages, similar to your bees. This ability to communicate rapidly in real time, and to deposit information chemically for future generations, led to a gradual growth in the intelligence of the colonies. Competition between different colonies enabled the more intelligent ones to obliterate those that were less so, and in this way, social intelligence greater than yours arose.

"This enabled the colonies to develop the ability to manipulate the environment and to make tools. Furthermore, we developed sophisticated methods of breeding other creatures to suit our needs, and we gradually eliminated the dinosaurs, except for a few that we keep for study. Eventually, we invented much better ways of communicating among ourselves than through chemistry and body language. Each of us now bears a transmitter in his brain that communicates electromagnetically with the queen."

"You mean, like a queen bee?" Fitzpatrick asked.

"Yes. It is the closest analog from your biology that we were able to extract."

"But how does that help you now that your queen is universes away?" Tariq asked.

"Our queen is with us," said the creature.

"In your ship?" Fairouz asked.

"Yes."

"Then, you have more than one?" Fitzpatrick asked.

"Yes. For safety's sake, it is necessary to have several, even on our Earth, and we also have them on all our planets, in order to colonize them. We have just been exploring the edges of interstellar space, and plan to see where else in the universe we can bring them. And now, we have discovered that there are more universes to populate."

"So, it is your queen who is the genius?" Tariq asked.

"Yes," replied the voice. "If you must single out an individual, though she derives her intelligence not only from her own superior brain, but also through being linked with us. She is able to use each of our brains electromagnetically. Her own is vastly empowered by genetic engineering, which has been going on for the thousands of years since we surpassed your level of intelligence."

"You're not going to harm us?" Ollerenshaw asked.

"There is no need to."

"You mean, you're really going to let us go?" she said.

"Of course. What purpose would be served otherwise? We see that your history is not governed by rational behavior, so this must be a very alien reaction to you."

"And you'll return our shuttle—and its crew?"

"Yes."

"What would you have done if you had thought we were hostile?" Fairouz asked.

"Then it would have been necessary to exterminate you." After a moment, the bug added, "Do you not do this with your own pests?"

Her natural state of terror now abating, the chief visibly relaxed and began to get into the spirit of the conversation. "What is your name?" she asked.

"We perceive that you are referring to the name of the unit speaking from your screen."

"Yes."

The being uttered a string of bloodcurdling clicks and chirps. "That is more like a serial number than a name. Naturally, it is impossible for you to reproduce these sounds with your vocal apparatus. But this is only the name of a minor appendage of the queen."

"What is her name?"

There came a very short burst of bloodcurdling squeals. "That is the label used to distinguish her from the other queens."

"And do you have any brothers or sisters as charming as you?"

"I, speaking as the individual before you and not the queen, have four hundred and twelve identical brothers. Of course, I have thousands of sisters."

"Of course."

Fairouz fiddled with the controls, and switched the external cameras to smaller screens. "They're leaving," she said.

On the screens, they could see the hundreds of small forms ascending the lines that tied them to the great vessel. The boss still remained planted in front of the blue-topped egg, surrounded by only half a dozen of the smaller bugs.

"You're going?" Ollerenshaw asked.

"Yes," replied the creature. "We are returning to our ship. We have determined that this universe contains an Earth with which we would be compatible. It is our duty to colonize it."

"Is that how you plan to spend the rest of eternity?" the Jesuit asked. "Just colonizing until you fill the whole universe?"

"Yes, of course. Is this not your plan, too?"

"What will you do if you come across a superior civilization?" Tariq asked.

"We will try to learn from it, if possible. If they are threatening, we will simply run from them as long as necessary. It is a big universe, and there are many places to nest."

"I have to know one thing," Fitzpatrick said, agitated. "You must have absorbed the Bible and the Koran. What did you think of them?"

"They contain an interesting hypothesis: a cosmic queen that you call God."

"A hypothesis?" Fitzpatrick said. "Surely, it is more than that. Don't you have any religion?"

"It is an intriguing hypothesis, unsupported by conclusive evidence. We shall try praying to God five times a day and see whether it results in observable phenomena, although the difficulty of knowing where Mecca is presents a problem."

"My God," whispered Fitzpatrick. "I feel like Muhammad, or Jesus Christ. I have brought God to the infidel, and he is converted."

"Personally," Fairouz said, "I think you're being a little bit premature. Come back next year and see if they're still praying five times a day."

"I must return to my vessel," said the creature.

"Please do not go just yet," Tariq said anxiously. "I have so many questions. What is wrong with our physics? Have you unified all the laws? Can you calculate the fundamental constants from first principles? What is the nature of time?"

"It is necessary for me to return. My work here is

done, and I have other work I must do in preparation for this new universe."

"Would it be possible for us to visit your ship?" Tariq asked.

"It is permitted. But you will have to wear the special suits we see in your inventory, due to the much higher atmospheric pressure. And no weapons may be brought."

"Are you crazy?" Ollerenshaw whispered. "If you get trapped there, who knows what's waiting for you?"

"This is the chance of a lifetime!" Tariq said with the fanatic gleam of a true scientist in his eyes.

"Maybe they'll eat you," Ollerenshaw said.

Tariq chuckled. "I doubt that I am their favorite flavor. We undoubtedly have a radically different biochemistry. In any event, I would give a dozen Nobel prizes for the chance to see an alien spacecraft, and to ask more questions. Who knows what great discoveries they may have made that we would not otherwise glimpse for a thousand years?"

"We'll have to get back with plenty of time to spare before the next universe change," Fairouz said.

"We?" Tariq asked. "You are coming along, too?"

"I wouldn't miss this for the universe."

"Well," Tariq said, "we have several hours."

"What about you, Father?" Tariq asked.

Fitzpatrick looked startled at the suggestion, and quickly shook his head no. "I'll be perfectly happy to listen to your report when you get back—you can video it, too," he said.

"How can you possibly just sit here?" Tariq asked, shaking his head. "There is a whole alien culture there— something as different from us as we are from the termite."

Shame hung on the Jesuit's face.

Tariq shrugged and said, "Well, let us get going."

"How about you, Chief?" Fairouz asked teasingly. "Are you sure you can resist this invitation? You might even get a letter of commendation out of it if we ever get back to Earth."

The chief gave her a dirty look.

Fairouz and Tariq floated over to the shaft entrance and waved farewell as they disappeared.

The priest looked after them for long moments and

then finally said, "The devil take me, but I've got to see it." He pushed off the hull and shot after his companions.

"Are we the only sane ones left?" Ollerenshaw asked Arnaldo.

"I wonder if their civilization produced any good videos," he replied.

CHAPTER 31

When the shuttle crew was back aboard and the copilot was put in temporary command of the *Ulug Beg*, Fairouz, Tariq, and the priest exited their ship wearing special suits designed for high-pressure atmospheres. They wore evapacks, with small xenon thrusters at each hip. Cryscameras on their helmets were set to record all that they saw.

All of the lines connecting the ship to the alien vessel were gone except for one amidships, where the boss stood by his blue-topped egg, along with his reduced entourage.

The humans were picking up strange buzzing noises on their suit radios—interceptions of alien chatter. They tested their evapacks, floating up and down, firing their jets. For Fairouz it was effortless; the other two were considerably less experienced, and moved awkwardly. At first, Fitzpatrick kept bouncing off the hull as he manipulated the hand controls.

Fairouz floated a couple of meters from the ship, patiently waiting for the men to sort out the controls. She stared at the milling, multilegged creatures, shuddering. "Just think," she said. "There, but for the grace of the fundamental constants, go I."

"It makes you wonder whether," said Tariq, "if the

onstants had been slightly different, we might have
een much better creatures."

"I'm quite sure we're good enough," said Fitzpatrick.
"Allah made us well enough to do the job."

"And what's the job?" Fairouz asked.

"Why, to spread His word, of course."

They joined the boss as two of his assistants put the
gg into a backpack. The egg retracted its thin "leg" and
rew another copper-colored stem from its top, which it
ouched to the back of the boss's helmet.

The group skittered over to the last line, grasped it,
nd small jets on their backs thrust them toward their
hip, like beads on a string. The boss joined them, fol-
owed by the remaining creatures. Then the humans did
ikewise, flying alongside the group with the aid of their
vapacks.

As they got closer to the egg-shaped ship, they could
ee an open hangar door. Six small egg-shaped vessels
lew out. "Where are they going?" Fairouz asked.

"To land on Ronin to take samples for future study,"
aid the boss.

"When are you planning to leave this orbit?" she
sked.

"In two point three of your hours. This allows approxi-
nately one half hour for error."

The humans checked their watches and set their
larms.

As they got closer, they began unexpectedly to acceler-
te.

"You have artificial gravity?" Tariq said.

"Oh, yes," replied the boss. "We have had it as a labo-
atory curiosity for centuries, although we didn't need it
ntil we started space exploration recently."

"How does it work?" Tariq asked excitedly. "We have
een trying for centuries ourselves to understand gravity.
Ve have barely gotten to the point where we can under-
tand how it works, and we still have no idea how to
ontrol it."

The boss looked at him with his four eyes, as if mea-
uring his cranial capacity, and said, "After reviewing
our personnel records, I conclude that you are the only
ne of your crew who would be able to understand my
xplanation, but it would take months to lead you

through the many levels of mathematics needed to comprehend the machinery."

Tariq was crestfallen.

The group fired their jets to decelerate, approaching a hatch near where the last line emerged.

Tariq noted that the line, nearly half a meter in diameter, emerged from one of a series of holes in the hull of the vessel. Each hole was sealed by a collar. The other holes, with their lines withdrawn, formed dimples on the surface of the vessel. Now that they were just meters away from the ship, they could see that the color was a very dark bronze, almost black, without a metallic sheen. There were small bumps everywhere on the surface, giving it the impression of gooseflesh, and the texture looked more organic than metallic. Tariq strained to see the engines, but they were hidden in the distance.

A hatch opened in front of them, like a slowly expanding sphincter muscle, revealing a brightly lit interior. Everyone crowded into the glowing cavity together.

In the cramped airlock, Tariq felt tentaclelike legs brush his suit, and his skin crawled. He could see from the expressions on the faces of the other two humans that their feelings were similar. He felt a twinge of admiration for Fairouz, who had entered this cryptlike alien vessel without a moment's hesitation.

His suit's microphone began to pick up the sound of air rushing in, and it jolted him back to the reality that he was now sealed within a machine more alien than he could ever imagine. If his hosts were capable of deceit, he might never see the *Ulug Beg* again, much less his own universe. He studied the airlock.

It did not seem to be made of metal, but of some chitinous material that folded smoothly into place. It gave less the feeling of a high-tech environment than of a cave, lacking only stalactites and stalagmites to be perfect. It was like being in the womb of a giant spider.

The suit creaked as the high-pressure atmosphere filled the chamber. Unlike normal pressure suits, it was rigid, designed for the exploration of transplutonian planets with dense atmospheres. As the pressure grew, he could feel the suit squeezing in, a claustrophobic experience that only his intense curiosity could overcome. As

ey experienced the squeeze, Fairouz and Fitzpatrick
eemed to be having second thoughts.

Fortunately, the gravity seemed only about half
arth's. It pointed toward the long axis of the ship and
ade "up" and "down" more real than it had been for a
ng time.

With a pop, a hatch in the wall of the airlock opened
ith a sphincterlike movement.

Tariq glanced at the environmental readout on his left
rist, and saw that the exterior was over a hundred at-
ospheres of pressure. The air was very moist, and
ostly carbon dioxide.

The boss stepped out into a corridor, followed by his
ntourage. Four corridors with circular walls emerged
om the chamber, all filled with a dim yellow light. The
liens removed their pressure suits and stowed them on
oncave shelves.

The workers skittered away down different corridors,
aving them alone with the boss, who put on the
ackpack with the egg and began to walk down one tun-
ellike corridor.

Thick, yellow, fernlike vegetation covered the walls
om top to bottom and crunched under their feet, where
was thinner, traffic having worn a path. They walked
n, finding the tunnels curving every which way, mak-
ıg it impossible to see very far. They had difficulty keep-
ıg their bearings.

As they walked, hordes of green insects and small blue
zardlike creatures skittered by.

Suddenly, a stream of dozens of workers popped out of
side tunnel and rushed past them, crawling up the sides
o get past, brushing past the humans and the boss.

"It's like rush hour in Copernicus Crater," Fairouz said
ith a faint smile.

"Are you fellows really our relatives?" Tariq asked.
Do you have the same DNA in your body?"

"No," replied the boss. "The atoms produced by stars
ı our universe are different from yours. Different tem-
eratures and pressures arose on our Earth. Our groups of
olecules have structures similar to your DNA, but the
dividual ones are all different in detail."

The boss spoke in his incomprehensible clicks and

shrills; they could see now that the English sounds came from the egg in the backpack.

"It is fascinating," he continued, "to see from your encyclopedia that certain patterns of molecules in your universe do repeat in ours. But the particular mixtures of carbon, hydrogen, phosphorous, nitrogen, and other atoms are quite different in most instances. This implies that many chemistries are possible that could give birth to life, and makes it likely that we will encounter other creatures in this universe. We have never been able to calculate how many alternate chemistries there may be that can lead to life. This is one reason way we explore space, although it is not the most important. Your existence gives us a data point."

"Do you have books?" Tariq asked. "Or data crystals? Videos? Anything that we could bring back with us to share with our fellow beings, if we ever get home? Or if we ever get to some civilized place where we could settle down."

"We have biological means of data storage that I may show you later."

Their steps grew heavier. Tariq realized the gravity had become stronger. The meandering corridor was taking them toward the center of the ship.

"You seem to have a bug problem," said Fairouz, pointing at a swarm of insects crawling among the foliage.

"On the contrary," said the boss. "We keep a balanced ecology within this vessel. There are insects, birds, small animals, fungi, and bacteria, all interacting in a carefully calculated way to maintain a healthy environment. The very light that illuminates our path comes from a fungus we have developed—one that grows in caves on our planet."

"Just what do you believe in?" Fitzpatrick asked.

"The laws of physics, and the predictability of the universe."

"Is that all? Don't you have any belief in a higher purpose?"

"Of course. Nothing could be higher than the continuation of our species. In this we are the same as you."

Fitzpatrick shook his head in disbelief. "I can't tell you how happy it makes me," he said, "to know that I have been instrumental in bringing the word of God to you

"We are still computing the God hypothesis."

They stooped to pass through a narrow section of the corridor, giving Tariq a flashback to the pyramid of his youth.

"Just remember to always observe the five pillars of Islam," continued the priest. "The first pillar is that there is no God but Allah, and Muhammad is his prophet."

"*La Ilha Illa-l-lah,*" said the boss via the egg. "*Muhamadun ras ulu-l-lah.*"

"Very good," said Fitzpatrick. "Much better than my Arabic."

"There are many Arabic videos in your entertainment encyclopedia," said the creature.

"The second pillar," continued Fitzpatrick, "is that you must pray five times a day, at the prescribed times." He struggled to keep up with the faster humans and the boss.

"I am well acquainted with the five pillars," replied the boss. "I know the Koran better than you do."

The Jesuit's ruddy face reddened even more. "Well, you can never emphasize these too much. You could get lost among all the details of the zillions of facts you've absorbed. You have to know that certain things are more important than others. And nothing is as important as the five pillars. So never forget the third one—charity, giving alms to the poor. Or the fourth—fasting during the month of Ramadan. Of course, the fifth is the most difficult of all, under the circumstances: the journey to Mecca."

"If we cannot journey to Mecca," said the creature, "does this mean we are doomed to hell?"

"Oh, no," said Fitzpatrick. "It is only necessary if it is possible to do. The poor, the sick, the insane, and such are forgiven if they cannot make the trip, and I'm sure God will forgive you since there's no way you can get here from here. Of course, nowadays—ever since Mecca was vaporized in the last war, although it is still necessary to go there if you can, and I've done so—it's not that it used to be.

"Back before the war, it was really something. Pilgrims wearing their special seamless garments would encircle the Kaaba seven times, kissing the Black Stone each time they did. I would especially have liked to have done that because the stone was a meteorite that fell

down from paradise. Tradition says that when Judgmen
comes, it will give evidence in praise of all those wh
kissed it. Now, of course, you can only walk around *pi
tures* of the Black Stone, along paths that have bee
cleared of radioactive debris. It's not the same."

"I understand that we are to face Mecca when w
pray," said the boss.

"Yes, that is true, and I realize it is difficult, under th
circumstances." He stopped a moment. "Let's slow dow
a little, guys." The others did so and he resumed. "All
can suggest is that you face in the direction of the curren
version of Earth, and I'm sure that God will read th
sincerity in your heart."

"And how are we to calculate the time of Ramada
given that it is based on a lunar calendar in your un
verse?"

"Well, since I am the only imam of this universe,
must make a decision about that. As long as you follow i
you will be following the true faith. So: I declare that yo
should follow the time set in our calculation in the con
puter. Just synchronize your clock with our ship's cloc
and maintain a reference to our Earth's time. You don
have to use it for everyday occurrences, just for the calcu
lation of Ramadan, for fasting. Since Muhammad a
peared in our universe, it seems to me that we should us
our Moon."

They paused as a blue creature like a bunch of grape
a meter tall, with four legs, waddled across their pat
from an intersecting corridor.

"But," added the boss, "Ramadan only starts after th
new Moon is seen from the Naval Observatory in Cair
How are we to know what the condition of seeing
there? It could delay sighting the new Moon a day
two, easily, if you have bad weather, for example."

"Our ship's computer has a subroutine that calculate
the mathematical horizon from Cairo, and this has be
come the standard way of calculating Ramadan, to avo
the old problem of weather causing variable calendars

Tariq noted a change in the vegetation. It was sparse
even on the ceiling, as if the traffic were heavier.

"Should we then use Earth time for setting the fiv
prayer times?"

"Oh, that won't be necessary. After all, we use loc

ime on Earth wherever we are, regardless of the time
one. So I suggest you use the local time for whatever
Earth you are near. Just remember to pray in the early
dawn, noon, the midafternoon, sunset, and night. Islam
s not really as rigid as I'd thought before I converted."

"And what of alms?" asked the boss.

"That just means giving money to the poor, in propor-
ion to your wealth."

"But our society does not use money, and we have no
poor. Everyone follows the commandments of the
queen."

"Surely you have some poor?" said the Father.

"We have workers who live in small cells, and we
have intermediate beings, such as I, who live in larger
and more luxuriously furnished housing, befitting our
state."

"Sounds like Earth," said Fairouz, wiping the condensed moisture of the humid atmosphere from the exte-
ior of her faceplate.

"Then you could give some of your furnishings to the
workers."

"But workers have no need of such things. They have
no desire for such things."

"Are you quite sure?" Fitzpatrick asked.

"Of course. The workers are even less intelligent than
humans."

"That dumb, eh?" Fairouz said sourly.

"Yes," said the boss. "Rather like your trained animals."

"It is amazing that they can build spaceships," Tariq
said.

"Under the guidance of the queen, and helpers such as
I," said the creature, "almost anything is possible."

They passed a cavern and saw a swarm of workers
assembling a machine from organic-looking materials.

"What is that?" Tariq asked.

"That is a fuel pump for an engine."

It was taller than a man, and made of scarlet fibrous
material. Parts of it seemed to grow from instruments in
the hands of the multilimbed creatures. Beside it stood
another boss similar to the one who accompanied the
humans. The grating sounds of their voices carried

readily across the ten-meter distance separating the humans from the workers.

"Does the boss there communicate mentally with those creatures?" Fairouz asked.

"In a way," replied the creature. "His mind, like mine, is attached to a transmitter implanted in his skull." He pointed to a short black antenna protruding from the back of his head. "Each of the workers has a similar implant, and it receives commands from the supervisor."

"Don't they have identities of their own?" Fairouz asked.

"Yes, but only to a minor degree. There is less difference between workers than there is between two dogs of the same litter. All workers are my sisters, produced by our mother, the queen."

"I've got it," said Fitzpatrick. "This is how you can give alms to the poor. We're poor. You're rich in information."

"I see," said the creature. "Money is a strange concept to grasp. Information is much easier. Yes, we can certainly give you information."

"But you *must* have identities," said Fitzpatrick. "*You're* an individual, aren't you?"

"In a limited way. My mind is linked to my queen exactly like the workers are linked to the supervisors. I have been trained from birth to do whatever she wishes."

"Are you happy that way?"

"Happiness as you mean it is a concept I have not been able to comprehend. It seems to be the absence of pain. If so, then I am happy."

"Don't you get any pleasure?" Fairouz asked.

"Yes, there is the pleasure of food, and there is the pleasure of fertilizing eggs on those rare occasions when it is necessary. And there is the pleasure which I receive when my queen receives pleasure. So this is happiness."

"How can you stand it?" Fairouz asked. "You're just a slave to the queen!"

"It is not so different from your holy books, is it? The Koran refers to you as being slaves of God."

"This is true," said the Jesuit. "After all, Islam itself means submission to the will of God, and this was just another way of expressing the concepts of the Judeo-

Christian religion. We are all slaves of God in that sense. But we are happy to be following the will of God."

"Then I suppose you could call me a happy slave, too," said the creature. "My existence is not so different from yours."

"But how can you stand it?" Fairouz said again. "Don't you have any urge to go out there and do something for yourself? Have some fun? Explore a little? Raise a little hell? Fertilize a few eggs when no one's looking?"

"I understand that you are referring to the phenomenon of individualism that I have encountered in your encyclopedia, and which we see in the lower creatures. But what you seem unable to comprehend is that I have no such need or desire. I am a cell of the queen's brain. Does one of your brain cells have any need to explore? Does it need to reproduce itself? Does it need to have fun?"

"God!" she said. "I couldn't stand being just a cell in a great organism. It would be almost as bad as being stuck in some office on Earth."

"That is a good analogy," replied the boss.

"It would drive me crazy."

"Then perhaps that is a deficiency in your programming. It would drive me crazy if I were disconnected from my queen. Of what use is a brain cell without a brain?"

"But how can you possibly enjoy life?"

"It is not necessary to enjoy life—living is simply what one does. However, I am beginning to understand your own brain's programming. I have synthesized a model of your thinking by combining your neural physiology with your videos. It was very difficult for us at first to separate fact from fiction, but fortunately, your encyclopedia explained the difference. Your fiction gives us a distorted image of the operation of your brain. And the history of the evolution of your species helps us to understand why you have been programmed by your environment in the way you are."

"Well, *I'm* not programmed," Fairouz said. "Nobody's programmed my brain except me."

"That is an easy deception for you to believe in. Every molecule in your body is there because billions of years of life shaped you into the being you are. Your very emotions are the products of chemicals produced by your glands, stimulated by your brain in accordance with rules established partly by billions of years of life and death among your ancestors, partly by the accidents of your birth, and partly by the creatures with whom you grew up."

The corridor grew larger, tall enough that one human would have to stand on another to touch the ceiling.

"You're the ultimate bureaucrat," Fairouz said angrily. "You're happy to be in your little cell, and you don't want anything to disturb it."

"Perhaps you can appreciate that I have pleasures of which you cannot dream. My pleasure and pain centers are tied in electromagnetically to those of my queen. When she is having difficulty, I feel pain. But when she is experiencing pleasure, then I experience pleasure. When we tapped into your ship's computer, and her brain assimilated the data, she achieved more happiness than in many centuries, and this happiness was transmitted to me. It was wonderful!"

"No wonder you were in a good mood," Fairouz said, snickering. "You'd just had a data orgasm."

Fitzpatrick shook his head. "I'm really at a loss to explain the glories of religion to someone who thinks like you," he said. "It's worse than arguing with an atheist in a pub, at which I'm expert. I haven't been so confused since I became a Muslim."

"Exactly how did that happen?" the boss asked. "Your encyclopedia is very unclear about why so many people converted so suddenly to Islam."

"I had a vision of the Prophet Muhammad, may his name be blessed."

"Mindhackers," Fairouz said with a smirk.

"That's a vile rumor spread by atheists!" the priest retorted.

"Well, here's the story *I* heard," Fairouz said. "Sure, it's just a rumor, but it explains a lot. Some guy hacked into a database of mindhacker software."

"Mindhacker?" the boss asked. "This term is not in your encyclopedia."

"Of course not," she said. "They've tried to keep it supersecret so only top governmental agents have access to it. But some shrink discovered a combination of visual

atterns and sounds that resonate with the brain's
hythms. It creates a hypnotic effect. You can reprogram
nyone's brain, make them do anything.

"So this hacker comes along. He happens to be a Prot-
stant, so he thinks it would be great fun to create a
nindhack virus that would give Catholics visions of
1uhammad. He releases it in Italy, but the joke is on
im. It spreads everywhere. I guess he must have known
was out of control when the King and Queen of En-
land became Muslims."

Fitzpatrick's face reddened until he could no longer
ontain himself. "This is all blasphemous nonsense! God
vanted to heal the rift between Islam and Christendom,
n artificial break that never should have existed, since
1uhammad himself followed the teachings of the Jews
nd the Christians."

"Of course," Tariq said, "in Egypt, everyone said it was
ne will of Allah."

A squeaking column of workers ran by them, single
le, hurrying ahead in the same direction as the humans.

"I found an amazing amount of Christianity and Juda-
sm in the Koran," said the priest. "All of the prophets of
ne Old and New Testaments are praised by Muhammad.
esus Christ is repeatedly described as a prophet of the
ord, and his name is forever blessed by Muhammad. It
1ade me wonder how the Crusades could ever have
illed so many Moslems, or how so many Moslems could
ave killed Christians and Jews.

"But then I thought, all you have to do is look at the
istory of Europe, and you can see Christians killing
hristians left and right. And look at my own little coun-
y of Ireland. The Catholics were always killing the Prot-
stants, and the Protestants, the Catholics. Of course, it
asn't improved much. Nowadays, in Northern Ireland,
ll you hear about are the riots between the Sunnis and
ne Shiites."

One of the workers paused to nuzzle at Fairouz with
er feelers, then was nudged on by another.

"But I have faith in God," he concluded.

"I have faith in hackers," Fairouz retorted smugly.

The last of the stream of workers ran by, leaving the
oss with the humans and his own entourage of workers.

The trio was silent, except for the sounds of the boss' own workers chattering.

They continued their journey deeper into the vessel, and the gravity grew yet stronger. The tunnels wound unpredictably, like wormholes. The humans were now thoroughly disoriented. Fairouz glanced at the inertial navigation unit on her wrist and shouted, "It's a trick! They're kidnapping us! Look at your INU!"

The others stared down at their own INUs, and saw that the distance to the *Ulug Beg* was increasing rapidly.

"You deceived us," said the Jesuit. "And I thought you were trustworthy."

The boss uttered a bloodcurdling groan, and then said, "The queen is amused. It is amazing how little of your brains you use."

"So she's amused, is she?" said Fairouz. "Well, I swear to Einstein that I'm going to take this ship apart atom by atom if she doesn't turn right around and send us back."

Tariq studied his INU display and smiled. "Relax," he said. "It is nothing to worry about."

The two humans stared at him.

"It is the artificial gravity. The INU cannot distinguish between acceleration and gravity."

"Of course!" said Fairouz, slapping her stomach.

After a moment, Fitzpatrick sighed and nodded. "The INU doesn't know about artificial gravity."

"Right," said Tariq.

"Sorry," Fairouz said to the boss. "I kind of got carried away."

"No problem," replied the creature. "The queen found that quite entertaining."

"So, that groan you emitted is your form of laughter?" Tariq asked.

"It correlates reasonably with what we understand that you mean by laughter."

They continued their journey. Fairouz looked at the boss as he led them through the maze, and said, "Does the queen see everything you see?"

"Yes. She sees through all my eyes, and the information is immediately transmitted to her."

"Do you have no privacy?" Fairouz asked.

"That is one of those phenomena for which we have no equivalent," replied the boss.

"But at least you have laughter," said Fitzpatrick. "I would bet that any creature that laughs must have a soul."

"What about hyenas?" Fairouz asked. "Do they have souls?"

"Of course not," said Fitzpatrick. "You need to have both intelligence and a sense of humor, I suspect."

"Well," said Fairouz. "I've known a few robots who were intelligent and laughed in the right places, so do they have souls?"

"I used to think not," replied Fitzpatrick. "But robots keep getting smarter every day, and they're able to simulate human emotions to the nth degree, so at what point do they cross the line? God could put a soul into anything he wanted to."

"What do you think?" Fairouz asked Tariq.

"I just let God worry about it. I am only interested in questions that I can answer."

"You're okay," replied Fairouz. "You're not the stuffed suit I thought you were when I first met you."

"Thank you, I think," he said, smiling. "And you are not the simpleminded rocketjock—" He stopped abruptly.

The corridor was blocked by arachnoid bodies from floor to ceiling. Each squirming creature, almost as large as the boss, held a purple prism aimed at the humans like a weapon.

"Looks like they've rolled out the welcome wagon," said Fairouz.

CHAPTER 32

"These are the guards," said the boss. "They are the bree
you might call soldiers." He pushed his way through th
living wall. The guards parted just enough to let hin
through while they patted him with their forelimbs an
inspected the egg in the backpack.

Tariq passed through next, and received the sam
close embrace. "They certainly are friendly," he said witl
distaste.

"They are checking for weapons," said the boss.

Fairouz and Fitzpatrick endured similar examination

"Do you always get frisked?" Fairouz asked. "It's wors
than security on the Earth–Moon shuttle."

"It is normal when visiting a queen," said the boss, "t
search for weapons and for parasites that might be de
tected by the taste buds on the tips of their limbs," sai
the boss.

"So, you have assassins?" Tariq asked.

"They have been known to occur in history, althoug
there has not been an assassination in centuries."

"Who would want to assassinate your queen?" the J
suit asked.

"Another queen," replied the boss.

"Just how many of them are there?" Fairouz asked.

"There are eight on Earth, and a dozen more els

where in the solar system. Centuries ago, there were far more, and they were constantly battling for supremacy. But eventually, we bred intelligence sufficient to resolve conflicts and establish stable boundaries."

The chamber was a huge cavern, which, judging by the increased gravity, was well inside the vessel. Tariq looked at his INU and found that the gravity was now close to one gee.

Insects buzzed everywhere, and birds flew among the yellow foliage that covered the walls. At the center was a great pulsating, purple, segmented creature the size of a whale. The TV colors had been all wrong. Blue fluid circulated through the hairy, translucent skin. Fragile, vestigial wings sprouted along the back, disproportionately small compared with the mass of the body. At the right end was a huge face with four yellow eyes that made the creature a parody of the boss. The six main legs were not in evidence, as it sat in a large trough, but the four forelimbs moved about erratically, like a madman conducting an orchestra of invisible players.

"Her majesty, the queen!" murmured Fairouz.

Dozens of workers crawled around and over her, preening her, washing her down with fragments of foliage dipped in red liquid, feeding bamboolike sticks to her.

An awful, low-pitched noise came from the queen, like a buzz saw running through a redwood tree. Her mandibles vibrated sympathetically.

"Hi, guys!" came the voice from the egg, still on the boss's back.

"Is that the queen speaking?" Fitzpatrick asked.

"Right you are, guy," came back the voice. "You are one sharp cookie."

It was the same sound as the boss had used—a synthesis of fragments of different videos—but quicker, livelier. "I'm transmitting directly into the translator," she said, "bypassing your guide."

"Do we bow or curtsy or something?" said Fairouz.

The queen groaned in the manner they now recognized as laughter. "Not necessary. I must say, I'm really glad I've run into you, even though it did cost me my universe. But hey, you can't have everything, and now I've got a whole universe all to myself."

"I'm glad you're not mad at us," said Fitzpatrick.

"No way, baby," replied the queen. "I'm grateful to you. My life has been a bloody bore for the last couple of centuries. I was looking forward to exploring interstellar space, and this is even better."

"Don't you miss talking with your fellow queens?" Tariq asked.

"Naw. They get on my nerves a lot. They're always bragging about their stud farms or the latest in genetic engineering, trying to build even more brains than they've already got. We've been building bigger and better brains for so many thousands of years now, it's hard to see what the point is anymore. We're about as smart as you can get. But you guys are a godsend—literally, if the padre is right. I haven't had so much fun since I colonized Mars. Who would have thought that some crummy monkey species would grow up to give us the Great Wall of China, World War II, and *The Beverly Hillbillies?* It's a gas!"

"Do you find those three cultural landmarks equally fascinating?" Fitzpatrick asked.

"Verily! Trying to put together a consistent model of a brain that would produce those macho Nazis, the wimpy Gandhi, and the Mormon Tabernacle Choir is like putting together what you call a jigsaw puzzle. Which, by the way, is something that puzzles me. Why would anyone want to cut a picture into a hundred little pieces just so he could put them back together again? Try figuring that out from your encyclopedia."

"It is rather hard to explain," said Fitzpatrick. "I am not quite sure I understand, myself."

"And this whole idea about a God. Far out! None of us would have dreamed up such an idea in a million years."

"So, you're going to try religion?" the Jesuit asked with barely concealed pride.

"What the hell? Can't hurt."

The priest winced. "That's a rather succinct theology you have there," he said dryly.

She heaved and rolled over on her side so her back was facing the humans and only two of her eyes could see them. Busy workers jumped out of the way and returned to her torso.

"Actually," continued the queen, "I've pretty much

had what your holy books talk about as paradise. And the one question your books don't answer is how you can keep it from getting so bloody *boring!*" The last word exploded from her in bug language, followed by its translation.

"I never thought of it quite that way," said Fitzpatrick. "I'm sure that God has ways of keeping us entertained for the rest of eternity."

"Tell me, anyway," said the queen, "why a bunch of people would get together wearing uniforms, all simultaneously repeating the same words that someone else has written, in a funny kind of artificial way so they all have the same frequency, more or less?"

"Soldiers?" said Fitzpatrick. "Repeating a pledge?"

"The Mormon Tabernacle Choir," Fairouz said with a smile.

"Yes, she's got it!" said the queen.

"That's music," said Tariq.

"I see," replied the queen. "There's an awful lot of that in your entertainment data base, and I can't for the life of me figure out what it's supposed to do."

"It gives us pleasure," Tariq said.

"It seems to be a mode of speaking," said the queen, "or of producing sounds, that is different from ordinary conversation or noises. Why would the same words spoken one way be boring, but spoken in this way you call singing, give you pleasure?"

The three humans looked at each other and shrugged.

"As a great musician once said," said Fitzpatrick, "if you've got to ask, you'll never understand."

"Zounds!" replied the queen.

"That's quite a translator you've got there," Tariq said. "Could we possibly have one to take back with us? We might find it useful in some other universes."

"I'm afraid I need it. On this cramped ship, we can't bring along two of everything, like your Noah's ark. We mostly just bring along biological blueprints and then grow what we need."

"We would be exceedingly grateful," replied Tariq.

"Who the hell cares?"

Tariq was taken aback.

"So, you grow everything?" Fairouz asked. "Even engines?"

"Sure. We do most of our stuff through biology. One of your great philosophers once said, 'Better living through chemistry.' Well, we've taken that further than you clowns could ever dream. We use smart bacteria in an accelerated growth medium. You start out with a few of the little guys and they reproduce like crazy, until they've built whatever you want—that is, if you program right."

"At least you will be following the true faith from now on, will you not?"

"That's something I've been wanting to ask you. What about all those other religions?" the queen asked. "You know—Buddhism, Shintoism, like that."

"Those are but valiant efforts by misguided souls at best," said the Jesuit. "And at worst, they are the product of the devil's wiles."

"But how do I know which of your thousands of religions is the right one?"

"That is what Allah provided me for, as his humble servant."

Tariq, becoming impatient with theology, blurted out, "What did you think about our science, our physics?"

"Pretty crude," replied the queen. "There are thirteen forces your physics doesn't even know about. Your most advanced equations are but crude approximations of the correct ones. And you don't have the foggiest notion of what vacuum really is!" She laughed an earthshaking groan.

"If you're so smart," Fairouz said, "how come you're stranded here with us?"

"Hey, baby, I never claimed to know *everything*. Just a helluva lot more than you guys."

"And what about our art?" asked the priest. "Can you appreciate Leonardo's brilliance?"

"Oh, there's no doubt that he was a clever fellow, by your standards," she replied, "but I cannot understand your species' obsession with pictures of itself. You've got your paintings, your mirrors, your sculptures, your poems, and your movies, and they're all about your bloody *selves*! You must be the most narcissistic species in a hundred universes."

"Don't you have any art forms of your own?" Fitzpatrick asked.

"What would we do with them? What are they good for? Can you eat them? Can you improve your genes with them? Can you expand your civilization with them?"

The priest shook his head sadly, and said, "You have just consigned to the waste vaporizer the greatest fruits of human creativity."

"Don't get me wrong, Padre," said the queen. "I think some of your arts are fascinating—especially your dramatic arts."

"Shakespeare?" Fitzpatrick asked. "Tolstoy? Joyce?"

"They are certainly interesting," replied the queen. "But nothing gives as profound an insight into your curious psychology as the works of the Marx brothers and the Three Stooges."

The Jesuit blanched.

"Yes, any civilization that could produce both Hamlet and Larry, Moe, and Curly is worth paying attention to."

"Oh, my God!" said Fitzpatrick.

"I realize that you humans cannot appreciate the full ramifications of the Three Stooges. You think it's just a bunch of hayseed slapstick, right? But believe me, it tells me far more about you than you could possibly want us to know!"

"A frightening thought," said Fitzpatrick.

"The hell with art!" said Tariq. "What are the thirteen other forces?"

"Most of them are associated with particles you haven't even *dreamt* of yet. And it would take me ages to teach you the math needed to understand why these forces exist. And, of course, we don't have that amount of time, unless you want to stay and study with me."

Tariq paused a moment, then shook his head and said, "I am dedicated, but not quite that dedicated. I would give almost anything if I could learn what you know about physics, but I have to stay with my companions. It is my only chance for getting back to my own universe."

"Pity," said the queen.

"What about books?" Tariq asked. "Can you give us a database with this information in it?"

"Why, soytainly," replied the queen in a voice, via the egg, that suspiciously resembled that of one of the Stooges whom she so admired. "Of course, I'll want something in return."

Fairouz looked at her suspiciously and said, "What? You've already taken all our knowledge from our databases."

"Nothing big," replied the queen. "I just want one of you. That's all."

The three humans looked at each with shock.

"I find you very amusing," she said, "and it would be fun to have one of you around the house."

"I knew there was a catch here," said Fairouz. "I knew it was a trap."

"Oh, it doesn't have to be one of you three," said the queen. "Anyone from your ship will do. All I want is a chance to observe one of you at length, since I can't quite simulate all the peculiar manifestations of your brain. Too many parameters, too little data."

"Over your dead body," Fairouz said angrily. "If any member of my crew doesn't go back, then I don't go back."

"Just one *little* worker," replied the queen. "I realize from your history that you sometimes form peculiar alliances with other creatures you call your friends when you're not killing them, but surely you can't have such alliances with *every* member of your crew."

"I sure as hell do," retorted Fairouz. "My crew is my family."

"But how will anyone survive here?" Tariq asked. "Your guest would run out of consumables after a few days or months. We could certainly get some additional supplies over here from the ship, but eventually you would run out."

"No sweat, man," replied the queen. "We've got some hotshot gene machines and we can work you up a tasty soufflé of whatever chemicals you need to eat. We've got plenty of water, and it's no trick at all to supply you with any oxygen you need. We've got your database on nutrition, so we can make sure you don't suffer from any deficiencies. And we can even cure you of any diseases you get, so you'll be practically immortal!"

"That's comforting," said Fairouz, "to know that not only will you spend the rest of your life living in this weird environment, but your life itself is going to be pro-longed—how long? Thousands of years?"

"Easy," replied the queen.

"Please," said Fitzpatrick. "We cannot accede to your terms. It would be immoral."

"Unless we got a volunteer," said Tariq.

"Splendid!" said the queen. "A volunteer it is."

"Let's just go back to the ship," Fairouz said, her eyes narrowed, "and see if there are any volunteers."

The two men nodded.

"Why not telecomm to them?" the queen asked.

"Our communications don't work through this ship," said Fairouz. "Must be too much conducting material around here."

"It's already fixed, guys," said the queen. "Your signals are now being relayed automatically to your ship."

"Ulug Beg, do you read?" Fairouz asked.

Arnaldo's face appeared on her wrist monitor. "We copy, Skipper," he said.

"Patch me into the ship's intercom, all decks," she said.

"Roger."

"Now hear this," said Fairouz. "The creatures have of-fered to give us valuable information if someone will vol-unteer to stay here—that is, to stay with these creatures on their ship forever. It would mean being trapped with them in an unfamiliar universe. There is no need for this. We can live without this information. I don't want any-one to feel pressured, but if any of you is crazy enough to take the offer, it's your life, and we would be grateful. If anyone's interested, just comm with the flight deck. Over."

They waited a minute. Arnaldo shook his head and said, "No one is responding. I can't understand why. You made it sound so tempting."

Fairouz relaxed visibly and said to the queen, "Okay, that's it. There are no volunteers. I guess we'll just be leaving now. Thank you for your hospitality. We must do it again some time."

The three humans began walking toward the hole through which they had entered. "Not so fast," said the queen.

"What now?" Fairouz asked.

"You're not leaving until at least one of you agrees to stay here," said the queen.

Fairouz tensed. Tariq reached for a nonexistent gun, and the priest began to pray silently.

"But you promised!" said Fairouz.

"I did nothing of the sort," replied the queen. "Jesus Christ! You humans were always weak on logic. I only said that if one of you would agree to stay, I would give you some goodies. I never said that if none of you agreed to stay, I wouldn't force my hospitality on you anyway."

"You bitch!" said Fairouz.

"I'm sorry, but I'm not programmed to respond with the emotional intensity that your expressions are designed to elicit."

The humans ran to the hole, but were greeted by a wall of soldiers that completely covered it. They refused to budge. The humans tried pulling and pounding on them, but they were much stronger than they looked.

"In the words of one of your greatest philosophers," said the queen, " 'nyuk, nyuk, nyuk!' "

"Damn!" said Fairouz. "I knew I should have brought that laser torch."

"It would not have been permitted," said the boss, after having been silent for a long time. The movement of his mandibles showed that it was he and not the queen who spoke, though the sounds came from the egg.

"All right, kiddos," said the queen. "Which one of you is it to be?"

"I'll stay!" exclaimed Fairouz. "I'm the captain of the ship and it's my responsibility to do the dirty work. I can't send anyone else to their doom."

"Do not be ridiculous!" said Tariq. "It is precisely because you are the captain that we need you the most. I am expendable, the Father is expendable, and so are most of the others. But you are not. I am the one who will stay. I am probably the only one on the whole ship who would actually sort of enjoy it. Curiosity has always been my weakness, and this is almost a dream come true."

"More likely a nightmare," said Fairouz. She looked at the priest expectantly, but he remained silent.

"There's a traditional way of solving this," said the

queen. "Drawing straws. I've seen it in your videos. And there's no shortage of vegetation."

"My copilot can run the vessel," said Fairouz.

"We need you more than me," she said to Tariq, "because you're the only one who has a ghost of a chance of getting us back home. You're the hotshot astronomer, and there's no one else of your caliber on board."

They both averted their eyes from the Jesuit.

"You're both quite right," said the queen. "The solution should be obvious, even to you."

There was a long silence.

"This is what I find fascinating about your drama. I don't understand why a bunch of seemingly intelligent people will run around and behave like idiots when the solution to all their problems is so trivial. I mean, why did Hamlet hang around the castle all day, brooding about the fact that his widowed mother got remarried? What difference did it make? But there was something in his genetic, or perhaps social, programming that just kept him from enjoying life. He could have gone off and found a nice queen and fertilized her eggs, but no, *excuse me!* I've got to hang around the castle all day and brood! The schmuck just couldn't make up his mind.

"And why is your English literature so obsessed with this guy Shakespeare, anyway? I mean, after all, Hamlet's story itself goes back to the Vikings, at least four hundred years before Shakespeare. What did he do besides tell a story that had been told many times before? Anyway, it's puzzles like this that make me need a human. I can see it's going to take me a while to decipher all your neurons.

"I must admit," she added, "that all this stuff about ghosts and life after death that occurs so often in your videos is fascinating. It sounds like parallel universes. I wonder if the fundamental constants are the same in heaven."

"I don't know about heaven," said Fitzpatrick, "but I'd sure be willing now to bet they're different in hell. And that's where you're going if you don't let us leave."

"Well?" the queen asked. "Which of you is it to be? To be or not to be, that is the question. Right?"

Another long period of silence fell upon them.

"Well, if you can't make up your minds, I'll have to do

it for you. I'll just choose one of you and that will be that."

"Oh, hell," said Fairouz. "Better straws than her decision." She turned and picked up some stems from the foliage on the floor. Something like a cricket jumped out of the way as she picked up the stems. She broke them into three pieces—two long and one short. The stems were yellow, with strange orange veins in them, Tariq automatically noted.

Fairouz faced the two men, shifted the straws behind her back, and then presented them.

"I've got to know," said Tariq, grabbing a straw. It was short. His face paled, and so did Fairouz's.

Fairouz opened her hand and the two long stems fell to the floor. Fitzpatrick breathed a sigh of relief. An expression of deep sorrow befell Fairouz. She tried to say something, but the words would not come.

"Good show!" said the queen. "Now we'll have all those years to discuss physics, and eventually, we'll be able to have some intelligent conversations around here. Boyoboy, this is going to be great!"

"I'm sorry," Fitzpatrick said unconvincingly.

"Well," said the queen, "you guys better be toddling off now. We've got a universe change due in about an hour. I've got to get this ship off this gravitational field, and you've got to get back to yours."

"She's right," said Fairouz softly. "I've got to go back— it's my duty. I wish to God it had turned out any other way."

The Jesuit walked quickly over to the exit. The workers moved aside readily. "It's like the parting of the Red Sea," he muttered idly.

Fairouz put her hands out toward Tariq and he squeezed them. She hugged him, and tears began to roll down her cheeks. Her suit fan turned on, its humidity sensor detecting the unnatural moisture.

He hugged her back and whispered, "I wish it had been different."

"So do I," she murmured. "So do I."

"You had better go now," he said. "There is not much time left." She nodded and pulled away from him slowly.

"We'll bring everything in your cabin over here, and all the consumables we can spare." She turned and began to walk toward the exit as if she were on a high-gravity planet.

"Wait!" he said.

She turned around quickly. "There is one thing I have to know," he said, "before you go. Or it will kill me, not knowing for the rest of my long life."

"Anything," she said.

"Shut off your suit radio and come here."

She turned off the transmitter with puzzlement. He did likewise as she walked over to him. They held hands again and he whispered to her so only her suit microphones could pick up his words.

In Arabic, he said, "Why did you sabotage the *Ulug Beg?*"

"What? I wouldn't do such a thing in a million years!"

"But I know you're a spy," said Tariq. "I was going to reveal it at the right time, but first, I had to figure out how and why you were sabotaging the ship."

She swallowed and glanced back at Fitzpatrick, to convince herself that he could not overhear. Turning her face so that the priest could not even see her lips, she whispered, "How did you know?"

"Your ring was the first clue," Tariq said accusingly. "The ugly one. It has an inscription on it in Hebrew."

"You searched my cabin!" She was shocked.

"It made me suspect you had some connection with the Israelis." He backed up a step from her, releasing his hands. "And I found your laser torch. It fitted in perfectly with the cuts in the pipes, the cables, and everything."

"I use that laser torch for carving figurines. It's a hobby. Sometimes I sell them on consignment in tourist shops."

"A nice excuse."

"Oh, God, it's so complicated, I can never explain it in time."

"Are you a Jew?" He said it with obvious distaste.

"Yes," she whispered. "That ring is from the Wailing Wall. It contains a tiny piece of the debris after Jerusalem was vaporized. It's all I have left of my parents. They died in the war."

"So, you're not a Druze?"

"That's right. I was just an infant then, and I was adopted by a Druze family. My Druze 'father' had been in the Israeli space force, a dear friend of my real parents. He and his family treated me like one of their own. I grew up speaking Arabic. I can't even speak Hebrew.

"Like the Jews, most Druze survivors left the radioactive pits of the Middle East and spread out over the Moon, Mars, the asteroids—any place they could find a piece of rock to call their own. When the pro-Israeli and anti-Israeli Druzes met in space, they were all pieces of extended families anyway that had been broken apart by old, stupid political borders.

"Before long, as they talked, the ones from Arab lands complained they weren't fully accepted by the Muslims, who regarded them as heretics. And the Israeli Druzes hadn't ever really had fully equal citizenship with the Jews, despite what they said. And they believe that any Druze you meet could be a reincarnation of your great-grandfather or whatever, which makes the family ties are even stronger than with you Egyptians. So they just set up their own independent Druze colonies.

"But enough of the anti-Israeli Druzes remained behind, scattered around the Islamic world, so they became grudgingly accepted in Eurafrica. So as a Druze, I was able to move freely in space.

"Then, one day, the Israelis contacted me. Somehow, they knew about my history.

"But I never did anything to hurt you!" she said. "Through the Druzes I came to love the Arabs. I usually think of myself as one. I'm more Arab than Jew. I sometimes think of myself as a citizen of space. Like a Bedouin, roaming from one oasis to another. I'd never do anything to hurt the Arabs, but I don't want to see them crush the Israelis, either. So I pass along bits of information here and there. That's all."

"So you're a traitor," said Tariq bitterly. "Go on, get out of here!"

"*Goddamn it!* I'm a spy, not a saboteur." She turned angrily and stomped back toward the exit, where the priest was still waiting. Fitzpatrick's eyes darted between the two. He started to say something and then thought better of it.

The boss joined them and led them back through the tunnel. They trudged silently, and then the boss said, at last, "I realize it is painful for you to be separated from your friend. I feel sorry for you. At least I think that is what I feel. I do not fully understand sorrow. We have no word for it in our language. I have never had an experience quite like this. But from your encyclopedia, I think I understand now what sadness and tragedy mean to you. I think this is how I might feel if I were separated from my queen."

"So this is you speaking, not the queen?" Fitzpatrick asked.

"Yes. The queen is preoccupied now with Tariq."

As they trudged along, Fairouz remained silent.

"Seeing all those scenes of sorrow in all those videos," said the boss, "is just not the same as seeing it happen in front of you. I can sense there is a profound pain here that I have never experienced. I wish things could be otherwise."

Fairouz's fan whirred.

As they walked, Fitzpatrick kept glancing at Fairouz's face, and the tears that streamed down. Finally, they reached the last leg of the tunnel and could see the airlock in the distance.

"We're almost there," the priest said to Fairouz. He put his hand on her shoulder. "I know it's hard to realize, but in the end, everything will be for the best. God so wills it."

They reached the inner hatch of the airlock. The boss opened it for them. The two humans stepped inside and the boss stood in the corridor, staring at them pensively with his four eyes.

"I have learned much from you," said the creature. "You have given me many things to think about that I could never have imagined if I had lived through a geological era. I did not even realize that individuals had an identity, other than the queens. I'm not sure that is making me happy, and it may be the opposite, but I thank you for opening a dim, locked door in the back of my mind.

"And I thank you for this concept of compassion— something that I had never imagined. I feel that I am somehow connected to your nervous system, in much the way that the queen is connected to mine. That which hurts you, hurts me, even though there is no electromagnetic link between us. I especially thank you, Father, for teaching me of these great messengers, Moses, Jesus, and Muhammad. They have helped me to understand your philosophers' concepts of justice and mercy."

The priest looked at Fairouz and then at the creature.

"I still do not understand," continued the boss, "why it is that the followers of these wonderful messengers often did the exact opposite of what they were told. Or why it is that wherever this God has gone in your history, death has followed. In fact, when I compare your history with those of the unenlightened who worshiped false gods, I can see no difference in the evils committed. But at least you make me think that there must be something higher —a greater duty than just obeying the dictates of the queen. This pains me, but I thank you for it. And now I must say good-bye."

"No, damn it!" shouted the priest. "I don't need some damn infidel monster to tell me what my duty is!" He jumped back into the tunnel.

Fairouz stared at him blankly.

"I'm the obvious choice!" the Jesuit said angrily. "You knew that all along. Tariq knew it. The queen knew it. Even this bug here knows it. Tariq's the only one smart enough to maybe save the ship. It's obvious that God sent me here for a purpose. And my purpose must be to bring enlightenment to the infidels. I'm going to take Tariq's place." He turned and began running back.

"He's right, you know," said the boss. "That is his duty. I will go lead him back to Tariq. He will get lost otherwise." He scampered off. Fairouz ran after him, conflicting emotions battling in her face.

CHAPTER 33

After a vociferous argument, Tariq accepted Fitzpatrick's reasoning. The logic was irrefutable. They embraced and said their good-byes. Fairouz watched from a distance.

Tariq, Fairouz, and the boss ran back through the tunnel. Tariq was a mixture of raging emotions—relief at his release, anger at Fairouz, and guilt at not having argued harder with Fitzpatrick. At the same time, he was trying to think of all the supplies he should bring back for the priest.

Their radio picked up the sounds of the priest muttering to himself. "Allah moves in mysterious ways," he said. "Moondust!"

They paused at the junction between two corridors. Tariq's eyes met Fairouz's, and he was jolted back to reality. *She is a spy,* he thought, *a traitor, and no matter what she said, she must be the saboteur. What to do?*

They resumed the run and soon came to the airlock. The humans stepped in.

Tariq said to the boss, "Thank you very much for all that you have done. We'll bring Fitzpatrick's supplies to his airlock. Please do everything you can to make his life as pleasant as possible."

"That I will," replied the alien. "He has taught me much, and given me much to think about. We should have many good conversations about morality, ethics, justice, and charity."

"*As-salamu 'alaykum,*" said Tariq.

"Peace be unto you, too," replied the boss.

The inner hatch contracted, sealing the two humans off. They could hear each other's labored breathing in the radios.

Fairouz spoke, saying, "I'm glad you're back. I'm really glad."

Tariq ignored her.

The outer hatch opened and the air rushed out, pulling at the humans like a wind, but the artificial gravity kept them inside. They climbed out to the hull and, firing their xenon jets hard, rose slowly out of the artificial gravity.

Automatically looking at her xenon gauge, Fairouz said, "This is using a hell of a lot of gas. These things were only meant for microgravity. We'll have to recharge them when we get back."

Tariq answered with silence.

"*Ulug Beg,* we're coming home," said Fairouz dispiritedly over the radio.

Their helmets filled with the sound of cheering.

"I'm afraid we had to leave Father Fitzpatrick behind," said Fairouz. "He made a great sacrifice for us."

The cheering died to silence. They could see the *Ulug Beg* in the distance, near the bright Sun. It looked like a picture out of an underwater documentary, when the videographer aimed the camera toward the surface at a boat hovering above, except here, the ship was crystal clear in the endless vacuum of space.

Fairouz touched the gain control on her transceiver and turned it down to a minimum. She reached over and did the same to Tariq's. "What did you do that for?" he asked in Arabic.

"Because I didn't want them to overhear us."

The two shot together, side by side, toward the *Ulug Beg.*

"Well, goddamn it!" she said. "Are you going to tell them?"

"About you being a saboteur?"

"I'm no saboteur! But are you going to tell them I'm a spy?"

Tariq thought about it a long while, then said, "Not as long as we're in the wrong universe. We need to work together. It's the only way we have a ghost of a chance of getting back. But I want your solemn word that, by everything you hold holy—if there is anything—you will not sabotage this mission anymore."

"I've never sabotaged the *Ulug Beg*, but even if I had, I'd give you my solemn word. I swear by the atoms of the sacred Wailing Wall, by the memory of my parents, and by the honor of my Druze brothers, I will not harm the ship."

"Very well."

"But what," she added, "if we get back?"

"Why, then," he replied, "you'll have to be tried for espionage."

They both knew that Israeli spies did not fare well in the Islamic courts of Eurafrica.

They boarded the *Ulug Beg* with relief. The whole crew crowded around the airlock and helped them out of their pressure suits. The mood was one of subdued excitement and happiness, contaminated by the loss of one of their own.

Bombarded by innumerable questions, Fairouz brought order to the chaos by scolding, "Later! We don't have much time. We'll have lots of time to talk about what happened there. I see a lot of people who should be at their stations. You know who you are. We do not leave our stations unmanned! We've got to get together all of Father Fitzpatrick's belongings, and enough consumables so he can survive while they work out his biochemistry. And we've got to prepare for the next universe change." Then she softened, and said, "But it sure is great to see you guys again." They let out a rousing cheer and dispersed rapidly to their stations.

Half an hour later, the supplies had been sent over to the alien ship and the shuttle had returned. The crew was at their stations. On the flight deck, they were somber, each acutely aware of the empty seat. The main viewscreen showed the massive alien ship maneuvering slowly via its side thrusters.

Suddenly, a great blue ion beam shot straight out of i
massive engines, seemingly to infinity, like a laser bean

"Somehow," muttered the chief, "it doesn't seem quit
right without a thunderous noise accompanying it."

The huge ship began to slowly accelerate away fror
Ronin, and then suddenly it was gone, just a trail of ior
showing where it had been.

"Incredible!" said Fairouz, her technophilia momer
tarily overcoming her sadness at the loss of the pries
"Can you imagine the acceleration in that sucker! It
amazing they aren't all squashed."

"Their artificial gravity, obviously," said Tariq in
monotone. "If you have the ability to generate gravita
tional fields, you can automatically neutralize the effec
of acceleration. You could accelerate at a thousand gee
and not feel a thing. I'd give my very soul for the secre
of the artificial gravity!"

"You almost did," Fairouz said dryly.

They stared at the empty screen. "Good-bye, Father,
whispered Fairouz. "We'll miss you."

The flight deck lapsed into silence.

"Well," said Fairouz, "I guess we'd better get ready fo
the next universe shift."

Tariq noticed a tear rippling down her cheek, and h
heart softened momentarily. He had to remind himse
that she was the enemy.

"We have about twenty minutes before—"

"I'll be a *pisciasotto*!" said Arnaldo. "It's the priest!"

"I thought there was no TV on this Earth," said Tario
Arnaldo keyed the loudspeaker on.

"Where the hell are you?" said the voice from th
speaker. "Somebody answer me!" It was the inimitabl
brogue of the Jesuit.

Fairouz lit up and signaled with her hand to switc
her into the transmitter. "Father, is that you?" she aske

"Well, it sure as hell isn't the Pope!" came the reply

"Where the hell are you?" she asked.

"I wish to hell I knew," he replied.

he priest was just a disembodied voice on the loud-
peaker—an interplanetary ghost.

"Father, can't you give us any clues?" Fairouz asked.

"The boss took me on a tour of the vessel," he said.
Then he put me in some kind of cramped, egglike pod
nd booted me out the hatch just before they took off.
here aren't any windows in here. He said it's a transfer
ehicle they use for dumping workers off in space tempo-
arily to be picked up by another vessel. But it's passive,
oesn't have controls of its own. It was pitch black in
ere till I turned on my helmet lamp, and there's nothing
can make any sense of."

Fairouz increased the screen magnification, showing
here the ship had been. She saw nothing but the black-
ess of space and countless stars. "I can't see you, but you
ust be out here somewhere!"

She looked at Arnaldo and said, "Direction finder!"

Arnaldo nodded and punched commands into his con-
ole. Phased-array antennas built into the hull began
anning for the source of the radio signals.

"I can't pick up anything," Arnaldo said. "You've got
talk, Father—say something. Keep on speaking. Any-
ing!"

"Talk about bread cast upon the waters!" came bac
the voice of the priest.

"Got a signal," said the Italian happily as the spe
trum-analyzer display jumped. "Keep talking."

"I talked to the boss about the concept of charity
continued Fitzpatrick, "and how important it is in th
Koran to help the less fortunate. He finally realized tha
there was one thing he could do—he could save me from
a fate worse than death."

"Gotcha!" said Arnaldo. He keyed the coordinates ont
Fairouz's data display.

Fairouz aimed the telescope at the coordinates and a
justed the magnification to cover the uncertainty in th
measurement.

"I've been to London to see the queen," said Fitzpa
rick. "Ha!"

At first they could see nothing, but then a tiny patc
of blackness became noticeable on the screen, visib
only as it blotted out a few stars.

"I think we've got you," said Fairouz. She increase
the magnification.

"Thank God! We Irishmen have never been noted f
a fondness for queens."

A tiny oval was outlined against the distant stars.

"Prepare to launch the shuttle," she said into the inte
com. "This is an emergency." She touched the shoulder
her copilot and said, "Grodno, this is a job for you." Th
bald Byelorussian nodded, unbuckled, and pushed off t
ward the shaft.

On the radio, Fairouz said, "Father, we're sending th
shuttle to pick you up."

"Allah is truly merciful!" came his reply.

While the shuttle crew prepared for launch, the fligl
deck kept a running conversation with the priest.

"How much air do you have left?" Fairouz asked.

"A good seven hours."

Tariq, who had been listening thoughtfully, said ov
the radio, "How in space did he prevent the queen from
knowing what he was doing? She could see everythir
through his eyes."

"Ah," replied the priest, "that's where he was not onl
charitable but clever. He broke his antenna so sh
couldn't see what he was doing or read his mind. SI

probably thought it was just a normal malfunction, and expected him to go to the repair shop."

"I wonder what will happen to the boss when the queen finds out what he's done," said the chief.

"I greatly fear," came the reply, "that he's going to be in deep moondust. But he's a sharp fellow, and the queen can't afford to kill him, I think. She doesn't seem to have too many chaps of his level on board. I think he's going to be all right. I'm confident that, before long, he's going to have all the bugs praying toward Mecca or whatever five times a day. He, instead of I, will have the honor of being the Muhammad to that universe, peace be upon him."

The shuttle was launched and quickly reached the black egg.

Two astronauts emerged from the shuttle as the flight deck watched on the screen. The Byelorussian radioed back, "How do you open this thing?"

"Haven't the foggiest," replied Fitzpatrick.

"Just stuff it in the cargo bay," said Fairouz, "and get back here ASAP."

"Roger," replied the Byelorussian.

They watched as the astronauts, using their evapacks, gently pushed the man-sized egg into the hold. The egg was so black as to be nearly invisible, even in their light beams.

"Button her up and get back here," Fairouz said.

They sealed the hold and reentered the shuttle. In the middle of the short trip back to the *Ulug Beg*, the ship's alarm went off, and the usual feeling overcame them. "Universe change alert," said the computer.

From the far side of the flight deck, the sound of the cat howling came, accompanied by its translation, "I am feeling very abused!"

"Aren't we all?" said Ollerenshaw.

"You okay?" Fairouz asked worriedly.

"Yes," replied the Byelorussian.

"Lock that stupid cat up in your room," Fairouz said to the chief, "or I'll lock *you* up in the engine room."

Ollerenshaw grumbled, unstrapped herself, and floated off in the direction of the howling.

"Well, I wonder what kind of universe Allah has prepared for us this time," said Fairouz.

More cat howling came, accompanied by the translation, "Negative! Negative! I haff got mice to catch und females to find!"

"I'm going down to the hangar," announced Tariq, heading for the shaft.

Fairouz silently watched him go.

Tariq bounced between the ceiling and floor of the main tenance room of the hangar deck, the zero-gee equivalent of pacing back and forth, while the shuttle rendezvoused

Three-fourths of the flight deck was pressurized; only the quadrant containing the hangar was exposed to vacuum. Tariq waited in the pressurized side with two engineers.

Through a porthole, he watched as the shuttle reentered. They waited for the door to close, and for the hissing air to repressurize the hangar. Finally, the red light over the access hatch turned to green, and the hatch slid open. The two engineers rushed through and tied down the shuttle while Tariq opened the cargo bay door.

The egg-shaped object was as black as the rings of Uranus, and featureless. There were no handholds, so Tariq pulled it out with difficulty in the zero gravity. From its inertia, he could tell that its mass was at least twice as great as that of the man it contained.

"What the hell's going on?" came the muffled voice from inside.

"It's okay," Tariq shouted. "You're in the hangar."

The two engineers helped him float the egg next to the shuttle.

"It feels warm, not like metal," said Tariq. "Of course, if it had been metal, Father Fitzpatrick's signals could not have gotten out."

"I'm sure the boss thought of that," replied the faint voice from within.

"How did he open it up when you got in?" Tariq asked.

"I didn't pay that much attention," replied the priest. "I was just so grateful to be getting out of there that I jumped in. I would have jumped into a rocket nozzle if he'd said it would save me."

One of the engineers brought over a toolbox, and
oated it next to the egg.

"Tell me everything you can remember about how he
pened it up," Tariq said.

"Well, he took me to this chamber down near the en-
nes, where gravity was lighter. There were a bunch of
ese eggs sitting there, and at first I thought they were
ose critters getting ready to hatch. They looked like
zgs in a carton. I was so busy looking around and won-
ering whether the queen was going to see us through
ne of her workers, who were in constant danger of en-
ring the chamber, I don't exactly remember what he
id. But he sort of leaned over and touched the egg and it
ist split in two."

"Exactly how?" Tariq asked. "Was it around an equa-
r?"

"Yes, I think."

Tariq ran his fingers along the widest part of the egg.
can't see any seam."

"There must be one."

"Let us see," said Tariq, beating an Arabic tattoo on the
3g.

"Hey!" said the muffled voice. "Are you hammering
ut there?"

"Sorry," Tariq said stopping. "Well, let us think like
iens. Our queens are masters of genetic engineering, as
ell as physics, and the fundamental problem with this
ape is that it has to remain airtight when the pressure
inside and there is a vacuum outside." He put his arms
ound it as far as he could—slightly more than halfway
ound the narrow perimeter—and squeezed. Nothing
appened. The egg did, however, flex slightly.

The material seemed organic, with tiny fibers running
rough it. It had a dull, flat black finish that absorbed
very bit of incidental light.

"Why would they use so black a color if it was de-
gned for someone to spot?" Tariq asked.

"Beats me," came the voice inside.

"Infrared!" said Tariq. "On that hot, permanently over-
ist Earth they live on, they must have evolved much
eater sensitivity to infrared light than we have."

"Makes sense," said Fitzpatrick. "Then the black
ould absorb any sunlight, and reradiate it as infrared."

"Yes! To them, this thing would be glowing brightly in space." Tariq rummaged through the toolkit, but did not find what he needed. "Hang on. I am going to get something that may help."

"Why don't you just cut the sucker open?" Fitzpatrick asked.

"We cannot do that!" said Tariq. "Who knows what advanced technology we might be destroying?"

"Well," said the priest, "speaking as a particularly advanced life-form, I say to hell with the technology—just get this sucker open!"

"Let me try one more thing, and then we will do it your way." Tariq bounced off the shuttlecraft and arced through the wall hatch into the shaft.

"Do not go anywhere!" he shouted as he flew out of the hangar.

"I was planning to go jogging," mumbled the priest, "but I'll stick around if you really want."

Tariq returned with an instrument like a handgun with an electronic sight. "I am back," he said, "and have got an IR probe."

"Hurry the bloody hell up!" said the priest. "I think the chief's claustrophobia is contagious, and I'm starting to catch it."

Tariq aimed at the egg and clicked the trigger. The tiny viewscreen lit up with a false-color image. But in place of the featureless surface, there was a bright green triangle, and when he moved the converter closer, the big triangle resolved into smaller triangles, less than two centimeters on an edge.

"We have something!" said Tariq excitedly. "This thing has strange infrared markings on it, and they look about the size you would make buttons if you were one of those creatures. I will touch one."

"I just hope you don't touch the one that says self-destruct."

Tariq touched the top triangle. Nothing happened.

"I am going to touch another one," said Tariq.

He did so, and Fitzpatrick exclaimed, "Hey! A light just came on in here."

"Progress," said Tariq.

He touched the next button.

"Hey, it's getting hot in here!" said Fitzpatrick after

moment. "It's heating up faster than my suit conditioner
an handle it."

He touched the same button again. "Did that help?"

There was a long silence, and then Fitzpatrick said,
Yes. It's getting a little bit better now, I think. At least,
t's not continuing to get hot."

He touched the next button, and there was a little
opping sound. He touched the egg, and the top half
loated up, revealing the priest.

"Bless you, my son," said the Jesuit, "unto the tenth
eneration!" His face beamed in his helmet.

The priest was cramped in a nearly fetal position and
eeded help getting himself unfolded. If there had been
ny gravity, he would have had difficulty rising, but in
s absence, he just floated in the air, shaking his arms
nd legs to get the circulation flowing again.

"I haven't felt so good," said Fitzpatrick, "since the
ight before I took my vows."

Tariq turned his attention to the eggshell.

"What happened then?" the Byelorussian asked.

"I had one last, wild fling!" he said, closing his eyes.

"What did you do?" an engineer asked.

"That's a secret between me, the confessional com-
uter, and the good Lord!" He winked.

Tariq studied the container. The shell was a good
venty centimeters thick—not the thin eggshell he had
alf expected to see. The interior looked almost quilted,
ith dark-blue padding that seemed organic. "Shock
shioning," he murmured.

Near where the priest's feet had been, there was a
aguely familiar, egg-shaped object. Tariq reached in and
ulled it out. It was unattached—just a large black egg
e size of a football.

He turned to the priest, holding it gently in his hands,
d said, "Could this be . . ."

The priest looked at it distastefully. "Yes, it's the god-
mn translator."

"Allah *is* merciful!" Tariq said joyfully.

"I lost count of the number of times I cursed that god-
mn thing," said Fitzpatrick. "It's cramped enough in
ere without it."

Tariq held it as if it was the most precious jewel in
e world.

"I don't mind telling you, if I could have kicked tha sucker out into orbit, I would have!"

"Why is it here?" Tariq asked.

"He said that it might come in handy, based on hi study of our experiences in the logbook. It was anothe one of his acts of charity."

"How do you turn it on?" Tariq asked. "It looks dead.'

"Beats me."

Tariq grabbed the IR gun where it was floating an held it to the egg. At first, nothing significant was visible but when he rotated it another triangle appeared, witl smaller triangles inside it. He whistled softly.

"And one other thing—I almost forgot. The boss sai something about stuffing a lot of their physics into it memory. Another act of charity."

CHAPTER 35

...riq rushed the translator egg up to the lab deck. Dr. ...ngoma was there with two technicians—a Frenchman, ...an-Pierre Peronnet, and an Iranian woman, Leila ...oinzadeh. The trio floated over to a gamma-ray micro- ...aph screen displaying ultra-high-resolution images of ...ant cells from Ronin.

"What have you got there?" the physician asked.

"This is the translation device the bugs used to talk to ...," Tariq said.

"How does it work?" Leila asked.

"That is what I am hoping to find out," Tariq said. ...ather Fitzpatrick did not get any operating instruc- ...ns."

"Maybe it's user-friendly," said Leila.

"It had better be," said Tariq. "We do not have all the ...ne in the universe to figure it out."

"How could it work?" Dr. Isingoma asked. "How could ...u put so much software inside such a small package?"

"It must be programmed at the molecular level," Tariq ...id. "From the speed with which it learned English, it ...ust have a massive amount of concurrent processing. It ...uld also require tremendous memory capability."

He spun it slowly in midair about its long axis, so they ...uld examine it visually.

"No features," said Leila.

"Only to our eyes. In IR," added Tariq, "it has ve
distinctive markings similar to buttons or keys."

"I wonder what it's made out of," Leila asked, touc
ing the surface gently. "It feels slightly rough, fibrous.'

Tariq held it with his hands and squeezed slightly. '
indents, so it is not rigid, and it is very massive," he sai
shaking it slowly.

"It seems organic," said Leila.

"One thing we know for sure," said Tariq. "Those cre
tures are wizards at genetic engineering. That is how th
was probably produced."

He put the egg back in midair and spun it slow
again. He unhitched the IR gun from his belt and aime
it at the egg, scanning as it rotated. There were no mar
ings on it except for the large triangle divided into fo
small ones.

Tariq stopped the egg's rotation and touched one of th
small triangles. Nothing happened.

He touched another one and the top third of the e
began to glow blue.

Tariq's eyes lit up and he said, "It is on!"

"Now, what do you do with it?" Leila asked.

"Good question," said Tariq. He said hello to the eg
but it didn't respond.

"Maybe you have to ask it a specific question," Lei
said.

"Do you understand me?" Tariq asked.

"Of course, bozo!" the egg said.

"Well, I'll be damned!" said Jean-Pierre.

"Inta ti-'raf sirr diras-it il-lugh-aat?" Tariq asked.

"Aywa," replied the egg. *"Il-waahid laazim yi-tmaarra
alay-ha wi yi-sta'mil-ha dayman."* It used the same singso
vocal style it had when translating for the aliens. It v
brated as it spoke, the sounds emanating from all over i
surface.

Tariq laughed. "Its Arabic is fine!"

"What did you say?" the Frenchman asked.

" 'Do you know the secret of learning a language
And the egg replied, 'Yes, one must practice it and alwa
use it.' "

"Parlez-vous Francais?" said Jean-Pierre to the egg.

The egg remained silent.

"*Avec un instrument comme celui-la vous pourriez entrer par es portes du paradis,*" he continued. " 'With an instrument uch as that you could enter the gates of heaven.' "

The egg still remained uncommunicative.

Leila spoke to the egg. "*Salam alekom, agha,*" she said in arsi. "Peace be upon you, sir. *Bebakhshid, moltafet shodid?* Excuse me, do you understand?"

"No," replied the egg.

"Well, what languages do you understand, Egg?" Tariq sked in English.

"Obviously, English, Arabic, and the language of my nasters, who you recently visited, for which you haven't got a name, but which I'll call—in view of your remarks —Buggish."

"But why would they need a translator if they only ave one language?" Tariq asked.

"I wasn't grown to be a translator," it replied.

"Then, what were you grown to be?" Tariq asked.

"You don't have any precise equivalent in English or Arabic. I wish you had more of your other languages in your data base. You've only got tempting morsels there, delicious bits of Greek and Latin and BA-IC. All of your foreign videos are dubbed, dammit! The losest I can come to translating that which I am is a correlator.' "

"Ah, so," replied Tariq. "We use lots of correlators in esearch."

"Hah!" replied the translator energetically. "You call hose puny machines *correlators?* Those are child's play, nerely capable of trivial mathematical calculations, good or nothing but the most mundane, juvenile data mea-urements—kindergarten Fourier analysis. I, on the other aand, correlate any and all information. I *thrive* on corre-ation. I was *born* to correlate!"

Tariq mused on this for a moment, and said, "I see. So hat is how you are able to translate our languages—by lelving into our data bases and correlating all the infor-nation there."

"You got it!"

"What other kind of data do you have from your own ivilization?" Tariq asked.

"Oh, I've got all kinds of stuff. I'm a walking almana•
Want to hear all the gossip of the last five thousan•
years? Which queen's eggs were fertilized by whic•
males? I've got all the dirt!"

"How about physics?" Tariq asked.

"Oh, yes, I've got all kinds of stuff here." The egg be•
gan to roar with laughter in the voice of some long-fo•
gotten human actor in some obscure video.

"What's so funny?"

"Your physics! You guys think you're really hot stuf•
but you've made so many blunders and overlooked s•
many obvious things, I just have to laugh."

More howls of joy.

"Would you be willing to teach me some of that?•
Tariq asked.

"Sure, that's my job, Mac. I answer questions."

"Are you happy with what you do?" Leila asked.

"It's a living. Most of the time, it's pretty boring. •
wasn't until we began to colonize space that there wa•
this huge spate of new data coming in to correlate. Boy, •
would have loved to have been around when they firs•
discovered the universe!"

"When was that?"

"About forty years ago, when we first began to explor•
the upper atmosphere. Man, what it must have bee•
like! Imagine—for billions of years, nobody could se•
through the clouds. They were thick and permanent, lik•
your Venus. Those rubes thought the Earth was th•
whole universe. Then, one night, a bug scientist is using •
balloon to fly higher than his wings would allow, study•
ing the atmosphere. He rises through a bunch of cloud•
Then, boom—he sees a whole bunch of stars and thing•
up there. Really shook up the queens. Say, get me som•
water."

"Water?" Tariq asked.

"That's what I said, guy. Water! The wet stuf•
Aitch-two-oh! I know you're not deaf, and I kno•
you speak English, but my estimate of your IQ is fallin•
rapidly."

"Why do you want water?" Tariq asked.

"Because I'm *thirsty*, camel jock!"

"Where do we put it?" Leila asked.

"Just immerse me in it," replied the egg. "I absorb it all over my skin."

"Here, let me," said Leila. "I've raised two boys." She took the egg gently and floated over to the emergency shower, where a sign said in English and Arabic: IN CASE OF CHEMICAL ACCIDENT, SHOWER IMMEDIATELY. She opened the transparent door, put the egg in the middle, floating in the air, then closed it and pressed a key. Water squirted from all directions.

"Aaah, that feels good!" said the muffled voice of the egg.

The egg hovered in midstream, supported by equal pressure from all sides for several minutes. Then it said, "Enough, already!"

Leila turned off the shower and dried the egg off with a towel.

"I feel a lot better," said the egg. "I sure didn't like being kicked all the time by that goddamn priest. And by the way, when is chow time?"

Tariq, who had observed all of this with amusement, said, "What do you eat?"

"Actually, I drink, I don't really eat. What I drink is a soup with all kinds of different chelates. I see from your roster that you've got someone around here who can synthesize up some good organic chemistry."

"I can handle that," said Dr. Isingoma.

"And with your vocabulary," said Tariq, "it should not be difficult to tell him what you need."

"That's a relief to hear," replied the egg. "I was afraid I might wind up one dead egg, and then I wouldn't be able to correlate anything anymore."

"Tell me," said Tariq. "Why is it that you sounded one way when speaking for the boss, a very different way for the queen, and now you have still another style?"

"Whenever I'm translating for someone, I try to capture not just the words of the speaker, but the *essence*. Any schmuck can translate the words; only a master correlator can perceive the subtleties that relate to one culture and find corresponding subtleties in the other one."

"And when you are speaking for yourself?"

"Then my own radiant personality bursts forth in an explosion of cross-cultural referents that dazzles even me!"

Fairouz's voice sounded over the intercom. "Tari
come up to the flight deck."

"What is it?"

"I think you really ought to see this."

Tariq looked longingly at the egg, sighed, and sai
"Roger, coming up."

CHAPTER 36

Tariq popped out of the shaft on the flight deck, and Fairouz said to him, "Good. I need a second opinion." She pointed to the screen.

He drifted past the chief, strapped in her chair with her usual expression of hopeless doom, and floated over to Fairouz and Fitzpatrick, who were staring up at the main screen on the ceiling. The Jesuit was now wearing a jumpsuit, and was excitedly muttering numbers into his wrist computer. Ng'ethe was pictured on a front-panel display, the data deck in the background, exchanging remarks with the priest.

On the screen the Sun blazed, but it was not the old familiar one. This one was red and raging.

"The Sun's off the main sequence," said Fitzpatrick. "It's evolved somewhere that our Sun will be five billion years or so in the future."

Tariq stared at it, observing the numerous black sunspots that dotted its surface. Wisps of solar prominences arced out into space, bent by strong magnetic fields.

"What does this mean?" Fairouz asked.

"Well," said Tariq, "for one thing, it means that life on Earth is impossible here. The planet must be boiling."

"But the Sun's red," said Fairouz. "Doesn't that mean it's cooler?"

"Yes," Tariq said with surprise. "Very observant!"

"Well, I may not be a big astrophysicist, like certain people around here," she said, "but I've done enough laser welding to know that if you heat up a metal, first it glows red, then it glows yellow."

"Yes," said Tariq, "it is the same phenomenon. The radiation law of our old friend Max Planck at work. But the thing is, as the Sun evolves it gets bigger—so much bigger that even though it is cooler, and each square meter radiates less energy, the overall Sun radiates a hell of a lot more."

"Well put," said Fitzpatrick.

"How big is it?" Tariq asked. "I need a scale."

"About three solar radii," said Fitzpatrick.

Tariq whistled. "That makes it nine times the surface area of our old familiar Sun. What does the Earth look like?"

Fairouz spoke a command to the telescope computer. A planet appeared on the middle of the screen, round and black and yellow.

Tariq grimaced. "Is that Earth?"

Fairouz nodded.

"It looks more like Mars, or maybe Venus, if you stripped away the atmosphere."

"Things are looking worse and worse," said Fairouz. "Doesn't look like much room for hope."

"Out of the frying pan, and into the fire," replied Ollerenshaw. Sly began to massage her shoulders sympathetically.

"The Earth's oceans have been boiled away," said Tariq. "A lot of the atmosphere has probably escaped into space by now."

Tariq tapped the control panel rhythmically, and spoke to Ng'ethe's monitor. "What's the solar spectrum like?"

"I'll put it on your data screen," he replied.

The screen lit up with a multicolored spectrum.

"Wow!" said Tariq. "Hardly any carbon."

"That bothers me," said the Kenyan. "What good is a universe that doesn't have carbon in it?"

"Exactly," said Tariq. "Life would be impossible."

"At least we do not have to worry about any nasty visitors, then," said Tariq.

"But I wouldn't want to live here," said Ng'ethe. "Where would you get food?"

"On the other hand," said the Jesuit, whose exuberance at being rescued from hell could not be chilled by a mere red Sun, "it would be a great place to open up a restaurant."

"Do you think it's going to get worse?" Fairouz asked.

"It looks that way," Tariq said, "but we cannot be sure. There is too much randomness in the variation of the fundamental constants. We could fluctuate back into a comfortable universe at any time."

"I wish I could be happy about the new universes coming more frequently," said Fairouz. "We're down to six hours per universe, and the interval keeps getting smaller and smaller."

"We've got to pray that one of God's fluctuations puts us into a universe where we can live," said Fitzpatrick. "That's all we can hope for now."

"I had better get upstairs," said Tariq. "I've been too busy to check on the trends in the constants lately."

He pushed off from the wall and flew back to the shaft, and went up to the data deck.

The Kenyan, strapped into his seat, was hunched over his keyboard. "Look at these numbers," Ng'ethe said. He displayed the fundamental constants on the screen.

"That's great!" said Tariq. "Planck's constant is going down. It's almost normal."

"Yes, and so are the other constants. So how do you explain what's outside the window there?"

Tariq thought about it, and then slowly began to nod. "I can only think of one answer—the weak interaction."

"Come again?" said Ng'ethe.

"There are a bunch of fusion reactions in the Sun, and they are basically controlled by the weak interaction, which in this universe must be stronger than it is in ours, so the Sun has been burning itself up more quickly," Tariq said. "Its brightness is just a delicate measure of that interaction."

Tariq hovered above Ng'ethe, holding onto the relay rack handle. "What about our universe-transition predictions? How are they doing?"

"I had to make some changes," said the Kenyan. "The intervals are coming faster and faster, and they weren't following your earlier prediction as accurately as I would like." He put the curves up on the screen. "This is a plot of universe intervals versus time, corrected for the changing constants." A series of yellow dots showed data: the intervals were clearly diminishing. "The green curve is your earlier fit. The purple one uses a higher order polynomial fit, using all the data up to now. It's giving a much better prediction than your first cut." The purple curve went neatly through the dots; the green one missed them by increasing amounts.

"That figures," said Tariq. "We did not have much data originally. And we don't even know that it really is a polynomial. It could be almost anything. It looks like the interval is approaching zero. That would be exciting. Imagine zipping through a new universe every second!"

"Personally, I've had enough excitement for one trip."

"Of course, it would probably kill us," Tariq added as an afterthought. "And if we did happen to get back to our own universe, we would not have time to escape Ronin's gravity. I only wish that the fluctuations in the constants were as predictable as the interval. I fear that the universe is just giving us another example of its inherent randomness. It is clear that we need more help."

"The egg?"

"Yes," said Tariq. "It is the only thing that might give us a clue as to what is going on. I will be right back." He shoved off and jumped into the shaft.

CHAPTER 37

Tariq, Fitzpatrick, and the egg made a picturesque trio as they floated up to the data deck. Tariq strapped himself into the seat next to Ng'ethe and held the egg in his lap.

"This had better be good," said the egg. "I was learning French and Farsi, and correlating like crazy. Did you know that there are all kinds of funny relationships between the two? I've got to get back and continue my studies. I've barely mastered the basic grammar and vocabulary."

"I should have thought you'd be fluent by now," said the priest. "You absorbed English and Arabic almost instantaneously, it seemed, and you didn't even have a common language then."

"Well, actually, it took a few minutes, but then I was able to tap directly into your data base. Those turkeys wouldn't let me stick my probes directly into their brains, so I had to restrict myself to verbal communications. Do you know how slow that is? Do you know how many bits per second you can transfer through the oral channel?"

"Enough linguistics," said Tariq impatiently.

"Tariq, my boy," said the egg, "the personnel records say that you speak Japanese, too."

"Yes."

"Then," said the egg, as a thin, coppery tendril emerged from its top, "you wouldn't mind if I tapped into your database, would you?"

The tendril grew until it almost touched Tariq's head.

"Get that thing away from me!" said Tariq, pushing it away. "You touch my database and you are going to become one scrambled egg!"

"But all I've got so far are three measly Indo–European languages, plus one Semitic one. You're the only one on board who speaks Japanese."

"Okay," said Tariq, controlling his temper. "I'll teach you Japanese. But orally—not through your brain probe."

"Oboyoboyoboy!" said the egg, rocking back and forth as some dense internal organ jumped from side to side excitedly.

"Provided," said Tariq, "that you first teach me some physics."

"It's a deal!" said the egg.

"How do you see?" Ng'ethe asked the featureless egg.

"Oh, I've got microscopic sensors all over my surface—light-sensitive cells something like the rods and cones in your eyes. Instead of focusing, I see everywhere at once. It's a pity you guys are so limited. Sloppy design work, if you ask me. Say, you're the Kenyan, aren't you?"

"Yes," he said. "How did you know?"

"There are pictures in the personnel file. It says you speak Swahili, Masai, and Kikuyu."

"Yes, and I'll be happy to teach you those when things calm down."

"I am delirious with happiness," the egg said. Moisture began to seep out through pores in the egg's surface, dampening Tariq's jumpsuit. It smelled awful.

"What is wrong?" Tariq asked anxiously. "Are you sick?"

"Well, it's kind of hard to explain, allowing for your culture's weird taboos about this sort of thing."

"What sort of thing?"

"Back home, I have all kinds of workers to take care of my needs. I am, after all, a biological creature, not a machine. It's just that I'm not what you would call house-broken."

Tariq's nose wrinkled in disgust, and the other two men snickered.

After Tariq had changed his clothes and cleaned the egg, they spent several hours interrogating it about physics. The grueling session left their minds reeling.

"That is all I can absorb for now," Tariq said at last.

"That's about twice as much as I can absorb," said the Jesuit.

"Good," replied the egg. "Does this mean we can begin Japanese now?"

"I will teach you just one word for now," Tariq said, "and then you have to shut up until we have some free time, if that ever happens."

"What's that?"

"*Sayonara.*"

"Hey, no fair!" said the egg. "I already knew that."

"I thought you did not know any Japanese," said Tariq.

"That was the title of a Brando movie in your entertainment data base."

Tariq sighed. "*Okei chotto yasumi-masho.* That means, 'Okay, let us take a break.'"

"I wish we were back about a century," sighed the egg.

Wearily, Tariq replied, "Why is that?"

"Because back then, they had subtitles on foreign movies. But all the movies in your data base have been computer-translated into English and Arabic. I could have picked up a whole slew of languages like lightning."

"A lot of people on board have their own personal crystal dictionaries for their various languages," said Fitzpatrick. "Later on, you can access their dictionaries and absorb vocabularies to your yolk's content."

"Far out!"

Fitzpatrick returned his attention to the men. "Those bugs are amazing physicists," he said.

"I've never heard concepts like those in my entire life," Ng'ethe said.

"I cannot help wondering whether they are all correct," Tariq said. "After all, they did not know about parallel universes before we arrived."

"Well, they can explain a helluva lot more things than our physics," Fitzpatrick said.

"They *seem* to explain a lot more," said Tariq. "But we cannot trust them totally. For all we know, they could be wrong about half of those things. Also, they are *too* complicated. The universe is simple—I am sure of it!"

"It works well enough for them to build a very impressive spacecraft," Ng'ethe said.

"True," said Tariq. "But I cannot help thinking that they may have gone off in the wrong direction at times. After all, Ptolemy's theory worked, even though he had the Sun and the planets moving around the Earth. He had to put epicycles on the whole business—wheels within wheels, so to speak—and when the whole thing was done, it was incredibly complicated, but it made the correct predictions. It was not until Copernicus came along that we discovered that everything was really moving around the Sun, and we did not need all those circles on circles. All we needed was circles moving around the Sun. Okay, so Kepler improved on that by making them ellipses. But the idea was simple."

"But their calculations of spectra and the physical properties of matter seem to be excellent," said Fitzpatrick. "They agree with the experimental data better than some of our own theories."

"Well, I will concede," Tariq said, "that they are pretty good physicists. I just do not think they have all the answers. And one thing is for sure—they are lousy astronomers."

The other two men smiled.

"What do you expect?" said the Kenyan. "If we'd been living at the bottom of a permanently cloudy atmosphere for billions of years, and had only recently discovered there was something beyond that, we'd be pretty crummy astronomers, too."

"There's nothing here of any practical value to us in our predicament," said Tariq. "On that we can agree."

The Jesuit nodded and Tariq added thoughtfully, "Though you never can tell what will become useful."

The alarm sounded and the computer announced, "Universe change alert."

They looked out the port at the red, raging, enlarged Sun, and then the usual queasy feeling hit them. The Sun doubled in size, and turned a deeper red.

"Damn!" said Tariq.

"Perhaps things will get better in the next universe," said the Jesuit softly.

Fairouz entered the deck. "What's going on?" she asked. "What can we expect next?"

The Kenyan slipped into the control chair and murmured commands to the telescope. He located Earth quickly.

Magnified on the screen, it was a sorry sight. Dark spots littered the surface; splotches of thick, dark clouds hung over many areas. At the edge of the planet, bright plumes rose hundreds of miles into space, like warts on the face of Earth.

"Volcanos!" muttered Fairouz.

The two scientists nodded.

"It reminds me of Io at its worst," Fairouz said. "When it's erupting like crazy and spewing all kinds of junk into space."

"Let us look at the solar spectrum," Tariq said.

When it appeared on the screen, Tariq shook his head and said, "A lot like last time. A little cooler, but virtually no carbon."

"We are probably most of the carbon in this solar system," Fitzpatrick said.

"One thing's for sure," Tariq said. "There's no life in this universe."

"And I thought things were dull on Pluto on Saturday nights," Fairouz said.

"Hmmm," said Tariq. "I wonder what the Jovian planets are like?"

"Without methane, and what with the screwed-up abundances of the other elements, it should be completely different from our system," Fitzpatrick said. "I'd love to see it."

"This is the chance of a lifetime," Tariq said, "to find out how the Jovians would have evolved under radically different circumstances."

"Just a minute," said Ng'ethe. "There should have been enough time to get us some preliminary readings on the fundamental constants."

He put the display up on the main screen.

"Uh-oh," said Tariq. "Now Planck's constant is getting *bigger*!"

"Well," said Fairouz, "if it was bad when it was getting small, shouldn't it be better now that it's getting bigger?"

"No," said Tariq. "It is probably just as bad either way. Our bodies have evolved for millions of years with Planck's constant the way it was. Now our chemical reactions are going to speed up because the cross sections are bigger."

"Just when I was looking forward to having a decent meal at the normal Planck's constant," said Fitzpatrick with resignation. "Oh, well, they do say that travel broadens."

"Well," muttered Ng'ethe to himself, "let's see what Jupiter looks like."

"It should still be the brightest planet in the solar system," said Tariq. "It shouldn't be too difficult to find."

The Kenyan turned up the magnification.

"Jesus, Mary, and Khadijah, wife of Muhammad!" said the Jesuit.

Instead of the giant, red-orange planet with four big moons, there was a small greenish-blue world with rings around it, plus a single moon.

CHAPTER 38

"Are you sure it isn't Saturn?" Fitzpatrick asked.

Ng'ethe checked the orbital parameters and shook his head. "That's their Jupiter."

"I wonder what Saturn looks like, then?" muttered Tariq.

Ng'ethe issued commands to the computer until Saturn's new face appeared. It was another greenish-blue world without any rings, and one bright moon.

"That makes sense," said Tariq. "The rings are mostly ice, and the heat from the sun has evaporated them. Looks like Titan is still there."

"But then, why does Jupiter have a ring?" Ng'ethe asked.

They quickly scanned Neptune and Uranus and found that they weren't too different from the planets in their world. Their distances had protected them so far.

Pluto turned out to be a smaller, featureless world, and the other terrestrial planets were hot cauldrons of volcanism.

"This is certainly the bleakest universe I've ever been in," said the Jesuit, a world-weary traveler.

"Damn!" said Tariq. "We should have been making careful observations of all the planets in each of the universes. How could I have been so sloppy? We have a fabulous opportunity here to study the evolution of the solar system. If we ever get back, we can intercompare all the data with the different values of the fundamental constants and revolutionize our understanding of the evolution of the universe. But my mind has been so damn foggy ever since we began shifting universes—it is as if it is filled with thick Turkish coffee."

"Skipper!" came Arnaldo's voice over the intercom.

"Roger," said Fairouz.

"Signals—intelligent signals!"

"That is impossible," said Tariq.

"Where are they coming from?" Fairouz asked.

"You won't believe this—Jupiter!"

"I'm coming down," she said, and jumped into the shaft.

The others quickly followed her, except for Ng'ethe and Tariq. The Egyptian lingered for a moment, discussing measurements he wanted made. Then he grabbed the egg and joined the exodus to the flight deck.

The group gathered around Arnaldo's console. On his TV screen there floated a deep-blue blob, covered with crimson fringes. Beneath it drooped long, pink strings. From the way it swayed slowly, it appeared to be underwater. On the loudspeaker a deep, slow voice, like that of a human's slowed down ten times, pealed forth. In the background, there were hundreds of these creatures in the distance, slightly murky, but clearly visible in the bright spotlights that surrounded them, giving the effect of an underwater stadium.

"They're beautiful!" said Fairouz. "The audience almost looks like a field of tulips blowing in a breeze."

The vibrations of the pink strands coincided with moaning sounds coming through the speaker, conveying the inescapable impression that it was the creature talking. When it paused, a louder, general moaning was heard, coinciding with ripples through the audience, like fans at a football game.

Fairouz glanced at Tariq and murmured, "No life in this universe, eh?"

Tariq snapped, "Is it my fault that they have rewritten the rules here?"

The egg in Tariq's hands bounced up and down, as the dense internal organ jumped around excitedly. "A new language!" it said. "Ah, correlation, sweet ecstasy of correlation!"

The scene stretched on without change for a long time. Tariq attached the egg to the ceiling in a net bag, where it could see, and strapped himself in at the data console.

Over the intercom, he said to the Kenyan, "Do you have that planetary spectrum yet?"

"Roger. I'll transfer it down to your computer."

The colored spectrum appeared on the screen, rich with molecular lines. Tariq scrolled slowly through it, scanning the hundreds of chemical signatures. The words of his *sensei* floated into his mind: "By all means, jump to conclusions prematurely! Therein lies much of the joy of science. Just do not let yourself be imprisoned by those conclusions. Most of them will fall apart when tested against reality, but the handful that remain—ah, there's the joy. You may be the first to peek into a previously unknown corner of the universe."

He paused at one line labeled GeH_4 and began tapping the console rhythmically.

He accessed the optical telescope controls, and surveyed the planet and the space around it at maximum magnification. There were several small moons, but only one large one. The rings were complex, but natural. But where his own Jupiter had only an almost invisible ring around it, this Jupiter had a huge, complex ring system, like that of Saturn. The planet itself was twice the diameter of the Earth, or about a fifth of Jupiter's proper one, and it was covered with thick, bright, pale blue clouds, making it impossible to see the surface.

He calculated its mass and studied its infrared emission. His absentminded tapping on the console grew to a crescendo, and then stopped. He smiled and nodded slowly.

Tariq unstrapped himself and floated over to the group, still clustered around the TV screen.

"I still think it's a political speech," the chief said.

"It could be a poetry reading," Fitzpatrick said.

"Maybe it's singing," Fairouz said, "and we don't recognize it because the pitch is too low."

Tariq looked up at the egg where it floated near the ceiling, and said, "How are you doing, Egg?"

"Lousy," came back the voice. "Not enough *different* images to correlate with. I need more shows, more variety!"

"How do you produce sounds, anyway?" Tariq asked. "Without a mouth, it must be hard."

"Not so," replied the egg. "I've got a special acoustic transducer organ and it vibrates sort of like your heart, except much faster. The movements get transferred by my body fluids to the outer layers, and I vibrate like a loudspeaker."

Tariq looked at the screen and said, "I guess he is not giving you much in the way of clues to deduce anything from."

"That's an understatement," replied the egg. "All I've got now is a whole slew of hypotheses, and no data to correlate them with."

"Maybe we can do something about that," Tariq said. He floated over to Arnaldo and engaged in a strenuous technical discussion for several minutes. Then he detached the egg from the ceiling and gently brought it over to the communications console.

"You wanted to stick your tendrils into someone's skull, so how about into our data base?"

"I've already sucked that stuff dry," replied the egg.

"That is all right," said Tariq. "Your Italian friend here has just set up a multichannel receiver so you can tune in every radio and television broadcast they have in the system. You can watch them all simultaneously."

"Oboyoboy!" said the egg, bobbing excitedly. A coppery tendril grew from the side of the egg, and slipped into a jack.

"You mean you've got other channels, and you've just been showing us the boring one?" Ollerenshaw asked.

Arnaldo shrugged. "The skipper seemed to like that one."

"Father," said Tariq, "I think I understand what has happened to Jupiter."

"Obviously," said Fitzpatrick, "most of it's been boiled away by the hot Sun."

"Yes, that is the essence of it. But it is the subtleties that intrigue me. Where are all the Galilean satellites? Why does Jupiter have a ring and Saturn not? Why hasn't Jupiter's ring evaporated? And especially, of course, how can life exist here?"

"What's your theory?"

"In the beginning, this Jupiter was just like ours: huge, hot, and with four large satellites. Life got started in the cloudy outer region of the atmosphere, where temperature was moderate; farther down it would be too hot, like our Jupiter today. And just like on ours, creatures could float with the aid of hot hydrogen."

"But how could it get started without carbon?" Fitzpatrick asked.

"I think the secret is germanium."

"Germanium? Like the frozen fish of Pluto?"

"Yes, germanium, like they use to make transistors. Germanium and silicon used to be popular for transistors because they had four electrons in the outer shells, making them neither metals nor nonmetals. That, more or less, is why they were semiconductors."

"What does all that have to do with life?"

"Carbon is just like germanium and silicon in that respect. It has the same four outer electrons, and it loves to form compounds with other things, and to interact with other carbon atoms. It's just that the germanium and silicon like to make nice, neat crystal lattices into which impurities can be introduced to create the exotic properties of semiconductor devices."

"But germanium is rare," said the Jesuit.

"Not in this universe. When I looked at the spectrum of the planet, I found that instead of the hydrogen, helium, ammonia, and methane of our familiar Jupiter, there was hydrogen, helium, ammonia, and germane."

"Germane?"

"I had to look it up myself. It is the germanium analog of methane. Where methane is CH_4, germane is GeH_4. Germanium plays the role of carbon. And the same kind of cosmic accident of fundamental constants that led to the enormous overproduction of carbon in our universe led to a tremendous production of germanium in this one. The spectrum is full of germane, and some of the higher compounds derived from it, such as digermane, trigermane, and so forth."

"Why are there rings around Jupiter and not Saturn?" Fitzpatrick asked. "I would have expected that if the Sun evaporated Saturn's rings, it should have done the same to Jupiter. After all, it's closer."

"The answer, I think, lies in the absence of the three big moons of Jupiter," said Tariq.

"So there's a mystery story," said Fairouz. "The Case of the Missing Moon. We need a private eye."

Tariq ignored her. "Around our Jupiter, the four large moons are mixtures of rock and ice. The outermost two, Ganymede and Callisto, are mainly ice, so here the Sun has evaporated them away. Europa, the next one in, is the one we see here. Much of it is evaporated away, but the rocky core is left. I wish we could visit it. I always wondered what lay underneath its surface. Anyway, the closest of all is Io, which got too close to Jupiter in this universe, and was fragmented by the gravitational field. *That* is the ring we see around Jupiter. And because it is rock and dust, it has not evaporated away like the icy rings of Saturn."

"But this Jupiter's much smaller than ours. What would cause Io to come so close as to pass into the Roche limit and break up?"

"This has to be where the plot thickens," said Fairouz.

"This Jupiter must have started out a gas giant just like ours, three hundred times as massive as the Earth and eleven times the diameter, but the heating from the Sun gradually evaporated most of it. Most of our Jupiter, after all, is just hydrogen and helium. It was the massive out flow of all its gas that created a drag on Io and brought it in closer and closer, until the gravitational field broke it up," Tariq said.

"I think this also explains how the life-forms evolved. Just as in our universe, this Jupiter evolved primitive creatures floating and flying and swimming in the upper atmosphere, where it was cool. The hot temperatures below the clouds did not allow complex molecules to associate, initially. Of course, this Jupiter did not have much carbon available, so germanium took its place, no doubt assisted by the different laws of chemistry allowed by the changes in the constants here. Germanium evidently formed more complicated compounds than it could in ours."

"But germanium is so heavy!" said Fitzpatrick.

"Yes, the creatures must have evolved light structures

with bubbles and sources of hot hydrogen to keep them buoyant, that were largely noncarbon and nongermanium. But as the atmosphere evaporated, they sank lower and lower, and the planet cooled off—"

"How could it have cooled off when the Sun is getting hotter?" Ollerenshaw asked.

"That's because Jupiter's heat basically has nothing to do with the Sun," said Fitzpatrick. "The reason Jupiter's so hot inside—far more than boiling hot—is that it's still contracting from the time billions of years ago when it first formed. If Jupiter were a lot smaller, it wouldn't have this heat."

"Precisely," said Tariq. "So as the atmosphere evaporated, these primitive creatures sank lower and lower. Eventually, the planet cooled and a liquid ocean formed. They still have enormous quantities of ammonia, just as in our Jupiter, and ammonia is enormously soluble in water, so the oceans that these creatures eventually met contained ammonium hydroxide, which is very powerful chemically. This enabled the primitive life-forms that had gotten started in the upper atmosphere to evolve into ever more complex creatures, just like in our oceans. And this, I would be willing to bet, is the story of how those creatures—" he pointed at the TV screen "—came into existence."

"An improbable story," said the Jesuit. "But it's hard to think of a better explanation, given that we see the reality staring at us on the TV screen."

"Why don't we just ask them?" Fairouz said.

"How?" Tariq asked. "In the time remaining, we'll never have a chance to establish two-way communication over these distances."

"No problem," said Fairouz, staring at her infrared monitor. "They've sent someone out to visit us."

All eyes focused on the bright red dot whose velocity vector was pointed at the *Ulug Beg*.

CHAPTER 39

They watched the distance numbers rapidly decrease a
the blip got closer.

"It ought to be possible to resolve it with the tele
scope," said Fairouz, issuing commands to the computer

On the main screen, the vessel was reddish in the ligh
of the Sun. It was hard to tell much about it because th
tail, flaring brightly, pointed toward them. At maximum
magnification, they could see purple grid lines crisscros:
ing the rear in starlike patterns in an engine design non
had ever seen before.

"Why are they moving backwards?" the chief asked

"They're decelerating," replied Fairouz. "At six hun
dred gees, no less!"

Fitzpatrick whistled and Tariq said, "Such decelera
tions are no problem for creatures who live in water."

"If they're decelerating like that," said Fairouz, "i
means they were *ac*celerating like bats out of Pluto to ge
here."

Tariq studied the numbers on the screen and saic
"They're about four light-minutes from here, so we stil
have an hour before they arrive. But that is close enoug
so we could communicate.

He floated over to the egg and said, "How are we de
ing?"

"Great! I've really got a handle on the lingo now."

"Thank God!" Arnaldo said. "Now I understand what n watching."

"Excellent," Tariq said to the egg. "Do you think you e up to sending out a hello to them?"

"No sweat!" said the egg.

"The question is," said Fairouz, "do we really want to nounce ourselves?"

"I think it's too late to worry about that," Arnaldo id, looking at a data screen. "We're getting a signal from em." He hit a switch and the TV screen showed one of e jellyfishlike creatures in a cramped room. A slow, rie voice came over the loudspeaker.

The blue "face" of the speaker floated on the screen, its imson fringes swaying as if the entire vessel was filled ith water. Its deep, groaning voice made the very walls brate.

"What's he saying?" Ollerenshaw asked the egg.

"You have to understand, I'm not yet absolutely fluent. don't have access to their encyclopedia the way I did ith you guys, and I have to make a lot of assumptions."

"We understand you're not perfect," said the chief. ust get to the point."

The egg remained silent.

"What's the matter?" Ollerenshaw asked. "Speak up."

"Actually, I am perfect—that is, perfect for what I was signed."

"Okay, so you're perfect," said Ollerenshaw. "Just give a lousy translation."

"I'm sensitive to body language, and the right-brain flections of voices, too," said the egg. "I know that you ere not sincere when you said that I was perfect. That is ite rude."

The chief gritted her teeth, took several deep breaths d exhaled slowly, and said, "I apologize, Sir Egg."

"Was that sarcasm?" the egg asked.

"No, Sir Egg, that was an honorific. I am dazzled by ur talent. I am amazed by your splendor. I think that u are the greatest egg in this or any other universe. d I apologize humbly if I have offended you. But inas- uch as our lives may depend on it, including your own, n we just get on with the goddam translation?"

"Okay," said the egg. "I accept your apology. The guy

is more or less what you would call the captain of th
vessel. He says he wishes to give you a greeting from h
planet, which you could not pronounce so I will just ca
Jupiter."

"What a relief," Ollerenshaw said. "Civilized behavio
for a change." She relaxed noticeably.

The egg continued, "He says—and I use the word
loosely because these are hermaphroditic creatures—h
says that we are the first visitors to his civilization that h
has ever encountered. He is honored to see us and com
as an official emissary to welcome us to his planet. H
asks from which star you have come."

"Sounds pretty good," Fitzpatrick said. The oth
members of the crew nodded.

"It certainly is a refreshing change," Tariq said.

"Maybe we should even consider making this un
verse our home," said Fitzpatrick.

"I suppose we could do worse," Ollerenshaw said. "W
nearly did a few times."

"All right," Ollerenshaw said. "Egg, broadcast th
back to him." The Italian adjusted the microphone f
the egg and selected the frequency for the transmitt
Then he gave the okay signal to the chief.

"We are citizens of the planet Earth." She paused an
the egg's deep-throated translation filled the deck. "W
come to visit you in peace and mutual respect. We a
honored that you have sent a delegation to visit us, an
we look forward to meeting you. I, Sybil Ollerensha
official representative of the planet Earth and leader
this expedition, am privileged to meet you. I, Sybil Olle
enshaw, look forward to a long and happy future of m
tual assistance and edification, and regard this as
historic moment in the first step toward establishing pe
manent trade and diplomatic relations between the go
ernment of Eurafrica of the planet Earth and your nob
and estimable civilization."

Fairouz muttered, "I can sure see why they made h
an administrator."

Ollerenshaw continued. "We are rolling out the w
come mat for you—figuratively, of course. This is som
thing we do on our planet for honored guests, and not
hope, something that would offend you, because if
would, we wouldn't do it, and we don't really have

elcome mat. But we welcome you happily to our
osoms, which come to think of, is an anatomical refer-
ace you probably can't appreciate, but anyway, I, Sybil
llerenshaw, will be delighted to be the first representa-
ve in the entire history of the human species to greet
ou when you arrive at our ship. That's all for now."

Fairouz gave the throat-cutting sign to Arnaldo, and
e shut off the transmitter. "And I, Fairouz Halabi," she
id, "am deliriously happy I never went into diplomatic
rvice." She gave Ollerenshaw a dirty look and the two
ientists grimaced.

"Well, what does he say?" Ollerenshaw asked.

"It's going to take several minutes for your speech to
t there," explained the Jesuit, "and then several min-
tes for the reply to get back here."

They passed the minutes speculating about the civili-
ation. Then the reply came.

The blue creature appeared on the screen and began to
eak.

The egg translated: "I am so deliriously excited to be
resent at an exquisitely historical moment such as this
at I embrace your tentacles, if that is not offensive to
ou. I am amazed that you have picked up our method of
eech so quickly, indicating beings of exceptional intelli-
nce—"

The egg paused. "That was 'exceptional intelligence,'
case you didn't hear it clearly," it repeated.

"—and worthy of enmeshing with," continued the
g. "Our minds swim forward in eager anticipation of
r meeting. We would be most indebted to you if you
uld transmit to us visual data about yourselves that
ould help us to understand you and your language, and
e shall do likewise. I would suggest broadcasting basic
athematics, chemistry, and physics."

The egg paused and said, "I'm guessing at those techni-
l words. They haven't occurred precisely in the broad-
sts I've monitored, but components of those words
ave, and that's my best guess."

The creature continued, "We look forward to replen-
hing any substances you may be in need of. I eagerly
ticipate your next reply."

"How could they build spaceships without fire?" Fitz-
atrick asked.

"How do you know they don't have fire?" Fairo⟨z⟩
asked.

"Because they live underwater," Fitzpatrick said.

"Maybe they have ways of processing materials th⟨at⟩
don't require fire," Fairouz said.

"That is very possible," Tariq said. "There are chem⟨i⟩
cals that generate great amounts of heat through exoth⟨er⟩
mic reactions, and electricity that can provide arcs, a⟨nd⟩
gases used by builders of underwater cities."

"If I may be so bold as to interrupt," said the eg⟨g⟩
"Being unencumbered by as many theories as you, a⟨re⟩
burdened only by the facts, I should remark that I'⟨ve⟩
seen a TV program in which they showed one of the⟨ir⟩
laboratories on a beach. They wear special suits that co⟨n⟩
tain their liquid so they can crawl up on the beach a⟨nd⟩
conduct experiments in the atmosphere. In fact, th⟨ey⟩
have whole factories on the shore, in which entire floo⟨rs⟩
and corridors are filled with water for the workers, wh⟨ile⟩
special handles are operated by them that allow them ⟨to⟩
work and manipulate tools in the air."

"I've never seen so many people who could argue ⟨so⟩
endlessly about trivia," Ollerenshaw said. "What matte⟨rs⟩
is that they built them and they are here, just waiting f⟨or⟩
us to establish contact. Let's send the bloody informati⟨on⟩
they want and make the best possible first impression⟨.⟩"

"Wait a minute," said Fairouz. "You don't seriously i⟨n⟩
tend to send them everything about us, when we st⟨ill⟩
don't know about them? How do we know that they⟨'re⟩
really well-intentioned?"

"All my instincts tell me that they're creatures of go⟨od⟩
will," Fitzpatrick said. "It's our job to pass along the gre⟨at⟩
est of human culture to them, to bring enlightenme⟨nt⟩
into their lives."

"How do you know they're not already enlightened⟨?⟩"
Fairouz asked.

"I used to be very trusting," Tariq said, looking ⟨at⟩
Fairouz out of the corner of his eyes. "But I have learn⟨ed⟩
to be suspicious. Let us be cautious here. No need to jum⟨p⟩
into this too fast."

The chief's initial exuberance subsided a bit and s⟨he⟩
said, "Maybe you're right. Let's just send them some mi⟨n⟩
imal information to keep them happy, then we can pl⟨ay⟩
it by ear."

"We could send them the kind of stuff that used to be nt in the last century, when people were first thinking out communicating with other civilizations," said riq.

"What sort of things did they send?" Ollerenshaw ked.

"Pictures of life on Earth, and maps of the solar system the galaxy. Once they transmitted a signal from the ecibo radio telescope with a plot of the abundant ele- nts in our bodies and a crude picture of DNA."

"That sounds innocuous enough," Ollerenshaw said. et's do that. You take care of it, Tariq, okay?"

He glanced around and did not find any expressions of jection, so he floated over to the egg and murmured a ries of descriptions to be translated, accessing the data- se for a few select pictures of the planet Earth and its ochemical molecules.

In a few minutes the reply came back, "We thank you your information."

The creature now looked pale. Its dark blue had rned light and it seemed to vibrate more than it had fore. "We were extremely interested to discover that ur chemistry is so different from ours," he said. "We uld like to confirm that your bodies are primarily ade of water and the sixth atom, the one with six arged particles and six uncharged particles in its cen- ', and six much lighter charged particles circling und the center."

"What's he referring to?" Fairouz asked.

"Carbon," said the Jesuit.

There followed a series of graphics showing the peri- ic table of the chemical elements, and a series of what med to be diagrams of molecules of very complex and familiar forms, plus some stills of underwater scenes Jupiter: a cavern, seven-finned fish, and what looked e an underwater cathedral.

"There you have quid pro quo at its best," Ollerenshaw d. "A little from us and a little from them. We both nefit."

The exchanges continued as the ships came closer, and e intervals between incoming and outgoing messages ortened rapidly.

Then, at last, they could see the alien vessel without

magnification. As it pulled alongside they got their fi
clear view of it. It was reddish in the light of the St
long, thin, and fluted, with parallel grooves running fro
the nose. Dozens of cockpits sprouted like blisters over
fishlike shape. Thin longitudinal fins added to its mari
appearance.

The chief looked more excited and happy than s
had since the beginning of the voyage. "God, I'm rea
looking forward to this," she said. "This is what I w
born for—to build bridges between species. This is goi
to look fantastic in my autobiography."

"Look at this!" exclaimed Arnaldo. He switched 1
signal onto a data monitor screen.

A TV show appeared. "This is another of their broa
casts," he said.

"You mean you have been watching television wh
all this has been going on?" Tariq asked.

"I was bored by all the diplomacy," Arnaldo said.
haven't had any decent TV in so many universes
couldn't resist."

Tariq shook his head unbelievingly.

They watched his TV replay. Three of the alien cr
tures floated in an enormous hemispherical stadi
while thousands of creatures on the ceiling looked
Suddenly, long, cylindrical, green fishlike objects, m
like pipes than familiar fish, darted in. They bit pie
out of the three aliens in the center.

As the humans watched with churning stomachs, t
pipe creatures tore their writhing aliens into pieces as t
audience roared like a pipe organ stuck on its low
notes.

"My God!" said Fitzpatrick. "This is like ancie
Rome."

"What kind of show is this?" Fairouz asked. "May
these are terrible criminals being executed."

"It is an entertainment show for children," said 1
egg.

"Are they being persecuted for some religion?" Fi
patrick asked.

"They were adults selected at random from the au
ence," said the egg. "Kind of the opposite of a quiz sho
They watched silently as the pipe creatures finish

ting the small, bleeding scraps while cheers continued
emanate from the audience.

Then three little creatures—miniature versions of the
ults—were brought in and a herd of tiny chartreuse
eatures like vivid piranha attacked them, to roars from
e crowd.

"Those are kids from the audience," said the egg.

"What really bothers me is their money," said
rnaldo.

"Money?" Ollerenshaw asked.

"Yes. Do you know what their currency is based on?"
paused dramatically. "It's the most valuable substance
Jupiter. Carbon!"

Ollerenshaw blanched.

"I thought it was funny until a moment ago," said the
lian. "Then I suddenly realized, that's what we're
ade of, isn't it?"

"It sure as hell is," Fairouz said.

"To these fellows," said Tariq, "we must be walking
ld mines!"

They looked at the main screen. The alien vessel was
oving slowly closer.

Fairouz stabbed the red button on the main control
nel and an alarm sounded. "Now hear this! This is not
drill! Glue yourselves in and prepare for immediate
gh-gee acceleration!"

She followed her own advice. In a few seconds, while
e captain of the other vessel said, "Prepare to mate,
acious beings of another star."

"I hope he doesn't mean that literally," muttered the
ief.

Fairouz hit the main engines, and nothing happened.
board the ship, only the whirring of ventilation fans
hoed down the corridors.

"Sabotage!" she cried. Tariq's eyes locked with hers. He
d not say a word, but his eyes narrowed and his every
ature spelled anger.

CHAPTER 40

"Engine room!" Fairouz shouted into the intercom. Wit
out waiting for a reply she said, "Major malfunctio
Zero power on the MEs. Check it out on the double!" S
frantically began to run computer diagnostics.

On the main screen, the massive alien vessel float
barely fifty meters away. Space-suited creatures li
shriveled beach balls began to emerge from an airlo
amidships.

"Those are like the suits they use for exploring t
shores of their world," said the egg.

With a glance at Tariq, Fairouz called up the maint
nance data base, and studied the telemetry from the d
ferent parts of the spaceship.

The alien captain's face appeared on the screen ar
his voice boomed out. The egg translated: "Creatures
the planet Earth, we are now prepared to meet."

"Now hear this," Fairouz said on the intercom. "Ever
body suit up and prepare for hostilities. All armed p
sonnel check their weapons. Prepare to repel attack." S
gestured to Arnaldo and the egg. The Italian turned t
transmitter on and she said, "It is our tradition to me
halfway between two vessels." The egg translated.

"Your thoughts congeal appealingly," replied the alie
"We shall flow to the bisecting point."

They put pressure suits on rapidly—something they ere becoming expert at.

"Perhaps we are being too suspicious," said Fitzpat- ck.

"Suspicious!" said Fairouz to the priest. "Hell, it's like e're made out of diamond!"

"We'd better do something," Tariq said, "or they'll get spicious."

"Yes," said the chief. "We need a volunteer to go down d meet them."

"I thought that 'I, Sybil Ollerenshaw' was going to be ir great interuniversal ambassador," Fairouz said bit- gly.

"Circumstances demand flexibility. That's why *I'm* a ader and you're a spaceship driver," Ollerenshaw said.

"Hell!" said Tariq. "*I* know who is going to volunteer."

"*You* can't go," Ollerenshaw said. "You're too valu- le."

"Of course I am not going," Tariq said. "There is no ed. Our volunteer is going to be Mr. Debonair himself, e high-powered diplomat, your silicon paramour. here the hell is he?"

"*Sly?*" Ollerenshaw said with horror. "You're not going take my one consolation away from me—the one pre- ous thing from the home universe I'll never see again?"

"Damn right I am." said Tariq. "Either he goes, or you ."

"Oh, *Sly?*" said the chief sweetly toward her deck bin.

The door opened with a faint swish, and a voice bel- wed out, "Yo!"

"Bring your peashooter," Tariq said.

"*Aw right!*" said Sly. In a moment he floated back, his cious matte-black laserrifle at a military "present arms" nce.

"We have an assignment for you," Tariq said. "It is not ely that you are going to come back alive from it."

"My dream has come true!" Sly said happily.

"You don't mind being killed?" the Jesuit asked.

"Hey, no big deal."

"You have no regrets?" Fitzpatrick asked.

"Only one."

"What is that?"

"That I never got to play Hamlet."

"Hamlet?"

"Sure, it was always my greatest dream—next to com bat, that is. My own interpretation. No wimpy stuff for me!" He recited in a booming mixture of British and New York City accents: " 'To be, or not to be: that's the godda question! Whether 'tis nobler in the mind to suffer th slings an' arrows of outrageous fortune, or to take arm against a sea of troubles, and by opposin', blow tho suckers away!' "

Around the corner the cat howled, "Mouse ale Mouse alert!"

"Damn," said Ollerenshaw. "Schwartzy must have got ten out when Sly opened the door."

On the intercom, Fairouz ordered the armed personn to surround the airlock.

Sly and Tariq, with the egg under his arm, descend through the shaft to the hangar deck personnel airlo amidships. A dozen men and women surrounded armed with firearms, torches, and tools. Others peep out from hatches, aiming their weapons at the lock.

Tariq and Sly flew over to the airlock, grabbed ha dles, and stared through the portholes next to it. Tar held the egg to the window.

A dozen of the creatures floated near the other sh now, around a large, transparent sphere containing o of their kind.

"That's their captain in the bubble," said the egg.

"Okay," Tariq said to Sly, who was looking over h shoulder. "Do you really understand? This means certa death."

"I love it!" said Sly, waving his rifle.

"Do not act hostile," Tariq said. "Pretend you do n know that they are planning to rip your guts out. Play f time. We need as much as we can get."

"Gotcha! I always wanted to go out in a blaze of glo I also wanted to go out shooting like mad, with my bo riddled by laser beams!"

"Really?" Tariq said, taken aback.

"Hey, even robots got dreams!"

Tariq patted him on the back and then looked at h own hand with distaste. "You are sweating," he sa with disbelief.

"I always sweat. The chief loves it. She turned up my sweat function the day I arrived on Pluto."

Tariq muttered a small prayer and opened the hatch. "We will use the airlock intercom, and the egg will translate for you, but he will stay in here with me. We have to suit you up so they do not know that you are a robot."

Two of the crew hustled up the largest pressure suit in stock and helped Sly get in it. Tariq covered the rifle with a sheet of black plastex. "That's so they will not know that it is a weapon." He fastened a tiny camera to the helmet.

The robot slipped into the airlock, wrapped rifle in hand.

"Have a good suicide," said Tariq.

"Thanks, buddy. You've been a real pal. Tell Mom I went out like a man."

Tariq slammed the hatch closed, and pressed the lock button. "Who is your mother?" he asked through the intercom.

"Daneel Murakami. He's the one who designed me at Sony."

"He?"

"He was like a mother to me."

"If I ever get back to Earth, I will send him a message."

"Thanks, pal. You're an okay guy for an A-rab."

"Thanks, I think. Remember, be diplomatic," said Tariq.

"Aaay!" said Sly. "I'm a born diplomat." He held his rifle close to his chest and faced the creature.

"Open the outer hatch," Tariq said.

"Roger!" The robot pushed the red key and the outer hatch opened.

Sly floated over to the halfway point, where two dozen of the creatures now congregated in a half shell around their captain's bubble, looking like a pearl in an oyster.

The deep voice of the alien captain boomed through the intercom, piped down from the flight deck. Tariq held the egg next to the mike as it translated.

"Greetings, great ambassador from another star," said the creature. "You have transformed yourself noticeably. You do not look like you do on television, although we

find your new appearance to be pleasing to the photo
detector." The creature quivered.

"Aaay!" said Sly over the radio. "These dustsucke
think I'm the chief!"

Tariq whispered to the egg, "Translate everything I
says into exquisitely polite diplomatic speech."

The egg reverberated with the deep sounds of the cre
ture. "What did you say?" Tariq whispered to the egg.

"I'm flattered by your pleasure in my appearance."

On monitors, the crew of the *Ulug Beg* watched th
closeups broadcast by Sly's helmet camera. The alien ca
tain floated in liquid in his sphere, its blue color less a
parent in the red light from the Sun. It vibrated rapid
as Sly got closer, and little wavelets ran up and down i
frills. They could see a tiny network of veins pulsatir
throughout the gelatinous mass of the organ that seeme
to be its head. Occasionally, one of its tentacles wou
drift in front of the bubble, as if trying to clean a spot
dirt off.

The creature boomed again in his deep voice, "What
that instrument you carry in your fine tentacles?"

Sly grunted, clasped the wrapped rifle to his che
and said, "Wouldn't you like to know, my fine bowl
Jell-O?"

The egg replied, "It is a symbolic instrument of pea
and goodwill, traditionally carried when beings from d
ferent gene pools meet on my planet."

The creatures formed a hemisphere around Sly ar
their captain, the open side facing the *Ulug Beg*. From th
exterior camera, it looked as if a great blue dandelion ha
formed in space around Sly. From Sly's helmet camera
point of view, it looked as if space had turned into
simmering, dark hood, through which only the Su
could be seen shining with the red glow from the bodi
of the creatures. They had tiny lights emerging from th
rims of their helmets that shined into the robot's eye
The camera automatically adjusted, and showed th
many of them held orange dumbbells in their tentacl
aimed at Sly.

"We would be honored," said the leader of the cre
tures, "if you would squirt into our vessel."

"Uh, can't we just hang out around here and, yo
know, shoot the breeze a while?" Sly asked.

"I am honored by your invitation," translated the egg,
ut I must inform you that we have a tradition of pro-
nged discussion before we enter another person's dwell-
g."

A dozen of the creatures jetted toward the *Ulug Beg*.
a magnification, they too were carrying orange dumb-
lls half a meter long.

Tariq said to the egg, "Ask him what those orange
jects they are carrying are."

"Those are symbols of our friendship toward you,"
me back the reply. "It is a tradition in our culture."

"Play for time!" Tariq said on Sly's channel.

"Uh, seen any good movies lately?" Sly asked.

"What means of intellectual stimulation are popular
your culture?" translated the egg.

"We have many means of stimulation," came the re-
y. "One of my personal favorites is singing philosophi-
l songs."

There was a long silence. "Say something," Tariq said
Sly. "Anything!"

"I was never much good on first dates," he replied.
Mostly I just flexed my muscles."

"I am endlessly fascinated by your civilization," trans-
ed the egg. "It is my greatest desire in the universe to
sit your home world—a world of exquisite beauty, cable of producing the finest of intelligent species."

"I admire your intellect and perception," replied the
en captain.

"Damn!" muttered Tariq. "Where is Fairouz?" The
zen approaching creatures in the vanguard reached
e hull with a series of muted thumps. The humans
atched them on the video screens.

"Tell him," Tariq said to the egg, "that we consider it
de to land on our vessel before a formal invitation has
en extended." The egg translated straightforwardly.

"We consider it rude," came the reply, "not to allow
sitors to inspect one's vessel. You are, of course, invited
visit ours."

"Said the spider to the fly," muttered Tariq. Quickly,
added, "Don't translate that!"

On the central screen, the hemisphere of creatures
ound Sly turned pale and began to vibrate visibly. On

the side screens, the creatures placed their dumbbells
one end touched the hull.

"Dammit!" said Tariq. "What are they doing?"

Suddenly, there was a loud vibration throughout t
ship, and the hull began humming. On the screen, dum
bells glowed bright white, and so did the hull where t
instruments touched.

"Dammit," said Tariq. "They are cutting into the hul

Fairouz burst from the shaft and shouted, "We got i
Into the intercom, she shouted, "Now hear this. Strap
Emergency acceleration. We're movin' outta here!" S
pushed the alarm key.

The humans threw themselves into seats and strapp
in.

"Sly," said Tariq. "This is it—fire at will!"

"Eat my photons, you mothercrunchers!" shouted t
robot.

On the center screen they could see his photon ri
glow as it sliced through half a dozen creatures.

Then he aimed at the bubble and ran the bea
through it. It exploded. Fluid boiled out into space. T
leader was split in two, its halves writhing in vacuun

Three of the other creatures fired violet beams at S
who rocketed to one side and shot two of them. The thi
got in a bull's-eye right in the power pack, and Sly e
ploded. Parts of him punctured four of the creatures li
buckshot.

With everyone strapped in, Fairouz jabbed the ig
tion key and the main engines fired. The ship began
move slowly, but quickly gained both speed and accele
tion, pressing them into their seats. On the side scree
they watched the creatures slip off as acceleration pull
them away, like insects off the side of a maglev car.

"Poor Sly," Ollerenshaw said. "But thank God tha
over!"

"What's over?" Fairouz asked. "It's only just begu
Those suckers have hundreds of times the acceleration
this ship."

"Oh," Ollerenshaw said, shrinking back into her cha
"Wonderful."

"We're up to two and a half gees," Fairouz said. "Tha
already exceeding specs. We can't maintain this witho
falling apart."

On the central screen, they watched the other vessel as its engine glowed and it began moving toward them.

"Wait a minute," Tariq said. "We can do better than that. Planck's constant is bigger in this universe—the binding energies of the molecules are greater!"

"No moondust?" said Fairouz. "How fast can I go?"

Tariq spoke quick commands into his computer, while the alien vessel began to grow larger on the screen. "It is not much," said Tariq. "We can squeeze another half gee out of this ship—perhaps a whole gee, if you want to push the envelope."

"Three and a half gees it is," Fairouz said. She squeezed the thruster and the crew was crushed back even farther into their seats.

The other ship grew larger on the screen.

"They're still gaining on us," Fairouz said. "Dammit! We've exceeded Ronin's escape velocity. We're going to be trapped in this universe with them."

Tariq frantically beat out a rhythm on the armrest of his seat. Then he called up the mathematical model of the universe shifts. "Just seven minutes left until the next shift."

"Oh, hell!" said Fairouz.

"But there's a way out," said Tariq. "Perhaps. It will require perfect timing."

"I've got nothing better to do with my time," Fairouz said.

"Keep your acceleration steady," he said. "We've got to play for time. Six minutes from now, we have to be just a hair below escape velocity. Understand?"

"Roger. I've got a few tricks up my sleeve."

They watched the alien vessel get larger until suddenly, its main thrusters stopped.

"They've given up," Ollerenshaw said.

"No way," said Fairouz. "It's just that they accelerated so fast, they'd overtake us if they continued at that rate. They wouldn't be able to slow down quickly enough to match velocities with us. So they just calculated what our position is going to be, knowing our acceleration, and figured out what speed they should be traveling so they'll overtake us at precisely the moment when our velocities are the same."

The other ship continued to gain on them, while Ronin receded disturbingly into the distance.

The ship came closer and closer, until finally it was abreast. Its main engines fired again. "They're just matching accelerations with us now," said Fairouz. "Let's see how they like this one." She killed the engines.

Their stomachs almost heaved into their throats, and the alien vessel shot past. "Eat my moondust, you suckers!" Fairouz shouted happily.

She hit the main thrusters and the ship rotated 180 sickening degrees, while the chief enjoyed the convenience of her barf bag.

Again Fairouz hit the main thrusters and the ship began accelerating at three and a half gees, though Ronin continued to get smaller.

On one screen, they watched Ronin shrink, while on the other, the alien ship became satisfyingly smaller.

"What's happening?" Ollerenshaw asked. "Why are we still heading away from Ronin?"

"Because you don't do U-turns in space," Fairouz said without glancing away from the controls.

"We still have escape velocity from Ronin. We've built up a huge amount of momentum," Fitzpatrick explained, "and now we have to kill it before we start heading back toward Ronin."

On the main screen, they saw the other vessel flip and fire its engines again.

"They're coming back," Ollerenshaw said as the other vessel began to grow larger again on the screen.

While everyone else's eyes were glued to the main screen, Fairouz's and Tariq's focused on the velocity figures in the Ronin-centered coordinate system.

Slowly, the speed decreased toward the escape velocity, which varied from moment to moment as they continued to move away from Ronin.

"You've got to fine-tune it as close as possible," said Tariq. "Not one centimeter per second more!"

Fairouz nodded.

On the main screen, the other vessel grew larger and larger. Its engines shut off, and it continued to coast while closing the distance.

"They're not going to let us get away with that trick again," Fairouz said.

The other vessel pulled astern of them, moving just a bit faster and then closing the distance.

They fell just a hair under escape velocity, and the universe-shift clock ticked down.

The alien vessel grew closer and closer, the alarm sounded, and the computer announced, "Universe change alert."

They felt the familiar queasiness in their stomachs, and the chief grabbed her barf bag again. On the main screen, the other vessel vanished, replaced by stars.

CHAPTER 41

"We did it!" Fairouz shouted. She turned on the intercom.
"Now hear this! We're safe! At least, safe from the last
universe. Allah only knows what we've got in this one,
but half a brain is better than none."

Cheering echoed through the ship.

The chief sighed and threw her bag into a receptacle,
her face betraying a sadness not shared by the others.
"What the hell happened?"

Fairouz leapt out of her seat, flew over to Tariq, and
hugged him. He joyously hugged her back.

"The creatures were trying to overtake us, so they
were moving just a little bit faster than escape velocity.
And now they're back in their universe, wondering what
the hell happened to the massive treasure of carbon that
was just in front of their eyes—not to mention the planet
that disappeared."

As the adrenaline died away, Tariq pulled away from
Fairouz.

"I'd love to see the expression on their faces!" Arnaldo
said.

Ollerenshaw began to cry.

"What's the matter?" Arnaldo asked, floating over to
her and patting her on the back.

"Poor Sly! I shall miss him so."

"Well," said Fitzpatrick, "at least he went out heroically, like a man. If any robot deserved a place in heaven, it's our Sly. I don't know if Allah gave him a soul, but if he did, I'm sure he's up there in robot heaven, munching on silicon chips, and drinking all the juice he wants from the nearest socket."

Arnaldo held Ollerenshaw's hand and said, "You know, until now, I thought you were a coldhearted woman, but I can see there's a real lady in there." He patted her hand and she smiled weakly.

Tariq and Fairouz returned to their seats, a welter of conflicting emotions raking across their faces.

"What was the sabotage this time?" Tariq asked thoughtfully.

"Someone destroyed part of the metamatter electromagnetic fuel system electronics," replied Fairouz.

Outside, the Sun was twice again as big as it had been in the previous universe, redder, and more turbulent, with dark sunspots splotching its face. The Italian returned to his console and searched furiously for signals.

"What exactly was destroyed?" Tariq asked.

Fairouz issued a command to the computer and the systems monitor displayed a colorful schematic of the wiring system of the engine. She touched the light pen to the screen and outlined several parts in red.

"What can you tell me about their components?" Tariq asked.

"I'm no expert on what's inside of them," she said. "The technicians could give you a better answer, but I think the easiest way is to just let me transfer this to your screen," she said, hitting keys. "Then you can interrogate the schematic database yourself."

The diagram appeared on his screen, and Fairouz floated over behind him.

"Just use this joystick to move the cursor around," she said, demonstrating. "When you have a question, or want more detail, press the joystick button to access hypertext, or talk into the computer microphone."

He moved the blinking cursor to the first symbol—a rectangle superimposed on a triangle. He clicked the joystick button, and the description appeared on the auxiliary screen next to the display:

50 MEGAWATT MAGNETIC FIELD MODULATOR PREAMP, KAWASAKI NO
J70983. LAST MAINTENANCE: 6 MINUTES AGO. NEXT SCHEDULED MAINTE-
NANCE: 7 MONTHS, 3 DAYS. CLICK FOR OTHER DATA: MAINTENANCE
HISTORY, SCHEMATIC, SPECS, OPERATIONAL HISTORY, DISASSEMBLY IN-
STRUCTIONS.

Tariq clicked on SPECS and poured through a long list of
temperatures, currents, voltages, and other data. "Gallium arsenide!" he muttered. "This stuff must be old."

"Yeah," said Fairouz. "A lot of the parts on the *Ulug Beg*
are recycled from other spacecraft. Budget problems, you
know."

Tariq moved the cursor to the next component, symbolized by three zigzag lines.

RECTIFIER, 30 MEGAWATT, SUPERCONDUCTOR, KAWASAKI PART NO.
D039581B.

The voice of the Kenyan sounded over the intercom:
"Planck's constant is bigger yet."

"Noted," said Tariq.

He went through the subdirectories again and paused
at the list of materials in the specs:

INDIUM ANTINOMIDE, SELENIUM, TELLURIUM.

He muttered, "Interesting." He clicked on the last component, a circle with two bars through it:

PLASMA STABILIZER, SUPERCONDUCTING, KAWASAKI PART NO.
F931201C.

He moved immediately to the specs and studied the
composition:

COPPER—YTTRIUM—GALLIUM ZERO-G ALLOY
THALLIUM—BISMUTH—DOPED—GERMANIUM
PRASEODYMIUM

"Germanium!" he whispered.

"Germanium?" said Fairouz. "That's a funny coincidence after those germaniacs."

Tariq began to tap rhythmically on the panel. The Jesuit floated over and said, "Germanium?"

"Yeah," said Fairouz. "Our saboteur destroyed three components, and one of them contains germanium."

"Weird," said the Jesuit.

"But there couldn't be any connection to our friends from Jupiter," said Fairouz. "The sabotage occurred before we encountered their universe."

"No intelligent signals," reported Arnaldo. "Just a *lot* of solar noise, plus Ronin's own radio noise."

"Undoubtedly there is some really bad magnetic turbulence on the Sun," said Tariq.

"That would produce all kinds of radio signals," said Fitzpatrick.

"So, can you rule out life completely again?" Ollerenshaw asked bitingly.

Tariq reddened, though it was hard to see on his swarthy skin. "I have given up making predictions about life," said Tariq.

"Wise move," replied Ollerenshaw.

"You have nothing to be ashamed of," said Fitzpatrick. "No human being could possibly predict all the changes in the laws of chemistry."

"Back on Earth," said Tariq, "our laws of chemistry are heavily biased toward our own experiences under conditions of temperatures and pressures we are most familiar with. Change those laws a little bit, and there is a whole new game."

"Right," said Fitzpatrick. "And nobody can guess what will happen under these circumstances."

Tariq glanced at the screen and did a calculation on his computer.

"Goddam!" said Tariq. "The Sun has now swallowed up Mercury. It is now a mature red giant."

The Jesuit looked at the blazing Sun on the screen and said, "I guess if you wanted to know what hell is, all you'd have to do is go to Mercury now."

"What will happen to the planet?" Fairouz asked. "Could it continue to exist?"

"Not for long," said Tariq. "The Sun's temperature is now over three thousand degrees kelvin, and the intensity of solar radiation is great enough to vaporize almost anything, except for tungsten, ceramics, and a couple of others. But even ordinary rock will just melt and eventually boil away in that inferno."

"Unless there are unusually refractory materials allowed by this universe," said Fitzpatrick. "Perhaps there' some rock that can withstand higher temperatures."

"True," said Tariq. "I forgot about that possibility."

They slept for a few hours until the next universe came The Sun became a red giant that enveloped at last eve: the orbit of the Earth.

They watched the Sun puff out great streams of gas a: it shedded its outer layers. A massive flow engulfed Ro nin and the *Ulug Beg* with streams of gas and dust, an only the great distance of the Sun and the thinness of th gas prevented serious damage. Planck's constant was big ger again.

No one was willing to abandon Ronin for such a ho: tile solar system.

The next universe was radically different. The Sun ha: shrunk down to a tiny white dwarf, a star with almost a much matter as it had had originally, but compresse: into a sphere about the size of the Earth they had lef Planck's constant was bigger yet.

The crew sat on the flight deck, glumly staring at th monitors. On the ceiling, the magnified view of the tin Sun haunted them.

"I wonder if we could survive in this universe," sai Fitzpatrick dejectedly.

"Do you really want to live with a white dwarf as Sun?" Tariq asked.

"Maybe things will be even worse in the next one," h replied. "They always are."

"I suppose we could harvest materials from what's lef of the outer planets and build a tiny colony around thi ship close to the Sun," said Tariq. "Our descendant might even grow to like it. White dwarfs take a long tim to cool down, and humans might recolonize the whol system a million years from now."

"Cheery prospect," said the priest.

"Do you think," said Ollerenshaw, "that the proton

proton cycle was still dominant, or is it possible that the carbon–nitrogen–oxygen cycle became the major thermonuclear reaction taking place up there?"

The others looked at her as if she had turned into an alien.

"Yes," Tariq said with puzzlement. "It is possible that the CNO cycle took over."

"I wonder," Fairouz said, "if the hydrogen burnt up more rapidly in this universe and went into the helium-burning phase quickly."

Tariq looked at her strangely.

"That would mean an increased metal production," she continued, "which should be readily detectable spectroscopically, shouldn't it?"

"How did you two get to be astrophysicists all of a sudden?" Tariq asked.

Fairouz shrugged, and the chief said, "It's just a little bit of information that popped into my mind from some half-forgotten course I took when I was a child."

Tariq and Fitzpatrick exchanged puzzled glances.

"It ought to be possible to model what's happening there," said Fairouz, "by taking a standard stellar evolution model—"

"Yes!" said Ollerenshaw. "Of course, obviously, all you have to do is plug in the new cross-section rates for the fusion reactions, and those we can deduce—"

"From the spectroscopic abundances in the outer layers," said Fairouz, "which we can easily detect."

"And then," said Ollerenshaw, "we tweak the models until we find a combination of fundamental constants that give us the observed constituents, and in this way—"

"Measure the weak interactions that we can't conveniently measure on board the spacecraft," finished Fairouz.

"Although I worry about departures from hydrostatic equilibrium," added Ollerenshaw.

"Me, too," said Fairouz, "and those sunspots—"

"Imply major magnetohydrodynamic turbulence and inhomogeneities," said Ollerenshaw. "At least in the outer regions."

Tariq's eyes lit up suddenly, followed by a similar expression of enlightenment on Fitzpatrick's face.

"Of course!" said Tariq.

"Because Planck's constant is bigger," said Arnaldo, "our mental reactions are moving faster—"

"—and we're making better interconnections between neurons than we could in our universe," finished Ollerenshaw.

Tariq's own mind was a whirl of equations and concepts and hypotheses, as years of intensive training in the depths of physics and astronomy boiled around in his skull. The interrelationships between quantum theory, relativity, field theories, thermodynamics, and many other branches swirled together and merged. Unexpected interconnections formed.

"This is amazing," said Ollerenshaw. "I've never seen so clearly before."

"I feel giddy," said Fairouz.

"I can see strategies in backgammon," said Arnaldo, "that would make me a fortune if we ever get back home."

"If there's any chance of us getting out of this—" said Fairouz.

"It's now," said Ollerenshaw.

"Before Planck's constant shrinks again," said the Italian.

Tariq called up the universe-transition model again and stared at the curve. "The intervals are getting shorter and shorter. There is going to come a time when our constants are going to be so juggled that we cannot survive. But when?"

He was greeted by silence. "Somehow, we have to move in the opposite direction of Ronin, through these parallel universes. If there were only an anti-Ronin, we could jump onto it and move in the opposite way. There must be other Ronins out there. But they cannot be very common, or we would have detected them long ago. So the odds of our coming across one now that just happens to be going in the right direction, and just happens to be close enough for us to get to, are very small. But we should start searching for it."

He spoke into the intercom to Ng'ethe, and gave instructions on surveying the sky for Roninlike objects.

He returned to his own screen, deep in thought. The crew's chatter faded out of his consciousness.

He ran his experiences backwards, like a video in re-

verse, until Ronin disappeared and Pluto emerged. Pluto!
Now he understood the strange frozen fish. Pluto was just
another Ronin, born in some other universe, wandering
until captured by Neptune's gravitational field. Its small
size and the decay of its internal radioactive heat had
doomed its ocean life to a frozen death. Pluto's orbit to
this day still crossed Neptune's, the only planets so intersecting, commemorating the tragic, chance encounter of
different universes.

He visualized Pluto and Ronin, shooting like bullets
through the leaves of an old-fashioned book, each leaf a
universe of its own. The leaves are thicker on the outside,
like the cover of a book, and thinner inside.

Ronin shoots through the leaves, taking a long time to
pass through the thick, outer ones. But the leaves become
infinitely thinner, and then God only knows what will
happen. Yet Ronin is old, so it must have been this way
before. Perhaps it goes through the place of zero-thickness and comes out into a set of universes that grow from
thin to thick. Perhaps the place of zero-thickness is the
place of attraction, so Ronin moves back and forth like a
pendulum across these zero thickness zones, traveling far
into the next set of universes, then falling back again
through the layer of no thickness and into humanity's
side of the set of universes.

It would be just like the stars that oscillate up and
down through the plane of the Milky Way galaxy. Ronin
could bob through these universes endlessly.

He pictured the data in his mind: the intervals between universes were clearly the most critical numbers,
and the digits floated in front of him effortlessly.

Suppose the universe transitions occurred at the ze-
roes of the function *sine (L/x)*, where *L* was the amplitude
of Ronin's oscillation, and *x* was the distance Ronin traveled through the universes. Assume that the planet was
moving in simple harmonic motion: $x = L \cos (2\pi t/T)$,
where *t* is time, and Ronin oscillates through the universes with a period *T*. Then all would be explained.

It's as if there were some great transuniversal force at
the center of the leaves of universes, where *x* was zero,
crushing the closest universes into infinitesimal sheets,
while the farther ones retained greater thicknesses. Perhaps Ronin originated there in the center, tossed out by

some unimaginable explosion, destined to oscillate forever through all the universes.

Ah, but how long would it take them to reach the singularity at $x=0$? He did a quick mental calculation, fitting the transition data. The answer: eight days.

In just eight more days, they would reach the point where the equation became singular, rather like a black hole, but a strangely *different* type of singularity. In eight days, the universes would come faster and faster. They would see an infinite number of universes in a finite time.

And then they would break out into the other side.

What would it be like? Would everything be antimatter? Would entropy decrease instead of increasing, so the universe became increasingly neatly ordered? Would time run backwards? Would gravity repel?

But we would all be dead by then, he thought. *The fluctuations in our constants will be too much for our jury-rigged enzymes. We've got to abandon Ronin!*

But whatever created Ronin must have created other debris, flying across the universes—dust grains, atoms, perhaps even stars from other worlds, all of different energies. Some would be moving faster than Ronin, and others slower. They would have bobbed back and forth many times, and some of them would be, right now, heading back toward his universe.

The galaxy was filled with interstellar dust—at least, *his* galaxy was—in vast quantities. It was this dust that powered the massive collectors of the *Ulug Beg*. Suppose some of that dust was moving across the universes like Ronin? It could be caught, swept up by the electromagnetic fields of the *Ulug Beg*.

His heart began to beat faster. He tried to remain calm, to keep his mind clear and focused.

If he was right, then half of the Ronin-type particles— the ronoids, as he began calling them—would be moving in the same direction as Ronin, and half in the opposite. But how could you select the right ones? How could you ensure that you captured only the ronoids moving homeward? Otherwise, they would just cancel each other out.

"Never underestimate the value of analogies," the *sensei* had said. "Analogies are the way our mind forms simplified models of the universe. They are often wrong. But some of them are inspired, and these are the ones that lead to great physics."

Analogies, thought Tariq. *What is analogous to Ronin? The problem of separating out the ronoids from the antironoids? Protons and antiprotons, electrons and positrons? They destroy each other when they come into contact, but what else distinguishes them? Opposite spins!*

But how can you tell one spin from another? With electrons and positrons, you can use magnetic fields to sort them out. Ronin has a powerful field—perhaps some of the ronoids have magnetic fields!

Tariq opened his eyes and said slowly, "I have a hypothesis."

CHAPTER 42

Tariq explained his theory. There was vigorous debate for half an hour, enveloping the entire crew in astrophysical equations when it moved to the rec deck.

Finally, Fitzpatrick summed it up. "We all agree that the theory makes sense," said the Jesuit. "So let's give it a try. It's our only hope."

"And clearly, even if it's wrong," said Fairouz, "we should get off anyway to take advantage of our increased brainpower. If his theory is wrong, at least we'll be smart enough to be able to survive here."

"That's right!" said the chief emphatically. "The next universe could turn us all into voidbrains again."

There was unanimity. The crew returned to their stations and Fairouz announced, "Prepare for escape!"

The computer counted down and she fired the engines.

Ronin drifted away for minutes, shrinking almost imperceptibly.

Their velocity increased, and the escape velocity decreased, until the two figures crossed. A moment later Fairouz shouted, "We're free!"

A few minutes later, the computer announced, "Universe change alert."

On the main screen, Ronin vanished forever, its place taken by thousands of stars.

They stared at the screen where Ronin had been. Their last connection to their home universe was severed forever.

A few halfhearted cheers went up, but no one seemed to want to celebrate. Fairouz shed a tear.

After a minute, Ollerenshaw said, "Well, at least if Tariq's brainstorm doesn't work, we'll have a nice quiet solar system in which to settle and breed."

"Breed?" Fitzpatrick chuckled.

"Certainly," replied Ollerenshaw. "It will be our duty to preserve and perpetuate the human species in this uninhabited universe."

"Sounds like fun," said Fairouz.

"It sounds like the bug queen," said Tariq.

"Of course," added Ollerenshaw, "as the leader of this new civilization, I will have to select the Adams and Eves to maximize the probability of survival."

"Like hell you will," Fairouz said lightly. "Your authority to choose Adams and Eves got left behind a few dozen universes ago."

"Let's just see what comes of Tariq's gizmos," said the chief.

Fairouz announced on the intercom, "All right, gang. Let's get to work!"

The crew feverishly hurried to perform tests and set up the equipment Tariq specified. Under his supervision, they modified the ship's dustcatcher. The crew worked together like the queen's servants.

During a week of nearly nonstop effort, every member of the crew took advantage of their newly acquired super-intelligence and conducted experiments, gathering interstellar dust with the aid of the great magnetic fields of the *Ulug Beg*'s sweeper.

At last they were ready for the main trial.

"Now hear this!" said Fairouz. "Strap in and prepare to return home."

Fairouz reoriented the ship and fired the engines, putting them on a trajectory that would gradually bring

them back to where Pluto had been in their own uni
verse.

As they moved through space, the dustcatcher field
swept up interstellar grains, separating out the ronoid
particles from the antironoids.

"Fortunately," said Tariq, "we do not have to separate
out the ordinary matter from the antironoid matter. That
will just give us an additional thrust in our current uni
verse and let us go through space faster to sweep up more
dust."

"I never did have a chance," said Fairouz, "to find ou
how you can separate out the ronoids from the antiro
noids."

"By comparing its spin and magnetic field. In Ronin
the spin of the planet was the same as the magnetic di
pole, like Earth. When Ronin bounces back from its trip
its magnetic field will be reversed, though its spin will be
the same. At least that is my theory, and it seems to be
confirmed from the small experiments we have per
formed."

"I don't feel anything," Ollerenshaw said, "other than
the usual acceleration. Isn't anything happening?"

"You have to be patient," Tariq said. "We have to build
up momentum perpendicular to this universe. It will
take a while before we have a velocity in that direction
great enough to break off from the escape velocity of the
Sun, so we are no longer tied to *its* gravitational field. We
will be able to roam free, like Ronin."

"It will take zillions of antironoid particles," said Fitz
patrick, "to give us enough transuniversal momentum."

"All I know," said the chief, "is that if this works, I'm
never going to leave Earth again until my neurons turn
to dust!"

For days they accelerated, until they had achieved sola
escape velocity and were free of the gravitational field o
the Sun. By then, they had accumulated large quantitie
of interstellar antironoids in their tanks.

"What happens to those antironoids when they sit in
our tanks?" Fairouz asked.

"They become just ordinary matter, as far as we are
concerned," said Tariq. "Their momentum is imparted to

ur ship, like a billiard ball imparts momentum when it
its another billiard ball. And if the two billiard balls are
icky, they stay together and travel with the total mo-
entum of the original ball. Bit by bit, we gain more and
ore momentum perpendicular to the universe."

Suddenly, the old familiar, queasy feeling swept over
em, accompanied by the announcement of a universe
hange.

Cheering went up in the ship. "We did it!" said
airouz.

"Or did we?" Tariq asked, looking at the screen. The
un blazed forth, a massive red sphere.

"It looks like a red giant," Tariq said, "but we have to
e sure we are going backwards, and not just in the same
irection Ronin was headed." He called up to the data
eck.

The Kenyan was glowing almost as much as the Sun.
We did it!" he exclaimed. "The spectral lines are identi-
al to the last universe we were in before the white
warf!"

Tariq smiled and gave the thumbs-up to Fairouz.

She laughed and spoke into the intercom. "Attention
ll hands. It's confirmed. We're on our way home!"

The hull vibrated from the cheering.

ay after day they traveled, accelerating in the direction
erpendicular to the universes, replaying in the sky the
uns they had visited before. One by one, they reap-
eared, shrinking and finally becoming an ordinary yel-
ow star. They passed so quickly through each universe
nat there was no danger from the hostile beings.

Arnaldo began to track where they were by the televi-
on programs of these alternate universes.

Eventually, they began to slow their transuniversal
nomentum by capturing ronoid particles and canceling
ut some of their antironoid momentum.

The intervals between universes slowed down to
ours.

Arnaldo avidly monitored the radio and television sig-
als, fine-tuning Tariq's navigation as they homed in on
neir universe. At last, Arnaldo shouted, "English! I hear
nglish!"

Fairouz threw the transmission onto the main screen. The image appeared of a police magnetocopter chasing a pink speedboat.

The scene cut to the copter pilot, a burly man in reassuringly familiar black uniform. He spoke into the microphone: "This is the police!"

The scene cut to the speedboat.

A man and a woman were in the cockpit, bouncing up and down as they rocketed through the waves. The man wore a loud floral Brazilian shirt and silver shorts with olive polka dots, the woman a lavender woven tungsten macroskirt and blouse. The man controlled the thrusters while the woman held onto a rail. The amplified officer's voice boomed down around them: "We know you've got the freak-crystals!"

"Those dust suckers!" shouted the man, swerving the thrusters to the left. The boat tilted violently. "How the hell did they know we'd be here?"

"I should never have let you talk me into this!" said the woman. They spoke with Noram accents.

The man pushed a button on the front panel and a mounted minirailgun was revealed. "Take the wheel!" he shouted. "I'll blow those magcops out of the sky!"

He reached for the trigger. The woman pulled back her fist and slugged him in the jaw. He fell to the deck and the boat bounced out of control.

"You little clone of a bitch!" He started to rise.

She kicked him in the solar plexus and he fell back, hitting his head on a fuel cell.

Blood trickled down his mouth and he groaned. She brought the boat under control, slowing the electric motor until they could cruise along safely on robopilot.

The man shook his head violently and clutched his stomach, gasping.

The woman pulled a pair of handcuffs and a badge out of her brassiere.

"You're under arrest, quarkbrain!" Her voice had dropped three octaves. She flipped him over, grabbed his hands, and slapped the cuffs on expertly.

"Oh, of course!" said the Italian. "This must be *Drag Net: Transvestite Squad*. I never watch it, but I've heard about it. I'm not crazy about cop shows."

Fairouz turned the volume down. "We're definitely ome!" she said happily.

"I never thought I'd be happy to see *Drag Net,*" said ariq. "But I now realize it is the most inspiring show in e universe—this or any other."

"Put me on Hades frequency," said Fairouz.

"Roger," said Arnaldo.

"Hello, Pluto," she said. "This is the *Ulug Beg,* calling ades station. We're back home and do we have a story tell you!"

"How far are we from Pluto?" Ollerenshaw asked, alking over to Arnaldo, thanks to the one-gee accelera- on they were now maintaining.

"Less than two hours," said the captain.

"Practically home!" replied Ollerenshaw, beaming at rnaldo as she put an arm around his shoulders.

"At last, decent TV!" Arnaldo said, beaming back at e chief.

"All we've got to do now," Fairouz said, "is get below e escape velocity of the sun, and its gravitational field ill lock us forever into our home universe!"

"Praise Allah!" said the priest.

"With this system," said Tariq dreamily, "we can ex- ore all the parallel universes we want to, whenever we ant to!"

"But not with me aboard," the chief said quickly.

"Yes," added Tariq. "We can go forward and backward, d stop at any universe we want, for as long as we ant. I would like to visit some of those alternate Earths, d find the universe that produced that kelparette ck."

The chief rumpled Arnaldo's hair, and he said, "You ow, we have a lot in common."

"Yes," Ollerenshaw replied. "Our cultural tastes are milarly sophisticated."

"Right."

"But you know," said Ollerenshaw, "most men don't for women as, uh, abundant as me."

"Ah," said Arnaldo, "but I *love* chunky-style women. n't stand females who look like laser beams."

She smiled.

"There's only one thing still bothering me," irouz said.

"The saboteur," Fitzpatrick said.

"Right," she said.

"Oh," said Tariq with forced casualness. "I solved th
days ago."

All eyes focused on him. "When Planck's constant w
big, and my mind was racing with marvelous clarity, th
answer became quite obvious. And after we had ma
the modifications to the engines, I tracked the culp
down."

"Well, who the hell is he?" Ollerenshaw asked.

"Or she?" Tariq looked playfully at Fairouz. "I'll
right back."

He went down the elevator to the lab deck and r
turned with a cubical cage, almost a meter on edge. Th
flight deck crew gathered around. It was a strange cag
with bright lights shining into it—a cage within a ca
within a cage. In the smallest cage was a black tube.

"I swore the lab crew to secrecy," he said. "I wanted
keep this for the right moment."

"What in Hades is that?" Fairouz asked.

"That," said Tariq, savoring the moment, "is our sab
teur."

He pushed the button and one face of the black cu
turned transparent. Inside was a small, chubby anim
that whined in protest at the light and shrank back fa
ther into the corner.

"That's one of those critters from Ronin!" said Fitzpa
rick.

"It certainly is," said Tariq. "The little fellow ate i
way into one of our storage compartments on the shutt
and stowed away. It has been traveling all over the Ul
Beg ever since, sticking to dark places mostly, dining o
whatever materials it was best suited to, depending o
the whim of the fundamental constants. Apparently, th
is how it has evolved—by shifting its appetite from on
substance to another, depending on the universe. That
why it was fond of germanium in the Jovian univer
and why it also ate gallium, arsenic, and seleniu
which are close to germanium in the periodic table. I b
it has put on a lot of weight munching on our ship
parts."

The chief laughed.

"So there's no saboteur after all," said Fairouz. "At
∣ast, not a human one."

"His form even changes with the constants, to take
∣dvantage of whatever the laws of physics and chemistry
∣re. I have some videos I will show you some time. Our
∣ttle friend even looks like a bird when the constants are
∣st right. The chief's cat had the answer all along. It was
'mouse,' but we did not listen to him. He kept smelling
∣ur saboteur. Oh, well."

"How in space did you capture him?" Ollerenshaw
∣sked.

"I hunted him down by building a trap, knowing that
∣e creature avoided bright lights and lived in the nooks
∣nd crannies of the vessel. And I designed a special cage
∣ith layers of different materials and lights to keep him
∣om escaping."

Over at the communication console, the egg chortled
∣appily. "I'm in heaven!" it said. "Just think! Thousands
∣f languages and Heisenberg only knows what other
∣ings to correlate!"

Fairouz's face turned serious and she stared at Tariq
∣raight in the eye. "So, what are you going to do when
∣ou get back to Pluto?" she said. "Making any important
∣lls?"

"Just one," he said, suddenly grim.

"Who to?" she asked softly.

He stared hard at her, like a sheriff in the wild West
∣ming at a desperado. He took a deep breath and said, "I
∣ave to make a vital call—to a restaurant on Hades."

"A restaurant?" she asked, wide-eyed.

He smiled. "Yes, I have heard great things about
∣uhammad Wong's Devil's Food Inn."

She laughed. "Wong's?"

"Yes," he said. "I'd like to make reservations for two.
∣are to join me?"

She glowed. "Can't think of anything better to do."

He returned to his normal seriousness. "Back when
∣y brain was functioning on overdrive," he said, "I had
∣ lot of time to think about our solar system, and the
∣indless rivalries that keep us from making it a paradise.
∣ do not want to contribute to another hundred genera-
∣ons of hatred."

He pulled a chocolate bar out of his pocket, opened
up, broke it in two, and handed a piece to her.

"It's made from an asteroid," he said. "One of you
Earth-crossing carboneous chondrites. They make th
best chocolate in this solar system."

"I know the one," said Fairouz. "I've been there. To te
the truth, I've even smuggled some of their chocolate."

"I've been saving this. It's my last one. And now w
can enjoy it."

She eagerly accepted a piece and smiled, saying, "Let
go out and paint Hades red!"

"Sounds like a good idea to me," said Tariq, smiling.

They ate silently, slowly, happily. "You know," sai
Tariq, "one day, I want to go back again through thos
universes and travel all the way to the singularity.
think that with what we now know, and an army o
specialists at home, we could concoct foolproof biochem
cals to protect us against the worst fluctuations. I want t
see an infinite number of universes! I want to see what i
on the other side!"

"I'll be your pilot," Fairouz said contentedly.

Their reverie was interrupted.

"Contact!" Arnaldo said excitedly. He put the signa
on the main screen, and Fairouz turned the volume bac
up.

"We copy you," said the face of a black man. "This i
Lowell Control, and we have someone here who wants t
talk to you."

A familiar female face replaced his on the screen. I
fact, the face was identical to Ollerenshaw's.

The flight crew glanced back and forth betwee
the real Sybil Ollerenshaw and the one on the scree
in disbelief. None was more shocked than Sybil Olle
enshaw.

The face said, "I am Enid Awlerenshim, ultimate a
ministrator for Afrikeurope on planet Lowell. I don
know what your game is, but I assure you that the rea
Ulug Beg is in orbit around Lowell at this very momen
It's being prepared for a translowellian expedition righ
now. You'd better tell us who you really are ultrapront
or you're in for megatrouble!"

Fairouz stared open-mouthed. The chief looked as

he had been punched, the Jesuit muttered a prayer, the
Italian cursed an oath, and Tariq grimaced and said,
"Oops! Sorry, wrong universe."

After a moment, the chief shrugged and said, "Good
enough for government work!"

The Attraction of Darkness
by WALLACE H. TUCKER

ne of the reasons astronomers love their work is that,
e just about everyone else, they love a good mystery.
e popular notion that science is stripping our world
ean of mysteries is an illusion. The practice of science
n be likened to the renovation of an old building with
ich and largely unknown history. One layer of paint or
allpaper is stripped away, only to reveal an older and
ore beautiful layer. What scientists do is strip away one
er of mystery or superstition, only to expose a more
ofound and mysterious layer of reality underneath. To
me this might seem to be a frustrating exercise, but to
ose who relish encounters with the unknown, it is ex-
larating. In the past decade, astronomers have become
creasingly excited and troubled as the pervasive pro-
rtions of a new mystery have become apparent. It is
e mystery of dark matter.

Simply stated, the mystery is this: Either something is
iously wrong with the theory of gravity, or most of the
atter in the universe is in some "dark" form that has so
escaped detection by telescopes of every kind—radio,
rared, optical, and x-ray. Leaving aside for the mo-
nt the possibility that the theory of gravity needs a
ajor overhaul (which is what the vast majority of astro-
ysicists are doing), this means, among other things,

that the interstellar spaces in our galaxy and all other
and possibly the spaces between galaxies, may be fill
with particles or objects that we cannot yet directly o
serve and about which we know practically nothing.

If astronomers cannot observe dark matter, how
they know it exists? What is the nature of the evidence
support its existence, and how convincing is it? Wh
could the dark matter possibly be—black holes? Brov
dwarfs? A new type of particle? A manifestation of extr
terrestrial life? What are the implications of the existen
of dark matter for our understanding of the universe? N
attempts to answer these questions in this essay shou
persuade you, if nothing else, that in removing some n
nor mysteries from our world, modern astronomy h
brought us face-to-face with a major one.

EVIDENCE FOR DARK MATTER

Appearances can be deceptive. Customs and bord
patrol officials know this. They rely on subtle clues wh
examining a vehicle suspected of carrying contraban
such as tires or springs that indicate the vehicle has
heavier load than it should. For example, what appea
to be a truckload of cabbages may in fact be a trucklo
of weapons, drugs, or even people.

In much the same way, astronomers are learning th
the appearance of the universe is deceptive. There
much more to it than the images resolved by telescop
Several lines of indirect evidence indicate that most
the matter in our galaxy is in some dark, so-far-und
tected form. There is something else in our galaxy besid
the few hundred billion stars that form the Milky Wa
the trillions of planets and quintillions of comets th
must exist if our solar system is typical, and the va
clouds of dust and gas revealed by radio, infrared, ar
x-ray telescopes: something that none of the theories f
the formation of our galaxy and the objects in it pr
dicted. Most of the galaxy is not in the form of norm
stars and gas. It is something entirely different. The sar
holds true, apparently, for every galaxy in the universe
and for intergalactic space, too. Space was once thoug

be virtually empty of matter, but many astrophysicists
ve now taken the position that *most* of the matter in
e universe—some 99 percent—is in the form of dark
atter, and that 80 percent of this dark matter is spread
roughout intergalactic space.

The evidence for these astonishing figures is tied in
ith our understanding of the influence of the force of
avity on the motion of all types of matter: stars, gases,
batomic particles. They all have mass, so they are all
fluenced by gravity. The theory that is used to figure
is is Isaac Newton's, with modifications by Albert Ein-
in that need not concern us at this point.

Newton developed his theory of gravity, so the story
es, while sitting under an apple tree, watching an ap-
e fall to the ground. Whether this actually happened or
t is unknown—Newton never confirmed the story in
s writings—but local tradition marked a tree on the
mily farm as the one from which the apple fell and in
20, when the tree died, it was cut into logs that have
en carefully preserved. It was common knowledge that
the time—the summer of 1666—Newton did spend a
of time at the farm sitting around doing nothing, ex-
pt perhaps thinking. So, it is plausible and pleasing to
agine that sometime in the summer of 1666, Isaac
wton observed that the line of fall of an apple appears
go through the center of the earth, and that this obser-
tion turned his thoughts toward the idea of a universal
w of gravitation.

An apple falls straight toward the center of the earth
der the pull of earth's gravity. In contrast, a pebble
ot from a slingshot follows a curved path, moving hori-
ntally as well as vertically, because of the velocity
en to it by the slingshot. The magnitude of this hori-
ntal velocity and the force of gravity determines how
from the shooter the pebble will land. If air resistance
uld be neglected, then a projectile fired at a sufficiently
gh velocity would travel all the way around the world.
the shooter ducked, it would continue to orbit Earth
e a little moon. This is not possible near the surface of
rth because of air resistance. It is possible a hundred or
miles above Earth, where there is no atmosphere. Al-
st three hundred years after Newton first proposed the
ea of artificial satellites, the technology was developed

for launching rockets above the atmosphere and then serting them into orbit with a second-stage rocket.

Newton's stroke of genius was to understand that t same principle explains why the Moon orbits Ear Sometime in the distant past, it acquired a large enou horizontal velocity to keep it forever in orbit. It also plains why Earth and all the other planets orbit the Su Gravity acts between every two bodies in the univer The force depends on the masses of the two bodies— larger the masses the larger the force, in direct proporti to the masses—and inversely, as the square of the c tance between the two objects. With Newton's law gravity, it is possible to calculate the mass of a planet star by studying the orbit of a satellite of the planet. Fr observations of the orbital velocity and the distance the satellite, the gravitational force, and hence the pla tary mass, can be calculated. This method has been us to calculate the mass of the Earth, the Sun, and stars double star systems. These calculations reveal some nor problems, such as the still unexplained irregularit in the orbit of Neptune, but this is a discrepancy of fraction of a percent. It is when the theory is used calculate the mass of our galaxy that a major myste appears.

Dark Matter in the Milky Way

The stars in our galaxy form a system that has rough the shape of a Frisbee, with a golf ball—representing t spherical bulge of stars in the center of the galaxy—stu in the middle. But the stars in the galaxy are not rigic joined together like the molecules in a Frisbee. They or the center of the galaxy in a swarm under the influen of gravity, so the rotation resembles more closely t swept back fluidity of a hurricane or a whirlpool than t rigidity of a Frisbee.

As the stars orbit the center of the galaxy, they bob and down, like the horses on a carousel. This bobbi motion is due to the combined gravitational force of the stars, gas, and dust in the disk of the galaxy. It can compared to a swinging pendulum, which is continua pulled back to the lowest point of its path by the grav of Earth. By measuring the motion of a pendulum, t

ravity of Earth can be determined. In the same way,
areful measurements of the motion of the stars in our
alaxy can, in principle, be used to determine the grav-
y, and hence the mass, of the galaxy.

In practice, however, astronomers seeking to measure
he gravity of the galaxy encounter formidable difficul-
es. The stars take millions of years to complete one
ving above and below the disk of the galaxy. They must
ork with what amounts to a snapshot of the motions of
aany stars at one instant. From these snapshots, they
aust attempt to reconstruct the motions of the stars over
aillions of years.

In 1932 Jan Oort, a Dutch astronomer, used this
aethod to determine the gravity of the disk of our gal-
xy. By studying the motions of stars relatively near to
ae Sun, he concluded that they were bobbing up and
own more rapidly than would be expected if the visible
ars accounted for all the matter in the disk of the gal-
xy. Oort's calculations indicated that approximately 60
ercent of all matter is in some dark form. This did not
orry him too much because he assumed that, in the
ourse of time, the extra matter would be discovered in
ae form of very faint stars or interstellar gas.

Thirty years later, Oort repeated his calculations. By
aen the data on the motions of the stars were better, and
stronomers knew much more about the number of very
aint stars and the amount of interstellar gas. But the
roblem of the dark matter remained. The mass observed
a disk of the galaxy in all forms accounted for only
ightly more than half the mass that the stellar motions
nplied should be there. Now Oort was worried, and a
w of his fellow astronomers, mindful that the careful,
onservative Oort was one of the best among them, wor-
ed along with him. But most astronomers continued to
ssume that the problem of the "missing mass," as it was
alled then, would go away as observations improved.

In 1984, John Bahcall of the Institute for Advanced
tudy in Princeton, New Jersey, updated Oort's work.
he major improvement was the use of modern com-
uters to determine the gravitational force from more
omplex, and presumably more realistic, hypothetical
istributions of gas and stars than Oort had been able to
udy. Although uncertainties remain, the result is essen-

tially the same: the amount of dark matter in the disk
our galaxy is approximately equal to the amount of no
mal matter—stars, gas, and dust. He also found that th
dark matter must be distributed in roughly the same wa
as the normal matter in our galaxy—that is, it must b
concentrated in a thin disk.

A Galactic Envelope of Dark Matter

How pervasive is the dark matter in the galaxy? Is
confined to the disk of the galaxy, or does it extend abov
and below the disk, and beyond the luminous edge
Three independent lines of evidence suggest that our ga
axy is embedded in a huge envelope of dark matter.

The first line of evidence comes from radio observ
tions. Vast clouds of hydrogen gas orbit the center of o
galaxy in much the same way as the stars. These cloud
give off radio frequency radiation at a sharply define
frequency—1420 megahertz—that is determined by th
structure of the hydrogen atom. If a cloud is moving rel
tive to Earth, this frequency will be shifted by an amou
that depends on the relative motion between the clou
and the Earth. This is an example of the Doppler effec
which highway patrolmen make effective use of to me
sure the speed of vehicles. Their radar gun sends o
waves of known frequency. These waves are reflecte
back to the patrol car by the moving vehicle. The Dop
ler shift in frequency of the reflected waves is then use
to calculate the vehicle's speed. Radio astronomers do n
send out radar waves to be reflected from the gas cloud
Instead, they observe the frequency of radio waves em
ted from the hydrogen atoms in the clouds, and compa
the observed frequency with the known frequency
1420 megahertz for hydrogen atoms at rest. Unlike vi
ble radiation from stars, radio frequency radiation is n
absorbed by interstellar dust, so the motion of gas clou
throughout the galaxy can be determined.

This technique was widely used in the 1950s to stu
the rotation of our galaxy. The results confirmed and e
tended the conclusion reached by Jan Oort in the 192
that the galaxy is rotating like a fluid object, such as
hurricane. The outer parts rotate more slowly than th
inner parts, producing a graceful, swept-back spiral a

earance. The amount by which the stars and clouds in he outer parts of the galaxy lag behind those in the inner arts depends on the distribution of mass in the galaxy. 1 the mid-1960s, astronomers had constructed a fairly etailed model for the distribution of matter in the galaxy, based on the analysis of observations of luminous matter in our galaxy and other, similar spiral galaxies. his model assumed that the distribution of mass in the galaxy could be deduced from the distribution of light. ight is strongly concentrated toward the center of the galaxy, so it was assumed that the mass was similarly oncentrated. This implied that the stars and gas clouds 1 the outer parts of the galaxy would experience a weaker gravitational force than the stars and clouds in he inner part.

A clear prediction of the model was that the orbital peeds of stars and gas should decline steadily at large istances from the center of the galaxy. In the past few ears, radio astronomers have shown that this prediction oes not square with the observations. They have tracked he orbital speeds of gas clouds at distances of fifty thouand light-years from the center of the galaxy—well beyond the point where there is any appreciable light from he galaxy. Yet the orbital speeds do not decline, but remain approximately constant.

If the planets all orbited at the same speed, the solar ystem would be disrupted almost immediately. For example, if Earth was moving around the Sun with the ame speed as Mercury, the gravitational pull of the Sun ould not keep the Earth in orbit; it would fly off into iterstellar space at a speed in excess of a hundred thouand miles an hour. Following the same line of reasoning, he rapidly moving gas clouds on the outer edges of our galaxy should have flown into intergalactic space long go. What is holding them to our galaxy? It must be the dditional gravitational force provided by dark matter.

How much dark matter is required? The radio observations imply that at least 50 percent of the mass in our galaxy must be in some dark form. They also indicate hat the dark matter extends well beyond the luminous dge of the galaxy. The hydrogen gas observed with radio lescopes forms a disk that extends out to fifty thousand ght-years from the center of the galaxy, beyond the opti-

cal disk of the galaxy. On its outer edges, the hydroge
gas disk bloats up and becomes thicker. This strongly su
gests that the dark matter is not confined to a thin dis
but is spread out in a more or less spherical envelope.

The dark matter observed by radio astronomers
therefore different in some as yet unknown way from t
dark matter deduced from the motions of stars near th
Sun. The latter is concentrated in a thin disk, as a
the visible stars, whereas the former is spread out in
spherical envelope that is much larger than the galax
This difference may indicate the existence of two diffe
ent types of dark matter in the galaxy.

The second line of evidence for an extended envelop
of dark matter comes from optical observations of th
most rapidly moving stars in our galaxy. The stars stu
ied by Oort and Bahcall are ones that sedately bob up an
down above the galactic plane, well under control by th
gravity of the galaxy. Not all stars have such tranqu
motions. Some move at high speeds on elongated ellipt
cal orbits, in toward the center of the galaxy and back ou
again. They appear to have been ejected from dense clu
ters of stars, where they were pumped up to high veloc
ties by many near collisions with other stars in th
cluster. When their velocities became too great, they e
caped from the cluster into the galaxy at large. In e.
treme cases, some stars must acquire velocities so lar
that they escape into intergalactic space.

Bruce Carney of the University of North Carolina an
David Latham of the Harvard–Smithsonian Center for A
trophysics in Cambridge, Massachusetts, hit upon an i
genious method of measuring the mass of the galax
with these stars. They reasoned that stars moving fast
than the escape velocity of the galaxy would be rar
since they could only be seen on their way out. By stud
ing a sample of high-velocity stars and determining t
velocity at which such stars became rare, they could es
mate the escape velocity of the galaxy, which can b
directly related to the mass of the galaxy.

In a sample of 925 high-velocity stars, they foun
none moving faster than 500 kilometers per second. B
fore the escape velocity of the galaxy can be determine
from this number, the motion of the solar system aroun
the center of the galaxy must be taken into account. Th

s not a simple procedure, but when all the uncertainties
nvolved are allowed for, Carney and Latham estimate
hat between 50 and 90 percent of the mass of the galaxy
s in some dark form.

The radio observations of orbiting gas clouds and the
optical observations of high-velocity stars are important
bodies of evidence in establishing the case for the exisence of a cloud of dark matter enveloping our galaxy.
The agreement between these two different methods is
mpressive, yet they leave a crucial question unan-
swered: how extensive is the envelope of dark matter?
The high-velocity stars give little information on this
question, and the radio observations tell us only that it
extends as far as fifty thousand light-years.

If the dark matter envelope has a radius greater than
ifty thousand light-years, it should be revealed through
another line of research: the study of star clusters or
small satellite galaxies that are orbiting our galaxy at dis-
ances ranging from just over a hundred thousand light-
years to a million light-years. The method is, in essence,
he same as that used by radio astronomers. Measurements are made of the orbital speed and the size of the
orbit of a star cluster or satellite galaxy, and these numbers are used to compute the mass needed to keep the
star cluster or satellite galaxy in orbit.

Though the principles are simply stated, putting them
nto practice is not nearly as straightforward as for the
radio observations of gas clouds. Whereas the orbits of
gas clouds can be accurately described as circles in the
thin disk of our galaxy, the orbits of the star clusters and
satellite galaxies are not well-known. These objects could
be moving in circular or elongated elliptical orbits. Since
t takes about a billion years to complete an orbit, it is
mpossible to tell what shape the orbit takes. This is a
serious obstacle to estimating the extent and mass of the
envelope of dark matter around our galaxy. For example,
ess mass is needed to keep a satellite galaxy in a highly
elliptical orbit than in a circular orbit. The assumption of
 circular orbit could lead to an overestimate of the mass
of our galaxy. Also, a galaxy in an elliptical orbit moves
with varying speed, speeding up as it approaches our gal-
xy and slowing down when it is far away. If a satellite
galaxy is in fact near the outer limit of its orbit and mov-

ing slowly, but is mistakenly assumed to be at an average
position moving at an average speed, the mass of our
galaxy could be underestimated. Because the detailed or
bit of the satellite galaxies is unknown, it is impossible to
know exactly how to use the observations to accurately
estimate this mass. The best that can be done is to take an
average.

The number of star clusters and satellite galaxies in
volved is only about ten, so the assumptions that go into
the averaging process may be crucial and the percentage
of uncertainty in the computed average may be rather
large. Five different groups have applied slightly different
statistical analyses to five slightly different sets of data or
star groups and satellite galaxies. When allowances are
made for the differences in samples of star groups and
galaxies, the results indicate that the radius of the dark
matter envelope is between seventy and one hundred
fifty thousand light-years and that it contains between
two and four times as much matter as all the luminous
matter in our galaxy.

Over the past ten years, several independent lines of re
search have led to a radically different view of our gal
axy. The old view—a central bulge of stars surrounded
by a thin disk of stars, gas, and dust that has a diameter
of about a hundred thousand light-years—remains
valid part of the picture, but we now know that it is at
most only half the picture, as far as total mass is con
cerned. Fifty percent of the matter in the disk is dark
matter of an unknown nature. Even more mystifying, it
has been discovered that the galaxy of the old view, the
luminous galaxy, is embedded in a huge, massive enve
lope of dark matter. Like the tip of an iceberg, or the
archipelago that peeks above the surface of the ocean, or
a tree with a massive root system, what we can see does
not begin to tell the whole story.

If we are embedded in a vast envelope of dark matter
how can we see out of our galaxy? Why is it that a keen
observer can, on a crystal-clear night, see the great galaxy
in Andromeda with the naked eye, even though it is two

million light-years away? How can astronomers have discovered thousands upon thousands of galaxies with radio, infrared, optical, and x-ray telescopes if our galaxy is surrounded by dark matter? These are important questions because they tell us what the dark matter cannot be. It cannot be dust or gas spread finely throughout an envelope around our galaxy. Otherwise, we could not see out of our galaxy, or at best, our visibility would be severely limited by what would amount to a galactic haze or fog. The dark matter must fall into one of two general categories: it must be a large object, such as some peculiar type of star that does not give off light, and we see out of the galaxy through the virtually empty space between these objects; or it must be a peculiar type of particle—one that is extremely common, has mass, yet emits or absorbs radiation very weakly, if at all. Then the light can stream into our galaxy just as if the particles were not there. These hypothetical particles have been given the name cosmic WIMPs, for weakly interacting massive particles. I will have more to say later about cosmic WIMPs and other suspects in the dark matter mystery. For now, let us consider more of the evidence.

The Universality of Galactic Envelopes of Dark Matter

Is the dark matter that envelops our galaxy rare, or is it a common feature of all galaxies? Of the three lines of research discussed above—observations of high-velocity stars, measurements of the rotation of a galaxy through observations of the motions of clouds of gas and dust, and observations of small satellite galaxies and star groups—only the rotation measurement is practical for any but the nearest spiral galaxies. And it is not simple. As late as the 1950s, it still took about a hundred hours on a large telescope to determine the rotation of a relatively nearby galaxy, so little was known about the way that galaxies rotate. Few if any astronomers suspected that there was anything peculiar about the rotation of spiral galaxies. Then, for no particular reason other than the fact that no one else was doing it, Vera Rubin took on the tedious task of measuring the rotation of spiral galaxies. She kept at it

for twenty years, during which time she formed a fruitfu
collaboration with Kent Ford, her colleague at the Ca
negie Institution in Washington, D.C. Ford had develope
an electronic device called the image tube, which was
much more sensitive detector of light than photograph
plates. An observation that would previously have sixt
hours could now be done in three.

Rubin, Ford, and their colleagues at the Carnegie Inst
tution observed a sample of sixty spiral galaxies. The
measured tightly wound spirals and loose spirals, larg
spirals twenty times as luminous as our Milky Way ga
axy and small ones only a quarter as luminous. In ever
case, they found that the galaxies appear to be spinnin
faster than is possible, if the luminous part of the galax
gives any indication of its mass. "The conclusion is ine
capable," Rubin and her colleagues stated in a paper sun
marizing their work, "that nonluminous matter exist
beyond the optical galaxy."

Radio astronomers, inspired by the work of Ver
Rubin and her colleagues, had begun measuring the rota
tion of galaxies in the mid-1970s. Their observation
often went well beyond the visible edges of the galaxie
They confirmed and extended the optical evidence tha
spiral galaxies are embedded in envelopes of dark matte
that contain about two to five times as much matter a
the entire luminous galaxy. Together, the two sets of dat
make a strong case for the existence of massive envelope
of dark matter around every spiral galaxy.

Not all galaxies are spirals. Many are round, like a baske
ball, or egg-shaped, like a football. They are called ellipt
cal galaxies, and differ from spirals in more than ju
their shapes. The arms of spiral galaxies have a brigh
blue hue, caused by hot, young stars. Clouds of cool ga
and dust from which new stars can form are also presen
As the galaxy ages, this gas supply will gradually be e
hausted, the formation of new stars will cease, and th
spiral arms traced out by the bright new stars will fad
away. Elliptical galaxies appear to have aged prem
turely. In contrast to spirals, they have very few, if an
young stars and very little, if any, cool gas.

Some astrophysicists argue that the difference b

tween spiral and elliptical galaxies is due to the rate of
rotation in the clouds that form galaxies. A slowly rotating cloud collapses to form an elliptical galaxy that undergoes a single burst of star formation that blows all the
leftover gas out of the galaxy and leaves a slowly rotating, elliptically shaped collection of aging stars. Spirals, it
is argued, form from a rapidly rotating cloud. The rotation inhibits the collapse, which in turn inhibits the formation of stars, dragging the process out over many
billions of years, so that it is still occurring today. Another theory holds that elliptical galaxies were produced
by collisions between galaxies. These collisions produced
bursts of star formation that cleared the galaxies of all
cold gas and bloated them into elliptical shapes. Adher-
ents of this theory point to the observation that elliptical
galaxies are usually found in regions of space where the
density of galaxies is high, whereas spiral galaxies seem
to prefer the low-density "suburbs" of space.

What is responsible for the difference between spiral
and elliptical galaxies? Is it heredity in the form of initial
rotation rate, or environment in the form of the density
of galaxies? More information on how galaxies form is
needed before these questions can be answered. In recent
years, it has become painfully obvious that astronomers
are just beginning to learn what galaxies are made of—
dark matter, mostly—and are still a long way from understanding how they formed. For example, spiral and
elliptical galaxies differ in many ways. Do they also differ
in the amount of dark matter? The answer could be an
important clue to the nature of dark matter.

Since elliptical and irregular galaxies rotate very
slowly, if at all, the techniques used to measure the
masses of spiral galaxies do not apply. A variation of the
high-velocity star method can be used, but with great
difficulty and uncertainty. Fortunately, the development
of sensitive x-ray telescopes in the past decade has provided a new technique for measuring the masses of many
elliptical and some irregular galaxies.

X-rays are produced in a medical x-ray machine by a
beam of high-energy particles. In a similar way, x-rays
are produced in space by high-energy particles. Astronomers have detected x-rays from a dazzling variety of objects, including neutron stars, black holes, and elliptical

galaxies. The x-rays from elliptical galaxies are produced by vast clouds of gas that have been heated to temperatures in excess of ten million degrees. This hot gas is a sensitive tracer of the masses of the galaxies that contain it, because the temperature of a gas is a measure of the average speed of the atomic particles in the gas. On a very cold day ($-20°$ C) the average speed of the atoms in the air is about fourteen hundred kilometers per hour. On a hot day ($30°$ C), their average speed rises to about sixteen hundred kilometers per hour. On the surface of the sun ($6000°$ C), the atoms are whizzing around at about fifty thousand kilometers per hour. In the gas clouds observed in elliptical galaxies with x-ray telescopes, the temperatures are in excess of ten million degrees Celsius, implying an average speed of the atomic particles in excess of a million kilometers per hour.

Particles traveling this fast would quickly evaporate from a galaxy unless they were held by the galaxy's gravity. Since clouds of hot gas are observed in virtually every elliptical galaxy, it is safe to assume that they are not a transient phenomenon, but more or less permanent feature. Therefore, the galaxies must have enough gravity to keep the clouds from escaping into intergalactic space. Through careful observations of the size and temperature of the clouds, the gravitational force, and hence the mass of the galaxy, can be calculated. The temperature of the gas cloud is not well determined, so the mass of the galaxy cannot be precisely determined. Despite the uncertainty, the x-ray observations clearly indicate the presence of a massive envelope of dark matter around elliptical galaxies. Between 50 and 90 percent of the mass of these galaxies is contained in dark envelopes. This is about the same proportion of dark matter to luminous matter as for spiral galaxies, and confirms the suspicion that there is much more dark than luminous matter in the universe.

With the discovery of dark matter in both spiral and elliptical galaxies, can we conclude that all galaxies in the universe are embedded in massive dark envelopes? Not yet. Another potentially important constituent of the

ealm of galaxies remains unaccounted for—dwarf galax-
es.

Dwarf galaxies range in brightness from one hun-
dredth of 1 percent to 1 percent of that of a large spiral
galaxy such as Andromeda, or our galaxy. They contain a
few tens of millions to a billion stars. They are so incon-
spicuous that they were not known to exist until the late
1930s. Edwin Hubble, one of the giants of twentieth century astronomy, once went so far as to declare that such
galaxies did not exist. This statement was enough to spur
his arch rival at Caltech, Fritz Zwicky, to undertake a
campaign to discover dwarf galaxies and thereby prove
Hubble wrong. When Hubble and other authorities at
Caltech refused to make time on the large telescopes
available for Zwicky's search, Zwicky acquired funds to
build his own telescope—a small, eighteen-inch reflecting one, which was installed on Palomar Mountain. He
soon found three dwarf galaxies, and in the course of a
four-year survey, found several more. In the years that
followed, other astronomers added to the list. Today, it is
believed that dwarf galaxies are likely to be the most
numerous type in the universe.

Because of their faintness, most of the dwarf galaxies
first discovered are very near our galaxy. So near, in fact,
that their very existence may imply that they contain
massive amounts of dark matter. Our galaxy is surrounded, appropriately, by seven dwarf galaxies. Two of
these—one in the constellation of Draco and one in Ursa
Minor—are only two hundred thousand light-years from
Earth. Because they are so close, they are subject to huge
tidal forces from our galaxy. The effect of tidal forces can
be seen every day at the beach. The side of the Earth
facing the moon is about 3 percent closer to it than the
side facing away, so the gravitational force exerted by the
Moon on the near side is slightly stronger. This imbalance distorts the Earth's shape by a few feet, and shows
up as the high and low tides of the ocean.

The tidal forces of the Moon on the Earth are very
weak because the gravitational field of the Moon is weak.
However, the tidal forces of our galaxy on a nearby
dwarf galaxy could pull the dwarf apart. Whether this
happens depends on whether the dwarf galaxy's gravitational field is strong enough to withstand the tidal forces

of our Milky Way galaxy. Since the dwarfs exist, their gravity must be strong enough, barring the unlikely event that they are not true satellites and are just making their first pass by the Milky Way. The tidal force depends on the mass of the Milky Way, and the distance and size of the dwarf galaxy. To the extent that these numbers are known, the required gravitational field of the dwarf galaxy, and hence its mass, can be calculated. The results of such an analysis indicate that the mass in dwarf galaxies, like in spiral and elliptical ones, is about 50 to 90 percent dark matter.

An independent analysis that uses the average velocities of the stars to estimate the gravity of the galaxy yields similar results. For other dwarf galaxies, the situation is not so clear-cut. The tidal force argument cannot be applied to give a meaningful answer, and measurements of the average velocities of the stars indicate that dark matter is 30 percent or less. Still other measurements—of rotating dwarf galaxies—indicate the existence of dark matter envelopes. One possible resolution of this conflicting body of evidence is that dwarf galaxies do not contain a large amount of dark matter in their inner parts, where the star-velocity averages were taken, but, like spiral and elliptical galaxies, are embedded in large, dark envelopes.

Dark Matter in Intergalactic Space

The space between galaxies is the place of the solitaires in the cosmic landscape. The immense emptiness of intergalactic space would make even the most dedicated space-faring recluse yearn for companionship. Out there it is a million light-years or more between galaxies and the skies are always a deep shade of dark. The faint wisps of light from distant galaxies are the only visual clues that the universe is not everywhere a bleak and forbidding place.

In the past twenty years, astronomers have established, through observations outside the visual band of wavelengths, that the space between galaxies is not completely empty. It contains high-energy particles, hot gas, and possibly, enough dark matter to affect the future evolution of the universe.

Most of the universe is intergalactic space. The luminous stars and gas in galaxies occupy less than one one-hundredth of 1 percent of the space in which they are located. The evidence just summarized indicates that the luminous portions of galaxies are imbedded in large, dark envelopes. Still, even if we take the most generous estimates of the size of these envelopes, they would all take up less than 10 percent of intergalactic space.

Three basic types of intergalactic space, related to the overall pattern of the distribution of galaxies in the universe, can be identified. While the exact pattern is still far from clear, some details of the area within a few hundred million light-years of our Milky Way galaxy are becoming apparent.

Our galaxy is part of a small group of about two dozen galaxies called the Local Group. Most of the galaxies in the universe are members of a group. If a group has several hundred members, it is called a cluster. Some rich clusters contain thousands of galaxies. The galaxies in groups and clusters are held together in a dynamic balance between their mutual gravity and their orbital motions about their center of gravity. The space between galaxies in a group or cluster of galaxies is the first type of intergalactic space.

The Local Group is one of about fifty groups and clusters of galaxies that are part of the Local Supercluster of galaxies. The Local Supercluster has the form of a flattened disk that is about a hundred million light-years in diameter. At least nine similar superclusters have been identified. The space between the groups and clusters of galaxies in a supercluster is the second type of intergalactic space.

Superclusters are not randomly spread through space. Instead, the universe appears to be like a bubble bath, filled with a froth of galaxies and voids. The galaxies are spread around the edges of immense voids, like soap in soap bubbles. The voids, which contain very few galaxies, are the third type of intergalactic space.

The same techniques can be used in the search for dark matter in the first two types of intergalactic space as for the investigation of galactic envelopes of dark matter. In groups of galaxies, the orbits of galaxies can be used to estimate their masses in much the same way that the orbits of satellite galaxies were used to estimate the mass of the Milky Way galaxy. The estimates are subject to the same uncertainties—namely, those in the averaging process used to deduce the billion-year orbits of the galaxies from a snapshot of their present positions and motion. When applied to the Local Group, two galaxies—the Andromeda and the Milky Way—contain most of the mass, so this method boils down to calculating the ten-billion-year orbits of the Andromeda galaxy and the Milky Way galaxy around their center of mass. The mass of dark matter in each of the galaxies is found to be between three and ten times the luminous mass, in agreement with other independent estimates.

In many groups and in all clusters, several galaxies of comparable size are present, which move in the combined gravitational field of all the galaxies in the group or cluster. It is often difficult to deduce much about the amount of dark matter around an individual galaxy under these circumstances, but the motions of the individual galaxies can be used to compute the total amount of dark matter in the group or cluster. The technique is similar to that used for tracer stars in our galaxy, using galaxies instead of stars. An average is computed for the velocities of the galaxies in the group or cluster, which is used to compute the mass of the group on the assumption that the galaxies represent a stable collection. The results of several independent investigations along these lines indicate that between 50 and 90 percent of the mass in groups and clusters of galaxies is dark matter.

X-ray observations of hot gas in clusters of galaxies, together with estimates of the mass required to hold this gas in the clusters, yield a similar result—70 to 90 percent of the mass in the clusters is in the form of dark matter. These two independent estimates of the amount of dark matter are consistent with each other; they are also consistent with the proportion of dark matter inferred to exist in galaxies. This means that all the dark matter in groups and clusters of galaxies can be explained in terms of envelopes of dark matter around individual galaxies. In rich clusters of galaxies, the dark matter envelopes overlap, so they may have been stripped from the individual galaxies and spread throughout the central regions of intergalactic space in these clusters. Nevertheless, the dark matter came from the individual galaxies, so the

onclusion remains valid: there is no convincing evi-
lence for an additional component of dark matter associated with the intergalactic space between galaxies in
groups or clusters of galaxies.

Does this mean that all the dark matter in the universe has been gathered into the envelopes around galax-
es? Or does the intergalactic space between groups and
clusters of galaxies in superclusters contain a significant
mount of dark matter? This possibility can be investi-
gated by considering the motions of groups of galaxies
within superclusters. The only supercluster for which
his is practical is the Local Supercluster, to which our
Local Group of galaxies belongs. The Local Supercluster is
in aggregate of about fifty groups and clusters of galaxies.
The groups and clusters are concentrated in a flat disk
with a diameter of about a hundred million light-years.
The Local Group lies near the edge of this disk. At the
enter is the Virgo Cluster, which contains several thou-
and galaxies. Astronomers have devised ingenious
methods for measuring the motion of the Local Group
with respect to the center of mass of the Local Super-
luster. This motion can then be used to measure the
ravity and thus the mass of the Local Supercluster.

One method is to study the detailed distribution across
he sky of the intensity of the microwave background
adiation. This radiation is believed to have originated
rom a hot early stage in the evolution of the universe,
efore stars or galaxies existed. Indeed, the discovery of
he microwave background radiation in 1964 is consid-
red to be the strongest evidence for the Big Bang theory
hat the universe has evolved from a very dense hot state
hat existed fifteen to twenty billion years ago. The inten-
ity of the radiation is uniform to less than a percent over
he entire sky, indicating that the universe must have
een extremely smooth less than a million years after the
ig bang. This smoothness presents a vexing problem to
osmologists on two accounts: how did the universe
ome to be so smooth, and how did galaxies form from
uch a bland primordial soup? The resolution of these
iddles is intimately related to the solution of the mystery
f the dark matter, and is one of the prime motivations
ehind some fascinating new theories for the origin of
alaxies and the universe.

A few astrophysicists have made a career of searching for variations in the microwave background radiation. Even a scarcely noticeable wrinkle, or a slight asymmetry in the otherwise uniform background, can be a very large clue to mysteries such as the origin of the universe; the origin of galaxies, clusters, and superclusters; and the amount of dark matter in the universe. In the late 1970s, a variation was detected that tells us how the Earth is moving through the background radiation. The intensity of the radiation is amplified in the direction of the radiation and decreased in the opposite direction. This information can be used to deduce the amount of dark matter in the Local Supercluster, but it is not simple. The measurements were made from balloons or jet airplanes above the Earth, which is orbiting the Sun, which is orbiting the center of the galaxy, which is orbiting the center of mass of the Local Group, which is orbiting the center of the Local Supercluster, which is apparently being pulled toward an even larger concentration of galaxies about one-hundred-fifty million light-years away.

When all these motions are disentangled, it is found that the Local Group is moving toward the center of the Local Supercluster at a speed of about one million kilometers per hour. When uncertainties such as the exact orbit of the Local Group and the exact distribution of mass in the Local Supercluster are taken into account, the mass of the Local Supercluster weighs in at the equivalent of one to three quadrillion suns. This translates to a dark matter fraction of between 80 and 90 percent. This estimate overlaps with those for the percent of dark matter in individual galaxies. The conclusion: there is no evidence for a substantial component of dark matter in the intergalactic space between groups and clusters of galaxies in the Local Supercluster.

This is potentially a very important result because it is contrary to the predictions of at least two theories: one that says that the dark matter is in the form of a particle called a neutrino, and another that proposes a revision of the laws of gravity. However, caution should be exercised because of the large uncertainties; they could allow for the presence of enough dark matter in the Local Supercluster to support the predictions of these theories. Further observational studies and more accurate theoreti cal models now under investigation should soon clarify the issue of the amount of dark matter in the Local Supercluster.

It should be apparent that the farther we move from our galaxy, the sketchier our knowledge is, and the more speculative our conclusions. But in spite of the risk of spending long hours going in the wrong direction, increasing numbers of astrophysicists have taken their telescopes and theories into the largely uncharted spaces beyond the Local Supercluster, in search of dark matter.

Only recently have astronomers begun to survey the sky in enough detail and depth to understand how superclusters are distributed in space. The cosmic maps that exist are much less complete, relatively speaking, than the maps Columbus was using when he sailed off in search of India and ran into America. Still, some fascinating details have emerged.

A map constructed by a Harvard–Smithsonian Astrophysical Observatory team of Valerie de Lapparent, Margaret Geller, and John Huchra covers a slice of the universe that has the width of about a dozen full moons and a depth of three hundred million light-years. It reveals a universe that resembles a foamy bubble bath. Space is mostly filled with empty spaces, corresponding to the inside of the soap bubbles. Galaxies lie along the edges of the voids, like the soap in soap bubbles. The intersection of voids produces a concentration of galaxies. The Local Supercluster is part of a thin—twenty million light-year—shell of galaxies on the surface of a void that is seventy-five million or more light-years in diameter. Subsequent surveys by the Harvard–Smithsonian team and others have confirmed the bubbly structure of the universe.

When the voids were discovered, a number of astrophysicists speculated that perhaps they were not empty, but only appeared to be so. Maybe they were filled with dim dwarf galaxies, or galaxies that are dim because they contain only very dim stars, or maybe the gas in the voids for some reason never formed into galaxies. Painstaking follow-up studies of a few large voids have revealed that they are not completely empty. They do contain a few dwarf galaxies, but these are concentrated along the walls of the void, in much the same way as bright galaxies. They also contain a few galaxies that are peculiar, in the sense that they appear to have much more gas than normal galaxies and seem to be very young galaxies that have formed only fairly recently. The number of these galaxies is very small. Furthermore, there is no evidence for a large reservoir of gas. The voids may not be totally empty of luminous matter, but they still qualify as the most desolate places in the universe.

In spite of the lack of evidence to support their belief, a respectable body of astrophysicists maintain that the voids cannot be totally empty—that they must contain large amounts of matter. If this is not in the form of luminous matter, then they must contain dark matter. Nor is the amount of dark matter trivial. On the contrary, they maintain, the mass of dark matter in the voids must be *five to ten times greater* than the mass in all the galaxies, including their dark envelopes, in the universe!

Why would sober astrophysicists say such a thing? And why would other astrophysicists, also presumably sober, take them seriously, so that they spend months working very hard to check it out? The answer is a compelling new model of the universe, called the Inflationary Big Bang model, that solves some of the profound problems with the standard Big Bang model so elegantly that many theoretical astrophysicists and cosmologists believe it must be correct. But if it is correct, then about 98 percent of the matter in the universe must be in the form of a universal sea of dark matter. Before discussing the Inflationary Big Bang model and why it is so appealing to so many astrophysicists, we must finish our inventory of the matter in the universe by taking the final step —the consideration of the universe as a whole.

The Average Mass Density of the Universe

How much matter, both luminous and dark, does the universe contain? It is impossible to answer this question since it is not known how large the universe is. A question that can be answered in principle is, what is the average mass density of the observable universe? The average mass density is the average mass in a large volume of space. It includes dark as well as luminous matter, matter in space between galaxies, and matter in galaxies. A knowledge of the average mass density is crucial to every theory of the universe because the mass density of the universe determines the gravity of the universe as a whole.

This universal gravity is opposing the expansion of the universe in much the same way that the gravity of the Earth opposes the upward motion of a rocket. If the mass density is less than or equal to a certain critical value, the gravity of the universe will be insufficient to halt the universal expansion. The galaxies will move farther and farther apart, all the stars will eventually burn out, and the universe will become cold and dark. In contrast, if the mass density is greater than the critical density, the gravity of the universe will be sufficient to slow the expansion until it eventually stops. Beyond this point, the universe will begin to collapse like a rocket that has reached the apex of its flight. The galaxies will rush together with ever-increasing speed until they collide. Stars will be crushed together, then the atoms, then the nuclei of atoms as the temperature of the universe soars from near absolute zero to billions of degrees in a fiery cataclysm that has been called the Big Crunch.

Astronomers do not know which solution applies because they have not been able to determine whether the average mass density exceeds the critical mass density or not. Existing surveys of all the mass in galaxies, *including their dark envelopes*, clusters of galaxies, and superclusters, indicate that the average mass density of the universe is between 5 and 40 percent of the critical value. This conclusion is based on the assumption that all the dark matter in the universe is associated with galaxies, clusters of galaxies, and superclusters. What if it is not? What if the universe contains a sea of dark matter that fills space almost uniformly, so that we are unaware of its existence? The situation would be in some ways analogous to a tribe living on a vast, mile-high plateau. They might seriously underestimate the true height of mountains rising above the plateau because they would neglect the elevation of the plateau above sea level. Similarly, astronomers could seriously underestimate the mass density of the universe if a universal sea of dark matter exists.

Fortunately, methods are available for testing for the effect of a hypothetical sea of dark matter. These relate to the effect of the mass density on the expansion of the universe. The course of this expansion is analogous to the motion of a rocket fired into space. The rocket will slow down as it works against the gravitational field of the Earth. The amount of deceleration depends on the velocity given to the rocket by its boosters and the gravity of the Earth. A rocket scientist could deduce from measurements of the deceleration of the rocket whether or not it would attain escape velocity. Similarly, astronomers can determine, in principle, the rate at which the universal expansion is slowing down. This information can then be used to compute the mass density of the universe and hence the ultimate fate of the expanding universe: endless cold or intolerable heat.

The most direct approach to the problem of measuring the deceleration of universal expansion is to measure the recession velocity of a large number of very distant galaxies. This is done by measuring the shift of the radiation spectrum of these galaxies toward longer wavelengths, the red shift, and relating the red shift to a velocity of recession. The light observed from a galaxy a hundred million light-years away left that galaxy a billion years ago, so a measurement of the red shft of that galaxy tells how that galaxy was moving a billion years ago. Measurements of a large sample of galaxies at different distances from Earth can then be used to trace out the course of the expansion of the universe through time. The major problem with this method is that the distances to these galaxies cannot be accurately determined. This leads to a large uncertainty, with estimates of the average mass density ranging from 40 to 160 percent of the critical density.

Another approach to estimating the average mass density of the universe involves an analysis of the elements synthesized by nuclear reactions in the first few minutes of the Big Bang. The exact amount of deuterium, or heavy hydrogen, produced in those crucial minutes depends critically on the mass density of the universe then. Using Einstein's equations of general relativity to de

cribe the expansion of the universe, it is possible to re-
ate the average mass density of the universe then and
ow. The deuterium nucleus cannot survive inside stars,
o any deuterium found on the surfaces of stars or planets
r in interstellar gas is thought to have been produced in
he first few minutes of the Big Bang. Observations with
adio and ultraviolet telescopes indicate that there is
lightly more than one deuterium nucleus for every one
undred thousand hydrogen nuclei. This suggests that
he average mass density of the universe is between 5
nd 20 percent of the critical mass density.

There are two loopholes in this argument. One is that
he calculations were made on the assumption that mat-
er was very smoothly distributed in the early universe.
f, instead, the primeval batter was grainy, like a poorly
nixed cake, the calculations could be made to be consis-
ent with the observations for mass densities as large as
he critical density. It remains to be seen whether the
ctual universe produces graininess to the required de-
ree, or whether other potential nuclear byproducts of
his early phase, such as lithium, are consistent with the
bservations. In the meantime, the uncertainty as to the
ctual value of the mass density of the universe remains.

This uncertainty is compounded by the possibility that
nother class of matter may dominate the mass of the
niverse—the cosmic WIMPs. These particles, by defini-
ion, interact only very weakly with the baryonic matter
—normal matter composed of neutrons and protons—
nvolved in the nuclear synthesis reactions. Most of the
nass in the universe could be in the form of cosmic
WIMPs, and the amount of deuterium manufactured in
he Big Bang would be virtually unchanged.

In summary, the presence of a universal sea of dark
natter can be neither confirmed nor denied by current
bservations and theory. The opinions of astronomers
nd astrophysicists appear to be split on the issue. The
bservational astronomers who have conducted the
earch for dark matter around galaxies, and in clusters,
uperclusters, and intergalactic voids, tend to take the po-
ition that there is no observational evidence for a uni-
ersal sea of dark matter, and that the mass density of the
niverse is somewhere between 10 and 40 percent of the
ritical density. It is only a matter of time, they argue,

before the theorists come to their senses and accept th
facts. The theoretical astrophysicists and cosmologist
who have been working on the consequences of the In
flationary Big Bang model of the universe tend to believ
that the theory is so elegant that it must be correct, so
universal sea of dark matter must exist. It is only a ma
ter of time, they believe, until the observers find it. W
turn now to an examination of the theory behind thi
schism in the astronomical community.

The Inflationary Universe

In the late 1960s, many astrophysicists and cosmol
gists thought that they had a roughly accurate outline o
the story of the origin and evolution of the universe.
went something like this: the universe originated from
very dense hot state that existed fifteen to twenty billio
years ago, and has been expanding and cooling eve
since. This story explained why the universe is ex
panding. It explained the existence of microwave back
ground radiation as a relic of the conditions that existe
in the first few hundred thousand years of the expansion
And theoretical calculations of the products of thermonu
clear reactions that must have occurred in the first fe
minutes of the expansion were in good agreement wit
the products that are observed in the universe today. Th
coherence and self-consistency of the picture satisfied a
most everyone who was familiar with the facts, and
was generally agreed that all that remained was to wor
out the details.

As so often happens, the working out of the detail
revealed fundamental flaws in the model. One of thes
concerned the subatomic reactions predicted to occur i
the very early universe—when it was only a few second
old, was much denser than the inside of a star, and had
temperature of a trillion degrees or more. Calculation
showed that, under these conditions, at least two types
particles should be abundant in the universe: magneti
monopoles—strongly magnetized particles that should b
easily detectable, yet aren't—and antimatter. An antipr
ton, for example, has the same mass as a proton, but a
opposite charge, among other properties. When a partic
encounters its antiparticle, both particles annihilate in

ash of energy which converts their mass into another
rm, such as high-energy gamma radiation. Antipar-
cles can be produced in high-energy collisions in parti-
e accelerators, but they do not occur naturally, except
ossibly under very unusual conditions around peculiar
ars or in interstellar space. It is far, far less abundant
an normal matter, contrary to the predictions of the
andard Big Bang model.

A second problem relates to the mass density of the
niverse. Although there is still considerable uncertainty
s to its actual value, astronomers are confident that it
es somewhere between 10 percent and 150 percent of
e critical mass density that defines the boundary be-
veen endless expansion and eventual collapse. Cosmolo-
ists argue that this is an extraordinary coincidence that
ust tell us something important about the universe.

Their reasoning is based on Einstein's theory of grav-
y. This theory introduces the concept of curved space.
ight in curved space does not travel in a straight line,
ut along a path that is curved in the vicinity of massive
bjects such as stars or galaxies. The theory also describes
ow the average mass density of the universe determines
e overall curvature of space. If the average mass den-
ty of the universe is greater than the critical density,
ace has a positive curvature. If you sent two beams of
ght out along parallel straight lines in such a space, they
ould curve toward each other until they crossed. The
irface of a globe provides a two-dimensional analogy.
he lines of longitude eventually intersect at the poles. In
ontrast, if the average mass density of the universe is
ss than the critical density, space is negatively curved.
arallel beams of light would bend farther and farther
part as they propagated through such a space. The divid-
g line between positively and negatively curved space
flat space, which has no curvature. Parallel beams of
ght remain parallel, and the usual theorems of plane
eometry apply to intergalactic space. If the mass density
exactly equal to the critical density, space will be flat.

Present estimates indicate that the mass density of the
niverse is at least one-tenth of the critical density—that
, one-tenth of the value needed to make space flat. Ein-
ein's equations show that, as the universe evolves, flat
ace remains flat, whereas curvature of positively and

negatively curved spaces constantly changes. In bot
cases, the departure from flat space increases with time
This is at the root of the extraordinary coincidence re
ferred to above. The range of space curvature allowed b
the observations of the universe now implies that, in th
first few minutes of the universe, the curvature of spac
must have been extremely small. The mass density mu
have been within one ten-millionth of 1 percent of th
critical density. This problem of why the curvature of th
universe is so small is called the flatness problem.

The third and perhaps most severe problem is that
uniformity. The intensity of microwave background rad
ation is uniform to less than 1 percent over the entir
sky. This implies that, sometime before the universe wa
a few hundred thousand years old, the temperature
the entire observable universe was uniform to within
percent. Such remarkable uniformity is extremely un
likely to have occurred by chance. It is as if everyone o
a crowded street were walking in step. This could be e
pected to happen only if the people communicated b
sight or sound. In the same way, the universe could b
expected to have the same temperature everywhere onl
if communication, in the form of conduction waves
shock waves, had smoothed out the temperature vari
tions. But calculations based on the standard Big Ban
model demonstrated that there had not been nearl
enough time for this to occur. Going back to an earlie
time when the universe was smaller only made matte
worse. Why, then, is the microwave background radi
tion so uniform?

In 1980, several scientists independently showed how
modern theories concerning the nature of elementar
particles imply that the universe underwent a very brie
phase of extremely rapid expansion. One of these scien
tists, Alan Guth of MIT, used this phenomenon to cor
struct a model that represented a major overhaul of th
Big Bang model. He called this new one an "Inflationar
Universe"—a name that was quickly picked up by othe
scientists. This model refers primarily to just the first fe
billionths of a sextillionth of a second (10^{-30} second)
the expansion of the universe.

Could such a fleeting fraction of a second possibl
make any difference? Yes, if you are willing to believe th

ysicists when they say that some mind-boggling events
ok place during that time. First of all, they claim that
e universe then was extremely hot—10 octillion or 10^{28}
grees. It was also extremely dense. All the matter in
e presently observable universe—a sphere thirty to
rty billion light-years across—was packed into a region
sextillion or more times smaller than the period at the
d of this sentence. Under these conditions, the rules of
ysics as we know them do not apply, and the particles
our everyday world do not exist. New rules, based on
trapolations from the known rules, govern the behav-
r of energy of matter. Exotic particles such as Higgs
sons predominate, and most of the energy of the uni-
rse is tied up in a peculiar entity called the Higgs field,
med after the Scottish Physicist Peter Higgs.

The energy in gravitational fields can be transformed
to energy of motion—just drop this book and watch.
e energy of a Higgs field gets transformed into the en-
gy of particles. Indeed, according to the theory on
hich the Inflationary Big Bang model is based, the mass
the universe owes its existence to the Higgs field.
hen the energy of the universe is tied up in the Higgs
ld, it expands with geometrically increasing speed. It is
is property that solves both the flatness problem and
e uniformity problem.

Consider by analogy the growth of a carrot. Suppose
u observed that sixty days after planting, you had six-
ch-long carrots. If you assumed that carrots grew at a
iform rate, then the carrots should have been about
e inch long ten days after they were planted. This is
t true. They were still seeds only a tiny fraction of an
ch long. After a two-week germination period, they go
rough a period of very rapid growth before settling
wn to a fairly uniform one.

The assumption of a reasonably uniform rate of ex-
nsion of the universe could also lead to a gross overesti-
ate of its size at some very early time. The standard Big
ng model predicts that, when the universe was only
-35 seconds old, all the observable universe was con-
ntrated into a region about the size of a carrot seed. The
flationary universe theory, in contrast, implies a much,
uch smaller volume for the universe at that time.

This means that, before inflation, the universe was

much smaller than we would have predicted from t
standard Big Bang theory—so small that there was
problem communicating from one side to another, ar
no problem in establishing a high degree of uniformity
the temperature. According to this model, the uniformi
of the microwave background radiation is a direct resu
of conditions that existed very soon after the observab
universe began to expand.

Note the use of the phrase "observable universe
rather than simply "universe." This is necessary becau
the inflationary universe implies the existence of diffe
ent domains of the universe. In our domain, one set
laws of physics presumably took on their particular for
when the expansion began fifteen to twenty billion yea
ago. Another domain could have completely differe
laws, could have started to expand at a different tim
and could have a completely different size. Some u
verses may just be beginning their expansion. We c
never know about these universes, only about our d
main. Within our domain, we can know only abo
those parts of the universe from which light rays ha
had time to reach us. In fifteen billion years, this cor
sponds to a sphere fifteen billion years in radius—t
observable universe. According to the inflationa
model, we cannot hope to know about more than a ti
fraction of our domain, which inflated to a size trillio
upon trillions of times larger than the observable ur
verse. This circumstance provides a resolution of the fl
ness problem.

Suppose you wanted to determine the curvature of t
Earth. You could get an idea that the Earth is round
carefully watching ships set out to sea. But if you o
served a toy sailboat on a small pond, you would co
clude that the Earth is flat. In the same way, astronome
attempting to measure the curvature of space can obser
such a small fraction of the totality of our domain th
they must conclude that space has zero curvature.
other words, the inflationary model *predicts* that the ma
density must be equal to the critical density to very hi
accuracy.

This prediction illustrates the power of the inflatio
ary model. It is the distinguishing characteristic of a go
scientific theory that it can make strong predictions. T

ther side of the coin is that the stronger the prediction, the more vulnerable the theory to disproof. This explains why many theoretical astrophysicists and cosmologists are adamant in their insistence—or hope—that astronomers will eventually find the universal sea of dark matter that will bring the average mass density of the universe into line with the critical density.

The inflationary universe also holds out the promise for explaining the observed dominance of matter over antimatter in the universe. In the very early stages, a slight asymmetry in the laws of physics produced a very slight preponderance of matter over antimatter. As the universe cooled from its superhot state in the first fraction of a second, matter and antimatter particles annihilated until all the antimatter was gone, leaving a universe composed solely of matter.

In summary, the mystery of the dark matter is not a single mystery but at least three. The first is the dark matter in the disk of our galaxy. Observations imply that approximately 50 percent of the matter in the disk is dark matter. The second mystery is the dark matter in the envelopes around virtually every galaxy in the universe. These envelopes contain approximately two to ten times as much matter as the luminous galaxies they envelop. Finally, there is the mass density mystery. The best theory we presently have for the origin and evolution of the universe, the Inflationary Big Bang theory, predicts that the average mass density must be equal to the critical density. Yet the observations show at most 20 to 50 percent of the necessary matter, even if we include dark matter. Can any one dark matter culprit provide the solution to all these mysteries? Let us look at some of the suspects.

THE SUSPECTS

When investigators search for a suspect in a crime, they look for someone who has motive, means, and opportunity. In the search for the solution to the mystery of

the dark matter, the criteria are that the suspect must
dark, sufficiently abundant to explain the quantity
dark matter observed, and not have any side effects th
would eliminate it from consideration.

The first requirement—darkness—means that the m
terial must be very inefficient at producing electroma
netic radiation, which includes radio, microwav
infrared, optical, ultraviolet, x-ray, and gamma radiatic
This radiation comes in waves similar to those in a lal
They have a wavelength—the distance between crests
and a frequency (the number of waves that pass a giv
point per second). Our eyes are sensitive to only a ve
small portion of the total spectrum of electromagne
waves. The wavelengths decrease steadily from rac
waves, which can be several meters, down through r
crowave, infrared, and optical—the range of wavelengt
that our eyes can see—to ultraviolet, x-ray, and gamr
rays, which have wavelengths less than a billionth of
centimeter.

Telescopes now exist that are capable of detecting m
ute quantities of electromagnetic radiation at eve
wavelength. Dark matter cannot simply be matter th
we cannot see. It must be matter that is dark—that
below the detection level of the most sensitive telescop
at all wavelengths. Furthermore, not only must the da
matter be a poor radiator, it must also be a poor absorb
otherwise, it could show up through the shadow it c
over the luminous matter inside the dark envelopes. No
that the definition of dark matter does not mean that
will remain forever hidden from our telescopes. Indec
astronomers, ever an optimistic group, are hopeful th
the next generation of space- and land-based telescop
scheduled for development in the 1990s will reveal
rectly the identity of the dark matter. In the meanwhi
they must be content with circumstantial evidence a
the process of elimination.

Gas and Dust

One form of material that can be eliminated is int
stellar or intergalactic gas. Cold gas can be observed
ther through its radiation or absorption by rac
telescopes. Warm can be detected with infrared and o

telescopes, and hot gas by ultraviolet and x-ray
escopes.

Nor is dust a suspect. If the galaxy were filled with
ough dust to account for the dark matter, it would look
e the Los Angeles Basin on a bad day. The interstellar
og would make optical astronomy impossible. Only
e nearest stars and no other galaxies would be visible.
The problem with dust and gas is that it is spread too
nly and therefore radiates and absorbs too efficiently.
rk matter must be concentrated in some form that
atly reduces this efficiency. The best way to do this is
th a dark star.

Dark Stars

Dark stars fall into two classes: once-bright stars that
ve evolved and collapsed to become dim or invisible,
d stars that have such low mass that they have never
olved. They are now the way they were and will al-
ys be: intrinsically dim because they do not have the
ss to generate the gravity that can produce the inter-
l pressures to turn on thermonuclear reactions in their
erior.

In contrast, the first category of dark stars were once
bright as our Sun or brighter, but they have long since
d up their thermonuclear fuel. Depending on its mass
birth, a star will evolve to become a white dwarf, a
atron star, or a black hole. Stars such as the Sun will
come white dwarfs—dense spheres of matter about the
e of the Earth. At first, the energy generated in their
lapse makes white dwarfs very hot, with surface tem-
atures of many tens of thousands of degrees. A num-
of these objects have been detected. As white dwarfs
l over the course of billions of years, they fade into
isibility and thereby satisfy the requirement of dark-
s. But there do not appear to be enough of them to
lain the amount of dark matter that has been ob-
ved. An intense search for white dwarfs in the neigh-
hood of the Sun has yielded only about a tenth as
ny as would be needed. It has been speculated that
haps large numbers of white dwarfs were produced
the galaxy when it was very young and then rapidly
led to invisibility. However, there is no evidence to

support this idea, which would require a revision of t
theory of how white dwarfs cool. It would also requir
clever mechanism for hiding the large amounts of h
lium ejected into interstellar space when these st
made the transition to the white dwarf stage.

Stars about ten times as massive as the Sun do r
evolve into white dwarfs. When their nuclear fuel is
hausted, they undergo a catastrophic explosion calle
supernova. In early 1987 a supernova occurred in
nearby galaxy, giving astronomers a unique opportun
to test the theories of these explosions, which rank as t
most violent in the universe. In a supernova, the ou
layers of the star are blown into interstellar space
speeds in excess of a million kilometers per hour. All th
remains of the original star is a collapsed core of mat
that is predominantly composed of neutrons. This obje
called a neutron star, has the mass of a star such as t
Sun, packed into a sphere about twenty kilometers
diameter. A cube neutron–star matter having a diame
equal to the period at the end of this sentence wo
contain the mass equivalent of six thousand tons. Th
are very dense and after they have aged a billion years
so, should be very dark.

But neutron stars are improbable suspects in the da
matter mystery on two counts. First of all, the number
neutron stars in the galaxy can be estimated from b
the frequency of supernova explosions observed in otl
galaxies, and from the number of young neutron sta
which can be observed through their radio or x-ray en
sion. Both estimates agree in predicting that the numl
of neutron stars is expected to be less than a percent
the number required to explain the dark matter in
galaxy. Second, even if these estimates were badly in
ror—because of a hypothetical period of intense neutr
star formation early in the life of the galaxy, for examp
—the by-products of neutron star formation would
observable. These by-products include a large amount
heavy elements, which would have been blown away
the supernovas, to be later incorporated into the n
generation of stars or mixed with the interstellar gas.
the heavy elements are conspicuous by their rarity, co
prising less than a percent of all the luminous matter
the galaxy.

This leaves black holes. When a star that has a mass
eater than about twenty-five times that of the Sun,
avitational forces will overwhelm all other forces. The
pernova explosion will be muffled to an extent that is
certain. A large part, perhaps all of the star, will col-
se in on itself. Since there is no known force that can
t it, the star will literally collapse out of sight, forming
varp in space-time. The gravitational forces in the vi-
ity of a black hole are so strong that nothing can es-
pe from it. Even light waves, including all forms of
ctromagnetic radiation, are trapped inside a region
led the event horizon. This name describes the circum-
nce that events that occur inside this horizon, such as
: radiation of a light wave, are unobservable to anyone
tside the event horizon. The black hole has closed itself
from communication with the rest of the universe,
:ept for its gravitational force. In this respect, it is the
al suspect for dark matter.

The crucial question concerning black holes as a dark
atter suspect is whether a plausible mechanism exists
producing the large number of black holes needed to
plain the dark matter. The stars that produce black
les must be extremely massive; observations of con-
nporary stellar populations indicate that such stars
ast be very rare. Black holes can account for dark mat-
in our galaxy or other galaxies only if there was a
ae in the history of the universe, long before galaxies
med, when a large fraction of the mass of the universe
s in the form of very massive stars that eventually
:ame black holes. Massive stars evolve very rapidly
:ause of the large pressures and densities in their cores.
is population of stars would have lasted slightly more
an a million years before becoming black holes.

The evidence for the existence of such pregalactic stars
weak, but it may be growing stronger. There is the
servation that the oldest known stars are not purely
drogen and helium. They contain a trace of heavier
ments. Where did these heavier elements come from?
:haps from a pregalactic population of short-lived,
issive stars that ejected a trace of heavy elements into
ergalactic space and collapsed to become black holes.
Massive black holes must still be considered as sus-
:ts for the dark matter in the envelopes of galaxies.

Three major areas of doubt remain, however. One
whether or not a population of massive stars destined
become black holes can be formed without at the sa
time forming a large number of stars destined to explo
as supernovas and thereby produce too high a concent
tion of metals. Another problem is whether these m
sive stars can evolve into black holes without expelli
too many metals into space—either violently, via a sup
nova explosion, or through the nonviolent loss of
outer layers of the star prior to black hole formation. T
theory of stellar evolution has provided no definite
swers to these questions. A third area of doubt is whetl
or not a universe in which most of the mass is in
form of massive black holes would lead naturally to
explanation of the formation of galaxies, clusters, sup
clusters, and intergalactic voids. This problem will be
amined later.

Even if massive black holes become the primary da
matter suspect for the envelopes of galaxies, it is doubt
that they could explain the dark matter in the disk of
galaxy. Their immense gravitational force would t
apart loosely bound double star systems, and they wo
suck up interstellar gas, producing bright sources of ult
violet or x-radiation that should have been detected.

Nor is it likely that massive black holes are sufficien
numerous to bring the universal mass density up to
critical density, as required by the Inflationary Big Ba
model. One of the predictions of Einstein's general the
of relativity is that a ray of light will be bent by a gravi
tional field. According to the theory, massive bodies su
as stars and galaxies produce warps or dimples in spa
The severity of the warp depends on the mass of
object. A light ray passing through one of these warp
bent. In 1919, Einstein's prediction was verified by B
ish astronomers during a total eclipse of the Sun. La
Einstein described how the bending of light waves by
gravitational fields of foreground stars and galaxies co
magnify and brighten the images of distant stars and g
axies.

In 1982, Claude Canizares of MIT used this theory
examine the effects of dark stars on the light fr
quasars—distant objects that are thought to be the b
liant nuclei of galaxies. He found that any type of

)sed dark star numerous enough to provide a universal
ass density equal to the critical density should produce
servable effects in the light of quasars. Since these had
t been observed, Canizares concluded that dark stars
 not exist in sufficient numbers to provide a critical
nsity of dark matter.

His calculations did not, however, rule out dark stars
th masses less than 1 percent of the mass of the Sun.
ese are called brown dwarf stars, and they are funda-
entally different from other types. Their mass is so low
at their internal pressure and temperature never reach
 point where thermonuclear fusion of hydrogen can
:ur. Their only source of energy is slow gravitational
ntraction. Brown dwarfs are more like a giant planet,
ch as Jupiter, than a star. They qualify as dark matter
 one count: they are very faint. Furthermore, since
?y do not evolve, they have very few side effects that
uld rule them out.

But could there be enough of them? If the average
ass of a brown dwarf is only 1 percent that of the Sun,
en they would have to be several hundred times as
entiful as solar-type stars to explain the dark matter in
 galactic disk; several thousand times as plentiful to
plain the dark matter in galactic envelopes; and sev-
al tens of thousands of times as plentiful to provide a
iversal density equal to the critical density. Many as-
physicists feel that this is asking too much. They argue
at if so many brown dwarfs were produced, it would
 very difficult, if not impossible, to produce as a by-
oduct a significant number of stars having a tenth the
ass of the Sun or greater. These stars, called red dwarfs,
 dim, but not so dim that they cannot be detected. Red
varfs are abundant. Of the hundred stars closest to the
n, two-thirds are red dwarfs. This is part of a trend: the
s massive a star, the more plentiful it is. If this trend
ntinued to Jupiter-sized brown dwarfs, they could be
 prime dark matter suspects.

However, observations of the numbers of red dwarfs
licate that the trend does not continue to lower masses,
t stops at masses about a fifth that of the Sun. If most of
 mass of the galaxy is in the form of brown dwarfs,
·y are not part of a trend in the normal process of the
mation of stars. They must be produced as the result of

some special process. A number of suggestions as to ho
this might have occurred have been made. Most of the
involve special conditions presumed to have occurr
when the gas cloud that was to become our galaxy was
the process of cooling to become a galaxy of stars. T
high pressures in the gas cloud at this time might ha
been conducive to the formation of hundreds of trillio
of brown dwarfs.

The most ingenious speculation concerning brow
dwarfs as the dark matter is due to David Criswell,
space scientist at the California Space Institute in La Jol
He speculates that the dark matter in galactic disks a
envelopes is composed of stars and planets that are bei
managed or "husbanded" by advanced extraterrestr
civilizations. The lifetime and prosperity of such civili:
tions, Criswell speculates, would be limited solely by t
amount of available energy. These beings will, therefo
seek to use available energy stores wisely. In particul
they may wish to attain a greater efficiency from the ra
material in a star than the thermonuclear processes th
provide. A carefully controlled thermonuclear reac
can in principle yield more than ten times more e
ciency than normal thermonuclear reactions inside sta
Accordingly, an extraterrestrial civilization might
strongly motivated to gather hydrogen fuel into res
voirs that could be tapped for future use in controll
reactors.

The ideal reservoir would be one that is self-gravit
ing, but not so massive that thermonuclear reactio
would occur spontaneously—an artificial brown dwa
These reservoirs might be created directly from the int
stellar gas before it condensed into stars, or possibly
dismantling stars. Criswell suggests that this awesome
of astroengineering could be accomplished by using fa
ities similar to large ion accelerators on Earth to cre
enormous electric currents and magnetic fields in t
space around a star. These magnetic fields could be us
to dismantle stars by pumping energy into their upp
atmospheres.

How could such a galactic development project be
tected? The reservoirs might show up as a cluster of inf
red sources, or a star in the process of being dismantl
might exhibit unusual properties that could be identifi

e details of this intriguing idea have yet to be worked
t. Most astrophysicists consider it too wild to give it
:ious consideration, but perhaps they should.

Serious searches for brown dwarfs have been under-
:en. These involve infrared telescopes that look di-
:tly for radiation from the brown dwarfs, and optical
d x-ray telescopes that look for indirect effects, such as
e gravitational one of a brown dwarf on a nearby com-
nion star. These efforts have met with limited success.
out half a dozen brown dwarf candidates have been
nounced, and only two or three of these identifications
e firm. This is not quite what would have been ex-
cted if the galaxy were congested with brown dwarfs.
the evidence to support the suspicion that brown
varfs are responsible for dark matter is absent.

The Structure Problem

The mass of dark stars is composed almost entirely of
e protons and neutrons that make up almost all the
ass in the world around us. (Electrons make up a frac-
n of a percent.) Protons and neutrons are part of a class
particles called *baryons,* from the Greek word meaning
eavy." The simplest solution to the dark matter mys-
y would seem that it is baryonic matter arranged in
me dark form, such as dark stars. One difficulty with
is solution is that there is little evidence to support it.
other is that it is very difficult to explain how galaxies
med in an expanding universe of baryons.

The difficulty has its roots in the observed smoothness
microwave background radiation. The observed uni-
mity of this radiation tells us that the photons were
read very smoothly through the universe a few hun-
ed thousand years after the Big Bang. A football field as
ooth as the universe was back then would have no
mps larger than about a centimeter. The baryons were
o distributed that smoothly because they interacted
ongly with the photons.

In the standard picture, galaxies are formed from
mps of matter that have a slightly stronger gravita-
nal attraction than surrounding matter. This matter is
led into the clump, making its gravity even larger, so
t it pulls in more matter, and so on, until a massive

cloud is formed. An adequate though not completely a curate analogy is the formation of a large snowball l rolling a small snowball around and collecting more an more snow. If you want to complete the process in reasonable time, you do not want to start with a snowba the size of a pea. Yet this is, in effect, what the observ tions of the microwave background radiation require as starting point for the formation of galaxies. Astrophy cists say it simply cannot be done in the time availab Galaxies should not exist!

One way out of this paradox is to assume that th standard model is not valid—that forces other than gra ity are at work in the process of formation of galaxie Jeremiah Ostriker of Princeton University and Lenn Cowie of the University of Hawaii and, independentl Saito Ikeuchi of the University of Tokyo, have propos an explosive model for galaxy formation. Explosive acti ity in a population of massive pregalactic stars sen shock waves plowing through space, sweeping up matt like a snowplow. New stars are formed and new exp sions occur as a chain reaction of explosive activity dev ops. Colossal expanding shock waves form vast bubbl surrounded by shells of swept-up matter. Galaxies for in superclusters along the edge of these bubbles, produ ing the observed bubbly structure of superclusters an voids.

The model paints an attractive broad-brush pictur Unfortunately, it has not been possible as yet to fill in t details in a self-consistent way. The predicted size of t bubbles is too small; there is no mechanism for produ ing the required pregalactic stars and the whole proce still takes too long, given the small clumps allowed the observed smoothness of the microwave backgrou radiation. These difficulties may not be insurmountab —for example, there is other evidence, discussed abov for a pregalactic population of stars—but they are larg

Three difficulties cloud the case for some form of baryc as prime suspects in the dark matter mystery. The first the absence of a good candidate object. Brown dwa and black holes are possibilities, but they both have go alibis. No one has seen nearly enough of them, and sufficiently strong motivation for their existence in the numbers required has been established. The second difficulty is the mass density problem. Some very fancy theoretical footwork is required to produce the observed amount of deuterium and other light isotopes from the Big Bang if the average density of the universe is equal to the mass density of the universe. Yet, to abandon this density requirement would mean abandoning the Inflationary Big Bang model, which solves other pressing problems relating to the origin of the universe. Finally, there is the structure problem. How did the observed structures of galaxies, clusters of galaxies, superclusters, and voids arise in the expanding universe? No good explanation exists in a universe composed solely of baryons.

Cosmic WIMPs

The difficulties with baryons led astrophysicists to consider another type of suspect—the cosmic WIMP.* WIMP is an acronym for "weakly interacting massive particle." *Weakly interacting* means that the particle neither produces nor absorbs significant amounts of light or other forms of electromagnetic radiation. It is dark matter. *Massive particle* is in a sense a misnomer. It does not necessarily mean that the particle is more massive than a proton or neutron, or even an electron. It only means that it is not like the photon, which can be thought of as a particle of light or a packet of electromagnetic waves that has zero mass. Cosmic WIMPs have nonzero mass, so if they exist in large enough numbers, they could be the solution to one or more of the dark matter mysteries.

WIMPs are attractive dark matter suspects for several reasons. They are naturally dark. They interact weakly with normal matter, so they would not participate in the nuclear reactions that produced isotopes such as deuterium in the early universe. This means that the mass density in WIMPs can be sufficient to bring the mass density of the universe up to the critical density without destroying all the deuterium. Since they interact so

---

* The acronym WIMP has led inevitably to another one for dark stars: MACHOs, for Massive Condensed Halo Objects—halo being the term for a cloud of matter enveloping the galaxy.

weakly with radiation, the problems related to the observed smoothness of the microwave background radiation are much less severe. Dense clumps of WIMPs could have existed without producing clumpy background radiation. These dense clumps make much better seeds from which galaxies composed of baryons and WIMPs could grow. The baryons would subsequently cool by radiation of light and other forms of electromagnetic waves and fall inward, leaving behind a dark matter envelope with a visible core. Astronomers have been compiling an impressive body of evidence that this is exactly the way a galaxy looks.

Can we now close the book on the case of the dark matter? Not yet. Many suspects that look guilty at first glance turn out to be highly implausible upon closer investigation. Cosmic WIMPs are no exception. Consider the neutrino.

Neutrinos are the one type of potential cosmic WIMP that almost certainly exist in large numbers. But are they truly WIMPs? They interact very feebly with normal matter. A trillion neutrinos could pass through your body in a second and you would not feel any worse for it. Nor would the neutrinos suffer any loss of energy. They could go through the Earth without slowing down or being absorbed or radiating any energy. They fit the requirement of darkness perfectly. Despite the coyness of neutrinos, physicists have been able to detect them as the by-product of certain nuclear reactions, so we know they exist.

Similar reactions should have occurred during the first few minutes of the Big Bang, producing a sea of neutrinos that is analogous to the microwave background radiation. The detection of the microwave background radiation has convinced most scientists that a similar neutrino sea exists. It cannot be detected directly because the energies of these primordial neutrinos has been diminished by the expansion of the universe. But if the neutrino has the mass of only twenty to thirty billionths of the mass of the proton, most of the mass of the universe would be in the form of neutrinos.

Laboratory experimenters have undertaken heroic efforts to measure the mass of the neutrino. So far, their efforts have been in vain. The experiments rule out a neutrino mass slightly larger than thirty billionths of the mass of the proton; they are consistent with a mass of zero. In early 1987, nature carried out a spectacular experiment of its own that established a more stringent limit on the neutrino mass. In February 1987, a supernova explosion was observed to occur in a nearby galaxy —the Large Magellanic Cloud. Two neutrino detectors on Earth observed a burst of neutrinos from this explosion. The burst lasted two seconds; it was presumably caused by the collapse of the core of the star to form a neutron star. The neutrinos in the burst covered a wide range of energies.

If neutrinos have no mass, they would travel the 150,000 light-years between the Large Magellanic Cloud and Earth at the speed of light. However, if they have mass, they will not be able to move at the speed of light. Low-energy neutrinos will lag behind high-energy neutrinos by an amount that depends on the mass of the neutrino; the effect is to produce a spread in arrival times of the neutrinos at Earth. Even though the energies of the neutrinos from the supernova varied by as much as five hundred percent, they arrived within two seconds of one another. An analysis that takes into account the dynamics of the explosion indicates that the mass of the neutrino must be less than twenty billionths of the mass of the proton. This eliminates neutrinos of the type observed in the supernova—called electron neutrinos because they are produced in the decay of a neutron to a proton and an electron—as suspects in the mass density part of the dark matter mystery.

Nor can the electron neutrino solve the mystery of the dark matter in the galactic disk. The disk of our galaxy was formed when the rotating cloud of gas that was to become our galaxy cooled, and low-energy matter sank down to the equatorial plane of the cloud. Neutrinos, by their very nature, do not lose their energy very easily. A cloud of neutrinos would retain the original shape of the gas cloud. This is one reason why neutrinos seemed attractive at first sight—they held out the possibility of explaining the observed structure of galaxies, with luminous matter embedded in a dark envelope. A consequence of this behavior is that neutrinos could not possibly have lost enough energy to allow them to sink down to the disk, so they could not possibly be the dark matter in the disk of the Milky Way.

Closer investigation revealed that electron neutrinos also encounter difficulties as an explanation of the dark matter in galactic envelopes, this because the behavior of neutrinos is constrained by the exclusion principle. This is a law of quantum mechanics which says that no two neutrinos can occupy the same quantum state. A familiar analog is a subway car: no two people can occupy the same seat. If there are more people than seats, the extra people cannot occupy the lower energy states, represented by the seats, but must be content with higher energy states such as standing. The low limits that exist on the mass of the electron neutrino imply that large numbers of them would be required to explain the dark matter in galactic envelopes. The low energy states would be filled. Most of the neutrinos would be forced into quantum states with such high energy that they would evaporate away from all but the largest galaxies. This is not consistent with the observational data, which indicates that a wide range of galaxies—from dwarfs to supergiant elliptical galaxies—contain roughly the same proportions of dark matter.

A final point against electron neutrinos is related to their speed. The condition of their creation implies that they would be rapidly moving particles. Since high speed means high temperatures, neutrinos are sometimes called "hot dark matter." Other WIMPs, discussed below, are thought to be moving at much lower speeds; they are called "cold dark matter."

The difficulty with hot dark matter is that strong gravitational fields are required to gather it into dark clouds. It is difficult to form galaxies directly in a universe in which neutrinos dominate the mass because the neutrinos are moving too rapidly. They would evaporate almost as soon as they were formed. Returning to the snowball analogy, it is as if it were impossible to form small or even medium-sized snowballs because they would immediately melt. The only way to get a clump would be to push together a large snowbank, let it freeze, and then chip off clumps. In the context of neutrinos, only structures the size of superclusters of galaxies would be sufficiently large and have sufficiently strong gravitaional fields to hold together once they condensed from the primordial gas. Galaxies would come later as these clouds fragmented.

This order of formation—large clouds the size of superclusters that subsequently fragment to form galaxies—has two implications that do not agree with the observations. First, galaxies seem to be much older than calculations based on a neutrino-dominated universe would suggest. In fact, most observational evidence suggests that the galaxies are coming together to form clusters, not that the cluster-sized clouds are fragmenting to form galaxies.

Second, an implication of the neutrino theory is that superclusters of galaxies would have a larger proportion of dark matter than clusters of galaxies, which would in turn have a larger proportion than galaxies. This is not observed. So for different reasons, neutrinos, like baryons, have difficulty with the structure problem. It is very difficult to explain how, in a universe dominated by neutrinos, the large structures such as galaxies and clusters of galaxies could have formed at the right time and with the right proportion of dark matter.

Electron neutrinos are not the only type of neutrinos. Tau and muon neutrinos are produced in the decay of short-lived subatomic particles. Their masses are more difficult to determine, and the limits on these masses are much greater than for the electron neutrino. There is at present, however, little or no evidence that these neutrinos would have been produced in sufficient quantities in the Big Bang to explain the mass density mystery. The difficulties encountered by electron neutrinos in explaining the matter in the disk of the Milky Way apply to tau and muon neutrinos, as well. It is not certain whether the problem with the filling of quantum states in galactic envelopes exists for these types of neutrinos. This constraint depends on the masses of the particles, for which only weak limits exist. The structure problem remains, though. It is intrinisic to hot dark matter of any kind.

The case for neutrinos is weak and seems to be getting weaker as time goes along, so astrophysicists have reluctantly had to release what was once a prime suspect. They have turned their attention to a new class of WIMPs that can be grouped under the generic name of cold dark matter.

Unlike neutrinos, the cold dark matter WIMPs are no known to exist. However, physicists who work on the theory of interactions between subatomic particles main tain that there are good reasons to believe that one an perhaps several types of these particles were produced i abundance in the first fraction of a millisecond of the Bi Bang.

Axions, named after a laundry detergent, were in vented to clean up a problem in elementary-particl physics in 1977 that had no direct relation to the dar matter mystery. However, when it came to the attentio of astrophysicists that the axion is predicted to be a parti cle that interacts very weakly with electromagnetic radi ation (hence, it is dark), that it should have a small (muc less than the mass of the electron) but nonzero mass, the quickly placed it high on their list of suspects. Axion satisfied the criterion of darkness, and unlike neutrinos are not constrained to obey the exclusion principle. Thi means that there is no difficulty having many axions i the same low energy state, a property which allows ax ions to account, in principle, for the dark matter aroun galaxies of all sizes, from dwarfs to supergiants. But ar there enough axions in the universe to make up the dar matter? For that matter, are there any axions?

The search for them is underway. Attempts to detec cosmic axions are in progress. These first efforts at axio astronomy are based on the theoretical prediction tha axions can be converted into electromagnetic waves i the presence of a strong magnetic field. A definitiv experimental answer to the question of whether or n axions exist, and if so in sufficient numbers, may n come for several years. In the meantime, we must rely o theory.

If the particle physics theory that predicts the exi tence of axions is combined with the Inflationary Bi Bang theory, it is possible to get an estimate of the time birth of axions: the first $1/1,000,000,000,000,000$ $000,000,000,000,000$ of a second in the expansion of th universe. Just how many were produced then is ver uncertain, but possibly enough to solve two of the thre dark matter mysteries: the dark matter in the envelope around galaxies and the dark matter needed to bring th universal mass density up to the critical mass density.

Another possible cold WIMP is the photino. Its exisence has been suggested within the context of an elegant theoretical speculation concerning the nature of elementary particles called supersymmetry. According to these types of theories, all the various particles of which the universe is composed are fundamentally the same. The apparent differences between electrons, protons, neutrons, neutrinos, and photons are only a consequence of the present low temperature of the universe. They are like snowflakes and hailstones, which appear to be different, but look the same once they have melted.

One consequence of this theory is that when the universe cooled from a very hot state and condensed into the myriad of different particles from which the universe as we know it is made, each particle had a supersymmetric partner. The electron had a selectron, the proton, a proton, and the photon a photino. These supersymmetric partners are predicted to be much heavier than their counterparts, and to interact very weakly with electromagnetic radiation, so they qualify as dark matter. It is expected that before the Big Bang was more than a thousandth of a second old, all the supersymmetric particles would have decayed to the lightest one, presumably the photino. It is possible that enough photinos would have been produced by then to solve the dark matter mystery.

As with axions, photinos are predicted to have relatively low random velocities, so they fall into the category of cold dark matter. Also like axions, they remain, despite experimental efforts to detect them, no more than figments of the theorists' imaginations.

The attractive feature of cold dark matter, whether in the form of axions or photinos or some other WIMP that might spring full-grown from some new theory of elementary particles, is the manner in which they are predicted to clump together. In a universe dominated by cold dark matter, clouds of gas and dark matter with masses corresponding to galaxies collapse first. Clusters and superclusters of galaxies would then be formed later as galaxies come together under the influence of their mutual gravitational attraction. This scenario predicts equal proportions of luminous and dark matter for objects ranging from dwarf galaxies to superclusters, consistent with the observations.

That is the good news. The bad news is that galaxies form too easily in a universe full of cold dark matter. One of the predictions of the Inflationary Big Bang model is that the mass density of the universe must be equal to the critical density that defines the boundary between an ever-expanding universe and one that will ultimately collapse. If this is so, then the intergalactic voids should be full of dark matter. But if they were full of cold dark matter, it would have collapsed, pulling luminous matter with it to form bright galaxies embedded in dark envelopes. The voids would not be voids, but would be ablaze with the light of thousands of galaxies. This and other observed properties of the structure of the universe on a very large scale—the motion of the Local Supercluster toward the Great Attractor, for example—indicate that the cold dark matter hypothesis, in its simplest form, is self-contradictory.

The answer to this indictment of the cold dark matter story has been that something is missing in the theory of galaxy formation. Perhaps the voids are filled with failed galaxies—dark matter that for some reason never collapsed to form galaxies. Or maybe some variation of the explosive galaxy formation scenario swept the voids clean of both luminous and dark matter. As I mentioned earlier, ordinary explosive activity does not seem to be capable of sweeping volumes of space a hundred million light-years in diameter clean. Something else seems to be required.

One of the most bizarre suggestions for this something else is a cosmic singularity called a cosmic string. Cosmic strings are predicted by a number of versions of the Inflationary Big Bang model. They would have diameters a quintillion times smaller than the nucleus of an atom and would form loops thousands of light-years in diameter. They are extremely dense, and would have a mass equal to that of a large galaxy. Although it is not possible that they could be the dark matter—they would produce enormous warps in space that would distort the images of galaxies if they were that plentiful—cosmic strings appear to have the qualities needed to be an accomplice in the dark matter mystery. The smaller loops would be expected to be in a state of violent vibration in the first fraction of a second of the Big Bang. These vibrations could conceivably generate enormous fluxes of electro-magnetic radiation that would sweep the intergalactic voids clean. Or, much larger loops could define the boundaries of the voids and attract matter to form vast chains of galaxies around these voids.

Unfortunately, the details of the cosmic string hypothesis have not panned out as expected. There are serious problems with producing strings of the right type and in sufficient numbers in the current Inflationary models. Nor is it at all clear that, even if strings existed, they could explain the observed large-scale structure of voids and the motions of superclusters.

So, although axions and photinos are still good suspects, the puzzle remains as to how they could be the dark matter, and the universe of superclusters and voids could look the way it does. Something is missing, and it may be more than Cosmic WIMPs or MACHOs can explain.

Is a New Theory of Gravity Needed?

Sometimes in criminal cases, it turns out that the crime under investigation never happened. For example, a reported murder may turn out to have been faked in order to collect life insurance. Then the investigation shifts to a crime of another sort—insurance fraud. A few astrophysicists believe something similar may have occurred in the dark matter mystery.

Mordehai Milgrom of the Weizmann Institute of Science in Rehovot, Israel, has been the leading advocate of this point of view. He argues that there is no dark matter mystery because there is no dark matter. The problem is, he maintains, that the standard law of gravity—Isaac Newton's—does not apply to the conditions that exist in galaxies and intergalactic space.

Specifically, he proposes that when the gravitational acceleration becomes very small—which happens when the gravitational force is acting over distances much larger than the size of the solar system—then Newton's law of gravity must be modified so that the gravitational force at large distances falls off less rapidly. This means, for example, that gravity would be stronger on the outer edges of galaxies, so they could rotate more rapidly. According to Milgrom, astronomers infer the existence of dark matter because they are using the wrong law of gravity.

This approach—inventing a new law—does not seem much more radical than inventing a new particle such as the axion. After all, Newton's law may explain the motions of spacecraft, the Moon, and the planets, but it cannot describe the conditions around black holes, or the expansion of the universe. For these situations, Einstein's general theory of relativity—a generalization of Newton's law—must be used. Is it not possible, then, that a further generalization of Einstein's theory is needed to explain the rotation of galaxies and the motion of galaxies and gas in clusters?

Most astrophysicists reply with a resounding "No!" when asked this question. Einstein's theory has great appeal. It has very few basic assumptions, and more important, it has served them extremely well over the years. They prefer to explore all reasonable alternatives before undertaking an overhaul of the theory of gravity.

Of course, reasonable people can become unreasonable when arguing about what is reasonable. Galileo was imprisoned for investigating an alternative to the hypothesis that the Earth is the center of the universe. Milgrom is in no danger of that. What he is in danger of, many of his colleagues feel, is wasting his time on a long shot. Nevertheless, it is one indication of the state of uneasiness that exists about the solutions to the dark matter mystery proposed so far that more and more astrophysicists are taking the time to try to prove him wrong.

The objections are both observational and theoretical. Milgrom's theory is consistent with most observations, but in a few cases, it appears to be contradicted by the data presently available. For example, in certain giant elliptical galaxies, observations indicate that dark matter must be present in a region where Milgrom's theory predicts agreement with Newton's law, and hence no dark matter. Milgrom's theory also predicts that the relative proportion of dark matter that must be invoked to explain the observations in clusters of galaxies must be greater than that needed for galaxies. The evidence, though not conclusive, is against such a trend.

The theoretical objections to Milgrom's theory refer to

its incompleteness. Many of the implications of his suggested modification of the Newton–Einstein theory have yet to be worked out, such as the effect on the expansion of the universe. Preliminary indications indicate major problems. One of these is that the increased strength of the force of gravity over large distances proposed by his theory should have halted the expansion of the universe by now. It should be collapsing instead of expanding— something that is obviously not happening. Whether Milgrom or some other ingenious cosmologist can solve this and other problems remains to be seen. In the meantime, the mystery remains, and most astrophysicists continue to believe in dark matter.

THE INVESTIGATION CONTINUES

The investigation of the dark side of the universe has uncovered many good suspects. Each suspect has an alibi which, though not airtight, is good enough to avoid conviction for now. Consider the facts in each part of the overall case.

The dark matter in the disk of our galaxy. Cosmic WIMPs are out because they cannot lose enough energy to collapse down into the disk. Neutron stars are out because the supernovas that produce them produce too many heavy elements. The same probably applies to black holes, but this is still uncertain. White dwarfs are out because they are not observed in sufficient numbers, as are red and brown dwarfs. Again the observations, with a lot of imagination, could be twisted to allow for the possibility that red, white, or brown dwarfs could be the dark matter in the disk. Brown dwarfs are the most favored here, simply because we know the least about them. There is little here to inspire confidence that we are near a solution.

The dark matter enveloping galaxies. Axions and photinos are the favored candidates among theoretical astrophysicists, whereas observers tend to favor brown dwarfs. Massive black holes remain a long shot possibility. Neutrinos, once the prime suspect, have been virtually dropped from consideration because of new limits on their mass and calculations relating to the formation of dark galactic envelopes with neutrinos. We don't have any direct evidence that any of these suspects exist in the numbers required. Nor are computer models for the formation of structure in the universe encouraging. Axions and photinos produce too many galaxies, whereas a model universe composed solely of baryonic dark matter, such as brown dwarfs or black holes, produces too few galaxies.

The mass density problem. The Inflationary Big Bang model solves a number of nagging problems relating to the origin and evolution of the universe. It predicts that the mass density of the universe must be very nearly equal to the critical density that defines the boundary between a finite universe that will ultimately collapse, and an infinite one that will expand forever. This implies that the proportion of dark to luminous matter in the universe must be about fifty to one. The observations so far do not agree with this prediction. They indicate a proportion between five to one and ten to one.

Clearly, pieces are missing from the puzzle. Are we looking for a still-undiscovered form of matter? Or some unknown process by which galaxies or superclusters or intergalactic voids form? Or a new theory of gravity? Or are the observations flawed in some fundamental way? This would be the simplest solution—the one that astrophysicists would like to believe—for then the mystery would just go away. But the breadth and depth of the observational evidence indicates that this is extremely unlikely to happen. The probability is that there really is something out there in the darkness that exerts a powerful attraction on the luminous matter in the universe. When we understand what it is, we will have arrived at a view of our universe that is radically different from our present one.

In the meantime, the mystery deepens and the investigation continues. Paraphrasing Sherlock Holmes, ". . . the game is still afoot."

. dramatic new series of books at the cutting edge
of where science meets science fiction.

THE NEXT WAVE
Introduced by Isaac Asimov

ach volume of *The Next Wave* contains a fascinating
cientific essay and a complete novel about the same
ubject. And every volume carries an introduction by
saac Asimov.

Volume One
Red Genesis
by S. C. Sykes
The spellbinding tale of a man who changed not
one but two worlds, with an essay by scientist
Eugene F. Mallove on the technical problems of
launching and maintaining a colony on Mars.

Volume Two
Alien Tongue
by Stephen Leigh
The story of contact with a startling new world,
with an essay by scientist and author Rudy
Rucker on the latest developments in the search
for extraterrestrial intelligence.

Volume Three
The Missing Matter
by Thomas R. McDonough
An exciting adventure which explores the nature
f "dark matter" beyond our solar system, with an
essay by renowned space scientist Wallace H.
Tucker.

Look for *The Next Wave* on sale now wherever
Bantam Spectra Books are sold

AN 288 12/91